Hidden Conflict
Tales from Lost Voices in Battle

Hidden Conflict
Tales from Lost Voices in Battle

Alex Beecroft
Mark R. Probst
Jordan Taylor
E. N. Holland

A Joint Venture of
Cheyenne Publishing & Bristlecone Pine Press

Cheyenne Publishing
Camas, Washington
www.cheyennepublishing.com

ISBN: 978-0-9797773-8-7

This work is also available as an eBook (ISBN: 978-1-60722-009-1)
available from Bristlecone Pine Press
www.bcpinepress.com

Not to Reason Why *edited by Sarah Cypher*

Blessed Isle, No Darkness, *and* Our One and Only *edited by
Leslie H. Nicoll*

Front cover designed by Jordan Taylor

Published by Cheyenne Publishing
Camas, Washington
Mailing Address:
    P. O. Box 872412 Vancouver, WA 98687-2412
Website: www.cheyennepublishing.com

Table of Contents

Blessed Isle

Alex Beecroft

Chapter One

I look on the man sprawled face down among tangled bed-clothes. The night air is sticky, airless, almost as hot as the day. I'm sat here at the desk, sleepless from the heat, as I will be until dawn brings a breeze from the sea, the scent of tar and ships, and a faint cool. I'll sleep then. For now, I'll light a candle, take out this journal and write. And look at him.

Gauze curtains hang around the bed, milky, ghostly, veiling him. He's kicked off everything but the tail end of a sheet and has hidden his face in the crook of his arm. His back is pale as milk and, in the candlelight, a sheen of sweat gilds his muscles with dim gold. He is a tall man, lithe and slender, and his black hair gleams like jet, curling into the nape of his neck, where a final lock kicks up like a drake's tail.

I lean down to rest a hand gently on his bare shoulder, and he shifts without waking towards the touch. I wonder then, how did I come here? What strange movement of the heavens or gamble of Providence marked me out to be so blessed?

I edge the sash a quarter inch further open, letting in lush, choking air and a multitude of Saint Sebastian's insect life. The pages of my journal lie limp and damp, and the ink sinks thirstily into them. Only a week ago, I examined a ship trading ice out of Greenland, crawled about the hold and parted the woven mats of straw to touch its sides and feel its burning chill with my fingertips. It was the first time I had been cold in almost a decade.

There might be some relief from this pressing humidity in the tiny boathouse beneath our dwelling. The thought of taking candle and journal and sneaking down there, to write in the cool, is appealing. But it would mean leaving him alone, and I begrudge every moment spent out of his presence. We have been forced to give up so much for this, our state of near married bliss. Best appreciate it now, lest tomorrow the hangman snatch it away.

Oak apple gall and vinegar scent drifts sharp from the ink. I sand the page again and smooth it as I wonder why I want to leave this record. Why not leave our story untold? It is dangerous to speak, let alone to commit the words to paper. My need to confess may be the death of us both. But it leaves a bad taste in my mouth that this love should go unrecorded; that posterity should judge men like myself—like him—by the poor fools driven out to grope strangers in alleys, all fumbling fingers and anonymous grunting. Those of us uncaught must perforce be silent. But one day, perhaps, when the world has grown kinder, this journal will be read by less jaundiced eyes. To them I will be able to say there was fidelity here, and love, and long-suffering sacrifice, and joy. To them I will be able to speak the truth.

I trim my pen and dip it. From the waterfront, the docks and warehouses all about us, comes the clap of rope against mast, and laughter; the riot of sailors trying to forget. In the town beyond, the notes of a *cavaquinho* fall like silver raindrops into the night. But, floating over all, from the hills of the interior comes a rumbling throb of drums as the slaves and the natives too remember their stories, keep their truths alive.

I should introduce myself. I am Captain Harry Thompson of His Majesty's Royal Navy. I began my life as a Norfolk wherryman's son. Pressed aboard the *Sovereign* under Captain Garvey at the age of fourteen, I took to the Navy as a bird, falling from its nest, takes to flight. It was my element and my delight. I filled my hours with work and study. Alone in my hammock at night, I imagined myself a great admiral, pacing the deck of a First Rate, his own flotilla following in strictly measured line behind him. By diligent study of those better born than myself, I polished my manners and my mode of speech, so that I could pass as a gentleman, and thus, in the year 1784 I was made lieutenant. The most junior lieutenant of the *Barfleur* under Sir Samuel Hood.

A man, like myself, with no family connexions, may serve his whole life as a lieutenant, but I was determined that should not be my fate. If I required either a miracle or an act of heroism to secure me a captain's rank, I would produce one. So when, some years later, a French cannonball shattered the railing of the *Barfleur*, bursting into thrumming, foot-long splinters of sharpened oak that sprayed the quarterdeck like spears, I was ready. I stepped in front of the Admiral and received through my shoulder the dart that would otherwise have pierced his throat.

I remember the blur of the sky, hazy, hot and deep, deep blue, all the masts bowing in towards me as if falling atop my face. I felt a crushing sensation as though they had indeed pinned me beneath them, and my mouth filled with blood. I am pleased to say, I could not have cried out even if I had tried. I fell silently into oblivion. And then I awoke in my hammock with a vast pain, and an Admiral in my debt.

Which may be taken as sufficient explanation for why, at thirty-four years of age, with a new wig atop my freshly shaved head, and a servant going on before me to carry my baggage, I took possession of my first, and last, command.

HMS *Banshee*, a sloop of war, swung about her anchor rope in Plymouth that day under gentle English May-day sunshine, and looked as though she had sailed straight out of my boyish dreams. Her paint shone bright azure and gold, and her company, drawn up for my inspection, stood neat and biddable, the officers glittering, the men like a country garden in bright check shirts and ribbons.

I found, later the same day, that she was elderly, had

been much knocked about in the Bay of Biscay, and was a leaky, wet ship. Always three feet of water in the well, no matter how we pumped. Always mildew on the food and in our clothes, and her finely dressed men wheezed and coughed as they worked.

My servant unpacked my things and did his best to make the cabin homelike, wiping the black bloom of mould from all the surfaces, installing my few belongings in this sumptuous, almost indecent, expanse of private space.

That week I was too full of work to see either officers or men as more than brief, bipedal shadows cast into the cave of my preoccupation. I had a convoy to organise. News had reached London that Captain Arthur Philip had successfully brought his fleet to Rio de Janeiro and, after reprovisioning there, had departed for Australia, his small payload of convicts largely intact. The birth of a new colony was underway, and I was directed to follow with a second fleet, comprising the convict transport vessels *Drake, Quicksilver,* and *Cornwall*, the supply ship *Ardent*, and the *Banshee* as escort and protector. All this I was to organise myself, and to achieve before the month was out.

In my zeal, I drove myself to achieve it all within the week. I wonder now, looking back, whether—had I taken longer, been more scrupulous—I might even then have seen the seeds of the great calamity to come. A bruise here, a livid cheek there, among the men and women huddled behind iron bars in the holds of the transport ships. Doctors assure me the malady could not have lain low so long, but I cannot help wondering…

Yet hindsight makes Cassandras of us all, encouraging us to cry out, "You should have listened," when it is far too late. Perhaps the doctors are right, and my fault came later. It is my fault, just the same.

The weighed anchor rose with a pop and a spout of bubbles from the Plymouth seabed. The day was fair, crisp and golden as white wine, and the breeze fresh. A Thursday, it was washing day aboard the *Banshee*, and we departed to our fate with the ensign flying, white sails bravely spread, and our rigging fluttering with shirts, small clothes, and stockings hung out to dry.

Now, I thought, taking a turn at the wheel to see how she handled—she wallowed like a swimming cow—*I have the time to get to know my ship, my men.*

The spray tangled like silver lace about the yellow haired, screaming woman of *Banshee*'s figurehead. The wind strengthened and the ropes of her rigging creaked with accustomed strain. By afternoon we were out of sight of land. Our little community of ships sailed alone on the deep blue waves of the Atlantic, under a sunset as juicy orange-pink as a peach.

A great burden fell away from me then, and I sighed as the wind nudged my back and whipped the ends of my ribbon against my cheek, the land and its scurry behind me, a long, long voyage before. *Now there is time to do more than merely work. Time to live.*

The washing came down from the rigging. The watches changed, last dog watch into first watch. Soft and silver over the sigh of waves, the ship's bell sounded out once. In echo came the sweet ring of the bells on *Drake* and *Ardent*, and a moment later the distant ting of *Quicksilver* and *Cornwall* further behind. Night fell with the lazy downward drift and the sheen of a falling magpie feather.

After eating my solitary dinner, I set my wig on its stand, took off my uniform coat and substituted an old grey short-jacket, disreputable and comfortable. I intended my officers to know at a glance that this was an informal visit. The officer on watch, Lieutenant Bailey, I believe, attempted to hide his lit pipe behind his back as he snatched off his hat with the other hand. I gave him a nod and walked past, pretending not to have noticed.

I have been down many a companionway—one hand for the ship and one for myself, leaning back to place my weight more firmly on the treads. I don't believe I was aware this was the last time I would do so in possession of my own soul. Not even when I paused outside the closed door of the wardroom at the sound of a voice singing, a voice as smooth and rich as a flagon of whipped chocolate, did I imagine that my life as I had known it was about to come to an end.

A wardroom servant, coming out burdened with dishes, held open the door for me, supposing me too grand to work the latch myself. I ducked beneath the lintel and froze there as if the air had turned to amber. I breathed in scented resin and eternity.

Scattered pewter plates reflected the light from lanterns swinging gently from the beams overhead. The hull curved in about the room like cradling palms. Down the long sweep of table, glasses glittered with pinpricks of silver, the wine within them burning red. *He* stood behind his empty seat at the head of the table, singing.

Braced, his long fingers curled over the back of the chair, the fall of his frock coat devastatingly elegant, he stood like the Archangel Gabriel before Mary. And his beauty was such that had he looked at me and said, like an angel, "Do not be afraid," I would have had to thank him for the needful reassurance.

Words cannot do him justice. What word is 'black' to describe hair as glossy as obsidian, as soft and thick as fur? He wore it in a loose mass of curls, collar length, informal, very modern. His top lip was the shape of a Mongolian recurve bow, only a shade or two pinker than his strikingly pale skin. A stubborn jaw outlined in shadow and a long straight nose. Black lashes and strong black brows. A masculine face, and yet exquisite; clear and glorious as a sword thrust through the heart. I gasped at the shock and ecstasy of it, and without faltering in his song—to this day I don't remember what it was he was singing; "You gentlemen of England," perhaps— he turned to look at me.

His eyes were dark brown, like his voice—like chocolate. Their gaze at first conveyed frankness, thoughtfulness, though with an element of wariness admixed. I saw them widen as he comprehended my interest. His song faltered. He licked his lips and a wave of heat and blood rose stinging and tingling to rush gloriously from the soles of my feet to my head. My heart beat twice in silence, the world falling away from our tangled glances, the two of us alone in the pupil of God's eye.

And then normality returned with a chorus of clinks as the slouching officers set down their spoons and cups, leapt to attention, mobbed me with welcomes and glasses of wine.

I couldn't remember his name! We must have been introduced a week ago. One of those dutiful faces beneath cocked hats must have been his. But, distracted by duty, I had been deaf and blind. Impossible though it seemed now, I simply had not noticed.

"Lieutenant Garnet Littleton, sir," he said, and gave me a wry, sensitive smile that made me choke on my claret. Dear God, so much for time! The voyage had only just begun and already I was doomed.

Chapter Two

You cannot guess how I am laughing in my heart. Well, why should you? I am dead and dust, and all you see is the change of writing from Harry's crabbed scrawl to my elegant hand. There will be fewer ink splots in this portion, I promise you.

Every night it is the same! We tryst with great mutual pleasure, and I, sated, fall asleep, only to be awoken in the grey of dawn by a flutter of curtains, a cold wind and the sound of his snoring. Yet again, he's slumped over the desk, tallow from the candle overflowing the tin saucer in which it stands and greasing his head and elbow. His fingers are in the ink. I have become quite the expert at hauling him from chair to bed and tucking him in without waking him.

Then I sit, and read what he has been saying, and chuckle to myself. He's so earnest! So pedantic. So convoluted in his meaning and expression! I love him for it, but still I laugh.

Look here where he has said, "I don't remember what it was he was singing." Is that not shocking? It reminds me of my father, trying to recount his own courtship over the dinner table. "Your mother was the most radiant creature I have ever seen," he would say, "in a blue satin dress that matched her eyes…"

"Darling, it was teal," my mother would reply. "And silk. I can't believe you can't even remember my dress. Thank God one of us was paying attention!"

And they would bicker for the rest of the afternoon, both of them with the same smug smile, taking great pleasure from their children's annoyance.

I feel a little like that now. For the song was *Give me but a Friend and a Glass, Boys*, and it was flung out like a net to see what I could catch. In case it is not sung where you are, dear reader, here are the words.

Give me but a friend and a glass, boys,
I'll show you what t'is to be gay;
I'll not care a fig for a lass, boys,
Nor love my brisk youth away.
Give me but an honest fellow
That's pleasantest when he is mellow
We'll live twenty-four hours a day.

You see? I was angling for a fish to bite, so I shall not rebuke him too much for being unaware of the lure, when he took it down whole and was hooked. Evidently he was so dazzled by my numerous and wondrous qualities, that my message utterly passed him by. I find I can forgive him for that.

Do you think I'm a fool? Yet it isn't folly which makes my words so light, and causes nonsense to spill out of my mouth like the notes of an aria. It's just that I'm happy. I didn't believe it possible to be this fortunate in life, being what I am. But I was wrong. Happiness goes to my head like wine. I daresay I am insufferable with it. If that's the case, I ask you to bear with me. I will become much more miserable presently.

I suppose I should cease this drivel and pick up the account where Harry has left it off. That momentous instant when Cupid's arrow pierced us both. Straight through one heart into the other, it flew. Metaphorically speaking, you understand, though, at the time, had I looked down and seen blood, I would not have been surprised. The rosy dimpled boy, having done his worst, clapped his bow back between his wings and flew off, chuckling. I was left trying not to smile, trying not to flirt or to stare. Trying not, in short, to get the pair of us hanged.

I had enjoyed the game of it, in the past. I did not enter the Navy because I feared to put myself at risk, and I have always found that life tastes sweetest with a slight spicing of terror. If you go looking for them, there are always men to be found, three weeks out of port, who are willing to take the chance of a quick fumble, a whisper misjudged so that the lips brush skin, the torment of squeezing by, just that little bit too close in a confined space. All this leading to a hasty climax on the cable tier or the spirit room. The gunpowder magazine, that's my favourite. Biting kisses and the little death in the dark, surrounded by all that slumbering fire.

I'm not a gambling man, despite what my present neighbours might tell you. But I believe the reckless compulsion a man finds at the tables, I found in this. Knowing I could be destroyed at any moment, loving the high stakes and the thrill.

And so I was singing in invitation when the door opened and Harry ducked beneath the sill. He has waxed lyrical over my charms. It is only fair I be allowed to do the same, lest you think that he is all the gainer and I the loser of this transaction. Nothing could be further from the truth. He was a broader man than I. Strongly built. Traces of the lower deck lingered in that awful jacket he wore and in his hands, made muscular and large by manual work, early in life.

I would not dream of a liaison with a tar. A crewman could not in all conscience say no to me, an officer. I could never be truly certain he was as willing as I, and so I have never dallied outside my rank. But I've looked. And I must say Harry's slight coarseness appeals. He has a pugnacious face, and keeps his hair cropped to the scalp. It is the colour of the stone called 'tiger's eye', a beautiful blend of brown and gold, and I wish he would let it grow, just a little. He says it irks him in the heat, but I would make it worth his while.

Yet it was his eyes I noticed then. An indeterminate colour, somewhere between blue and green, as though the Creator had taken the pale blue of the English skies and added a liquid wash of gold. They changed from shadow to light, from expression to expression. I thought I saw a different me in them; a man I liked better than I had liked myself hitherto.

I drew out my own chair for him and made him sit. He toyed with his wine, his tanned face white as if freshly painted. I thought he looked thunderstruck as I; still deafened and dazzled by that moment of the divine. No wonder Jove's lovers burned up entire when he revealed his full power to them! We had seen but an instant of it and we were as shaken as a toddler by the blast of his first cannon. Such a physical thing, I could have fallen on my arse from the recoil, and bawled for fright.

He looked afraid too. Instinctively, once I had made my introductions, I found a patch of shadow in which to sit, and let the Second Lieutenant, Angus Kent, fill up our silence with a long account of those things our old captain used to do, which he supposed our new would wish to continue.

Harry nodded in appropriate places. I saw his eyes stray to me. I wondered why there was no crack, no snake of lightning following the path of them, for I felt it in me. Every fibre of my frame clenched and then released with a strange tingling snap.

He snatched back his gaze when he saw me watching, and coloured. His jaw hardened. "Well, gentlemen," he said, "I honour your captain's name, and he seems to have run a taut ship. But I go my own way. I will keep those traditions I find useful, but I do not intend the hand of a dead man to guide me. You must reconcile yourselves to change."

A firm voice, a frank stare. They were impressed. But I had noticed that after that first glance he did not look my way again. His eyes travelled from one side of the room to the other by way of the table, avoiding me. I sat in a notional abyss cut out of the wardroom by his will, consigned to Coventry or to Hell, whichever would suit me best.

Oh, I thought, feeling the chill of it already, *so that's the way of it. He means to reject this. The most extraordinary event of my life, and I'm sure of his, and he intends to pretend it did not happen?* I will admit that grudgingly I was pleased he was wiser than I and more self controlled. But I was wounded to the quick in my pride.

To be so easily dismissed was more than I could bear! *Oh no*, I thought. *You do not feel the thunderbolt of Jove, and go on as though nothing has happened. The gods punish hubris such as that. You do not have the strength to fight against Olympus.*

Look at me again, sir, I thought. *You do not want to make them angry.* But he would not, and neither of us would have believed the retribution that was to come.

Chapter Three

So now you know what I have to deal with—this bundle of antic superstition and high self regard, which does not think to ask a man before commandeering his private journal and making light of his secret thoughts. He is gone now to his work. With his gracious manners and good looks, his well bred courtesy and flair for the dramatic, he is amply in demand by the diamond exporters of Brazil to negotiate with and translate for their English clients. Part guide, part spy, part bodyguard, it is an occupation not without its danger. Scarcely a day goes by without an attempted robbery on the warehouse both from land and sea, and on the individual persons of the company as they walk about town. I believe that too contributes to Garnet's ease here. He could not be content in a less perilous employment.

I have another hour in which to savour my coffee and *pão de queijo*—which is a kind of heavy bread with cheese—before I go to my own work at the customs house. I sit in the little roof terrace of our house with herbs in pots about my knees, and the distant shape of the sugarloaf mountain casting a shadow like a sundial across the waterfront of Flamengo.

I believe some inner reluctance is preventing me from continuing the story. Indeed, I do not like to think on the days between our first landfall here and our second.

Rio de Janeiro is a common port of call for vessels of all nations; a final experience of cosmopolitan civilization and a chance to refresh one's men and restore one's ships before rounding Cape Horn, or the Cape of Good Hope. If we had known what was to come when we arrived here fresh from England in August of the year 1790, so many lives could have been saved. So much suffering averted.

I see Garnet attributes our ill fortune to my resistance to his charms. How like him! He is, I am afraid to say, a poet: a great habitué of the opera and the theatre, and a haunt of every bookshop in Brazil, scraping up ancient love verses and modern sensational fiction with promiscuous abandon.

Do I agree with him that the gods were angry? No, not at all. I believe he makes that excuse to avoid accusing me of the gross mismanagement of which otherwise I must be suspected. I should have noticed sooner. I should have bowed earlier to wind and weather, turned west sooner. Then perhaps when the disease came upon us, we would have still been strong enough to fight it.

And perhaps he is right in this—that had I not been so busy resisting him, avoiding him, repressing my thoughts and desires and emotions, then possibly I would have had more energy and attentiveness to spare for my work.

And yet I had the convicts taken on deck under guard to receive the benefits of fresh air. I had their bedding destroyed and replaced with new, their apartments fumigated and scrubbed. They were fed meat and fruit to keep them from scurvy. I examine my conduct nightly and I am satisfied that, in that respect at least, I could not have done more.

But I am getting ahead of myself again. Enough of this. In future I will tell the story plain, with none of these intrusive musings. And you, Pest, if you read this, must endeavour to do the same. I shall not attempt to keep you out of my private journal. I know now how futile such an endeavour must be. But pray at least make yourself useful while you are here.

So then. A hot, tropical sun shone upon us as we anchored our small fleet off Isla das Cobras off Saint Sebastian, the great city of Rio de Janeiro. Our ensigns drooped heavy in the windless air, and the men in the boats before us, towing us into place, drooped like the flags, gasping. The sky curved like hammered gold above, and across it there flew, cawing like crows, a flight of birds so blue they looked like little machines of enamel and brass, too vivid for life. The wind smelled of rank swamps and green, growing things, smoke and sewage and fish.

I stood at the rail and marvelled at the fine stone walls and forts of the city, the extraordinary mountain on its peninsula, very like indeed to a loaf of sugar stood upright on a dish. I watched the little boats set off from the shore; peddlars in skiffs laden with yams and persimmons, acerola and guava, melons, bananas, and carambola. Whores piled onto rafts, rowing towards us with brawny bare arms, bared breasts gleaming with oil.

Men lined the rail on either side of me, leaning over, waving and grinning, proffering kisses and pennies. I tapped the arm of the marine sergeant Elliot, making him start and drop his shilling into the snatching hands. "Ready the launch, Mr. Elliot. I'm going ashore."

Elliot turned away from the saucy lass he had been eyeing, and looked at me with no great goodwill. I was unrepentant; I expected the men to sate themselves in whatever way they could, but I expected my officers to exercise a little more decorum. After all, I had had to exercise restraint through three weeks of subtle provocation from a certain black haired lieutenant, and I was in no mood to pander to Elliot's whims.

Out of the crush of folk on deck, the said lieutenant appeared like a dutiful shadow, joining me at the rail. He moved aside to let the purser heave aboard a sack of bread, and 'accidentally' touched his knee to mine. He shifted, and our thighs were in contact. The atmosphere of unbridled lust aboard hit my nostrils like opium smoke, making me reel. He saw it and leaned in, smiling, to murmur some pleasantry I could not quite catch, my heart so thundering in my ears.

"Step back, Mr. Littleton," I said, my voice harsh from being forced unwilling through a closed throat. "This is not a cattle market. What do you mean by crowding me like this?"

Our eyes spoke; his expression hurt, puzzled, a little defiant, as if to say *I know you want me. Why won't you take me? I don't understand.* Mine, I hope, stern, unrelenting.

"Forgive me, sir," he said. "I only wished to enquire if I might come with you into the town. I speak Portuguese fluently. Spanish too. I may be of some help."

We had not spoken of this thing between us. In truth I had avoided him, hoping that he would have the sense to leave it alone; that the attraction would die of its own accord for want of encouragement. But it seemed he had not the sense, and for all my neglect it would not die. Perhaps it was time to face it, head on. For me to tell him outright it would not do.

"Very well," I said, as repressively as I could. "You may accompany me."

He smoothed down his hair then, and smiled at me, like a tomcat eyeing its prey.

I will not deny that I was glad of his company. I had had my servant polish everything it was possible to polish in my uniform and my starched neckcloth was choking me. It was my first visit to a foreign country as a Captain of His Majesty's Royal Navy, and at the sight of the fortifications on *Ilha dos Cobras*—even though they truly looked to me more sugar-pastry than stone—I became convinced that courtesy required me to introduce myself to the Governor. But in doing so, I would bear, on my inadequate shoulders, the dignity of my country and my king. I, a bargeman's son, without a drop of truly gentle blood in my veins.

The *Casa dos Governadores*—the Governor's House— was a long, white building, reassuringly severe. I remembered to wipe my hands on my handkerchief and not on my coat, and I went in with such an assumption of dignity and so straight a back I must have walked like a heron in a pond,

cold eyed and dainty, hiding my inadequacies by a show of
pride.

I believe I had begun to struggle, with my gutter Portuguese—picked up in the tavernas and bawdyhouses of Lis-
bon—through an utterance resembling "I come, bring hello
his Great George," when Garnet stepped into the fray, bowed
with just the right amount of civility and rattled off the im-
probable names and titles of the Governor and his staff as
though born to the idiom. He charmed and smiled and trans-
lated, briefly and succinctly, leaving me with little to do but
to stand and look the part. This I could manage.

Even when the formalities turned into an unwelcome invitation to dine, he enabled me to play the part of "picture of
silent strength" rather than the clown I must have otherwise
appeared. My gratitude for his aid was such that when we
spilled, a little merry from wine and port, out of the dining
room and into the clinging damp velvet of the Brazilian
night, I nodded indulgently at the first thing he said.

In the avoidance of diplomatic disaster, I had forgotten
the other, larger disaster that loomed like a lee shore beside
us both.

I began to have an inkling of it again as he led me past
the fountain that played so decorously in the square before
the Governor's House—its severe symmetry speaking of reason and enlightenment and self restraint—and out, ducking
through narrow alleys and long shuttered streets that cut
across the *Calhabouco* point, the fortress on our left, the land
rising on our right into a noble tree clad hill. The military
hospital glowered like a further crag atop it.

Paving gave way to channels of dust. The torches, which
had burned in front of the civic buildings, guttered out, and
only the moon hung, ivory-gold and swollen above the whispering trees. Something, an ape maybe, chattered in the profound darkness outside the city, and others answered it,
whooping. I looked at Garnet, and the pale topaz light
sleeked lips turned in as if to smother a smile. His eyes

gleamed like the moon.

"Where are you leading me, Mr. Littleton?"

"Just here, sir."

A mud-brick building, visible in the darkness only as scattered yellow dots of light, lay like a rockfall on the side of the hill. My eyes adjusted, picked out the gaps where dirt had fallen from an angle, and lamplight shone through the chink. The roof was all holes, like a colander turned over a lantern. When the door opened, the whisper of human voices was added to the sea and trees, and a drum began to thud out a dim irregular heartbeat. Something like a lute, sweet and stringed, picked out a lazy, meandering melody, now approaching the drumbeat, now drifting apart, like a long silken pennant falling, twisting and fluttering from a high mast.

Within, it was dim; a tawny, confiding, ill-lit place. They crammed us into a little stall like a donkey's at the back of the room. Indeed, I believe the place may have been a stable-block once, now tricked out as something else; a ballroom, a bawdy house, I wasn't sure. A woman with long hair straight and black as poured tar and skin the colour of polished rosewood put down before us bowls of some kind of stew, and flagons of wine as raw as vinegar. I took off my hat and turned my coat inside out to hide the gold, but as I did so, the small stir caused by our entrance evaporated. One by one the onlookers took their fill of watching us and looked away.

The music began again, like rainfall.

The table gave us scarce room to put down knives and tankards together. Behind it, we needs must touch. The buttons of Garnet's pocket-flap poked me in the hollow of my hip. Our elbows jostled as we ate, and the stew was spiced with little red flecks that bit my tongue like fire, until I had no option but to quench it in long pulls at my wine.

I drank too much, too quickly. Sweat beaded on my scalp and itched beneath the wig. I took the damn thing off, wretched horsehair and sticky pomade and authority abandoned all together.

Peeling out of my coat too, I sat on it to keep it safe. And all the while that heartbeat went on pounding, lazy and hot and sweet, until the room reeled about me, and I could not get the scent of Garnet out of my mouth, no matter how burned. It wound about me, like the music, every time he moved; some modern cologne, orange blossom and rosemary, overlaid atop of tar and sweat and heat.

"This…this is a mistake," I said, not quite sure whose mistake it was; his or mine. I should not have followed him here, let alone come through the door. I did not know why I had, except that I had very much wanted to.

A little ripple of applause went through the room. Voices called out in soft encouragement, and Garnet leaned over to whisper, like a friend with a confession, his lips just grazing my ear, his breath warm on my skin, raising all the little hairs on the nape of my neck with shivery, appalled desire, "On the contrary, it's most carefully planned. There is even a bed waiting upstairs."

"We're in a crowded room!" I snapped, shocked, and realised too late that my shock was itself a confession. An innocent man would have taken Garnet's word only as an invitation to get very drunk; the assurance one would not have to walk far to find a bed in which to sleep it off. I, who was not innocent, could no longer pretend not to catch his meaning. If I wished to break off this courtship before it started, I had now lost my chance to lie.

He understood this too. "You can't tell me you are anything other than what I am, sir. You can't say you didn't feel what I felt; that day."

I had no need to ask him which day, and that shook me. So he had experienced it too, had he? That revelation, utterly unlike the infatuations to which I had been subject in my youth—he had shared it. A kind of bitterness against destiny and the unfairness of the world, and the bloodymindedness of youth, which would not see or acknowledge the inconvenient impossibility of its desires, made me look away, his frankness unanswered.

But looking away was another mistake. A couple had begun to dance to the music; she in a white blouse and no stays, her great full skirt billowing about her like a wheel, he in a pair of white breeches and nothing more. I cannot attempt to describe how lascivious was the sight. They swayed together, their hips moving in the rhythm of the drums. Came together, he pressed tight to her back, their bodies moving as one, then swirled apart, catching one another by the throat for a kiss, breaking away and dancing alone, flaunting themselves, taunting one another with their beauty and their pride.

The breeches rode low on the man's hips. Along the hollow of his flexing spine his sweat gleamed like amber, and his black skin bore a fine dew like the bloom on the skin of a plum. He drew himself up and clapped a staccato rhythm, making the music his own, making my heart drop and then soar. So beautiful! So masculine; so ready to lay claim to what he wanted. And she, so complicit, her eyes full of answering fire, challenge and amusement.

Garnet's hand on my thigh was almost my undoing. I turned and surprised the same look on his face; a yearning, inward, sensual look—a defiance and an invitation. He wanted me to be that for him; to be a man, for him. "You can't say you don't want this as much as I do."

His hand moved, sliding up to curve about my yard. The blood drained from my skin and my lips became cold. Oh yes, I wanted him with an intensity that crossed the line into pain. I shoved back the bench on which we sat and reeled away, spilling hat and coat and wig to the floor, my teeth chattering. "It ca—it can't happen!"

"But *why?*" He pouted like a spoiled child, and I wished I didn't find it so adorable.

"You need to ask?" *They'll pillory us and pelt us with excrement. They'll mock and laugh and whisper. They'll take away the twenty years of my life I spent working for this: my rank, my ship, my duty, my king and country. My pride.*

Garnet drew himself up with a lithe and heartbreaking arrogance like that of the dancers. His unselfconscious smile was an anchor in a racing tide. "Am I not worth the gallows?"

I cut myself loose, stumbling out into the crowd, and thence to the door, pursued by his gaze as by a shark. I feared he might yet eat me if I stayed longer. "I am not afraid to die," I said. "But the man is not yet born who could tempt me to endure the possibility of disgrace."

Chapter Four

By God, I'd forgotten what a prig Harry was in those days! Ungrateful bastard, and after I saved his sorry arse from making a laughingstock of himself in front of the Governor and the *ton* of Saint Sebastian. I will admit the whole incident somewhat dampened my ardour. Weeks of denial and anticipation, wondering where best to take him, savouring in advance the thought of our first time. How sweet, how intoxicating a thought…and now this.

Though I picked his discarded garments from the floor before I too headed back to the ship, I made certain to drag them through every scrap of mud upon the path.

Disgrace, eh? I grew up in disgrace. How could it be otherwise, being the youngest of five sons, with no other way to attract my parents' attention? I have stood in the corner of the schoolroom very still for hours on end while my brothers and sisters played outside. I have been cuffed and birched and caned at home, and in the Navy I have been mastheaded, left spread-eagled in the rigging and kissed the gunner's daughter a thousand times.

I like to be admired, but I don't *care* very much, within, what people think of me. Not with the kind of soul-deep care that Harry seems to feel. I didn't understand it then. I'm not certain I understand it now.

I see he has called me 'Pest' and admonished me to keep to the story. What shall I say about him then? Brute! Do you truly think you can still give me orders now?

Still, it was in a sober frame of mind that I returned to my cabin. As was no doubt his intent, I pondered the reject-tion for some days. Weeks, indeed. Until my hammock became a torment to me, sleep being far off, and I could have mapped the position of every knothole and nailhead in the deck above me blindfolded. How could I fight this bugbear of disgrace? Why should I trouble myself thus over some ape of a creature with whom I had scarce exchanged a dozen words? Who was this man to have such a hold on my imagination, with his coarse hands and his cowardice?

No man of resolution would be turned back from his course by such an ephemeral threat. Good God, no man of fashion would still be wearing a wig these days! I should have known from that alone that he had the dash and the moral precepts of my grandfather.

And then I would dream of him, his hair grown long and soft. I would put my lips to it, and it would taste of crème caramel. I'd wake hungry, in every sense, and begin again the endless battle to hate him for his fear.

This was an anxious and a fretful time for us all. We re-provisioned at Saint Antonio's busy docks, payed the seams of all the ships afresh with new caulking, emptied and pumped out each hold to check for damage to the hull. We scraped the worst of the crud off *Banshee's* copper bottom, and careened the other ships to rid them of weed and worm. Then we reloaded the ballast and stocked the holds carefully to ensure each ship sailed to the best of her ability. All this at the breakneck pace for which the Navy is justly praised. Time was drawing on. August passed into September, and though here the days might pass as balmy as ever, down at the arse-end of the world, where we were going, the change of seasons would be reflected in changeable weather, uncertain winds, and currents.

Time and tide wait for no man, they say. Neither waited for us.

We left Rio on the fourteenth of September, *Banshee* leading, *Drake* and *Ardent* a cable's length behind, *Cornwall* and *Quicksilver* behind them in formation. It had been—the dart of Cupid apart—an uneventful voyage, and Angus Kent said as much as we sat down to dinner in the wardroom in the second dog watch.

I told him to mind his mouth, and all around the table I caught the flutter of movement as lieutenants, marines, and warrant officers made little gestures to avert the bad luck. But I think I've said before that the gods frown on hubris, and we'd scarcely hours to wait before this was proved true again. At six bells in the middle watch...I beg your pardon, dear reader. If you are no sailor, that is at three of the clock in the cold hours before dawn, the fresh wind that had carried us out of harbour veered. The sails fluttered at the edges with a sound like giant hands clapping. The fore course blew out aback.

Tumbled out of my hammock at the great crack, I raced up the companionway barefoot, in my nightshirt, found Harry already there, already bellowing orders. Lieutenant Bailey, who was in my opinion the greatest idiot the Lord ever gifted to this world, could not apologise enough. He smoothed his whipping grey-blond hair. The wind carried his ribbon away. His pale eyes bulged: the shift in the weather had taken him by surprise, he said. He would have had the sails under control in a moment. He was covered in shame that the Captain had been forced to wake, but really it was not his fault...

A rain had driven in on the wind. It plastered my shirt against me and dripped into my mouth. I drew breath to tell him exactly what I thought of his seamanship, and Harry took hold of my arm, the heat of his hand like a spot of white light on my elbow.

In the distance, but still too close, lightning tore a booming path across the sky, showing Harry's eyes, vivid green, blue, gold and then darkness. To think, I was all but nude before him—the old linen shirt drenched and clinging—and I was too furious with Bailey to take advantage of it. I missed an opportunity there, and it was the last one I would have for many terrible weeks to come.

But first I need a drink. I taste those days in the back of my throat and they cling there like mildew. I half expect to find a crop of hands and limbs and organs, all furred and soft with rot, growing deep inside my chest...But that's—no. That's just a nightmare I have at times. Wait a moment.

There. It's better to write this out of doors, under an awning in the marketplace, surrounded by women dressed in fabrics of such riotous colour it looks as though someone had smashed a stained glass window over them. An escape route at my back, the ocean in front of me, placidly blue, and a glass of *cachaça* to hand. There's nothing like that taste of grass and pepper and eye watering alcohol to strip the stench of death from your mouth.

The contrary winds remained with us. By tacking and tacking and tacking again we inched down the coast of South America. At first we attempted to uphold morale with endless rounds of ship visiting. Such officers as each transport could spare dined with us, and then the next day we would row over to them, and repeat the process in return.

But mine seemed not to be the only bruised heart aboard, for the atmosphere of these visits was awkward at best, poisonous at worst. I suppose the grandeur of our wardroom in comparison to theirs left them feeling out of place and abashed. At any rate, as the journey wore on and our weariness increased, these visits fell off. We Banshees were left alone in our splendour, and our little fleet drew in on itself, surly and uncommunicative and tired.

The *Banshee* herself was a cold, wet creature; at the best of times like a coffin buried in a marsh. Now, the planks of the hull separated as she worked against the wind. Cold sea water trickled endlessly down the walls. The decks, too, gaped as she wallowed, and rain and brine showered on all of us sleeping below. I would wake for my watches like a prune, my skin shrivelled by wet blankets. Salt sores opened on my back and legs and buttocks.

And I was privileged of course, for I had access to better
rations than the men, and I did not have to pump, day in, day
out, the rattle of it after a time as inaudible as one's own
breath.

A month of this passed, and the sea chilled as we picked
our way south. I slept in my coat now, my cot clattering
against the wall without waking me from my sunken stupor.
We were entering the treacherous Scotia Sea—the maelstrom
of hot and cold currents and capricious winds that makes
Cape Horn so feared.

By this time we had hoped to be far, far East of this, with
Africa to larboard, rounding the Cape of Good Hope and entering the Indian Ocean. But though we worked the sails until men fell from the rigging out of mere exhaustion, we
could not make easting worth a damn.

On the twelfth of October, Joe McCall fell from the
foremast topsail yard and broke his back on the deck. He was
our third victim of sheer weariness, and I remark it only because I thought for a moment he had made a boom like a
cannon when he fell. I had joined the men hauling on the
running rigging, and it was the boy Stirling who cried "Sir!
Sir!" and drew my attention to the second gun and signal
from the *Drake*. They were asking for Doctor Mortimer to be
sent to them, and as they had a surgeon of their own, Harry
sent me too, to see what was amiss.

Dear God, it was dark. I remember that. The skies,
though midday, were heavy as iron, smeared with a hint of
rust. For once all winds had fallen, though a dirty emerald
light flickered on the horizon. I could hear the silence as I
swung up the side of the convict transport ship, and my skin
crept. The smell hit me first. You've smelled slave ships, I
trust? That reek of human fear and ordure and misery? If not,
I encourage you to do so. It may change your mind on many
things. One voyage, they say, and you may yet come away
human, but sign on for a second and you will lose some part
of your soul. This was worse. This did not give a man a sec-

ond chance. It hit me in the face like the moist wind on the opening of a hot house door, and I bent double and vomited over the side.

"Not pretty, eh?" said Joseph Barnes, the Master, as I straightened up, holding my handkerchief to my mouth.

"What…" I asked, looking out over a deserted deck, ropes lying in tangles, sails unmanned despite the livid sky, marines sleeping in the bow netting rather than go below. "What is the cause?"

"Death." Dr. Mortimer came aboard with his servant behind him. "That is the smell of death, and…" he sniffed the air as a gourmand might sniff a fine bottle of wine, sifting through the various flavours. His jowls drooped, and he hugged his bag to his chest as though it were a sleeping child. "Typhus, I believe." His smile looked winched up by thin lines. "The bouquet of Newgate."

"Gaol fever, he means." Barnes was a starving bulldog, his skin hanging in folds, almost green in the eerie light. We followed him below, to a bare and silent mess deck. Hammocks, each sewn closed about a human form, piled up in the stern. A speckled arm lolled from a cot still swinging from the deck above, and Mortimer picked it up with professional interest, looking pleased when its owner screamed.

The smell filled every orifice, oozed almost visibly into one's footsteps. Not like battle, that's a bright smell, sulphur and hot brass and fresh meat, coppery and clean. This was foul.

"Yes," Mortimer dropped the arm and proceeded to the cage built into the bows. "Typhus." No movement stirred behind the bars. Down in the hold where the less privileged had been confined, there was no sound. Only that fetor, sliding up the stairway like a snake.

"A storm is coming," I said, numb with the horror of it. There must have been lanterns, I expect. I believe Barnes had one in his hand. But I remember the scene pitch black, as though we stood in a pit. "How many men do you have to man the ship?"

"Not enough." Barnes drew in a wheezing suck of breath.
"We was tired to start with. All this fucking tacking upwind,
sir, we was fit for the knackers weeks ago. Then this started
and we dropped like flies. Four of us left, sir, fit and healthy,
counting the marines. Ten with the remaining prisoners, but
they're women."

I looked back at the pile of hammocks in the stern, the
lowermost already seeping with putrefaction. The topmost
was barely two feet in length, sewn carefully to the larger
form beside it. Barnes caught me looking and dropped a
hand onto its swathed head. Tenderly, so as not to wake it.
"That 'un's Martha, my daughter. And this 'un's my wife."

"I will send over crew from the other ships. At once," I
said, looking away so that he might weep in peace. It would
be a near thing, but I believed we had just time to transfer
men enough to get her through the storm. Maybe time to
heave that pile of corpses overboard first, if we rushed. A
nine day blow with them tumbling about the ship like grisly
skittles did not bear thinking about.

Disaster has a funny way of breaking upon you by fits
and starts; too large for you to comprehend the entirety at
once. Dr. Mortimer set a hand in the small of my back.
Which I resented, I must say. He was always one for these
little liberties. He muttered, "Sir," in that tone these people
reserve for tragedy and large bills, "We arrived healthy at
Rio. This must have come aboard there. Given the amount of
socialization between ships in the first weeks out, I feel it
incumbent upon me to say…"

The first tiny wave of the oncoming storm lifted the sea
around us. I could feel it passing beneath the keel, shivering
up through the planks of the hull. A change coming. An
omen. I did not lift the doctor by his lapels and shake him. I
hope you'll agree that was very restrained. "It's in the other
ships too?"

"Undoubtedly, sir. And also our own."

Chapter Five

McCall's fatal tumble from the rigging had made my mind up. No matter our determination we could not sail directly into the wind. We would have to dare the Horn. I would give the order to turn west the moment Garnet returned.

Driving rain had begun to lash horizontally across the greasy grey swells of the building sea. Garnet's body, as he scrambled aboard, made a hole in this wall of water. His lips were blue and beneath his sable hat his hair whipped forward, thrashing like black tentacles. The pupils of his eyes were wide and dark as if from opium smoke. "They're dead," he said. "They're all dead."

"Get a grip, man!" I exclaimed, twisted within at his distress. But I needed him back, under control and at work more than I needed to give sympathy. "What the hell kind of a report is that?"

As soon as I got the true story out of him, I roused our own invalids on deck. We fought our way to the limping hulks of the transports, grappling and pulling them close one by one. The poor remnants of crew from *Drake* and *Cornwall* amounted to no more than ten exhausted men bent double against the strengthening wind, speechless and cadaverous and dappled with livid red spots. I would not abandon even the violent convicts, much less those whose crimes had been merely to be hungry and desperate, and so as the waves mounted I sent the marines to swarm across from one ship to the next, breaking open the barred doors and bringing every human creature who still drew breath into the *Banshee*.

Lashed together with *Quicksilver* we plummeted down

the troughs of waves that had become mountainsides. The sky had met the sea, and we breathed water only a little less dense than the ocean. The tear and smack and boom of lightning raced towards us on clouds like boiling black tar.

Banshee wailed like her namesake as the unmanned *Quicksilver* wrenched at her, turning her broadside into waves that smashed down upon her like rockslides. I grabbed the arm of the last convict, scraped him over the rail, dropped him on the deck and hacked at the cables holding the dead ship to our living one. They parted, and as I screamed orders to set *Banshee* running before the wind, I saw the three abandoned vessels of my little fleet heel over, the sea swamping aboard them. A wallow, a moment's smoothness on the surface of that raging ocean, and they were gone.

Happy the man who dies in the middle of a storm—who never reaches the safety and sanctuary of calm; who never has time to contemplate the ruin he has just suffered. For there was my career and my reputation gone in under a minute, and if I'd had time to think about it then, I might not have had courage for what was to come.

But the wind veered and hauled about us, and the wheel bucked beneath the helmsmen's hands like an unbroken stallion. Lightning hit the water next to us in a bang and plume of steam, lanced down again and we heard a shriek like the gates of hell opening, saw one intense, vivid image of the supply ship, *Ardent* lit up, dazzling white against the black abyss of sky and sea. Everything blazed, etched in burning bright lines and fathomless dark. And then she was behind us too, a suggestion of flame in the gloom.

Michael Franklin at the wheel gave a high pitched gurgling scream. He must briefly have let go. The wheel had spun and the spokes caught him in the stomach, beneath the ribs. His body tumbled past me as I crawled, bent double against the wind, to grab the helm. It almost lifted me from the deck. I clung on, every muscle in my back and belly tearing with the effort of holding it still, fighting the pull of the sea, the insolent, easy, veiled strength of the wind.

It blew for nine days.

I remember very little of the end of it. Hands, on mine, eased my claw-like grip off the spokes. I recall my puzzlement as to what this warmth could be about my fingers. Looking up, I saw a face where I had been used to see the sky. "Sir," this face said, "it's safe for you to sleep now. Come on."

It was Garnet, of course.

I had been somewhere far away from humanity, from speech and thought and regret. As he got a shoulder under my arm and peeled me from the helm I felt my senses were being darkened—I had become the ship. I had forgotten what it was to be a man.

"Come now," he taught me to walk again, guiding my uncertain steps into the cabin. "It's over and we're through it. Go to sleep, sir."

Between the two of us—I daresay I was very little help— I was tumbled into my cot and covered with blankets. As I spiralled into unconsciousness he leaned over and kissed my brow, his lips like sandpaper and his hollow cheeks furred with a ten day's growth of beard.

~~~

When I woke, a day later, I had stiffened in every limb. I shuffled, bleary eyed, out of the cabin, wondering what a captain had to do to get a cup of coffee and a hot breakfast after he had steered his ship singlehandedly through the storm.

A pearl gray sky floated above us, wisps of cloud hurrying from the east. The foremast lay, in a cat's cradle of fallen rigging, over the bow, dragging at us like a sea-anchor. Why was no one attending to it?

Zachary Walsh stood asleep at the wheel, and on all the rigging and the rails of the ship drowsed hundreds of seabirds exhausted by the storm. We were covered over with bundles of white feathers, but there was no other human being on deck.

"Zachary! Zach!" I whispered, my voice as stiff and overstrained as my muscles. As I reached out to shake him awake, his head tilted gently with the roll of the ship and I saw the hectic flush, the red rash of typhus that spread beneath his chin. Casting a hitch about the wheel to keep us on course, I caught him before he fell and hauled him laboriously to the companionway stair.

"Lieutenant Kent! Dr. Mortimer!" I called, trying not to let the panic enter my voice. "Where the hell is everyone?"

The answer met me on the gun deck; long rows of swathed shapes, and a shorter row of invalids hanging in their hammocks. Someone had opened three of the gunports and a wet, cold breeze blew in, making the stench endurable. I like to think my first thought was not *not Garnet—please say he is still alive!* But that thought was very present, adding a newly personal twist to my feeling of helplessly falling.

A sound of knocking came up from the orlop deck beneath my feet—metal on wood, the clatter and glissade of chains. I will admit my skin crawled. I thought myself dead, the captain of a ghost ship condemned to sail these bitter waters for all time as a warning against...

But there my imagination faltered, and the door to the wardroom opened, proving me not quite abandoned, yet. Garnet came out, with a kind of calmness in his demeanour that spoke of having endured madness and won through it, sailing shattered out of the other side. He had even shaved.

He had even shaved! I could have kissed him for that act of defiance, of humanity in the face of this utter ruin. But Mortimer came out after him and so I did not.

"Captain," Garnet said gently, and took hold of Zach's trailing legs by the knees. Together we manoeuvred the man into a waiting hammock. Garnet turned aside to find a blanket, tucked it in around the unconscious sailor with a fatherly tenderness I had not anticipated in him. He was so reassuringly in control of himself that I found it easy to imitate him—to click back into place like the rudder sliding back onto its pintles, ready for use. Affection for him swelled up and almost filled the hollow place the state of my ship had opened in my chest.

"This happened during the storm?" I asked, nodding at the line of casualties, without taking my eyes from the edge of his lips. He had a little scar there. Perhaps he'd split it, fighting as a child. It glimmered silver. I thought the skin must be thinner than in other places, the pulse beneath hotter, and at the thought life came thundering back into my veins, scalding sweet. I regretted the dead—their names are in the beginning of this book and I read them over every night— but the same life that breaks the shell, that sends the sap of trees hammering into the sky, demanded its recognition from me. We were not dead, either of us. We were alive, and I ached to prove it.

Garnet responded to my gaze. His nostrils flared and his mouth opened a little. He inched forwards. If we had been alone I believe we would have rutted there amid the corpses, and it would have been...It would have been holy, in some way: life's victory, an affirmation that love was greater than death.

But we were not alone. Garnet wrenched himself away, cleared his throat. I sat down shakily on the nearest cannon. And Dr. Mortimer, who looked like the skin of a sausage after the meat has been squeezed out, said "I've no doubt the disease has been aboard some time, manifesting itself only as a general malaise and lowness of spirits. But the storm taxed our resistance too greatly. We could no longer keep it in check, and it has spread..." his smile, even now, was not without an element of scientific interest, "with extraordinary rapidity and completeness."

"So I see." I stood, lifting up along with my bones the weight of responsibility for all of this. "There is no one on deck. How many men do we have fit for duty?"

"Six." Mortimer did not attempt to soften the blow. "The three of us, Lieutenant Gregory—the commander of *Quicksilver*—Taff Walsh, foretopman out of the *Cornwall*, and Ben Hough, one of the jailers, also out of *Cornwall*. They are asleep, but I can rouse them if you wish."

"No, let them rest. I've no doubt they need it."

"If, under Providence," Mortimer went on, with a careful note of hope, "we are permitted another week of calm, then I believe I should be able to provide you with a further nineteen convalescents, capable of light duties."

"Very well," I said, quailing inside. Six exhausted men to handle a three masted ship as she negotiated her way into an unknown harbour in potentially foul winds? Yet we could not stay at sea. Not here in this perilous southern ocean, where storms came regular as the tick of a clock.

As I thought this, there came again that deep, indistinct groaning from the hollow of the hold beneath us; the rattle of chains and something that sounded almost like speech. My wits had settled and this time, though the hair still stood up on my arms, I took a lantern from its nail in the bulkhead and edged slowly down the stair. The noise stilled. The light ran away from me, illuminating the ribs of the hull like the belly of a whale, and revealing blackened, shabby, hunched things that moved, shuffling forward until their chains twanged taut. Their eyes glistened in the light of my lamp.

"Get us out of here!" He was a flash of teeth in a tangled beard. A distinguished looking man once perhaps, but goblin-like in that half light. I've never seen eyes before or since that had such a red light in them, but his words were reasoned enough. "Please, Captain! You are the captain, ain't you? Please, we can help! Just let us out."

"You've been fed?" I asked, while inside, my heart seemed to turn to brass, its beat jerky and far more terrified than I had ever been facing the French.

"Oh aye," said he. "And watered like cattle when they could spare the time. But we've all had the fever, ain't we, and come out the other side, fit and healthy, and you need us."

I didn't like his smile. The records of his offence had gone down with his ship, but if he had not done murder in the past, I believed he was contemplating it now.

"I will think on it," I said, and went out into the open air with the sense that I was running away.

"There are twenty-three of them, sir." Garnet had followed me, and now he leaned into the wheel for support. "Twenty-three men, with nothing to look forward to at our destination but dust and chains. And six of us. If there's a single man among them with knowledge of navigation, we'd be signing our death warrant to let them free."

I took a glass and climbed to the mainmast top-mast yard, scouring the three hundred and sixty degrees of horizon for land. Given nine days running before a wind of twelve knots or more, we must have rounded the Horn in the storm. America should lie to the east—the long hospitable coast of Chile, where we could land and nurse our invalids back to life, rest and eat and regain our strength, and draft in any adventurous Chilean lad who cared to sail with us. If there was but a blue, cloudlike shape on the edge of sight, a change in sea and clouds, we might yet be saved.

A smudge darkened the edge of the world to starboard. My heart leapt into my dry throat as I peered and peered through the little circular window at that low… ridge of hills in the distance? Or might it be a reef? Was there a line of white beneath it where the surf broke on the shore? The log had gone over the side in the storm along with the midshipman who was trying to read it. All I knew was that we had been tossed like a thrown stone steadily west north west. How far we had travelled I had no idea, and would not until the skies cleared enough to show us the moon. But it *could be* America, over there. It was not beyond the bounds of possibility. *God almighty, have mercy on this sinner now. Let it be land. Please, let it be land.*

The wind blew still nor' nor' west, away from what I thought must be the coast. If it was land, that smudge of black should be growing fainter, dipping slowly beneath the horizon.

It flickered white. I took the glass from my eye and rubbed the strain from my face, and when I looked again the shape was larger, darker, more defined. I felt then as a man must who is alone and wounded in the woods and hears the first howl of the wolves, a kind of paralysis of terror and disbelief. The thing was flying towards us out of the east. Ten minutes more and I could see it as boiling black thunderheads, piling up one on top of another. Their undersides drew down into strange, demonic dugs, stained crimson and weeping rain as red as blood.

Courage drained from me. I closed my eyes and clung to the rigging, resting my cheek against the worn fibres of the shrouds, and I might have stayed there until the storm overtook us, blew me into the air like a child's kite, had not Garnet beneath me suddenly begun to laugh.

I climbed down, startled. The thrum of the sea through the hull had already strengthened and the lines popped and hissed as they tightened. Garnet looked up at me, the distant lightning reflected in his eyes. "Dear God, sir," he laughed, his smile wide and bright, "it isn't often you get to watch your own death flying towards you across the water. It's just as the poets say. It's sublime!"

His joy leapt the gap between us like a flame travelling down a fuse. It touched something within me and exploded, filling me with light and heat. I thought him a magnificent madman, and he filled me with awe and delight. In that moment I knew for the first time that I loved him.

His lunacy infected me. I wanted nothing so much as to drive him into the cabin, lock the door and couple as the ship was ripped apart around us, dying as we'd never dared live.

But I was the captain and below my feet there slumbered still a score of my crew and twenty-three other human souls whose well-being was my responsibility. Half in love with death as I was, I would not let them perish without doing my utmost to save them.

"All hands on deck, Mr. Littleton if you please." I brought the keys of the manacles out of the stern locker in which they had been stowed and passed them to him solemnly. He grasped my fingers with them and pressed, clasping my hands for a long moment, knowing what I was going to say. The wind picked up and shrieked in the rigging and the first spatterings of that bloody rain smacked aboard, hailstones rattling down with it.

"All hands please, Mr. Littleton," I said. "Including the prisoners."

"Aye, aye sir. At once."

Chapter Six

You felt that too? I wish I'd known! I still think there could be no better way to die than that—the glory and the ecstasy of it. Maybe when we grow old? When the aches and pains begin, you lose your teeth and I my hair, we can buy a sloop and fit it out like an emperor's tomb and run it into the maw of a black squall. Let the sea tear apart that which it brought together? Better than dying in bed, incapable, incontinent and wrinkled, buried in separate graves by mourners to whom the survivor would never be able to tell his grief.

But yes, yes. I dare not risk your rebuke. I have remembered I am supposed to be telling the story and not embarrassing you with my thoughts.

They came up the companionway steps like black dogs, hunkered over, stiff, scarce able to walk from their long confinement in chains. They paused at the top, straightening with exquisite care, squinting at the light and snuffing the racing, water laden air. I can't find it in me to blame them for what they did. I'd have done the same had I been caught scrumping apples, confined in darkness for months, tossed and forgotten as human ballast in the utter dark and freezing cold of the underwater hull. If I'd gone in to that a man, I'd have come out a monster. I can't blame them.

Harry a little I can blame. He should have known. But I think he did. I think he knew they would turn on us, but he wanted to give them a chance at life anyway. The heart of a hero beats in the breast of that man, even though he does look so much like a bailiff's enforcer.

It did not begin immediately. It took three days. The first

day, our prisoners were still too cramped in themselves, unaware of their opportunities and blasted out of their mortal
concerns by the rising, enfolding seas. Landsmen all, they'd
never seen anything like this. They thought nature something
to subdue; a field to plant, a steady place under their feet.
Now man's sheer insignificance in the world was brought
home to them by the terror and power of the sea. When Nep-
tune rages one cannot reason with him, one can only hold on
and hope to endure. For some, it is a strangely intoxicating
freedom. For others, it loosens their wits and makes them
grovel on the deck, blind and helpless as maggots. There are
few unbelievers on the sea—the gods are there, visible in all
their power, and a man must live with them, or die.

Harry lived up to his name and harried them at every
turn, sword in hand—for the powder of a pistol would have
been drenched beyond use in seconds—giving them the will
to move. He pitted himself against their terror and won, driving them to work the sails, to set loose the wreckage of the
foremast, to hold down the wheel. We taught them—we had
to teach them—to read the compass and the flags, to keep the
ship running, running fast in front of the wind.

By the end of the second day, you could see it in their
faces, behind the smear of weariness, the thought, *This is not
so hard. We can do this.*

That was when I put the barrel of water and the wax-
paper wrapped parcel of hard tack in the pinnace and loosened all the ropes that held her tight to the deck. I'm not certain even now whether this was forethought or cowardice. I
know I dared not tell Mortimer or Lieutenant Gregory what I
had done, lest they should take it for defeatism or even mutiny. What can I say? I like to have an escape route prepared.

On the third day the wind fell briefly, and a gleam of yellow sunshine pierced the cloud. From yards and rigging our
convicts looked up and cheered, light tender over battered
faces. Steam rose in frail curls from the decks as the hot
sunlight dried them.

Gregory put a hand on the scuttlebutt, dipped me out fresh storm water. He was a lovely creature, not above nineteen years of age, smooth skinned and rosy as a girl. You'd have thought he rouged his lips, they were so pink, and he was leggy and eager and charming as a new colt. God knows what he must have suffered, growing up in the Navy, but it had made him wary. He glanced down at his reflection, up again at me. "This…this is it, isn't it, sir? The moment they turn on us."

The clouds thinned and streamed away to the west, a sky of cerulean blue dreamed hot above our heads. The scuttlebutt blazed silver, a perfect mirrored circle, and the air filled with the scent of wet hemp. One by one, like fruit too heavy to stay on the bough, men came down from the rigging. The soft thud of their bare feet sounded on the deck all around us.

"They'd be fools," I said. Then loudly, "Can't you see the second front following on behind?" I pointed out east, and indeed there hung a second black line, thin as a pencil stroke. "Can't you taste the lightning in the air? This is only a temporary respite. It'll be on us again in minutes."

We'd had to give them axes with which to clear away the fallen foremast and its tangles of snagged rigging. We hadn't dared to ask for them back. Now the leader of the convicts, a man named Nathanial Carter, walked over to us, took the cup from my hand and dropped it on the deck.

I had been working beside them for the past three days. My hands were swollen, bleeding and black from rope burns. I had slept perhaps twenty-four hours in the past fortnight. I had begun to see the phantoms of our fleet keeping pace with us, their crewmen all in grey, rags of black flesh about gleaming bone. I saw one now, behind him, and it was Joseph Barnes, who had gone down with the *Drake* rather than leave his wife and child.

A month-long fury boiled the blood within me. I slammed the heels of both hands up and under beneath Carter's breastbone. The blow lifted him off his feet, sent him sprawling on the deck, winded, struggling for breath and shocked at the swift response. As he lay there, glaring at me, I made to kick him in the balls.

"Mr. Littleton!" A tearing noise behind me and the seams of my coat parted as Harry grabbed on to the material and hauled me away. I still think he was wrong to do so. Perhaps he had not seen the blatant, deliberate challenge to my authority, and therefore he supposed I had started it. I had not. But I thought, even in my rage, that reacting at once and with maximum force we might yet have cowed them. Harry, Geoffrey, and I had swords; we were military men, we'd fought all our lives. I think we could have taken them. Four or five down, dead, and the rest would have thought better of it.

But Harry...Harry was a little too gentle for the rank he inhabited. He saw, perhaps, something of himself in the prisoners. Understood their station in life better than I, and wished to talk. He hoped we could all come through this somehow together. An admirable sentiment, but naïve.

"How could you instigate this now?" He spun me around, put himself between me and the slowly closing ring of prisoners. The fury on his face matched mine—he was terrified. "The second half is coming!"

It sped upon us almost at his call. The first outlying wave of the next storm built under *Banshee's* abused hull until it groaned, and the lines thrummed. Carter rolled to his stomach, pushed himself up onto his knees and spat on the good clean oak of his Majesty's deck. "We don't need these buggers any more," he yelled. "It's our ship now. Our rules. Give 'em what they deserve, lads. Twelve fucking months in chains, they owe us! Now get them!"

He came for me, teeth bared. My sword was already in my hand. I cut his throat without a second's thought. A lukewarm mixture of rain and blood spattered my face as the temperature plummeted and the sea bucked beneath us.

Wind screamed in the rigging so loud I could not hear the

convicts gasp as Carter thudded to his knees and thence to the deck. But their faces changed. It recurs to me in dreams, the way heady hope, gleefulness, became grim at the sight of that fountain of blood pumping out of his throat.

My own heart choked me, as if it was trying to follow suit. I took a breath and they were on us. They piled on Harry first, because he had seemed weaker than I. Ten of them at least set about him, like a village football match, all gouging hands and kicks and elbows. Three of the bravest edged towards me, fanning out so that I should not be able to defend against all of them at once. Behind me, I could hear above the wind the tiny, tinny noise of steel-on-steel as Gregory fought for his life. Above us the unmanned yards creaked round and the sails blew out, thundering and snapping uselessly.

We tipped over the crest of a wave. A wall of water slammed across the deck. I grabbed a flailing line, watched with triumph as one of my attackers was swept away, flapping in the grip of the water like a minnow poured out of a jar. Wrapping the rope around my wrist, I swung out, caught the second man in the chest with my heels. He spiralled away like a sycamore seed in the gale.

Banshee slid sideways down the wave, the relentless gale heeling her over, her port rail below the water. I darted a glance to starboard and saw a wall of water some fifty feet high, deep emerald green, flecked with racing dots of foam. We slid down its side, broadside on, and above us the crest of the wave built and bent over. Tons and tons of water mere seconds away from falling like boulders atop us, crushing us, filling us up and foundering us.

A tang of copper in the air. Gregory's yellow-haired head flew like a cannonball overboard. I felt almost glad. I knew now that it was over. We were lost.

And then the wind fell, cut off by the enormous wave. The dead, damp air filled with Harry's voice, calling out to me. Possessed by a kind of red raw, death or glory strength, I

ran up the inclined deck of the ship, stabbed two of his as-
sailants in the back and grabbed a handful of uniform coat. It
was like stepping into a shower of knives—edges every-
where. I slashed a red-haired man in the stomach, hauling
Harry with all my strength towards the boat.

Something tapped me on the leg. I saw a brief, blazing
glimpse of Harry's face, eyes wide and green as the sea, a
molten star of white rage within them. He leaned past me. A
whisper of movement as his sword passed within inches of
my face, and then a man behind me was stumbling to his
knees, clutching at his eye, blood seeping through his fingers. As he fell, something tugged again where I had felt the
tap, and looking down I saw a marlin spike driven all the
way through my thigh from one side to the other.

I recall thinking I had never seen anything so comical in
all my life. When I pushed Harry against the boat, drew up
the tarp that covered it, to indicate to him that he should get
in, I seem to remember I was laughing too hard to speak.

Shadow fell black on the ship. Columns of solid water
pelted the deck like ammunition, and then one of the convicts screamed, a high pitched pig-like noise that echoed
strangely in the trough. Solid water curled above us. Spray
whipped away horizontally, as the glassy roof paused before
it fell.

Instinctively, the convicts turned their faces towards this
greater threat, and in that split second pause Harry dived into
the boat. I scrambled after him. For a moment I was stuck,
the marlin spike caught on the tarp. Then I wrenched it out
and used it to saw through the pre-weakened rope that held
the boat to the deck. The rope parted. We ground slowly to
port across the deck. Harry lashed the tarp closed. The sound
of tons of seawater spewing through *Banshee's* port side
gunports rumbled like thunder beneath us. She rolled further
over and our speed picked up. We felt the slatey grind and
shudder of our keel against the deck. The boat's oars
bounced about our shins.

And then a smoothness beneath us and a roar above. The tarpaulin bowed inward. Water spurted from between the knots. We held it closed and felt the deep cold against our fingers. Everything not strapped down within the boat rose and tumbled against us, oars and barrel and biscuit and ropes, bailing bucket and the discarded, blood stained spike. It slowed as we drove deeper. Cold and silence encompassed us, but for the creaking of the boat's timbers. Water seeped in through the lapped planks.

We were underwater, pushed down by the breaker towards the seabed, maybe to smash there like a dropped egg on a flagstone. We held our breath and looked at one another for a long motionless, breathless moment.

And then with a rush and bubbling we burst back onto the surface. With a final clatter everything settled into its place. Like men possessed, we peeled back the tarp, set up the mast and the single small sail, double reefed, working with speed and strength I don't think I could consciously equal again.

The scrap of canvas caught the wind and, collapsing to sit by the stern, I felt life go through the rudder. She had steerage way. I turned her to run before the wind and she sped like a kite up the mountainous sea.

Harry looked back until we were over the streamers of spray and scudding back down the next trough. I did not. I could see the reflection in his eyes, his pupils two dark mirrors. There was nothing behind us. *Banshee* was lost; capsized and gone under, taking all her invalids with her.

He is a well set up man, Harry. Broad shouldered. The kind of man you'd put money on at boxing. But at that moment a careless touch might have shattered him. He sat down as though his bones were made of glass. Looking at me, he opened his mouth, then shut it again, dumb in his desolation.

"Go to sleep," I said. "I'll take the first watch."

With a great struggle, some words surfaced. He crouched forward, laid his hand on my knee. "Your leg…"

I looked down in surprise. Truth be told, I'd forgotten about it. No one could have been more surprised than I to see that my white breeches were now crimson and my stocking gummed to my leg with dried blood. That was, of course, the point that it began to hurt. "Oh," I said—I'm aware it was not the wittiest of ripostes—"oh damn!"

He tore the arm from his shirt to make up a pad of linen and bound it on firmly with his cravat, his hands shaking. His bent head was furred with a stubble of hair that shadowed the shape of his skull and picked out the vulnerable nape in tiny glints of gold. Everything seemed miraculous to me then, limned in the kind of vivid high relief they say is a characteristic of the sight of eagles. I brushed my palm over his head from forehead to nape and back again, feeling how the bristles fought me one way, accommodated the next.

Harry sat back on his heels with a thud. "Don't do that!"

They say I'm not a tactful man, and perhaps I did think, "You can hardly be worried about greater disgrace than this!" But give me credit. Even with the searing, scouring pain that was working its way up through the marrow of my leg and into my stomach and spine, I did not say it. I said, "Why not?"

"Because I don't want you to."

I think of all the wounds I'd had that day, that one was the worst.

Chapter Seven

I was angry with him, you see. And with myself also. His impulsiveness had cost me my ship; had cost Mortimer and Gregory and Chapman and Kent, all the surviving marines and tars, even the convicts, their lives. So I thought at the time. I hadn't realised that Carter had been the one to start it. That makes a difference. I wish you had told me before! I should not have been so resentful over the years.

But I digress. I was at the time furious, and hurt, and deeply, burningly ashamed. I wished I had gone down with my ship—my first command!—and died. I blamed him for saving my useless life, and myself for letting him do so. I loathed the fact that I wanted to let him carry on petting me while I fell asleep with my head in his lap. We neither of us deserved that.

"Can you watch?" I asked at length, reluctantly. "How do you feel?"

"I feel splendid." He grinned at me, white teeth in a face speckled with red gore. "Better than fine. I feel…exultant."

I couldn't answer that. I lay down by the mast, thoroughly repelled, and fell asleep in an instant.

When I woke, my head seemed full of oakum, and my body an iron structure, partially rusted together. Before I opened my eyes, I thought from the sound of the wind that the storm had abated a little. Though I lay in a pool of rainwater, its rate of descent had slowed. A rhythmic scrape and shush lulled me back to oblivion, and when I woke again it was distinctly drier beneath me.

I looked up. Garnet sat in the stern, his black hair blown

54

forward over his face, the tiller under his arm and the ropes of the sail in one hand as he bailed with the other. He lacks at least ten of my years, and at that point he looked, against the breaking dawn, young and weary and beautiful.

He turned his head to look at me. It seemed an enormous effort. His face was white as paper and those brown eyes of his looked black to the rim. "Harry. I'm tired."

My heart twisted within me. Even with the desolation it seemed I had space for a fresh pain; how could I have blamed him for what was my fault? How could I have been angry, when I knew what he was? I knew he was young and proud and reckless and arrogant and hot tempered, and had that aristocratic certainty that everything he did must be right. I knew it, and I had not restrained him. It was my fault.

Creakily, my bones protesting the movement, I found water and hard tack, passed them to him. Then I got him by the shoulders, and as he had done for me earlier, I eased him away from the tiller. He yielded to me, heavy and limp and confiding, not an ounce of strength left in him.

"I have a niece," I said, my arms about his chest, settling him down into a sitting position beneath me. His head drooped onto my knee, his eyes closed. "Betsy. My sister and her husband let her sit up to hear my tales, when I am in port, and she falls asleep just like this; draped all over me. I can lift up her little arm and let it fall, and she does not wake."

He gave an "hmn" of amusement, tried to open his eyes and failed. I should have known the battle vigour would wear off and leave him watching over me, injured, alone and rebuked, with both our lives in his hands and no word of thanks.

"Not angry?"

I threaded my fingers through his hair and teased out the tangles of blood and salt. A wearying inner voice told me we should not be talking so—like lovers, stirring drowsily in the early morning, warm beneath the blankets. But why not?

Who was there here to see? We were ruined and dying, and together. And for the first time in my life—since, at the age of ten I began to suspect there was something strange about me—I felt free. At peace. "No," I murmured, watching his fingers open, and the biscuit he had taken up fall out into his lap. "I'm not angry. Or at least, only with myself. I'm sorry, Garnet. I'm so sorry."

By midday, the storm had slackened to become a fine following wind, the swell had decreased, and the sky above turned the most translucent of whites. A glow like a hot pearl concealed behind those filmy clouds showed me the sun, finally, enough for me to take a guess at our direction. Still mostly west with a little northing. I thought perhaps, with a little luck, we might yet strike Tahiti and be saved, though luck had not been the greatest distinguishing feature of this trip so far.

Garnet slept all day, while I thought about my life. All my striving for success and it had come to this: nothing— worse than nothing. If we made it back to England, by some outrageous miracle, a court martial would be waiting for me, as it was for any captain who lost a ship. I had lost four. An astonishing degree of failure that deserved to be punished with the utmost rigour, *Pour encourager les autres.* The irony of it! All those years I had feared to reach out lest I bring disgrace on myself and here it was, inescapable. It seemed that should I not drown, then I must indeed be destined to hang.

Steam rose off us as we travelled onwards. Our coats dried on our backs. Garnet woke sunburned, his face flushed pink, staggered to the heads and then to the barrel of water to drink thirstily. When he settled himself to the tiller I did the same, brought the bucket back and set it, upturned, between his legs so I could sit there, leaning back against his chest. He gave a snort of amusement, and pressed his smile to the crown of my head. "I like you better like this."

"I find I no longer need worry about the propriety of a relationship with an officer of inferior rank. If I'm not hanged for incompetence, when we get home, I'll be turned before the mast for sure."

"You think we'll get home?" He placed a kiss on the tip of my ear, startling me into laughter.

"At this moment I don't very much care."

I felt his low, rich chuckle through the muscles of my back and it warmed me like the sun. Setting an arm around me, he idly unbuttoned my waistcoat from top to bottom, and though I eagerly wished to know whether he would move on to other buttons after, I had fallen asleep before I could find out.

Sometimes those first weeks come back to me in dreams as a glimpse of paradise. We were hot and cramped and thirsty, filthy, dishevelled, sick of hard tack, and the barrel of water grew staler by the day. Yet what I remember is the solid warmth of him in my arms, drowsing, peaceful and contented as we drifted onwards under the light of the stars. It was the first time I have ever been so purely happy.

We talked. I learned about his family; a mother and father so devoted to each other that the children had always known they came second. He detailed all their different ways of attracting attention, from the ostentatious perfection of the eldest, to Garnet's waywardness. He too had nieces whom he adored. "I was bringing home the most beautiful packet of silk for Constance's first ball dress. She will be coming out soon, and that shade of jonquil would have brought out the chestnut in her hair."

His brows creased. We had unpicked his cravat and made a line, bent a pin into a hook and threaded on it the juiciest, whitest, most energetically squirming maggot we could shake out of the bread, and he was sitting dangling this impromptu fishing rod over the side. He shifted it into the other hand, rubbed his forehead, squeezing his eyes shut. "The silk is at the bottom of the ocean now. And I may never see her again."

Something took the bait. I saw the line whip out through his fingers and lunged for it, catching it just before it hit the water, landing an ugly, wide mouthed warty creature, a toad of the fish world. "Yes!" I cried, elated at still being able to achieve something. "Yes. I got one! You nearly lost him, you sluggard!"

He had not re-opened his eyes. "My head hurts," he said. "The light is too bright."

I used to be a steady sort of man, but Garnet has always had this ability to tip me from overweening joy, to despair, and back again. I left the creature flapping in the bilges and pressed my hand to his face. He all but scorched me.

Savagely, I shoved back the wool of his coat, the loosened neck of his shirt, and saw the fierce red blush where no sunburn should be. There on the hot smooth flesh stood out the little mottled circles of typhus.

I'm told Job in his trial never once sinned by being angry with God. I was not so restrained. I stood by the mast and screamed my voice hoarse at him, shaking my fist at the heavens and dredging up every obscenity from my childhood I had ever carefully purged from my speech. There came no reply, and in the end Garnet had to beg me to stop, for I was making his headache worse.

I sat down again squashed flat, like an ant under a man's foot. I was no doctor, and even if I were, I had no medicines. I had nowhere to go. The storm had thrown me off my reckoning so far I had no hope of guessing our longitude. The empty ocean stretched out from horizon to horizon, featureless, and I knew the islands on which I pinned my hope were scattered in the Southern Ocean like a handful of sixpences on a desert of white sand. Should the wind blow one degree this way, or that, we might pass by them without even seeing them, blow onwards, adrift, a funeral barge under a black sky full of the points of teeth.

Looking back on it now, it occurs to me that I too may well have been delirious from the heat. It seemed such a relief to give up, and yet I was weeping as I tied off the sail, put a hitch round the rudder and made as comfortable a pallet for us both as I could, out of rope and our coats. I lay down there. There seemed a ceremonial to it, as a woman of India lies on the pyre of her husband; perhaps not willing, but resigned to being consumed with fire together with her beloved. Gathering Garnet's lithe frame into my arms, I pressed my wet cheek against his forehead to cool him. He lifted his chin, instinctively offering a kiss. His mouth was dry, his lips hot and rough. His breath against my face came in short bursts of fire. "Hate you," he said. "All this time... You have to pick now. I'm too tired."

"Ssh," I said, "go to sleep." It must have been the end of everything, because there was such a feeling of rightness, of coming home, simply to lie there with his skin against mine, our breath mingling, our hearts slowly coming into time with one another. I closed my eyes and waited for the end.

Let no one say death comes on demand. I woke suddenly, as if, at some instinctual level, I recognised a change. The oars dug me in the back, and my chest and thighs were clammy and damp from being pressed against Garnet's sweating heat. An urgency had me by the heart, but it had not reached my mind. *Damn it!* I thought, *you weren't supposed to wake up afterwards!* But I disentangled myself nevertheless and crawled back to the stern to look out.

Night had fallen and the cool refreshed me. The sea ran on with barely a swell; a long, idle rolling motion, smooth and black. Above us shone a spill of stars, pale gold and silver and white. I thought they twinkled. But something about that flicker kept me braced against the gunwale, gazing up. Was there a sound? A peeping? A low, restless whirring noise?

Yes! Yes there was!

I bit down on my lower lip and the cracked flesh parted. Blood oozed out, salty and thick as I peered up into fitful darkness. I caught fluttering, clapping, clicking noises, an impression of swooping. Birds! And not gulls. These were a great flock of tiny, black, plover-like birds; the kind that make their nests ashore.

I took the tiller in my hand, the ropes of the sail in the other, and turned up into the wind to follow them.

Hours passed. The birds, flying fast against the wind, scudded away before me until I could no longer even guess at them. My heart failed, but I held my course, and then, two or three hours later, I felt that unexplainable sensation a sailor gets when there is land nearby. For me it is a kind of jangle of the nerves, and a breathlessness. The water feels shallow beneath me and the waves feel wrong. The air hangs heavy, as though in an old, unopened room.

The sky had turned to slate, grey-blue, in the east, and sunlight filtered upwards through the sea like a candle in too thick a green glass lantern. I muffled my breathing behind my hand, strained my ears and heard it: surf. The long, uninterrupted swells of Oceania breaking on a distant shore.

"Garnet!" I cried, nudging him with my foot. He rolled side to side limply and I, with my heart beat held in suspense, hunkered down and shook him violently by the shoulder. "Garnet, wake up! That's an order, Lieutenant. Help me find the land!"

His eyes were half open, a slit of white eyeball beneath the fringe of dark lashes. But he clung to life, still. He gave a little mutter, and his pulse raced visible in his scarlet throat. I caught up the bailing bucket, filled it in the sea—the sound of breakers growing stronger in the tricky pewter twilight of dawn—and dashed the water over his face.

Several doctors have since told me I might as well have stabbed him in the heart. The fever should be encouraged to grow and reach its climax, I now understand. This sudden cooling might have proved catastrophic. But he looked so hot, so sunken away where I couldn't reach him, and I wanted him to wake.

Well, I'll know next time if, Heaven forfend, there

should be a next time. I could not check to see what damage I'd done, for as I knelt there, the sun came up and the wind freshened. The boom of the sail creaked around above my head and, as I caught it, I saw over the deep dark blue of the sea a line of turquoise, more vivid than the gem. Breakers dazzled in the newly minted light, and a shallow rise of land showed above them, green with trees.

I stood out to sea once more and sailed cautiously along the line of shore, looking for a place to safely run the boat through the breakers and bring it to land. The dazzling white beach was narrow as a ribbon—scarcely a shelf before falling away into deep water. The shore curved in like a horseshoe. I discovered it was an island little more than a mile long, the main wooded spine of it curled about a central lagoon. If I could steer the pinnace into that, we would have a gentle landfall.

But out from that central spine curved two long arms of dunes and reefs. The water moved like serpents over them, and the breakers rolled in, lifting themselves up and crashing down on the submerged rocks. Risk the waves hurling us down to smash on the narrow rock beach, or risk the deceitful currents and razor edged boulders buried in the inlet to the lagoon?

I looked at Garnet. The heat in him was such that already his clothes were dry again, his face like blood. No more prevaricating. I furled the sail, shipped the oars, and rowed into the inlet.

Had there been two of us—one to row and one to watch—we might have done better. I pulled for four hours or more, from dawn 'til past noon, finding the sandbanks by grinding gently into them, and the rocks by bumping off. My back and arms passed through cramp and into pain, and thence to a kind of thin, red, torn sensation. A little after noon, when I had, for yet another time, run up what looked like a promising channel and come to a dead stop, the sea swelled under the keel. The tide had turned and begun to build beneath us. I had now to fight not to be flung forward too fast. The seas rose and foamed about me, crashing down into the open boat.

As I bailed and struggled to row at the same time the swell picked us up, threw us down, jarring atop a reef. An oar splintered, tearing itself out of my hands. The boat shuddered, grounded, scraping itself along a ridge of rocks. Planks buckled beneath me and sprung wide, admitting rough volcanic rock grown over with corals. Then a second wave lifted us off again, washed us over the bar, through and out into the sapphire waters of the lagoon.

The boat sank beneath us. I held Garnet in one arm and swam for the shore.

Chapter Eight

My poor Harry! Such heroics, and I not conscious enough to applaud. Had it been me, I would have resented my audience's lack of interest, but he is a better man than I. Oh, don't argue, you know it's true.

As for me, I had been dreaming, though horribly real it seemed at the time. I found myself the newest recruit on the Flying Dutchman, and they would keep making me work too hard—I being the only one left in possession of enough of a corpse to handle the sails. Seizing a sudden opportunity to escape I had dived off, into the sea, their insubstantial hands clutching at me. So when I opened my gritty eyes to find myself washed ashore on a dingy pumice beach, I thought at first I was still asleep.

But the waves tickling up my body were exquisitely cool; cool like a mouthful of elderflower iced-cream, sweet and fresh and clean. I breathed in and felt the air move unobstructed in my chest. Splinters of coral dug me in the buttocks with edges like shattered glass. If this was a dream, it was altogether more embodied than I was used to.

With much labour I turned my head, my spine having been replaced by seaweed and my flesh with jelly. There lay Harry, quite exhausted, his mouth hanging open and holes in his stockings. No hat, no shoes. Urchin-like, bruised about the face. The sun shone yellow on his bronze and brown stubble, and the eyes that, even closed, looked too thoughtful, sceptical and sad, in that harsh face.

Beyond him, the sun shone like adamant on a lagoon the unnatural, iridescent blue of a peacock feather's eye.

Through the dazzling light and colour there lazily sailed towards us the black, triangular tip of a cruising shark's fin.

I don't know how we got up the beach, both of us so spent, but you can be assured we did. And fast—stumbling and falling and dragging one another up, out, away from the water. After perhaps five feet, the beach gave way to moss. Dwarf trees rustled about our waists and the light danced in gold-green stars upon our feet. Harry clutched my upper arms as we fell down together for the final time. "You…" he gasped. "You…!" A wild glitter of the eyes and then he lunged forward and crushed me, his hands knotting painfully in my hair as he sobbed into my neck. I, being weak and ill and not immune to sentiment, began to cry as well. Partly because I felt so dreadful, partly because of everything we had lost. Mostly, I believe, simply because he had begun it and I could not stop.

If you think this was unmanly, dear reader, I challenge you to do better under similar circumstances.

We shared what must have been the world's dampest kiss—tears and seawater and snot between us as I held on to his ears for comfort. We shifted closer, little by tired little until we were lying entangled. Then we slept in the dappled sunshine for a day and a half.

And thus began our eight months as castaways. For such a long time, there's little to tell of it. Well, it was a little place. The main island lay like a sausage curled in a pan, somewhat less than a mile long, and narrow. Five minutes walk across, and nowhere was it possible to get away from the sound of the sea. From the ends of the main island curled causeways of sand and rock, underwater at high tide, but perfectly dry at low, and if one faced the lagoon, at the end of the left hand causeway lay two smaller wooded isles. I estimate perhaps a hundred acres of green land, all in all. A hundred and fifty if one counted the sandbanks.

When we woke, that first morning, we made love. Nothing needed to be said; we both understood it would happen as soon as we had the physical resources to allow it. It was sweet and weary and gentle, and afterwards I held Harry tight and mourned for all the things he had had to lose to make this possible. I wished I might give his prudishness and his confidence and his career back to him. And in a petty part of myself I wished he might have come to me despite them, instead of needing to be ruined first. But I will say that holding on to him afterwards, in the warm glow and satisfaction of coitus, I entertained the inexcusable thought that the past months had been worth it.

The island where we found ourselves proved exceptionally suited to life. The trees were of two sorts, the one with small white flowers the shape of octopus tentacles. The other with leaves that turned round as buttons where the salt water dashed against them. In one sheltered spot, the trees grew to eight feet in height, like honest, decent English trees. Beneath these, we made our camp. But the majority of the forest, though composed of the same species, was stunted by constant storms and spray.

Both kinds of tree bore leaves which, we discovered from experimentation, might be eaten, though those of the button plant needed to be stewed first. And both sorts provided wood fine-burning for fires, and heavy and durable as iron for tools.

Birds nested everywhere. Grey birds nursed their eggs in shallow scrapes beneath the trees. Black plumed seabirds dozed on the sandbanks in raucous chattering heaps. Among the branches of the trees darted slender white birds with sloe-like black eyes, like ghostly crows. And all of these were innocent, trusting creatures who never learned to flee at our approach. Good eating.

I suppose you think we did nothing but eat and fuck the whole time. Hah! Well, that wouldn't be so far off the mark. Yet we did improve our domain. Once I had recovered from my fever, and my leg so far improved that I could limp and swim, we returned together to where the boat had gone

down—one of us to retrieve what could be salvaged, the
other to keep the sharks away.

This, I loved. You have to picture it: the water is clearer
than glass, its depths turquoise. Little fish swim about us and
we have not troubled with clothes. Harry swims like a mer-
man, all of him tanned light biscuit brown. I'm looking up, at
the shafts of light through a silver dancing roof and watching
them slip like tongues over the planes of Harry's chest and
belly and privates.

And then the shark comes, and it's all a game of speed
and teeth and death. Can I strike him in the gills strong
enough, hard enough, to deter him while I go up to breathe?
Will he turn and tear my arm off? Well, as I am here writing
this, I think you can guess the answer to that.

In this way we salvaged the tarp and the sail, the marlin
spike, bucket, barrel of water and numerous ropes. Our
campsite in its hollow became positively civilised as we
rigged the sail for a joint hammock and the tarp over it for a
roof. We used the bucket to boil things, warming stones first
in the fire and dropping them in. The resultant stew inevita-
bly tasted of ash, but one got used to that.

Water was our greatest physical problem. When we first
crawled ashore we found numerous pools of it, but over the
next few weeks they gradually dried up. We realised then
that there was no source of water indigenous to the place.
Yet even this was not a great trouble, except on one occasion
I will detail below. For in general rain came at least once a
fortnight and replenished our pools, our barrel and our rudi-
mentary well.

Thus in every bodily sense we were provided for. Indeed,
our cups ran over with plenty. Plenty of food and drink,
though not very fine. Adequate sunshine and shelter and
firewood and peace and liberty to indulge our natures with
no condemnation and no risk.

Harry spoke of it as a Blessed Isle, like Avalon. His face
would shine, and everything braced in him soften, until he

looked as though he had indeed regained his youth. And when he did so an unnamed emotion would slither in my breast like an adder, poisoning my mood for days. I began to feel a sympathy for all those poets who have written about spleen and black bile and the dark hound that sits at the door of the soul, gnawing away at its joy.

Though it grew from day-to-day, I did not speak of this to Harry. It would have been like snatching the slice of birthday cake from a child's hand and stepping upon it. But the melancholia would not be ignored. I took to wandering off in search of solitude, having to suppress violent anger when he sought me out. There was no place in the tiny speck of land to which one could withdraw and be certain of remaining alone.

Harry must have sensed my uncharacteristic surliness, for he became solicitous, trying to draw me out, make me talk. Seeking me out when I tried to find a moment's peace. This was the state of affairs between us when the water began to fail.

Three weeks passed without rain, and then a fourth. The shallow pools dried. The well yielded less each day; a cup between the two of us, and that salty. We angled the tarpaulin above us to allow morning and evening dew to drip into our barrel, and at dawn harvested a mouthful each, brown with oak tannin. We pulled green leaves from the trees and chewed them to keep our parched mouths moist. The chicks had hatched and grown. There were no more eggs to harvest, no more sooty broth. We ate our meat raw and sucked out the blood.

When the next storm rode up from the north—racing waves, boiling clouds and solid sheets of falling water—we danced for joy, naked, coated in mud and altogether savage. Rain splashed and gurgled and murmured all about us, slicking our skins, filling the well, filling the barrel and overflowing as Harry pinned me against the slick grass with a hand to the back of my neck. We coupled in the downpour, the storm's violence echoed in our blood.

Afterwards I looked at myself in one of the many pools that remained. Steam smoked up from them and wound about the boles of the trees. Silver misted the leaves above my head, where white, doleful eyed birds sat on black branches looking down at me. In this ethereal setting I looked into their mirrored surfaces to learn who I was, and I was utterly shocked at the result.

Had you asked me what I expected to see, I would have said "Hyacinthus." I had, for some time now, given up the wearing of clothes. I thought to see the long smooth lines of classical beauty. The winsome youth who tempted Apollo. You'll say I'm vain, no doubt. Perhaps I am. But I have been called handsome too often to claim not to know it.

I thought to make a charming rustic picture, nude as an Arcadian shepherd, with my black hair artfully tousled and a few well placed leaves. Instead I saw a Caliban. My hair and beard stood out in elf-locks all about my face, solid with mud and twigs, matted and nest-like. When I rubbed the caked dirt from my cheeks I found my skin had tanned quite brown. Grazes and a gouged red wound showed where, in the vigour of our pleasure, I had not noticed myself being pressed onto stones. My limbs had lost their graceful smoothness and become corded with unsightly sinew and muscle. My thigh was banded with red twisted scars that might have been scattered worms.

I looked like something that had crawled half way across England, sleeping under hedges all the way, to collapse in tears at the workhouse door. I appalled myself. Seizing my uniform and weapons I ran to the lagoon to bathe.

"What ails you?" Harry came gently out of the blue shade of the woods as I was sharpening my sword. He too looked roughened by the wind and sun, dried and withered like a piece of old leather. Like an ape with human eyes. All my accumulated days of melancholia burst upon me at once, and the last few coins of fairy gold turned to ashes in my hand. So this, this ugly and meaningless world, this was the truth, was it?

"Nothing." I bowed my head and did my best to shave with the edge of my sword.

He sighed, sunk onto his heels in a patch of shade and watched me. His gaze itched up my spine like a file of soldier ants. It settled on the bruise on my cheek. "Did I hurt you?"

"Oh, please!" The edge of my blade dug into my skin. "Do not treat me as though I was a woman! You could not hurt me if you tried."

"I treat you," his frown deepened. Its shadow darkened his changeable eyes from green to blue. "Like someone for whom I care a great deal. If I have not hurt you, something has. What is it? What's wrong?"

His concerned voice irritated me. Our ship had long gone down, and he was no longer my captain to demand to hear my thoughts. "Go away, Harry," I sawed beneath my chin, pulled out double handfuls of beard. "Leave me be. I need peace, space. Away from you."

He actually winced. I felt a sense of achievement, and shame, as I gathered my things and walked out along the causeway to the smallest wooded islet. Behind me my footprints filled with water. The tide flowed in.

We called it Ardent Isle, the little one, after our smallest ship. There, I finished my toilet. I bound back my hair, shaved as best I could and dressed carefully in my salt stiff, clammy uniform. Every piece of clothing put on chafed. The buckles pinched and the waistcoat buttons choked me, climbing up to my throat. And every one came with its own individual ache of regret.

I stood and looked out from the southern shore while breakers of burning whiteness seethed over the silver beach not five feet below me. Behind their dazzle, the ocean receded forever in lines of lapis lazuli towards a sapphire sky. Somewhere before the horizon the two vivid blues merged as the bowl of the sky sealed us in, like a brandy glass pressed over a captured wasp.

Since there seemed no reason to do more, I was still standing, gazing out, when the tide turned. Gradually the water drew away, leaving a flat expanse of barren grey rock with reflections of the sky shattered and scattered across it. Trees sighed around me and stones slipped and settled. The seabirds squabbled as they had since we fetched up here, an endless backdrop of complaint. And then Harry's arms went about me from behind. He pulled me in close and rested his chin on my shoulder. His knees were wet and cold against the backs of my legs. Evidently he had not waited for the tide to go out fully, before literally wading back into the conversation.

But his embrace was comforting. I liked to feel him, solid, capable and gentle, breathing with me.

"You want to go home," he said, quietly.

"I am forgetting how to be human." I feared to look him in the face. So, of course, I did so at once. He too had washed and groomed himself and dressed. No beast now, thank God, simply thin and weather-beaten and concerned.

His smile came cautiously, slightly bemused. "It isn't a thing you forget."

"No?" I took both his hands and held them in my own, drew them up so I could kiss the calloused knuckles. "I feel like Odysseus, come to an island where men are changed to pigs. What have we done here but eat and rut and sleep?"

"And talk," he shrugged. "What else is there to do?"

The sun was going down, the horizon banded with livid orange light, purple above it, intense and unnatural. I turned away from it and found Harry in his white shirt and breeches, with his ink-smudge eyes, like a watercolour man in an oil painting world. I smiled, because he was the only thing that looked right to me then. "My point exactly. What makes a man human? Is it not art, culture, the discourse of other minds? Friendly society. Even enemies.

"I miss," I swallowed, and my need lodged in my throat like an iron ball. "I miss… *Everything.*"

The dam broke and the words came pouring out of me. "The opera. The theatre. I miss music, and balls. And women! I miss talking to women. And gaming and riding and hunting. And carriages, and…" I fingered brocade in my mind, my touch drinking in the slippery, soft, heavy luxury of beautiful fabric. "Visits to the tailor. New suits. Sitting in a coffee house of a morning, reading the news. I miss drinking in the wardroom and rolling my eyes at anecdotes that grew stale three months ago, while across the table from me my drinking partner is laughing up his sleeve at my antics.

"I miss books. Other people's ideas, bringing me to a standstill because here is something I never thought before. The *smell* of colliers and sewage and stockfish and hemp and cologne. I miss other people, Harry. I am…sorry, but much as I love you, you cannot be a sufficient replacement for all civilised society."

He stepped back. He looked dumbstruck. Something tender and fragile changed behind his eyes. It took me longer than it should have to realise it was only the reflection of moonrise. "You love me?" he asked, bemused. As though this was unexpected.

"Did I not say so? I thought I had."

"You," he sat down heavily on the edge of the grass. The light grew silvery behind him as the great shield of pitted moon began to shine in earnest. "You most certainly did not. I thought myself a challenge to you. A sport. You are…you cannot say that your demeanour gives a man any confidence in the seriousness of your affections."

I walked away, collected a few branches as an excuse to turn my back on him. It's true. That too I have been told a number of times—that I seem a gadfly. A flirt and a tease, without a heart. But it seemed intolerable to me that Harry, of all men, had thought it too.

He had cleared the ground when I returned. I stacked the

wood and set to work making a fire-drill, avoiding his eyes. If we were telling the truth now, some old resentments of my own could do with an airing. "I know you don't care for me."

An ember dropped into the pan of the drill. I tipped it into a double handful of dried grass and bent over it, blowing until it caught. My hands were full of fire. The flaring flame showed his face, red gold against a sky of dark, Imperial purple. I thrust the tinder into the heart of the stacked wood and the small sticks caught and crackled. "You had to have everything else taken from you before I became something worth valuing. No doubt you only tolerate me here because there is no other alternative. I help pass the time, I suppose."

He laughed at this; a little bark of surprise and mockery. "Don't be an arse. Will you force me to say it in so many words? Very well. I love you too. There. Does that satisfy?"

I could have kicked the fire in his mulish face had I not lost my shoes somewhere at sea. He expected me to believe that? A declaration of love phrased like a complaint? "Oh yes," I flung a log atop the burning pile. Sparks swarmed. "I was convinced of your regard when you were willing to risk nothing at all for me. This love you feel you would feel for anyone with whom you were confined long enough. It has no reality. It will vanish like a phantasm, should we ever escape."

The night grew colder, and a water-laden wind flowed over us. The tongues of the fire fluttered like the pennants of a ship. Harry came to sit beside me, his hand resting on my knee. I did not move it aside, but I did not clasp it either. "You think this is not real?" he asked, as if clarifying a concept strange to himself. "This place and what we do in it, you think it is an interlude while the real music plays on, out there?" He flapped a hand in the direction of the rest of the world.

"Yes."

"To me," he turned his head to watch as salt in one of the

branches burned up with a hissing, blue, ghostly light. His voice was very calm and sure. "To me, *this* is the reality. Out there they make us pretend. They force us into lies or hiding. Here I've been free to be myself for the first time in my life. You and I, it's the first honest thing I've ever done. And that's because this place has given me the freedom to do it." A little sigh of amusement mingled with melancholy. "Your prison is my refuge."

I leaned back and watched stars bloom overhead, so clear you could see their colours, faint and pale. Harry's words turned my understanding of our situation inside out. If this was a refuge, what must his normal life have been? Could a man be so sensitive to the criticism of others as to feel *better* when every last human soul but himself was gone? I did not understand it, but I grieved for him.

Yet now a reason for my affliction had been brought home to me, I did not know how I would continue to bear it. "It is making me insane."

He took a deep breath, like the sound of wind and sea, leaned in and kissed me beneath the ear. "Tomorrow we will try a final time to raise the boat. If that isn't possible, we will build a raft. I'm still firmly of the opinion we are somewhere in the vicinity of Tahiti. If we carry on northwest we must eventually strike New Guinea, or even Asia. We must think of provisioning. Water will be the main difficulty there."

I was slow to recognise this as the declaration of love for which I had wished. But as he continued to work out the details of our onward journey it did finally occur to me that he was giving up his refuge, his true self, for my sake. He was facing again everything he feared, simply because I wished it. I gave a smile somewhere between tears and laughter and covered his hand with my own.

Chapter Nine

A full week has passed now since I began this account, and I am sitting on the terrace of the *Passeio Público*, looking out over Guanabara Bay. I am not completely easy in my mind at the thought of bringing such an incriminating document out-of-doors, but it is a habit that Garnet has acquired, and I am too weak-willed to put an end to it. It will please me when it's finished and can be locked away to be found again only after we are both dead.

Still, it is pleasant to sit here after a day spent creeping through the bowels of fishing boats with my fellow customs men, up to our necks in shrimp and swordfish, looking for contraband. My employment, I am afraid, is a great deal less glamorous than Garnet's, and I appreciate the evening breeze to take away the stench.

Children shriek behind me, chasing one another up and down the many pathways and through the falling water of the *Fonte dos Amores*.

A man selling coconuts has just accosted me—I had to buy one so that he would go away. Once more, following Garnet's precepts has led me into more danger than I am comfortable with. But perhaps I like it that way, for if I did not, surely I would learn better?

And now it is I who interrupt the story! Forgive me. The truth is that while I wish I could claim such selflessness as Garnet has claimed for me, the thought of leaving our blessed isle had been growing on me too. I did not wish to go, but I did wish to find out, if possible, the fate of *Ardent* which had become separated from us in the storm. The great gnawing of my heart would have been eased if I had known that one at least of my charges had survived. I wanted too, with a strange penitential desire, to stand my court martial and maybe—this was my hope on those nights when I could not sleep—to have the court rule that only storm and sickness was at fault in causing our disaster, not I.

These concerns would not have been enough to goad me into attempting an escape if Garnet had only been happy. But having him there unhappy was intolerable, and so we had to leave.

I would not like to think it of myself, but perhaps the decision was so easy to reach because I had no real belief in its success. We had tried to raise the boat, which was lodged fast between two boulders, and failed. I could not see that circumstances had changed in the meantime to make our success more likely. And from the weight of the wood we took from the island's trees, I suspected it would not float at all.

This indeed proved to be the case, but Garnet was not deterred. "We can break the boat in half, recover the pieces as they float to the surface, and then mend her."

With rocks for tools and sharks circling overhead, this plan seemed impracticable. But I had not reckoned on Garnet's gift for getting his own way. Those gods he is always talking about? I believe they favour him too much. That or the sheer power of his personality bends the world to suit him, as a lens bends light. However it was, we had not been three days on the work before everything changed.

I was hauling the boat's broken mast and a chunk of worm-riddled keel up the beach when Garnet's excited shout pealed on my ear like a church bell. I looked up, saw him perched like an incongruous bird in the branches of the tallest tree on the isle. Framed against the pellucid sky, he was waving his white shirt like a flag.

I dropped the mast and ran, leaping up the inclined ground, excitement and sick dread warring for possession.

Garnet had set a fire going, covered it with leaves, and smoke was beginning to filter through the canopy of branches. The island's birds hurtled into the sky in a twisting, protesting flock dense enough to set the lagoon in shadow. But neither of these signals was needed, for barely quarter of a mile from the long, north side of the main isle a three masted frigate was riding at anchor. They had already begun to heave out the boats.

Garnet and I looked at one another. Without another word said, we flew into a frantic state of tidying comparable with that of a new wife when her husband's mother makes an unexpected call. Ah, no, even his metaphors are rubbing off on me. I mean we tidied like a ship's crew, whose captain has seen the admiral put off from shore for a surprise inspection. We dressed to perfection, rolled up the hammock, swept the clearing, set the lid on the water barrel and covered over the two plucked plovers we had meant to roast for dinner. Then we stood side by side, at attention, and I think from his quick, nervous breathing, that despite his smile, he shared something of the shattering strangeness I felt on seeing other people again for the first time in so long.

They burst into our clearing, rifles in hands, their faces closed and grim. Incredibly, they wore British uniforms, and behind them on their ship the Red Ensign fluttered in the wind like a long stemmed poppy. The marine's red coats hurt my eyes, so bright they were. Men ringed us both, keeping the guns levelled upon our faces, and my astonishment and joy at unlooked for rescue faltered at the look in their eyes. "Gentlemen," I said, watching the same doubt dim Garnet's big grin, "you are an unbelievably welcome sight. How did you know to come for us?"

"None of that." The marines parted and a lieutenant strode through. He examined the clearing, and us, and raised disapproving eyebrows at the single hammock. I reeled. I could not believe any of this, and it was a while before I collected myself enough to notice he still wore his cocked hat.

"I am Captain Harry Thompson, of HMS *Banshee*," I straightened my coat. The buttons had tarnished in the salt air, but the gold braid still shone bright. "I expect you to uncover before me, sir."

His mouth writhed like a serpent. He turned and fixed me with a snakelike gaze from pale and piercing eyes. "What is this fucking impertinence? Uncover before *you*, pirate? On your knees!"

"I beg your pardon?"

"Sergeant." The word was the only warning I had before a rifle butt to the back of my knees made me stumble and fall forward. As I struggled not to sprawl on my face, someone caught my arms and manacled them behind me. The sound of a scuffle and Garnet shouting, and then the butt of the gun was driven into my skull and the world came apart in a burst of black fire. This was proving to be an unorthodox rescue indeed.

~~~

I woke. Even as I pieced myself together with clumsy fingers, long before I opened my eyes, I knew we were at sea. The rocking might have been dizziness, but that damp wind and the creak of sails, the turn of the wheel, the ting of the bell and knock of rope on mast was unmistakeable. The sun shone acid bright at the corner of one shut eye. Beneath the other ran holy-stoned deck planks and a line of caulking, tacky in the heat. Voices spoke dispiritedly above me until a racketing, metallic din cut them off and they grumbled into silence.

For a moment I lay, lulled by the familiar sounds, and a profound relief went over me. We were home. I would see my family again, and Garnet would attend his niece's coming out ball. I would receive my judgment from a court martial board of my peers, and perhaps be absolved of responsibility for all those deaths...

"You must let us out!" Garnet's voice put an end to these idle thoughts. He sounded close above me, weary and hoarse and patient as though he had said these things a thousand times, and was prepared to go on saying them until he was heard. "I am Lieutenant Littleton of the *Banshee*. This is Captain Thompson of the *Banshee*. We were shipwrecked. We have *nothing* to do with this."

"What...?" I struggled to my knees, my head swimming, and he was with me at once, arms about my shoulders, steadying me. I almost closed my eyes, rested my world of aches against his strength, but as I looked around, I noticed for the first time the latticework of iron bands that sur-rounded us. I had woken in a cage, one of a dozen men crouched uncovered, unsheltered, on the quarterdeck of this unfriendly ship. Our fellow prisoners were watching us. Out-side the bars the lieutenant and midshipman of the watch had turned, regarding us like curious beasts in their very own menagerie.

It was as though, through long disuse, I had lost all the callous on my soul. I felt their judgment as an unhardened hand feels the rope burn and cut as it pulls through. Over half a year, I'd had, to forget I was anathema, to forget I was a pervert, to forget I was something less than scum. I stiffened in Garnet's arms, unable to bear their scrutiny. Looking down on me, he gave a little choking laugh, and let go.

I wanted so much to kiss him, and I could not. I had for-gotten what that felt like. I had forgotten it profoundly and thoroughly, or I should never have agreed to come back.

He knelt back on his heels, his face shuttered and the ex-pressive body I had learned to read so well held still, as if in pain. "Are you recovered, sir?"

"What...what is...?" My mouth had dried, and tongue and mind stumbled together over our predicament.

The lieutenant untucked a cane from beneath his elbow as though he meant to beat the bars again and silence us. But he refrained. He was not the man who had struck me, on the island, and there seemed to be a lurking fear in his eyes. His conscience, perhaps, sat uneasily within him.

"We are aboard HMS *Pandora*, sir," said Garnet. "Captain Edward Edwards. Apparently HMS *Bounty* suffered a mutiny earlier this year, and the *Pandora* is hunting the mutineers down to bring them home for trial. We had the bad luck to pitch up on an island close to where the ship was lost. Now they think we were involved."

"That's..." I grasped the bars and pulled myself upright, pleased that after a moment of drilling nausea my head and stomach settled. "That's nonsense. You, sir, what's your name?"

The lieutenant was a young man, plump and blond, with a placid face and a haunted look. "You aren't supposed to talk," he said.

"Then how am I to persuade you I am speaking the truth?"

"That's rather the point," he licked the worried smile off his lips.

"Listen," I let go of the cage, pulled my uniform coat straight so that he could see the insignia. "I have served on the *Pearl*, the *Yarmouth,* and the *Savage*, and lately on the *Barfleur*. My lieutenant here has served on...?"

"*Dragon, Inconstant,* and *Dreadnaught*, sir."

"You should have no difficultly finding, among your crew, a shipmate who can recognise at least one of us. Unless you want to face the most appalling legal stink when we reach London, I suggest you make every effort to do so. Then let us out of here at once."

I looked down at my fellow prisoners. They had expanded into the space where I had lain. There was now no place to sit not already occupied by legs. Mutineers. If that was not irony upon irony. Should we be convicted of mutiny, we would hang as though we had been convicted of love. What then had been the point of all my pretence?

As *Pandora's* lieutenant turned away, crooked a finger to summon one of the powder monkeys, I reached out and took Garnet's hand. It surprised him into a smile that was quenched immediately, as the doors to the captain's cabin opened and a severe, dark haired man came out.

I released Garnet's hand with a speed that must have seemed suspicious, but I think the man's mouth was compressed so much it could not tighten further. It dragged down at the sides as though fitted with an invisible bit.

"Captain Edwards?" I said. His hard gaze passed over my face like the beam of a searchlight, and moved on. He turned his back, cutting me dead. Rage consumed me—a lifetime's rage, composed of all those moments as a tar I had been treated like this, like something inhuman. All those moments, struggling up the long ladder of my career, thwarted at every point by men like him. I burned with fury, and he strolled about the quarterdeck as though he was taking the air.

"Cheated by every servant, mistrusted by every commander, betrayed by every lover," Garnet whispered. "If he's ever had any at all."

I do not wish to speak ill of my service, and indeed I have found many great and gallant men in the Navy. Men cheerful in the face of adversity, generous and even playful in every day life, magnanimous in victory and undaunted in defeat. But I have also known too much of this—the petty tyranny, the grinding, unrelenting disrespect. The moment Captain Edwards turned his back on me was, I think, the moment I fell out of love with my career.

It is too late now to cut a long story short, but I will endeavour not to protract it for very much longer. On Edwards' fifth turn about the deck the powder monkey returned, bringing with him, up the companionway, a rusty-aproned surgeon, and, leaning on his arm, a man I knew. Ned Compton, coxswain's mate in the *Yarmouth*, now holding in his bursten belly with a cut down pair of lady's stays. "Oh, aye, I know Mr. Thompson, sir. Lieutenant in the *Yarmouth*, he was. Did hear he'd made captain of the *Banshee*. Congratulations to you, sir."

"Thank you, Ned. It's good to see you again."

He chuckled. "Aye, main glad you must be right now."

Things became a little more comfortable after that. They let us out. We were given hammocks to sling in the wardroom, and a change of clothes from the slop chest. Either by way of apology, or as a scheme to investigate us further, Edwards invited us to one of the most painful dinner parties I have ever attended, scrutinising my table manners, peppering us with suggestions of what we should have done to prevent the disaster to our fleet. "Also, I wonder," he said, "what you found to occupy yourselves with, all that time alone on so blasted an isle."

We made him some noncommittal answer but the thought lodged in my mind. As we plunged back into human society, played cards in the wardroom, stood watches for fellows who were grateful to take a few hours extra rest, the thought of what I had lost began to grow on me like a canker.

I became acutely aware of the space that separated me from Garnet. My hours of solitude, or in the company of other men, seemed grey and barren. Yet my hours with him were a torment of constant awareness and yearning. Without him in the hammock beside me, hot and restless and fidgeting in his dreams like a big dog, I could not sleep. My heart seemed to beat in a cavern within my chest, its tiny flickering unable to fill the dark. A constant squirm of anguish lodged there, like a worm in the flesh.

We breakfasted together and sat next to one another at the wardroom, and yet it felt to me as though he was dead and I was not being allowed to mourn.

Pandora worked her way slowly through the islands of this little known part of the world. The mutineers sweltered in their cage by day and shivered through the exposed nights. I found myself drawn to them, and would spend much of my free time standing by the ship's rail as near to the cage as I could come. I knew I deserved to share their fate, and in sharing their penance I felt a little calmer.

On our last night aboard as free men, Garnet joined me by the rail. The fitful wind veered into the east. About the bow the water broke into twin curves of luminescence, and the wake stretched out behind us in a sheet of pale green light. A moon like hammered gold hung above us. Other than ourselves, only a midshipman occupied the quarterdeck, and he drowsed by the capstan. From the forecastle came a mutter of voices speaking low and tense. I had noticed a great deal of whispering aboard *Pandora*. She was not a happy ship.

Garnet turned his head to listen, and the faint gilded light flowed across his face. Something in the line of his throat, the shadow beneath jaw and cheekbone, and the little inwards tuck his mouth made at its ends, stopped me dead. Pure beauty, almost too glorious to endure.

He looked at me, puzzled, as my mouth opened and my hands began to tremble. Such dark eyes, intimate as a man's own fantasies. "Sir?" he asked, briefly uncertain. And then he understood. His mouth curved up, and his face lit with delight. He tugged me forward by the cuff. I swear to you I felt his touch on the material of my sleeve as though it were on my yard. I was mad—I freely admit it—mad with loss and need and regret. I think perhaps I wanted to be caught. I had tasted freedom and knew I could no longer live without it.

We made it no further than down the quarterdeck stair before he pulled me into the shadow of the great cabin, where between the ship's boats and the arch of deck above lay a patch of shadow so dense we could not see each other, let alone be visible to others.

I hope those ladies who read this will forgive me for the comparison, but, ever had to piss? Ever had to hold it in so long it passed through pain to making you think you were going to die of internal strangulation if you did not let go? Ever have one of those dreams where you cannot find the privy, no matter how you search? You'll sympathise with my state then. I wasn't thinking, I'd got so used to having him when I wanted, I just couldn't hold on any longer.

Dear God the bliss! We were all mouths and teeth and heat, and his hand's in my hair and the other hand's down my trousers and he's going "I never thought... oh Harry... I never thought I'd play this game with *you*." And then the doors open and the captain comes out and everything shatters into smithereens like a plate dropped on a stone floor.

Disgrace. Edwards paced up and down behind his desk, hands linked behind his back, lips pursed as though he had bitten into a lemon. Marines behind us, and our wrists tied with rope, and the cabin seemed to pulse ruby red with the force of everyone's disgust.

I'd been afraid of it all my life, and here it was— exposure, ridicule, abomination, like being flayed and laid skinless on a nest of ants.

"My God," Edwards turned and glared at us. "In front of my very cabin. Do you have no control at all? No self re- spect?"

There's a kind of joy on Garnet's face, and seeing it shifts everything inside my head. By gradual stages, like sail- ing out of a fog, the obstruction cleared, my confusion light- ened, my shame thinned and lifted: I understood. Garnet needed no refuge, no hidden isle moated all around by im- passable sea. Inside himself, where no one else could touch him, he had learned how to be free. How not to be ashamed. "We thought you might like to watch, sir," he said.

Edwards' disapproval flickered for a moment. Something intense went through it, fast as lightning. It looked to me a lot like panic. The effort of compressing his mouth back into scalpel thinness made him dab at his forehead with his hand- kerchief. Reaching for his logbook, he opened it, took out the sheaf of ill written notes that marked the latest page.

"I am," he rustled through them, brought a sheet out and pressed it to his lips, "a little behind with my paperwork. I have not yet written up my log of the past fortnight." Setting his elbows on the table, he steepled his hands, as if praying. "There is nothing in here to suggest we ever picked up two castaways from Ducie Island."

I could all but hear the creak of strain as he winched his mouth up at the ends into the straight line of a satisfied smile. "Until I have recorded that fact, you are legally missing, presumed dead." He crumpled the sheet on which, I guess, his record of our rescue lay scrawled, looked at me with the triumph of a man dismissing inconvenient tedium. Then he threw the only evidence of our existence out of the stern windows, where it bobbed for a while like a duckling in our wake, before sinking.

"If I never record it, there is no legal proof that you were ever here. This frees me of the necessity to bring you back to England for trial. For your guilt, I have the evidence of my own eyes." Over my shoulder he exchanged a glance with the sergeant of marines. "There can be only one appropriate punishment. You will be hanged from the yard arm until you are dead, and your bodies disposed of in the sea."

"Now, sir?" the sergeant asked, with what seemed to me excessive eagerness.

Edwards patted his forehead again with that limp handkerchief. His mouth reassumed its habitual downward tug. "Nonsense. You may manacle them both and secure them to the deck. We punish on a Saturday in this ship, gentlemen, come hell or high water. There is no reason to disturb the ship's routine for something as sordid and unimportant as this."

The night I spent shackled to the deck—the width of the ship between myself and Garnet—was, I think, the most formative night of my life. A Thursday night. I had two full days and nights to live. I was in the situation of which I had been afraid all my adult life, and every sailor gave me a kick or a curse as he passed. Yet, as the hours wore on, a sense of peace stole over me. I felt my heart beat in my chest and the blood course through my limbs. The stars still shone above me, and the black and silver sea bore me up as it always had. The sails creaked. The ship grumbled on to herself as though nothing had changed.

I had thought I would be crushed, did anyone ever find out about me. I thought the world itself would condemn and swallow me up. Instead, there was the moon gleaming like a sickle above. As its light hit the water, there came a great heave of silver, and a whirr, like wings, as a school of flying fish leapt out of their element and flitted beside us as though God was skipping stones.

Fear lifted off my chest like a boulder. I watched the sunrise with the eyes of one newly born. The worst had happened, and look, it was not so bad.

As soon as there was light to see, I caught Garnet's eye and smiled. Had we been closer I would have thanked him for persuading me out of my solitude and into this more fundamental freedom. I had been a coward for a very long time, and he in his absurd way had shown me how to be a man. His smile in return was dimpled with delight. I don't believe he ever was afraid of anything.

They did not trouble to feed us. But, about midday, when both the captain and Lieutenant Hallett had gone below, Ned Compton gingerly brought us a dipper full of water each. As he leaned down to let me take the thing in my manacled hands, he made as though to scratch his nose, concealing his mouth beneath his hand. "You knows how to navigate, don't you sir?"

My peace stirred into a kind of puzzlement, threaded through with hope. "I do."

"Your boy too?"

"My b—Mr. Littleton, you mean?" *My boy?* as though we were spoken of together. As though the world knew us for a couple. It perhaps should not have done, but it filled me with insufferable pride. "Yes, he's a very capable navigator."

"Suppose you was plotting a long journey. What d'you need?"

I kept the dipper of water before my mouth as I answered, wondering if this was mutiny. Something about these seas appeared to encourage it. "To know where we start. Compass, charts. Sextant. A good watch. Maskelyne's tables, if possible."

"Right you are." His withered eyelid drooped in a confiding wink, but he stood and hurried away before I could scratch the itch of my curiosity. As the day passed, I kept my eye on him and saw as a result that an understanding seemed to exist between Ned and a number of the *Pandora's* tars. Meaningful nods abounded; the occasional slapped shoulder and raised eyebrow. There seemed more men busy tying down the ship's boats, to me, than was strictly necessary in this weather.

But again, I let my tendency to prose on run away with me. I will be more succinct. I fell asleep with a feeling of anticipation, and was woken at three bells of the middle watch by a hand on my shoulder, and the vibration of a crowbar working the pin of my chains out of the deck. One of the ship's boats was being swung out on the crane and lowered gently and quietly down. In another, already in the water, two shadowy shapes were shipping her mast while other men packed barrels under the thwarts and sat, waiting.

I opened my mouth to say, "Not mutiny, then, but desertion?" and Garnet slid a silencing hand over my mouth and led me down into the stern of the second boat.

Pandora had been working north up the coast of Australia, intending to return to England via the Endeavour Strait. Knowing this, we chose to brave the empty Pacific once more. We set the boats before the wind and scudded away into the East, making for Chile.

I shall not tell you the details of that long journey, for they are repetitive and dull. Our companions' endurance for their evil-tempered captain and cold-eyed lieutenants had been pushed beyond healing by one too many insults. They had been planning their escape for some time, held back only by the knowledge that they had nobody among them capable of plotting an accurate course. Our appearance, with those very skills, had been taken as an indication that God was with us, and thus they found themselves happily inclined to ignore our crime.

There were fourteen altogether. Fourteen souls whom I brought safely to landfall in Chile. There we parted with them. I do not know what happened to them after, but I notice with some satisfaction that neither does anyone else. They cannot have been caught, at least.

Pandora herself—I learned later—sailed at night onto one of the many reefs off Australia and was wrecked. These two things were a salve to my self respect. I had brought at least this tiny crew alive to shore. I was not the only captain ever to lose a ship. These things I tell myself regularly, and they help a little, at least in the daytime.

I wind slowly down to my conclusion: having parted with our fellow deserters, Garnet and I—claiming to be brothers—signed up as crew members on the *Mafalda*, a Portuguese trading ship bringing Chilean Muscatel to Europe, and pisco and aguardente to the miners of Brazil.

I believe it was a hard time for Garnet, who had been used to being instantly recognised as Quality, and treated as such. To be tanned and calloused and coarse as a sailor of the lower deck was as abhorrent to him as the thought of exposure had been to me. He bore it well, however. And I experienced, in this return to my roots, another kind of relief. I do not like to lie, and it seemed to me that my efforts to become a gentleman had had some taint of falsehood about them all along. I was learning now to accept myself for what I was.

We docked at Rio and they paid us off with a handful of *réis*. To celebrate our hard earned wages, we returned to the tavern we had visited when we first touched at Saint Sebastian. It was exactly as I remembered it, yet everything had changed. It was comparable to putting on a pair of spectacles for the first time. Inside one's head, something shifts, and all the little cogs mesh together, functioning as they were designed. Everything becomes clear.

I drank too much, and let my mind dwell on the dances. Candlelight could not have been warmer or more golden than Garnet's soft voice in my ear. The music slid between us like warm oil. He was full of smiles, and all the more so when I dragged him outside by the collar and had him, up against the wall in the moonshadow of Corcovado Hill.

I remember the scent of that evening: lime and salt, mud-brick and heat, and that peculiar throat closing, acrid green scent of the deep, wet jungle. We clung to one another in the aftermath of passion, slid gently down to lie entwined. Scrub brush closed over our heads, and the drumbeat of the music filtered through the wall at our backs. I set my mouth to Garnet's throat and his heartbeat pulsed in time.

"We're not really going home at all, are we?" he whispered, gently as if he feared to break me. But I had been thinking the same thing. Once *Pandora* returned to England all that would await us there was a trial for sodomy, or desertion. Our families must have heard by now of our disappearance. They would have mourned and moved on, happy in the knowledge that we died doing our duty. What good would it do to any, to return from the dead only to bring disgrace? To force our relatives to witness our hanging would be the utmost cruelty.

"No," I wound my hand into his hair, worked my kisses up from throat to jaw and thence to his lips. "I've had enough journeying. I think it is time to stop."

It is surprising what a man can give away and still remain himself. With that decision we lost our family, our friends and our country, but as I rolled onto my back and looked up at the stars, I felt as though I had in some small way received my island back. *No man is an island, entire of himself,* says John Donne, but two may be, together, needing nothing else.

I look up and here he comes, clad all in black velvet and silver lace. He has a silver topped stick in one hand, and the whiteness of his linen bids fair to rival snow. I had meant to tell you of his daring rescue of Pedro de Lancastre da Silveira de Castelo-Branco Sá e Menezes, the Count of Vila Nova de Portimão, which set us on our present route to mild prosperity, but I find I can pass over it with a sentence. In our first month here, Garnet was fortunate enough to rescue this personage from footpads, and the Count, in gratitude, was instrumental in securing us our present employments.

Garnet has a downcast look. In the pavilion beyond, Maria Margarida Fernandes and her family sit eating ices. She is a lady of a certain age, a great fondness for gossip and a large acquaintance, many of whom we have made our own over the last few years. He dips his hat to her, and I can tell by the meek cast to his face and the droop to his neck that he feels it is a good time to restage our one remaining piece of deception.

"You have the look of an errant dog slinking back to its kennel, sirrah," I will say when I can no longer pretend not to have noticed him, and he will flare up, throw down his hat, and the subsequent conversation will go very much like this:

"What is that to you, brother?"

"You've been gaming again! I know the signs. How much have you lost this time?"

"I earn five times as much again as you. I wish you will not keep on badgering me about my few entertainments."

"You may earn five times as much. You lose six times! What, have you reduced us to penury once more? And our savings? Damn you! How will either of us ever afford a wife?"

Such a pantomime! Garnet, of course, enjoys it, as he enjoys all theatrics from the grand opera to the Punchinello plays. I see the need. For our first year here, once we were respectably settled, we were much plagued by the attentions of unmarried women. Nowadays they merely ask me sadly why I do not wash my hands of my profligate sibling, and I shake my head and say in a weary tone, "What can I do? He's family."

I am resigned to the deception, but still I resent it. I would be honest, if I could. I am an honest man, it is only the world that forces me to lie. But we stand at the turning of the century, and already the revolution to come is breaking out all over the world. The rights of Man. In the nineteenth century perhaps the baseless persecution of men like myself may end and we too join in *Liberté, Egalité, Fraternité, ou la Mort.*

To that end, I am sealing this completed diary and depositing it in my bank, to be released when we are both dead. I think of it as a message in a bottle, cast out into the seas of time. May the future reader know what we have not been permitted to say in the present: that we were happy. And that we were true to one another through the loss of all things. It is important to me that someone should bear witness to our love.

As for my own future, I foresee a staged argument, a time of austerity, sympathy from our neighbours and Garnet's amusement at a long standing joke. I am content. And I think…I think I shall grow my hair.

Not to Reason Why

Mark R. Probst

Dedication

To my mother,
who died not knowing who I really was,
and who, I believe in my heart of hearts,
if she were alive today,
would be proud of me,
just as I am.

Theirs not to make reply,
Theirs not to reason why,
Theirs but to do and die:
Into the valley of Death
Rode the six hundred.

-Alfred Lord Tennyson

Fort Abraham Lincoln, North Dakota
May 15th, 1876

Brett was peripherally aware that Mrs. Kerrigan had just spoken to him. "Hmm?"

She smiled demurely. "I said, would you like some more tea, Brett? And whatever are you thinking about? You were a million miles away right now."

His cheeks warmed and he looked down at his teacup. It was nearly empty. "Yes ma'am, I will have a little more, thank you." He scooted the cup toward her. She refilled it, looked at her husband, then glanced at the clock above the mantel.

Seated to Brett's left, Sergeant Dermot Kerrigan gently wiped the crumbs from his mouth, then placed the checkered napkin back in his lap. His long, slender neck rose above the yellow neckerchief to a smooth-shaven, deeply cleft chin. His sideburns squared off just above his jawline and were a much darker shade of red than his hair, which he parted neatly on the side. His eyelashes were so blond they were white.

"A man couldn't ask for a lovelier or more gracious wife," he said.

A hint of a smile passed over her lips. Just a shade over five feet tall, Dermot's wife barely came up to his shoulder. She was petite and fair-skinned, and her hair and eyes were very dark. She was somewhat plain, but her inner beauty shone through and created an illusion of outward beauty. In the eighteen months they had been married, they doted on

95

each other. Dermot treated her like a queen and she was impossible to spoil. Though the cavalry required them to be separated for long periods of time, Sarah was a soldier's wife through and through, an office she performed dutifully and proudly.

Sarah stood, gathered the few remaining desert plates and the teapot, and carried them to the kitchen. Dermot leaned closer to Brett and spoke in a low voice, sharing a joke about a saloon girl and a virgin. They were chuckling over the punch line when Brett suddenly realized that Sarah had reentered the room. Dermot's back was to her so he couldn't see the icy stare directed at Brett. The reprimand he could see in her expression caused him to scoot away from Dermot and pick up his teacup. She retook her seat, her countenance once again sweet and smiling in front of her husband. Brett was always welcome in their home and Dermot invited him to dinner often, but he seemed oblivious to the fact that his wife sometimes resented the intrusion.

"Oh no. I was hoping it would be a while longer," Sarah said.

Brett had missed something. "What would?"

She reached over and touched his shoulder. "Oh Brett, you're daydreaming again."

"General Custer's back. Just arrived from Washington this morning," Dermot repeated.

"Oh, then I guess we'll probably be marching again," Brett said, moodily. The past two months had been a reprieve for the soldiers of Fort Lincoln. During Lieutenant Colonel George Armstrong Custer's absence the fort had been under the command of Major Marcus Reno, and everything had been peaceful, the soldiers at ease, and the wives happy. Most of the soldiers and their families wouldn't have minded if Custer and his ambition had just stayed in Washington D.C.

"I think it's miraculous that he managed to get the president to give him back his command after all those nasty accusations he made," Sarah said.

"He did stir up quite a hornet's nest." Dermot beamed with pride, straightening his neckerchief in a subconscious gesticulation. "Accused Belknap of graft and then proceeded to name off a whole list of congressmen on top of that. Even accused the President's brother of accepting bribes! Blew the lid off all the corruption in Washington."

"Is it true?" Sarah asked. "I mean was Custer telling the truth?"

"I don't doubt what he said was true." Brett fidgeted with his teacup and avoided looking at Dermot. "Congress seemed to think so. They impeached the Secretary of War based on his testimony. But however true his accusations, I think he really just wants to make sure Congress doesn't look too closely at *him*."

"I really don't understand what you all have against the general," Dermot said.

That was Dermot for you. He was just about the only soldier in the fort who actually admired the man, and insisted on honoring him by referring to him by his earlier pro tempore rank.

"It's just I think he takes too many risks," Sarah said. "I know he wants to be the next president, and I sometimes wonder if maybe winning a few battles isn't sort of a campaign for him."

Brett was impressed. Sarah was no empty-headed housewife.

"Nonsense, darling," Dermot said. "He is simply doing what needs to be done to keep this country safe. He may want to be president, and why not? He's earned it. If it weren't for him, the Indians would be running wild and scalping every settler west of the Missouri River."

Brett thought it was more likely that the dissent among the Sioux and Cheyenne was in retaliation for Custer's raids and the government's constant reneging of its treaties. But there was no use arguing these politics with Dermot. His patriotism was unflinching.

Brett finished off the last of his tea, then rose from the table, grabbing his forage cap from the hat-rack by the door. "I'd better be getting back to the barracks. Thank you ma'am, for the fine dinner." The news of Custer's return had soured his mood. He had planned to spend more of the evening with the Kerrigans, but now he didn't feel like socializing. They said their goodbyes, Brett gave Sarah a light kiss on the cheek, then turned to Dermot and gave his shoulder a friendly squeeze. He donned his cap and stepped out into the night air.

~~~

He and Dermot became friends six years prior on the day that Brett first came to Fort Rice. He had been a bit guarded and not inclined to socialize when Dermot approached him and asked him if he played poker. It was only after Brett had managed to win all his money, that Dermot really took a shine to him. They were so much greener then. They spent whatever little free time they had together, roughhousing in the barracks, or going drinking, and often on payday they would try to start up card games so they could try and win a bigger chunk of the payroll.

When they were reassigned to the new Fort Lincoln, Dermot met Sarah, the daughter of an army colonel. And with Sarah, Dermot reformed himself. His attention went to her. Brett was still his best buddy, but Sarah became his bride. Sarah, for her part, liked Brett right from the start, and sensed that the friendship between him and her husband was significant, but as time carried on her warmth towards Brett cooled. Most of the soldiers envied Dermot a wife like this, thinking him the luckiest man at Fort Lincoln. Brett however, was jealous of *her*.

As he slowly strolled to the barracks, he turned and looked back at the light emanating from the windows of the Kerrigan home. He wished he could live there. In the simple and rather barren quarters assigned to married men and their wives, Sarah had dressed up the room with curtains, table-cloths and braided rugs. The kerosene lamps bathed the dark wood of the walls and floor in a warm glow. He imagined the two of them in bed together. Dermot snuggled up behind her, with his strong arms wrapped around her waist, gently nuzzling the nape of her neck with his soft lips. What he wouldn't give to be in her place, just once.

When Dermot had bunked in the barracks with Brett and all the other unmarried enlisted men, there were nights when Brett couldn't sleep and he would quietly sneak over to Dermot's cot and just stand in the dark gazing at him while he slept, in the tranquil repose of a boy who had played him-self out. One summer night, when the moonlight though the window illuminated his face, his sharp, smooth features breathtakingly handsome, Dermot had kicked off his covers and his undershirt was unbuttoned nearly all the way down. The pale skin on his chest was sleek and free of blemishes; his young body had yet to grow hairy. Brett had realized that he was truly smitten. He visualized Dermot in his present state, his body now matured—his arms encircling and pro-tecting Sarah, that hairy chest nestled against her form—a form that held no interest for him.

He returned to the barracks, quietly undressed and hung up his uniform, and climbed into his bed—alone .

~~~

Brett was awakened by the soldiers' chattering and rum-maging. The bright sunshine through the window meant that he had overslept. Why hadn't he been awakened by reveille? Something was amiss, and the men all seemed to be excited about something.

"What's going on?" he asked Daniel, his nearest bunk-mate. The young private was now pulling on his trousers.

"We're marching at dawn tomorrow," Daniel said. "Gen-eral Custer has given us leave for the day. Most of us are go-ing into Bismarck to whoop it up while we can."

Brett flopped back against his pillow. Shit. Another expedition. Since President Grant had created the January 31st deadline for all the Lakota and Cheyenne to be back on their reservations or be considered hostile, the 7th Cavalry had been on several expeditions to round up the so-called hostiles. Now three and a half months past the deadline, it was starting to bother Brett. The two months that Custer spent in Washington had offered some reprieve, but now that he was back the expeditions would start all over again. Brett only had a year to go on his army contract, and unless things changed drastically, he wasn't going to reenlist. He really needed to find a new livelihood.

Since he was off duty for the day, he decided to stay in bed awhile. He reached over to the crate he used as a nightstand, picked up his tobacco pouch and cigarette papers, and rolled himself a smoke. The sun had warmed the barracks considerably, so he got on top of his bedcovers, put his arm behind his head and watched the soldiers preparing to leave for town. He took a deep drag on the cigarette. Most of them were still green. The expeditions had been routine, and most of these boys had seen little combat.

He wondered if these youngsters looked at him and saw an old man. He was only twenty-eight, and though younger than Dermot, he hadn't managed to hold on to his youth so well. He already had some premature gray hair sprouting at his temples, which stood out plainly against his short-cropped, dark brown hair. He had also put on a few extra pounds, and though he was by no means fat, he looked stocky for five-foot-ten. He was proud only of his beard, which had been part of his countenance ever since he had been old enough to grow whiskers.

"You coming along, Corporal?" Daniel asked, "There's bound to be some poker games."

"Nah," Brett said. "Not this time. I'm just going to rest

up. If we're pulling out at dawn, I don't feel like doin' much today."

He wondered if it would be rude to spend the day with the Kerrigans. Since this expedition would likely last a couple of months, they would probably appreciate some time alone. Or maybe he could spend part of the day with them—he would drop by later in the morning just to see how they received him. If he sensed they wanted to be alone, then he wouldn't stay long.

~~~

That afternoon Brett found himself at the Kerrigans' front door. Dermot answered his knock.

"Hey there, you all ready for the expedition tomorrow?"

"As ready as I'll ever be."

"Yeah, me too."

"You think you might like to go into Bismarck for a while? Get a drink or something?" Brett couldn't help but stare down at his feet. It didn't feel right to try and steal a man away from his wife on the last day before a long separation.

"Afraid I can't, Sarah's got a picnic lunch planned. We're going down by the river. Why don't you join us?"

"I..." Brett shifted his weight from one leg to the other. "I don't know if I should."

Sarah appeared in the doorway, a scarf tied around her hair and a basket of food hanging on her arm. "Good afternoon, Brett."

"Ma'am." He removed his cap.

"Brett's going to join us for the picnic, dear." Dermot put an arm around her and guided her out of the house.

"Wonderful," she said, "It's a good thing I packed extra."

Try as he might, Brett tried to detect falseness in her tone, but it just wasn't there.

~~~

After lunch, Sarah remained sitting on the blanket laid out under a fir tree, watching while the two men walked up-river, picking up stones and vainly attempting to skip them across the flowing water.

"Did you see that?" Dermot said. "I actually got one to skip."

Brett laughed and tossed one himself, only to have it swallowed immediately by the river. He longed for the old days back in the barracks when he and Dermot wrestled with each other and got drunk and spent most of their off-duty time together. His thoughts returned to his decision not to reenlist. Leaving his friendship behind would be difficult. But might it not be better for him? To free himself from this unnatural attraction so he could find himself a nice girl and get married. Even the thought of normal domesticity brought a wave of depression over him. If only what he truly desired were possible, how happy he could be. A small pinecone suddenly struck him in the head. Dermot broke into laughter.

"Damn you!" Brett charged at him, knocked him down, and tried to pin him. Dermot continued to laugh and struggled to get up but Brett had both of his wrists pinned to the ground as he lay on top of him and refused to let him up. His face hovered inches above Dermot's. He could feel the heartbeat beneath him.

Dermot stopped struggling. "Okay, okay, I give. Now let me up."

"Not until you apologize for braining me with that pinecone."

"I'm sorry. Now please let go."

He didn't want to let go. He wanted to prolong the contact. For a split second he considered holding him down as long as he could, but Dermot wasn't laughing anymore and the joke was over. Dermot's grimace told him he had gone too far. He let go and they got up and brushed the dust off their uniforms. Brett glanced back towards Sarah. She was standing with her hands on her hips, watching. He felt just like he did when his mother had caught him being naughty with himself behind the outhouse.

May 17th, 1876

By sunup, twelve companies of the 7th Cavalry were mounted in formation on the parade ground of Fort Lincoln awaiting the orders to march. An immense mule train, loaded down with supplies and ammunition, was lined up against the fort wall on one side, while on the opposite wall were lined up dozens of covered wagons with teamsters and the families of the soldiers who would be accompanying the 7th to Camp One for a final farewell before turning back the following day. Brett spotted Sarah in a very visible yellow dress and bonnet among the wives.

The little square wooden fortress with its two-story palisade seemed claustrophobic at this moment, and he was anxious for the bugler to sound the marching order. Open country awaited. Custer was near the open gates, conferring with his superior, General Terry, while Major Reno and Captain Benteen waited nearby. Dermot sat at attention and was oblivious to his horse's restless bobbing. Brett and Dermot, along with every other soldier in company E, rode white horses. The company had unofficially been dubbed the "Gray Horse Troop."

Colonel Custer finished with General Terry, then turned to Reno and Benteen to relay orders. After a few minutes they broke apart and climbed up on their mounts. Custer drew his sword, pointed it at the open gate and shouted the order. The bugler took up the call, and one by one the companies filed out through the gates.

Once outside the fort, they fell in to a long procession with the Gray Horse Troop somewhere in the middle. When they got further away from the fort, Brett glanced back past the endless procession of mounted soldiers—lettered guidons evenly separated the companies, and behind these, the mule train and wagons were still emerging. He was suddenly astonished by the sheer scope of this operation. The soldiers had been told very little in the briefing. Only that they were to rendezvous with both Colonel Gibbon's and General Crook's troops in late June for a three-pronged attack on the renegade Sioux. This was big. Most of the young soldiers were champing at the bit for action. Brett was queasy inside.

At midday, Custer called a halt. The wagons pulled up alongside the ranks and the men dismounted and began helping some of the women down from the wagons. Many of the younger ones and some of the children were forced to walk, as there wasn't room in the wagons for all.

"What do you think about farming?" Brett said. "I've heard that down south there's some really fertile ground."

"Huh?" Dermot anxiously looked back at the dusty trail for the stragglers, Sarah among them.

"Tobacco or cotton would probably bring the best prices, but I'm thinking more of wheat."

"I guess so." Dermot spotted her in the distance.

"Are you even listening to me?"

Dermot knitted his brow and said nothing.

When she caught up, Dermot kissed her discreetly and stuck by her side. She'd found the wagon where she had stashed her basket, and they found a nice spot beneath a fir tree to spread out a blanket for a picnic lunch. Brett took this opportunity to lead his and Dermot's horses to the river for refreshment. He felt like they expected him to look after the horses. Sometimes it was like he was invisible around them. She tended to dominate Dermot's attention.

He stroked the horses' manes as they gratefully gulped from the river. He knelt between them and bent down to splash the cold, clear water over his face to wash off the trail dust. It tasted clean and rich in minerals—so much better than the stagnant water in his canteen. He took off the cap, poured it out and refilled it with river water.

When he returned to the picnic, Sarah already had all the food laid out. She had roasted chicken, beans, and biscuits. She looked up at Brett and laughed.

"What?" he asked, knitting his brow.

"Why Corporal Price," she chortled, "your beard is dripping."

Brett laughed and dried his chin on his sleeve. He and Dermot sat down on each side of her and began helping themselves to the meal. The food was cold, but it still tasted delicious. He hadn't eaten since the day before.

They hadn't even finished the last biscuit before Custer gave the order to mount up. Brett was annoyed. Women needed more rest than that, especially the ones who were walking. But Sarah quickly gathered the plates and started to fold up the blanket without complaint.

"Let me help you, darling," Dermot said.

"No, no. You two go along. Mustn't keep Chief Yellow Hair waiting."

Dermot hugged her and gave her another heartfelt kiss, and then he and Brett dashed back to their horses.

~~~

The rest of the day was a hard ride. The terrain was often hilly, and the river always nearby, but the air was just warm enough to be uncomfortable. The pedestrians were starting to fall behind. Eventually the wagons slowed to wait for them, but the 7th moved on.

By nightfall, they stopped to set up Camp One. By the time the wagons and those on foot showed up, the soldiers had finished pitching all the tents in organized rows across the flat prairie on the bank of the Heart River. Everyone worked together to collect wood for the campfires, and then the women began to cook the farewell feast.

The horses had been groomed, fed, and bedded down. All the officers had gathered for a conference in General Terry's tent. The wives dished out bowls of hot stew from kettles hanging on spits over the campfires and the men found places to sit wherever they could, on rocks, logs or just on the grassy ground. Sarah joined Dermot and Brett near one of the campfires. They sat on the bare ground, Brett with his knees drawn up and Dermot squatting on his haunches, as they sampled the cornbread and waited for the stew to cool. Sarah gingerly plopped down beside them. For a woman who was usually poised, she had no qualms about roughing it in situations like these. She had managed to retain her femininity unlike other military daughters who were inclined to become tomboys, but she still knew the ins and outs of military campouts.

They ate their food in silence. The night sky was black and the sparks from the fire looked like shooting stars against it. Sarah laid her plate on the ground, her food not even half-eaten.

"Who is that man lurking about General Terry's tent?" she asked. Both men followed her gaze. A thin man with dark hair and long sideburns stood near the opening to the tent, smoking a cigar and shifting his weight from foot to foot. He kept glancing into the slightly parted flab.

"That's Mark Kellogg," Brett said. "He's a reporter from Bismarck. Sort of a correspondent for this expedition. He's been following the colonel around like a lonely puppy."

Sarah's eyes seemed to lose focus as she stared into the fire. Brett wondered if she took Kellogg's presence as a bad omen. He had observed her at these partings many times, and he usually couldn't sense that she was ever troubled. Tonight was different: He could detect just the faintest glimmer of fear in her eyes.

"I guess they think this patrol is going to be newsworthy," she said softly. "Perhaps even historic?"

Dermot finished his stew and laid his plate beside hers. She rested her head against his shoulder, staring blankly into the fire. She unconsciously brought her hand up, stroked his chest, and held it there. He instinctively put his arm around her. Brett knew he should look away, but he couldn't—and it didn't matter because they were barely aware of his presence.

When he could bear the low fire of yearning no longer, he turned to see what was happening at the general's tent. The officers had emerged and were all being served plates of food by Mrs. Custer. Colonel Custer was having an earnest chat with Mark Kellogg. Kellogg was intent on every word. The discussion finally ended with a hearty round of laughter and they joined the other officers and Mrs. Custer for dinner. He turned back to Dermot and Sarah and saw that they had got up and moved to the edge of camp and were facing away from him, Sarah in front of Dermot and encased in his protecting arms as they both gazed up into the starry night sky. Their need for privacy was apparent. He couldn't help but wonder if his watching them had made them uncomfortable.

~~~

By eight a.m. the camp was completely packed and the wagons were loaded. The only soldiers who hadn't mounted up were the married men. They were making their final farewells to their wives and children. Brett observed many a young wife break down in tears. He could hear old Mrs. Farrell's shrill fussing over the sergeant. "Don't you be a overdoin' it! You ain't young no more and you got to be extree careful not to get yourself hurt. If the army sees fit to still havin' ya, then that's their business, but I say don't you be takin' no extree chances. Let the young ones do most of the fightin'..." Brett stopped listening and looked toward Dermot and Sarah. Dermot gripped both of her arms as he talked to her. His voice was too low for Brett to hear what he said, but he could well imagine what Dermot might be saying.

"It won't be too awful long, my dear. I'll think of you every day. Try not to worry so much. Spend a lot of time with the other wives and try not to dwell on the dangers. You know how very much I love you."

She stared into his face, unwavering, and didn't shed a

tear. The bugler was already sounding assembly.

"I'll bet you wish you could be in his place now, eh, Corporal?" Daniel said. "A pretty young woman like that, who wouldn't?"

"Have some respect for the lady, Private!" Brett was more annoyed at himself than Daniel.

"Sorry, sir." Daniel looked a bit hurt by the rebuke. The poor kid was rakish, thin, twenty-one, and surely didn't mean any harm. He was the guidon, and the letter E flapped in the wind above his head on the pole he carried.

Dermot walked up and Brett handed over the reins to his mare. She bobbed her head and snorted in excitement.

"There, there, girl." Dermot patted her neck. His voice sounded thick. He climbed up on the mare just as "Forward, ho!" was relayed back though the line. As the horses began to move, Sarah stood firm and motionless, hand at her breast. Every parting was possibly the last time a wife would see her beloved alive, though none of the women ever dared speak of it—to do so would be bad luck. Brett saw a melancholy solitude in the lone figure this time that he had never witnessed before. As the horses were spurred into a gallop, her stoic figure shrank into the horizon. The image haunted him. As much as he envied her, this was one time he wouldn't want to be in her place.

They marched along the rough, dusty terrain for hours. The overhead sun beat down mercilessly, and the Dakota plains were hilly and mostly treeless. Some of the younger men, enthused at the prospect of action, broke out into army marching songs. The infectious nature of the singing spread through the ranks as all eventually joined in the singing of the well-worn melodies.

Finally in the late afternoon, Custer called a halt to rest and water the horses. Dermot and Brett guided the horses to wade into the Heart River and hopped down. The cool water came up to their knees. Daniel stopped at the bank, got off his horse, planted the guidon in the river mud, and pulled off his boots and socks.

Dermot laughed. "The water's not going to hurt your boots, Dan."

"No? Well I paid ten dollars for them boots, and I ain't takin' any chances." He hopped off the bank into the shallow water and bent over to splash the sweat off his face. He ventured out a little further, and then gave a yelp. "Damn rocks are sharp!" He lifted his foot out of the water and grabbed it with both hands to massage it, then lost his balance and fell over backward with a splash.

Brett and Dermot doubled over, laughing hard. When he regained his composure, Dermot extended a hand to help Daniel up. Daniel grabbed his hand, but instead of coming up, he deliberately pulled Dermot down into the water on top of him. All three started laughing again, drawing the attention of the nearby troopers. Before he even realized what he was doing, Brett dove in on top of them. The three of them wrestled in the shallow water, laughing uncontrollably, and appearing to have taken leave of their senses. Some of the men chortled at the good-natured fun, others nervously looked up the river worried that Custer or one of the other officers might notice and disapprove of the shenanigans.

They finally settled down, remembered that they were soldiers and not schoolboys, and trudged up the riverbank, sopping wet, Brett with his arm around Dermot's shoulders. Daniel stopped to pull on his socks and boots, but Brett and Dermot snatched up the reins and led their horses to the mule train, to see if they could pilfer some bread and a can of fruit from the supplies. Brett was grateful that the afternoon heat would dry their uniforms quickly, before any of the officers had a chance to notice their indecorous conduct.

May 29th, 1876
    They march in long columns, through heat and dust toward a blinding orange sun. They climb over precipices and

descend through gullies, pushing on at a relentless pace but seeming to get nowhere. Brett feels something bad will happen to Dermot. He saw it in Sarah's eyes when they left her behind and now he feels it himself. The sun is so enormous in the sky that the sweltering heat is scorching their backs. The guidon falls and the pennant lands in the dirt; the column of troopers tramples over it. Brett knows that Dermot is in danger. He must get to him and divert this disaster. The bugler sounds the charge and an arrow pierces his lung; the note is cut short. Brett is now certain of disaster. It was madness for him to have ever considered leaving Dermot behind in order to take up a new life elsewhere. He searches for Dermot among the columns of sweating, dust-covered soldiers. He must find him quickly, before it is too late. Sioux warriors are dropping into the ranks—slitting throats, severing limbs, and stabbing hearts. Brett is frantic in his search. Dermot is sure to be among the slain. He will never recover from the loss. He must find Dermot and then never let him go. He is enveloped in a throng of bleeding, crippled soldiers. Finally they part to let him through. Dermot is there. He has his back to him, his rifle in the crook of his arm. He turns and sees Brett. A wave of relief rolls over him as he runs to Dermot and catches him in a tight embrace. They fall to the ground, oblivious to everything around them. He smothers Dermot with affection until at last their lips are locked in an insatiable kiss. Their uniforms melt away and their naked bodies undulate together in blessed gratification. The melding of the two physiques is so complete that Brett's hold is viselike. He is determined to not let go, but the warriors find them and grab onto Dermot's feet, trying to pull him away. He is losing his grip. He cries out. His shoulder is shaking.

"Brett, wake up."

He opened is eyes to see Dermot hovering over him. His tent flap stood open where Dermot had just entered. He felt cooling sweat on his forehead and moved his hand down to cover the erection in his pants.

"You were making a lot of noise—calling out and thrashing around. Must have been some nightmare."

Brett swallowed hard. "Yeah. Real bad. Indians trying to... kill everyone."

"You're okay now. Try to stay awake for a while. It helps to keep you from going right back into the same nightmare." Dermot squeezed his shoulder and went out, tying the flaps back down.

June 10th, 1876

Brett wiped the sweat from his forehead with the back of his hand. His cap was soaked and he wished he could remove it so that the breeze could cool his head. The past few days had been grueling. Custer was determined to get to the Sioux camps as quickly as possible, and had allowed almost no rest. The horses were tired and frothing and the men were downcast and irritable from the heat and lack of rest. They couldn't go on like this much longer. Only Dermot was taking it all in stride. Though he appeared a little worn, he never uttered a grumble or a cross word—his duty was his virtue.

Up ahead, a group of officers had broken formation and were conferring with Custer's personal Ree guides and the six Crow guides assigned to the expedition. The long column of soldiers began to compress like the bellows of an accordion as they slowly came to a halt near the officers' conference.

"What's he saying?" Custer turned to his half-Sioux interpreter, Mitch Bouyer.

"Sir, he says the great summer council of the Teton Sioux always happens about this time every year."

"What's this rubbish? I've never heard tell of any Indian *summer council.* If such a thing were happening, don't you think our Indian agents would have reported it?"

The Crow guide hung his head, hearing the skepticism in Custer's tone.

"That's what he says, sir." Bouyer wore a calfskin coat and an ostentatious fur and feather cap, and was looking seriously into Custer's eyes. "He says last year they gathered in the land of the Dakotas, but the miners have now taken that land, and this year the council will be further west."

"General," Captain McDougall interrupted. "About the mules, sir."

Custer held Bouyer's gaze for another moment, then narrowed his eyes. He still looked skeptical. He suddenly turned to McDougall. "The only thing I have to say about that supply train, is that you keep those scavengers away! We've lost far too many food supplies to these back-hills bandits, and I want all scavenging ceased!"

"General, if you might assign a few more men to the supply train…?"

"You have enough men for the train, Captain McDougall. See to it that they guard those supplies!"

"General, if I may," Major Reno interjected.

Custer spun on his heel to face him. "Well?"

"The men need rest, sir. Morale is down and the horses are worn out. At this rate, the troops will be in no condition to face the enemy."

"Time is of the essence, Major. We need to return these Indians to the reservations before they spread out even further."

"But you're pushing the men too hard. What's a couple more days?" Major Reno spread out his hands in query.

"We've got to get this battle won by June twenty-eighth and by God we're going to do it! Gentleman this meeting is adjourned!" Custer turned away followed by the ever-loyal Kellogg.

Once the officers remounted, the troops began moving again and slowly spread back out.

After riding beside Brett in silence for a few minutes, Dermot, knitting his brow, turned and asked, "I wonder why it's so important to be done with all this by the twenty-eighth."

"The Democratic Convention," Brett said, glumly.

~~~

At sundown Custer finally called a halt. The exhausted troopers climbed down off their horses and began preparing the camp. Brett had lost count. He couldn't remember if this was Camp Twenty-three or Camp Twenty-five. The tents were slowly erected and the campfires soon blazing.

After supper, the exhausted men of the Gray Horse Troop lazily sat outside their tents to smoke and unwind. The plain was an ideal campsite, at least, and Brett sat flat on the grass with his legs splayed out, leaning on his palms. More than half the troop had already retired for the night. Those who remained were too fatigued to get a card game going, so like Brett, they just sat or lay on the grass in quiet conversation. Daniel slipped a flask out of his coat pocket, took a long swig of the rye whiskey and then passed it around. The liquor burned going down, but its effects were more than welcome. Even Dermot wasn't above imbibing after the past few days. Once the flask was drained, Daniel took it to his saddlebags, refilled it from the secret cache for which he had traded the last of his pay, and returned to start a whole new round.

The alcohol was like medicine. The more they consumed the better they felt. Weariness transformed into levity, and for some even giddiness. Jokes began to circulate and sloppy laughter occasionally erupted, always followed by an ardent shushing from the more sober men.

Daniel took a long swig from the bottle, passed it to the next soldier, then stood up. He swayed slightly before regaining his equilibrium. "Men," he mimicked, a finger high

in the air. "I will have *order* in this outfit!" He stuck his chin
out and clamped his hand on his hip. He ran his other hand
down the back of his neck, smoothing his imaginary long
blond hair. "I will not tolerate drinking in the ranks! As long
as I am in command, the 7th Cavalry will be a *dry* outfit.
Any man caught drinking on duty will be flogged within an
inch of his life!"

Not even Dermot was able to keep a straight face.

Lieutenant Smith appeared out of nowhere. "Having a
good time, men?"

They all jumped up, stumbling and wavering, in their
best attempt to salute. Daniel, swaying back and forth, tried
his best to keep his composure, but a snort escaped his nose.

"At ease," Smith said. Brett could tell by his expression
that he was amused. "Everything seems in order here. May I
request that you all try and keep it quiet, so's not to disturb
those who are sleeping?" He winked and headed off to his
tent.

They collapsed back onto the ground quietly chuckling
and whispering. Several of the men patted Daniel on the
back, teasing him about his gaffe. Even Dermot was laughing and having a good time. Brett couldn't keep his eyes off
of him. The men were so drunk now that none of them even
noticed Brett's gaze. He inhaled deeply, hoping the cool
night air would clear his swimming head. It didn't. It only
made him dizzier, and Dermot's handsome features were
more appealing than ever. As the men exchanged slurred stories and jokes, and threw their arms around each other's
shoulders or playfully slapped each other's knees with Dermot deep in the midst of it—to Brett, in his uninhibited state,
it seemed more intimate than it really was. He couldn't re-
frain from watching the men, their masculine forms; their
bodies becoming more appealing as he fought the urge to
reach out to them.

Then Daniel stood up and staggered over to where Brett
sat. He teetered as he held out the bottle to offer Brett an-

other drink. Brett reached out to take the bottle and his fingers touched the back of Daniel's hand. The skin was young and soft. He paused for a moment before taking the bottle. He studied Daniel's slim form before him; his coat was unbuttoned and hung open to reveal perfectly proportioned waist and hips. He wanted to touch, to feel, to hold that body. But no! He mustn't. To allow himself that luxury would be dangerous—possibly even fatal. He accepted the bottle but his self-control gave way. The bottle slipped from his fingers and dropped to the ground. He lurched forward onto his knees and flung his arms around Daniel's legs, burying his face into the private's stomach, and held on tight. Daniel steadied himself by resting his hands on Brett's shoulders. It felt good—the well-formed thighs engulfed in his embrace.

He heard laughter. A soldier's voice rang out, "The corporal's so drunk he thinks the private is a dancehall girl!" The joke brought on another round of raucous laughter. Daniel shoved at Brett's shoulders in an attempt to free himself and Brett released him and slumped to the ground feeling his cheeks color as he wished he could fall through a hole and disappear.

The fires died down, as did the high spirits, and one by one the soldiers tumbled off to bed before they passed out. Dermot got up, stretching his long legs and yawning.

"G'night, Brett." He turned away.

"Night. Sleep well." *My love.* Brett watched him walk away. His tall, lean body, powerful thighs, rounded backside... *Oh dear God, why must you torture me by making me this way?* He sat alone in the dark as the last glowing embers of the fire extinguished into nothing but smoke.

June 21, 1876

It was just after sunset when Brett poured black-as-mud coffee into two tin cups and handed one to Dermot. As they blew into the cups, Brett surveyed the camp. General Terry's headquarters was aboard the *Far West,* a small steamer anchored in the Yellowstone at the mouth of the southern-flowing Rosebud. Straight rows of tents lined its banks, and supper was roasting on spits. Weeks of travel had finally brought them to this destination—the mouth of the river where the massive campaign was to be launched. Terry and Custer would be separating their forces into two prongs to surround the Sioux renegades. The plan was for Custer to move south along the Rosebud, Terry to swing west following the natural southern curve of the Yellowstone, and both forces were to meet up with Crook's army, which was expected from the south. All three were to come together in a surprise attack on the twenty-sixth and trap the Sioux.

The smell of roasting game filled Brett's nostrils, making his mouth water. He sipped the coffee. It was so strong he nearly spit it out, but the image of Sarah spewing coffee entered his mind so he swallowed the bitter brew instead. Why did he care how he appeared to Dermot?

"Christ, this coffee isn't even fit for the mules. I hope that meat they're cooking is as half as good as it smells. I don't know how they expect us to fight on these pitiful rations."

"Are you trying to say you miss my wife's cooking?" Dermot asked.

"Right now I'm so hungry I'd even settle for *your* cooking." Brett took another sip of coffee and winced.

"Let's go see what we can scrounge up." Dermot led the way to the cook's wagon. They each grabbed a plate and fork and reluctantly stabbed at the half-cooked game set out on the table. They were hard-pressed to guess what it might have been when it was alive. At least the bread looked appetizing; and they could expect a little flavor from the beans, too.

Brett cautiously took a bite of the meat. It was tough and grisly, but didn't taste as bad as he thought it would. From a distance came the sound of hoof beats.

The whole camp jumped to respond, ready to arm themselves and fight. But one of the sentries announced that it was only the returning scouts. Major Reno and a full company of men rode swiftly into camp and dismounted. While the troops unbuckled the saddles and let the sweaty horses drop and roll in the grass, Major Reno headed straight for Custer's tent, maps tucked under his arm, to deliver his reports.

"Do you think they found any signs of the Sioux?" Brett said, alternating bites of beans and meat.

"Hard telling. We've got to be getting close. Haven't you noticed how fidgety the Crow guides are getting?"

Brett looked towards the Crow campsite some one-hundred yards away. They sat in a circle passing around a pipe and scratching images in the ground.

"How do we know they're really on our side?" Brett said.

"Does it really matter?" Dermot mopped up his beans with the rest of his bread. "Their job is just to lead us to the Sioux. Once we get there six more Indians against us ain't gonna make a wit of difference."

Brett knew that Dermot's indifference was only a shield against his fears. Through the years he had observed that the closer they got to battle the more pragmatic he appeared.

They finished their meal, cleaned and returned the plates, then stretched out in front of the campfire. Major Reno left Custer's tent and headed over to have some supper. Pretty soon Colonel Custer and several officers emerged from his tent and headed to the *Far West*, where they hopped aboard and disappeared into the cabin.

"What you reckon they're up to?" Brett said, lying back with his hands behind his head, gazing up at the stars.

"Gambling, probably." Dermot lay on his side with his arm perched on one knee.

"There's an entire nation of Sioux out there waiting for us, and the colonel is going to spend the night playing poker?"

"Sure," Dermot pulled off his cap then scratched and messaged his head. "Gambling relaxes some men. Maybe it takes the general's mind off his worries for a while so he'll have a fresher approach in the morning."

Brett wasn't sure if Dermot was making excuses or if he really believed what he was saying. The fires were starting to die down and the troopers began to settle in for the night. A few still milled about, but the Crows and Rees had all disappeared. Dermot yawned.

"I guess we had better turn in, too," Brett said. "The colonel will surely want to make an early start in the morning."

"You're probably right." Dermot got to his feet, reached down for Brett's shoulder, and gave it a friendly shake.

Brett basked in the touch. He wished it could last longer than just a fleeting moment, but he tried to hold on to the sensation in his memory even after Dermot disappeared into his tent. Brett sighed and lumbered off to his own tent.

~~~

Brett woke to something pelting the canvas of his tent. He was disoriented and couldn't figure out what the sound was. He poked his head out of the tent and was taken aback. Tiny pellets of hail were bouncing off the ground. He shuddered at the gust of freezing wind. How terrifically bizarre. A few days ago it had been sweltering, and now, in the middle of June, they were having a hailstorm. What were the odds? He lay back down and listened as the clatter continued. The sudden night freeze and ice spewing from the heavens seemed like a sign. Even after it finally stopped, he found he couldn't fall back to sleep.

Sometime later he heard boots crunching around the

campsite. He sat up and parted the tent flap just a sliver. The ground, covered in hail, almost looked like snow. Custer and several officers had returned from the *Far West* and were gathered around the entrance to Custer's tent. They spoke in hushed tones so as not to arouse the camp. Brett could barely make out what they were saying.

"Will you take along the Gatling gun attachment?"

"And get McDougal to pick out the strongest mules. We are taking as much ammunition as they can carry."

Custer ducked into his tent and the officers disbanded. Lieutenants Wallace and Godfrey were headed towards him, so Brett let the tent flap fall shut. As they passed, Brett heard them clearly.

"You've made out your will, I presume," Wallace said.

"Do you think that's going to be necessary?"

"I have. Just in case, you really should have things in order. It's so much easier for your family, that way."

"I'll do it tonight, then."

"Godfrey, I believe General Custer is going to be killed."

"Why?" Lieutenant Godfrey momentarily froze in his tracks.

"Because...I've never heard him speak in that way before."

As the crunching of the officers' boots faded into the distance, Brett sat in his tent and a shiver passed through him. Not just from the physical cold, but from terror. He needed to talk to Dermot. It would be cruel to wake him at this hour, but it couldn't wait until morning.

Outside Dermot's tent flap Brett softly called his name. Inside was gentle snoring, but no sounds of movement. Brett untied the straps, opened the flap and peered inside. In the darkness he could just make out Dermot's lanky form under the covers of his bedroll. He inhaled deeply and felt a quiver in his chest. He leaned into the tent's opening and allowed his hand to come to rest on Dermot's thigh, just above the knee. Through several layers of material he could feel its shape and solid muscle. He wanted to run his hand along the full length of Dermot's leg, but resisted the urge. The snoring was so soft, it was more like rough breathing. Brett crouched in the darkness for a moment, watching Dermot's abdomen rise and fall with each breath. Stop it, he told himself. He gripped Dermot's thigh and shook it briefly.

"Wake up, Dermot."

Dermot sprang up in the terror that was natural to all soldiers who are forced awake. "Wha? Who's there?"

Brett knew that Dermot was too disoriented with sleep to make out who he was. "It's just me, Dermot."

"Brett, what's the matter? Surely it's not morning yet."

"Not yet. I hated to wake you at this hour, but I need to talk to you about something."

Dermot cocked his head and peered around Brett's shoulder. "What the heck, is that *snow*?" He was staring though the open flap.

"Naw, it's hail. Didn't you hear the hailstorm?"

"I musta slept right through it. Hail in June? I'll be damned." Dermot rubbed the sleep out of his eyes.

"I heard the officers talking. I think we're all in for some real trouble."

"How do you mean?" He yawned.

"A lot of the officers are making out their wills."

Dermot sat in silence, staring at Brett in disbelief.

"I think this battle is going to be bigger than anything we've ever seen before. Well, maybe not for you, since you fought in the war against the Confederates, but I'm afraid a great many of us may be killed. I think maybe Custer might be on the wrong side of this one.

"Wrong side?" Dermot frowned. "How can you say that? There is no wrong side against the Indians."

"I mean wrong side, in that it may not be the victorious side."

"There's nothing wrong with dying to protect your country."

"Dermot, haven't you ever noticed how these things are reported in the newspapers? When *we* win they say it's a victory, but when *they* win they say it's a massacre."

Dermot opened his mouth to issue a protest, but nothing came out.

"Perhaps you should make out your will? It might make it easier for Sarah, just in case."

"What about you? You gonna write one?" For once, Dermot's eyes reflected fear.

"I've got nothing to leave and no one to leave it to. I'll help you with yours though."

"Thanks Brett. There's no one I can count on more than you."

June 22nd, 1876

Reveille jolted him. Last night after helping Dermot mentally sort out all his possessions for his will, Brett had barely fallen back to sleep before the damned bugle blasted him awake again. The cold breakfast was served in a rush and the camp was now completely dismantled and packed away. Brett and Dermot stood by their horses wondering how on earth they were each expected to carry a hundred rounds of ammunition for their carbines, twenty-four rounds for the pistols, and ten pounds of oats for their horses. The poor mule train had it even worse—the twelve strongest mules had to carry twenty-four-thousand rounds. Custer certainly didn't want to take any chances on running out. Brett packed his ammunition with great care. He filled his saddlebags as well as the bag attached to his belt so that the cartridges were straight and lined up for easy access. He slung the sack of oats over the saddle and tied it on securely. He believed if he could keep his saddle in order, his life would follow. General Terry, Colonel Gibbon and Colonel Custer were near enough that he could hear their conversation.

"Colonel Custer, you're sure about the Gatling guns?

They'll come in mighty handy should you run into any trouble," Terry said.

"No, no," Custer waved his hand. "They'd just slow us down. I can't be lolling around waiting for them to keep up. My scouts have assured me that we're getting close to the Sioux village and I don't want to give them a chance to scatter."

"Okay, then. If you're sure."

"I am." Custer turned to leave.

"Now Custer," Gibbon spoke up and the colonel stopped and looked back. "Don't be greedy. Wait for us!"

Custer shook his head. His expression was one of irritation, without a scrap of humor, and he resumed walking away.

Their loads secure, Brett and Dermot mounted their horses just as the bugler sounded "boots and saddles." The procession filed out of the clearing to follow the Rosebud. Terry and Gibbon stayed behind. The rendezvous would be in four days.

The march was brisk and the morning air was still cold from the overnight hailstorm. As the column began to spread out, Brett and Dermot were soon beyond the hearing of the other men.

"Do you think the general was wrong not to bring along the Gatlings?" Dermot asked, not altering his gaze from the horizon.

"For our sake, yeah." Brett glanced up at Dermot then dropped his gaze back to his saddle horn. Brett couldn't ever remember hearing Dermot second-guess Custer. If even Dermot had doubts, it was more confirmation than he needed that things were looking grim.

"Those Gatling guns sure could have made the job a lot easier," Dermot said. "Just imagine if we had had them back when we were fighting the Rebs in the war."

"Do you think that's fair? Spitting out bullets so fast that the enemy doesn't even have a chance to fight back?"

"But look at it this way, Brett, if we had been able to conquer the Rebs quickly in the beginning, the war wouldn't have lasted for four years and a lot of men wouldn't have had to die."

"Do you really see any honor in killing men that can't fight back?"

"The Indians are no different. You know they'd use the Gatling guns against us if they had them."

"I'm sure they would." Brett sighed, conceding the argument.

~~~

Thankfully the march was a short one. Brett was so weary from lack of sleep that he was grateful when the column pulled up into a small timbered area, which was shielded by a tall bluff a few miles out.

"Why are we stopping already?" Dermot asked Lieutenant Smith, who was passing by on his way to the officers' bivouac.

"Major Reno's scouts report that this is the last good grazing area before the Sioux camps. It seems the Indian ponies have chewed all the grass to the nub further on," Smith said. "Try and get some rest while you can. We're likely to be moving out again tonight."

Smith walked away and Brett looked back at the procession of mules, slowly making their way. The overburdened caravan of beasts stretched out for over a mile.

"Look at that mess." Dermot shook his head. "The general didn't think that Gatling gun attachment could keep up, but they'd have been way ahead of that sorry lot."

Brett could see the soldiers cursing in the distance, trying to keep the stubborn animals moving. The cooks were already clanging pots and pans in preparation for an early dinner. By the time they unpacked their gear and settled in, the meal was ready. They had a quick bite of bread and cold meat, then settled into their bedrolls and were fast asleep before the day's last light was gone from the sky.

~~~

The sentries scrambled around the camp and shook each soldier from his sleep. Brett opened his eyes to find himself face to face with young Daniel. It was still dark.

"What is it, Private?" he asked.

"Time for assembly. The general's ordered no more trumpets this close to the Indian camp."

"What time is it?"

"Three o'clock." Daniel moved on to wake up Dermot, who lurched up in terror.

Breakfast was served cold and the camp quickly packed up and moved out by five a.m. As the shadows shrank back, the clear morning revealed marshy bogs inside the river bends. As the bluffs loomed ever nearer, the trail crossed over the thin stream of the Rosebud five times. After eight miles, it finally straightened out and opened into patches of forest at the base of some bluffs.

They drew up into a large flat area on the bank of the Rosebud and found some of Custer's scouts waiting for them.

"Look at this place." Dermot stood up in his stirrups and quickly surveyed the entire settlement. "It makes my flesh crawl."

Large circles of packed earth marked where Sioux lodges must have recently stood. The buffalo skins had been removed from the wikiups, and what remained jutted up from the landscape like skeletal ribcages. For miles around the grass had all but been obliterated by the Sioux herds, bitten off at the roots. The landscape was copiously decorated with animal droppings.

As Custer conferred with his officers and scouts, Brett and Dermot guided their horses away from the column and wandered toward the center of the campsite. A very large circle in the earth indicated where the council lodge had stood. All around the dirt was packed with moccasin-prints where the Sioux had participated in tribal dances. Piles of dry bones, cracked and splintered for the marrow, were scattered about. Blackened ashes were all that remained of ceremonial bonfires.

Brett swallowed hard before he spoke. "How long ago do you think they were here?"

Dermot slowly climbed down off his horse and picked up a bone from the pile. Beetles scurried in all directions. He then kicked over a dried horse dropping, and examined the bugs crawling inside. "I'd say at least a couple of weeks ago."

"Then maybe they're all gone now—far away—but you know Custer's still gonna go chasing after them."

"No doubt." Dermot climbed back onto his mare and Brett followed him back to the ranks.

Custer had finished with the scouts and sent them on ahead, and had given the order to move on. As the troops passed through the southern end of the camp, Brett noticed the tracks of the unshod Sioux ponies, and deep scores in the earth from hundreds of lodgepoles being dragged behind.

In the miles ahead, they did not run into any Sioux or Cheyenne. What they did find was more deserted camps. All the same, with chewed-off grass all around, heaps of bones left over from tons of consumed meat, and the abandoned bent willows from the wikiups. The discovery of each new campsite caused Custer to push ahead with new vigor. The pace became downright maddening. The mule train, under Captain Benteen's command, was now so far behind that they had completely lost sight of it. Brett noticed a general uneasiness among the soldiers and the scouts. Each new abandoned campsite seemed to bring a sense of foreboding. The men said very little as the miles wore on, but glanced at one another to gauge their expressions and silently confirm their worst fears. The Crow guides were solemn, and had stopped trying to mask their skittishness.

Dermot had broken formation to go ahead and find Lieutenant Smith, in hopes of getting information from him. Now he returned, and the look on his face was solemn and determined. Was there fear hiding underneath the surface? He wondered if he ever showed Sarah his true feelings.

What did he say?" Brett asked.

"He said the general seems to think we're gaining on them."

"Dermot, you know as well as I do, all these campsites aren't from the same tribe." Brett's voice wavered in spite of his efforts to control it. "Whoever left these camps left at about the same time. And they're getting closer together. We're now passing one in just about every river bend. One tribe couldn't make that many camps so close together and eat that much meat."

"I know," Dermot said. "I didn't want to say anything to the lieutenant, but I think there might be a heck of a lot more Indians around here than the general's expecting."

As they passed several more deserted Sioux camps—the packed earth, scored trails, piles of broken bones and chewed-off grass seeming ever-more ominous, Brett decided a change of subject might take his mind off it.

"Do you ever think about times you were really happy when you were a boy?" Brett asked.

"Sometimes. You thinkin' about that now?" Dermot guided his mare around a large rock and moved in closer to Brett's side.

"Yeah."

"Tell me about it."

"One winter when I was about nine. There was a blizzard that kept us snowbound in our cabin. Me and Sam couldn't even get out anymore to go sledding." He thought of Pa sitting in the corner rocking chair, whittling on a piece of driftwood, bored and disgusted that he couldn't make it to work in the coal mines. Ma had sat in the opposite corner of the cabin, sewing until her hands got tired, and then reading one of her tattered novels. The Christmas tree had been coarsely decorated with homemade paper ornaments and strung with threaded popcorn. "So we just played by the fire. We loved the new painted wooden soldiers that we got for Christmas. We built a lop-sided fort out of kindling for the soldiers, and pretended to go to war against the Indians." He could still remember how he and Sam had stuffed themselves with the bread pudding that had been their special Christmas treat.

Dermot smiled, seeming grateful for the pleasant distraction. "You miss them, don't you?"

But the question reminded him of less happy times. Times he didn't want to think about. Like when his Pa had been trapped in a collapsed mine, and suffocated before they could dig him out. That was right before the war. *The war.* He remembered the day the army had come and taken Sam away. Ma, then a widow, had pleaded with them not to take her son. She had said that her sons were all she had left good in the world. But they wouldn't listen, and besides that, Sam *wanted* to go. He was itching to go and fight the Rebs and probably would have volunteered in a year or two even if he hadn't been drafted. Those years had been painful for his mother. He did all he could to help her. But the old hens never seemed to lay enough eggs and the cow never seemed to give enough milk. She did what sewing she could for other folks, but the war had been a burden for them all and they couldn't give her much in the form of payment.

The day the war ended Ma had hung on to the last shreds of hope that Sam would be coming home. Even though she hadn't received a letter from him nor heard anything about him in two years, she wouldn't let herself believe the worst. If he was dead, his name would have been on the lists that were posted every few weeks in town square. When he still hadn't returned six months after the war, her hope began to ebb and she took to withdrawing to her bedroom, having little appetite and refusing to socialize. There was no joy left in life for her and her will to live had perished. The years of hard work and the mental anguish had weakened her body, and just two months after accepting that Sam wasn't coming back, she died.

Brett was an orphan and not yet eighteen. What few kinfolk he had did not live nearby and he had had no intention of imposing on their hospitality. That's when he had decided to join the army. Partly because he had felt guilty that he hadn't fought in the war, when many others his age had, and partly because he missed his brother and hoped that maybe he would be able to learn what had become of him.

"Yeah. I miss them a lot." He took a deep breath and tried not to think anymore.

After traveling some thirty-three miles for the day, Custer finally made one last crossing to the river's right bank and set up camp facing the lightly forested hills and deep ravines. The 150 mules with Captain Benteen were still some six miles back and weren't expected for hours.

~~~

The men had been ordered to put out the fires as soon as supper was finished. The last of the mule train had finally rolled in around eight-thirty, and most of the men were asleep by the time the stars were fully out. With no crackling fires, the camp was eerily quiet. Because he dreaded facing the seclusion of his lonely tent, Brett asked Dermot to sit by him in the dirt, just about a hundred yards from the nearest camper. Looking up, the vastness of the starry night sky overwhelmed him. He felt like a mere speck in the universe. A mote that could be wiped out effortlessly, without anyone noticing.

"I'm really scared, Dermot."

Dermot looked at him but didn't answer, then looked away.

"I'm scared because I don't think Custer knows what

he's doing and a lot of us are going to die. You've seen the signs. I'm afraid there are more Indians out there than seven hundred soldiers can handle."

After a few moments of silence, Dermot finally turned back to face him. Tears were beginning to brim in his white lashes. "I know you're scared. I'd be lying if I said I wasn't scared too."

"I'm not ready to die. I don't even know the reason why we're fighting these Indians. Just because they don't want to live where we tell 'em they have to? I can understand why they wouldn't like that. It's not their way."

For once Dermot didn't argue. He dabbed away the tears with the palm of his hand and his mind appeared to be on other matters. Brett wanted to somehow provide comfort. Hell, he wanted to be comforted himself. Tomorrow they could very well ride into battle and one or both of them could be killed. He wanted Dermot to know what was in his heart. He ached for Dermot to know how much he cared for him. What was the risk if he told him? If Dermot learned the secret and then was killed, it would die with him, but at least he would have known the truth before he died. But if Brett were the one to die, what harm can come to you after you're dead? He closed his eyes and said a silent prayer. *Please God, forgive me, but I must do this. I can't take the chance of losing him without ever letting him know.* He turned to face Dermot, and gripped both of his forearms.

"I must tell you something. It's hard for me to say it, but I need you to know because tomorrow we may both be killed."

Dermot met his gaze and looked a little bit bewildered. "Okay. Tell me, then."

"I love you. I always have and I always will."

Dermot smiled. "I don't know why that would be hard for you to say. Of course I love you too. You're my best friend in the world. You know I'd do anything for you."

"I don't think you understand." Brett let go of his arms and dropped his head.

"Hey, what's to understand?" Dermot put his arms around Brett in a tight embrace. "Best friends love one another and will do anything to see that the other one is cared for."

Brett squeezed Dermot as tight as he could, his chin resting on Dermot's shoulder. He never wanted to let go. "I just wish I could make you understand. You mean the world to me."

When he felt Dermot release the embrace, he pulled back slightly and looked him square in the face. His tears had dried and he had a peaceful look in his eyes. Three days worth of red stubble gave his jaw a slightly bearded look. *Oh hell, if this doesn't explain it to him nothing will.* He leaned in and gently caught Dermot's lips with his own. Dermot's eyes widened and Brett felt a very subtle flinch, but Dermot didn't push him away. He let Brett kiss him. In fact, the letting turned into kissing. Dermot closed his eyes and seemed to enjoy the sensation. Brett didn't know if Dermot was imagining he was kissing Sarah, or if he was truly thinking of him. He wasn't sure it even mattered. The moist softness of their lips sliding together, their tongues lightly touching, and Dermot's hands kneading his back was enough to fulfill the yearning.

He wanted the kiss to last forever and secretly he willed Dermot to hold on. But it was he himself who broke contact. He shifted his position so that they sat side by side, Dermot holding him with one arm as he nestled his head on the strong shoulder. This was what it felt like to be in Sarah's place. Oh, that it could be permanent. Brett had no idea how much time passed. The night was nearly silent save for the chirping of crickets. The intimacy of close contact with another human body was a comfort to both though for Brett it was more.

"Brett." The sound of his voice pierced the silence. "I have a favor to ask of you."

"Anything. Just name it." Brett gently placed his hand on Dermot's knee.

"It's a lot to ask of anybody, but I think maybe... not so much from friends as close as we are."

"Tell me. What's the favor?"

"If I am killed..." Dermot swallowed hard, "...and if by some miracle of fate you make it out of here alive..." With his free hand, he lifted Brett's hand from his knee and held it. "I want you to take care of Sarah for me."

Brett moved away from Dermot's shoulder and looked into his eyes, still holding his hand tightly. His pale green eyes reflected the stars. Brett saw in them pain and desire and desperation.

"How do you mean? Surely you're not asking me to marry her, are you?"

"Well why not? If she'll have you, then by all means, I give you my blessing. But if that is not her wish, then please just look out for her for me and see that she is cared for."

"Okay."

"Do you promise, Brett? Promise that you'll take care of Sarah for me?"

"I promise."

Dermot took him into his arms and held him tight. With his mouth next to Brett's ear, he said, "Thank you. I could never have had a truer friend than you."

Brett squeezed him even tighter. The two of them sat under the stars, hanging on to each other for dear life. As freely as Brett had made the oath, he wasn't sure what good it would do, for in all likelihood they might both be slain in battle tomorrow. He pushed the grim thoughts from his mind and prayed that he might spend the whole night in Dermot's arms.

~~~

The sentry kicked Brett in the foot to wake him up. The pale light of dawn streamed into his pup-tent. The memories of the previous night came flooding back to him like a warm bath soothing tired muscles. He and Dermot had sat out together in each other's arms until they were too drowsy to keep sitting up. He barely remembered stumbling back to his tent and losing consciousness.

Brett couldn't help but yawn as he tried to rouse himself. However much sleep he had gotten, it wasn't nearly enough. "What's happening, Private?"

"The scouts found a fresh trail of the Indians, sir." The young, lanky soldier, probably still in his teens, could barely contain his excitement. "The general wants to move out right away."

"Is there even time for breakfast?" His stomach felt as empty as an old hen's nest.

"Cook's already preparing it, sir." The boy trotted off to the next tent.

Brett rubbed the sleep out of his eyes then proceeded to pack his bedroll and tent. What had happened last night? Whatever it was, he was sure it was unlikely to ever happen again no matter how much he desired it. The memory would have to be carefully preserved and guarded in his brain for the rest of his days. He wondered if Dermot would cherish the memories of last night—or perhaps just the opposite. He might even try to forget them.

He carried his neatly packed tent and bedroll to the clearing where the horses had been bedded down. The camp was now thoroughly roused. After depositing his gear, he joined the rest of the troops at the cook's wagon. Dermot was in line looking none the worse for wear, though Brett could see his eyes were still vacuous from lack of sleep.

He accepted a bowl of mush and cold bacon and leaned against one of the wagons while he ate. The young recruits buzzing around the camp were wide awake and eager, many of them laughing and boasting in their excitement to engage in what for many would be their first battle. How innocent they were. After serving an entire career in the army, fighting and killing and maiming, they'd change. Perhaps they wouldn't have regrets, but they'd definitely lose some of their enthusiasm, and glory and valor would soon turn into remote and increasingly conditional ideas.

In less than an hour they moved out. Custer seemed as eager as his young recruits. As soon as they arrived at the trail the scouts had discovered, he forged ahead, leading the foremost troops and disappeared into the dust.

"There goes Hard Backsides!" Dermot said quietly, grinning.

"Aptly named," Brett said. They spurred their horses in a futile attempt to keep up.

It was perhaps the most miserable march of the whole expedition. They rode endlessly without rest. They were plagued with buffalo gnats that bit their faces. Some of the soldiers suffered bites on their eyelids, making it near impossible for them to see through the swelling. Brett wanted to scratch his face off it itched so fiercely. And if the humans were suffering, the horses had it worse—the deerflies bit their haunches, and they were going the whole day without water. The heat was stifling and there were times Brett would have welcomed a warrior arrow straight into his heart just to end it all.

The dust was so thick that it was impossible to tell what was happening ahead. The procession slowed and then began making frequent halts.

"How do the Indians stand it out here with all of these damned bugs?" Dermot fiercely rubbed the back of his neck.

"I've heard they spread themselves with bear grease."

"That would certainly work, but who wants to go around smelling like a stinking bear?"

"You gotta choose one, Dermot: itchy or stinky."

"Not to mention greasy—yeesh."

Brett couldn't help but laugh. He wondered if Dermot wasn't purposely avoiding any mention of the previous night. Or perhaps in this hell-march, it wasn't even in his thoughts. He looked to the west. "The sun's getting low. I reckon it must be near five o'clock."

"We've got to stop soon. The horses are about to drop from thirst."

Reprieve came fifteen minutes later as the column crossed the Rosebud, stopping briefly to let the horses drink, then crossing into freshly deserted Sioux encampments. They followed the trail for another two and a half hours then came to a halt under the protection of a large bluff. Word was relayed back that they were stopping to make camp.

They gathered near together under the bluff, and Brett hopped down from his mare, his knees buckling from the stiffness. He began to loosen the saddle strap and stopped short at Lieutenant Smith's yell.

"Horses are to remain saddled. We won't be camping long."

Brett met Dermot's gaze and sighed. Would they be able to get much rest at all?

Supper was hasty; campfires were small and put out as quickly as possible. The ravenous soldiers devoured the small meal, and hoping to catch quick naps, they tossed bed-rolls on the bare ground and collapsed upon them.

~~~

It felt like he had only just closed his eyes when Lieutenant Smith's voice woke him. He sat up and through bleary eyes saw Dermot rising up onto his elbows and blinking, still half-asleep.

"Corporal, Sergeant. I hate to cheat you out of your rest like this, but get yourselves up and go grab some coffee. We're moving out again."

"Sir?" Brett looked up at the sky. The tiny sliver of new moon was just about to set on the horizon; he knew it couldn't even be midnight yet.

"The Crow scouts found them, all right. A Sioux camp of at least four hundred lodges. The general wants to get as close as we can before daybreak."

Four hundred lodges? In one camp? Brett did some mental calculating. *My God, that must mean one to two thousand warriors.* Would they even have a chance against those odds? They weren't due to rendezvous with Terry and Gibbon until the twenty-sixth—the day after tomorrow. He felt sick in the pit of his stomach.

Silently he got up and tightly rolled up his bed. All around him he could hear the snoring of the soldiers yet to be awakened.

"I guess this is it, then," Dermot said.

"Yeah." Brett hung his head. He longed for the intimacy of the previous night to soothe his fears, but knew it wasn't practical. Instead, he reached over and grabbed Dermot by the shoulders. "We're gonna make it. We'll come through, none the worse for wear, and Colonel Custer will have his victory and we'll be back at Fort Lincoln in less than a month."

Dermot smiled in the moonlight and cuffed Brett on the ear. Brett wished he could believe his own words of encouragement. They secured the bedrolls to the horses and then downed cups of boiled coffee before mounting up with the rest of the camp, hastening to be ready for Custer's orders.

~~~

The march earlier that day may have been miserable, but marching in the middle of the night in near-total blackness seemed even worse.

Brett and Dermot rode side-by-side but could barely make each other out in the thickening cloud-cover. The only way they knew to guide the mares was by listening for the clip-clop of the horses' tread ahead of them. They had left the river-bottoms behind and were climbing the eastern side of the divide. Brett's mare faltered, nearly losing her footing and almost pitched him out of the saddle.

Hearing the quiet curses, Dermot moved in closer and reached out and touched Brett's shoulder. "Just making sure you were still there." His voice was nearly a whisper.

"I nearly wasn't. She must have stepped in a rabbit-hole or something." Brett kept his voice low. He wanted to ask Dermot how close he figured they were getting to the Sioux camp, but was afraid talking would make too much noise. The constant clanging of canteens and tin cups permeated the darkness, making him very nervous. The mule train was well behind them, but the hungry mules kept braying. *Dear God, please make them shut up, any Indian within five miles is bound to hear us.* Brett had never heard of warriors attacking at night, but he couldn't help but think that this would be the perfect opportunity to catch the cavalry in an ambush.

After hours of slow, clumsy plodding, Brett finally spoke. "You still awake?"

"Barely. The general sure seems keen on getting us to this Indian camp in a hurry."

"Yeah." Brett thought again of two thousand warriors against their band of seven hundred. Surely the colonel didn't mean to attack before Terry and Gibbon's regiments arrived the day after tomorrow? He didn't want to think about it anymore. "Dermot, you know it's only nine more days 'til the Fourth of July?"

"The Centennial," Dermot said. "There were plans for a big celebration at the Fort. I don't think we're going to make it back in time."

Or at all. Brett couldn't keep this thought from his mind. "Well, even if we don't make it back to the fort, we can have some sort of celebration on the way. I think there's enough whiskey and food supplies that we could make quite a party.

I know a couple of privates who brought along their mouth organs, so we could even have music and dancing."

"Sarah would have loved the dancing. I couldn't dance without her being there."

"With no ladies available, we'll just all have to dance with each other."

Dermot quietly chuckled. Brett knew he must be smiling. He imagined himself dancing with Dermot, their hands clasped, Dermot's right arm around his waist and his left hand on Dermot's shoulder.

They nearly bumped into the horses ahead. The ground had flattened out and Brett could barely make out a huge blackness that was a tall bluff, under which their column had stopped. The troopers spread out under the protection of the bluff and dismounted. They led the horses to nearby pools of water that were fed by a creek. The thirsty horses eagerly dipped their heads for a drink but recoiled, snorting at the alkaline stagnation.

"Water's no good here," Dermot said, unbridling his mare so she could at least get some moisture out of the grass.

Brett unsaddled his horse and used dried grass and weeds to wipe down her sweaty back. Dermot did the same for his horse, then flopped down on the ground. Using his saddle for a pillow, he was fast asleep in minutes.

Brett sat down opposite him and lay back against his own saddle, but found he couldn't sleep. In the clouds above, faint highlights of gray began to hint that dawn was near. He watched the officers at Custer's tent, flitting to and fro. Didn't the man ever sleep? Men half his age were plumb tuckered out and yet he seemed tireless. In fact Brett was becoming so unnerved by the relentless drive of the man with his unquenchable thirst for victory, pushing harder and further than many soldiers could abide, that thoughts of insubordination began to emerge.

After the camp quieted down Brett did manage to catch a few minutes of sleep, but kept waking up because of bad dreams. He was up at daybreak when the Ree scout, Red Star, galloped into camp carrying a message that the enemy had been found. Brett watched Custer's tent with trepidation. It didn't take long. Custer was soon roused and in his excitement mounted up and rode though the camp himself, buckskin-fringe flying, to shout the order to prepare to march at eight o'clock.

Dermot was startled out of a sound sleep at the shouts, his face a mass of confusion. "Are we marching out again?"

"In a couple hours," Brett said. "I should think some breakfast would be in order. If we're going to battle today, at least we should do it with a full stomach."

"Wake me as soon as it's ready." Dermot laid his head back down and dozed off again.

~~~

Since Custer wouldn't permit campfires, breakfast was raw bacon and hardtack. Brett could barely stomach the raw meat, and somehow felt savage eating it. The hardtack had no more flavor than a burlap sack, but it fueled his empty stomach.

At eight sharp the troops moved out behind Custer, fresh in a clean blue shirt and his buckskin coat. As they climbed the divide, the thin clouds gave them a little bit of protection from the scorching sun, but the heat quickly grew intense. They could barely hold the horses back—thirst was driving them mad to find water ahead. By ten-thirty they had climbed some ten miles up the divide. They stopped at the base of the lookout point where the scouts who had spotted the Sioux camp were waiting. Custer and Red Star left them to climb the peak and join the scouts.

~~~

In less than fifteen minutes Custer and Red Star had vanished from view from the troopers who were packed in a hidden ravine at the base of the peak. Though it was still early, the air was already stifling. Brett mopped his brow and watched the peak wondering just what it was Custer would see over the other side. Hundreds of tipis and thousands of warriors preparing for battle? Taking a small tribe into custody was one thing, but for this he wasn't prepared. Surely Custer had the sense to wait for the other two regiments.

His mare bobbed her head and nickered restlessly. Her eyes rolled with panic and thirst. A cool stream is what she needed. It pained Brett to know she was suffering. He stepped down from the saddle and untied the sack of oats, scooping up a handful and holding it under her chin. She tried to eat them, but they fell dry from her lips.

The ravine was small and well-hidden by foliage. As the mule-train began crowding in, it became cramped. Brett left his mare and threaded his way through the horses to find Dermot. He was by himself at the edge of the ravine, sitting erect in his saddle, peering up at the top of the peak.

"The horses aren't going to last long without water." Brett said.

Dermot looked down to meet his gaze. "I suppose not."

"Can you see anything up there?"

"No, I was just waiting to see some sort of movement when they come back down."

"The river's on the other side. I sure hope we come to the river before we come to the Indians."

"Yeah." Dermot pulled off his cap and his red curls were drenched with perspiration. He ran his fingers through his hair to aerate his scalp.

Sensing his discomfort, Brett rested his hand on Dermot's thigh. "You're worried, huh?"

"I just wish I knew what we were dealing with over there." He fanned himself with his cap. "Ah well, it's no use frettin' over it. The general will be back soon enough to let us know what he saw."

Dermot got down off his mare and they tried to find a little bit of shade to sit down and wait. The ravine was so still and hot, that it felt like they were suffocating. The few drops of water left in their canteens weren't enough to keep their tongues from swelling.

"Perhaps it would be better if we thought about something else other than what's waiting over the divide." Brett sat with his arms resting on his knees.

"Like what?"

"Like after this is all over and we're back at the fort. Wouldn't you like to leave the army, Dermot? I don't mean right now, but later, when your contract is up. You know, do something else for a change. Farming, raising pigs, anything but this."

"Brett, you already know the answer. The answer's the same. It's never going to change. The army is what I am."

"For your whole life?"

He smiled impishly. "Until I'm an old fat general who's too slow to move anymore and they force me out."

"But what about Sarah? Surly she would be happier to have you closer to home and out of harm's way."

"Sarah's just as much part of the army as I am. She's been in the middle of it all her life and fully understands it... and me."

Brett realized it was useless to try and counter the argument. As much as he wanted Dermot to come away with him and begin anew, it just wasn't in the cards. He scratched his whiskers. The sweat made him itch. The air was so stifling in this ravine; even a tiny breeze would have been a welcome relief to help cool him down.

For the next fifteen minutes they sat in silence. Random thoughts swirled though his mind—a military ball at the fort. All the ladies wore flowing dresses but strangely had papooses strapped to their backs, while the men were in full military dress but wore headbands and feathers and warpaint.

Sergeant Curtis broke the quiet when he came galloping into the center of the ravine, out of breath and flustered. Captain Yates asked him what had happened.

"I lost some of my clothes from my saddleroll 'bout a half-mile back, so I skedaddled back to find it, and I done found three redskins all gathered 'round a box o' hardtack that must've fallen out of one of the mules packs. They done took off back to the Little Bighorn when they seen me, but the Indians know we're here. They've seen our tracks and you know they've run back to tell the chiefs all about it." The sergeant finally took a breath.

Brett's blood froze. If the Sioux didn't know of their presence before, surely they would be alerted now. Their only chance had been with a complete surprise attack, but there was little hope of that now. He suddenly realized that during Sergeant Curtis's report he had reached out and clasped Dermot's hand and was still holding it. His face flushed red and he withdrew his hand. Dermot appeared not to notice, but Brett knew he was just being polite by ignoring the indiscretion.

The troops quieted down and waited. Waited for Custer to return and inform them what was over the divide, waited for how he would react when he heard the report that the Sioux knew of their presence.

Finally, movement was spotted below the peak, and all the troopers got to their feet to watch Custer descend the slope with the scouts in tow.

After he refreshed himself with water from a canteen offered by one of his officers, Custer gathered all the men around to give his report.

"Men, it's not as bad as the reports made it out to be. Mr. B-Bouyer and Mr. Reynolds have reported that they saw thousands of Sioux ponies penned near th-the Little Bighorn. Mr. Bouyer insists that the biggest Indian camp he has ever heard of is down there. Now I'm telling you all, my eyes are as good as any man's here, and I have looked through the very same binoculars and-and-and I didn't see a goddamn thing! Furthermore I don't believe any of the scouts up there sa-saw anything either. In their excitement they've just let their imaginations run wild. Indeed there are Indians out there; we have tracked them this far, and in fact I've just been informed that Sergeant Cu-Curtis met a few of them this morning, and I'll be damned if you all think I'm going to let them escape us now! I assure you their numbers are small and by the time we sit down to supper t-tonight we shall have defeated them! Now mount up and await your orders! Victory is at hand."

Some of the older men looked deathly pale, but managed to keep their composure. Brett felt his stomach lurch and knot up as he watched Dermot and saw him cheering along with the younger recruits, many of them pumping their fists in the air, eager for their first fight.

Brett felt as though every nerve in his body was exposed and raw. With much more haste than he would have liked, the entire regiment of 12 troops had climbed to the saddle of the divide. There was nothing but rocks and dirt and dry vegetation. To the west lay the valley of the Little Bighorn River.

Custer called a halt while he organized the troops. He called Captain Benteen over and the two of them stood face-to-face in heated discussion. Benteen kept looking back at the troops then shaking his head. Brett couldn't make out their words but he could tell an argument was ensuing. Several times, Custer pointed to the ridges toward the south and Benteen would look, but then jump right back into the argument. Finally the matter appeared to be settled and Benteen called out in a loud voice, "Companies D, H, and K, you're with me! We're moving on!"

To Brett's dismay, Captain Benteen mounted up and led the three companies south. *What the hell?* Brett thought. *Where is he sending them? Surely they're not leaving us! We barely have a chance as it is with all the forces together, but with three troops off to God-knows-where, it's suicide plain and simple. What is Custer thinking?*

As D, H, and K disappeared over the ridge, Custer walked over to confer with Major Reno, who jumped down from his mount and listened earnestly while Custer pointed at different locations in the valley below. Reno nodded earnestly and seemed to accept all the instructions and maneuvers that Custer laid out to him.

When they were finished, the colonel and the major shook hands and Custer raised his voice to address the remaining troops. "Companies A, G, and M, you are now under Major Reno's command. C, E, F, I, and L, you are with me."

Custer and Reno remounted and started to lead the eight companies down the western side of the divide. Only the mule train was left behind under the charge of B Company.

As they stumbled down the rough terrain of the coulees, Brett noticed that Reno's three troops began to veer south and a growing gap of distance began to separate them. Soon there was no doubt but that once again, Custer was dividing their ranks. It was unthinkable. Three more troops—a hundred and twenty men—were as good as deserting them. Brett couldn't fathom the reasoning behind these tactics.

The descent down the rocky slope was slow and cumbersome as the horses often lost their footing and stumbled. The valley came into view below with the Little Bighorn River snaking back and forth across it and light patches of forest peppered the landscape. They were still too far away to make out the Sioux camps.

"Did you expect the colonel to divide us up like this?" Brett leaned towards Dermot and spoke at a low volume.

"No, I didn't know what to expect, but I'm sure he has good reason. Damn it Brett, have a little faith in the general! He's probably the best army man around when it comes to fighting Indians and he wouldn't have done it if it weren't necessary."

Brett was a little wounded by the rebuke and delayed his response for a minute. "I hope so. But I think he should have waited for General Terry and Colonel Gibbon like he was supposed to."

"That's all water under the bridge now." Dermot leaned over and grabbed Brett's arm looking deep into his eyes, the whole time bouncing from the rough gait of his horse. "Just remember our pact, okay? About Sarah, if... well you know."

"I haven't forgotten any of it." He tried to stress the word "any" hoping that Dermot would pick up his hidden meaning. "But if only one of us should survive, I hope it's you."

Just up ahead many of the Crow and Ree scouts had doubled back and were flocked around Custer, with Mitch Bouyer interpreting for them. Custer's angry voice rang out clear. "What do you mean they say they won't fight!"

Brett couldn't make out what Bouyer was saying. He broke ranks to move closer. Bouyer was saying something about the Rees being told that they only had to find the Sioux, not to fight them. He guided his mare around a grouseberry bush and was close enough to hear Custer speak.

"If they won't fight, then t-take away their guns and horses. They can just walk back to their squaws!"

The scouts stood their ground and conferred among themselves, finally agreeing only to help capture the Sioux ponies, but not fight the warriors. They moved back into the advance, heading back to Lieutenant Varnum and the rest of the scouts. Brett rejoined his troop.

~~~

Late that afternoon, the five companies halted on the bluffs above the Little Bighorn. Far below, the Sioux camp was now visible just across the river. To the left, they could see a long trail of dust rising off the river bottoms. Major Reno's companies were charging the encampment from the southeast.

Brett held his breath as the dust cloud slowly approached the camps. It was impossible to make out any figures or hear any sounds of battle. He closed his eyes; he wasn't a praying man, but this was one time he would make an exception. His mare strained at the bit, crazed for the river below; the blazing afternoon sun burned the back of his neck; and finally the first reports of the carbines from Reno's troops reached his ears. It had begun.

~~~

They slowly worked their way down the rough gullies. A drizzle of a creek and some scum-covered pools were enough to temporarily halt the horses. Brett's mare nearly gorged herself sucking away the top-layer down to the muddy bottom. The gunfire and puffs of blue smoke below riled up the soldiers, who began spurring the thirsty horses forward before they could even get their fill. Brett had to push his mare to keep up. The slope was now less precipitous and the horses began to pick up speed. The Gray Horse Troop did its best to keep the horses in some semblance of formation as they broke into an all-out gallop. Daniel began to charge ahead of the company.

"Whoa there, Private!" Captain Smith barked. "There'll be plenty of Indians down there for us all."

He fell back into the line. "Sorry sir, I just didn't want to miss out."

To his right, Brett saw Custer near the head of the charge, standing in his stirrups, gallantly leaning forward, the fringe of his buckskin jacket whipping in the wind. The incline had nearly flattened out now, and foliage became denser and greener the nearer they got to the river. Looking across the line of horses in full gallop, Brett was momentarily reminded of a horse race, or perhaps a fox hunt. But the sound of men shouting, hooves pounding, and stones clattering was soon diminished by the rallying drumbeat in his chest. The air was hot against his cheeks and the dirt kicked up by the horses smelled fresh.

He had a sense of Dermot somewhere off to his left.

Turning to look, he saw his face was expressionless and con-
centrated on the target ahead. Brett saw no joy in Dermot.
No bloodthirsty lust for battle that so many of the younger
recruits possessed. Just calm determination and raw bravery.
While Brett's own impulse was to wheel his horse around
and run back to the divide, he knew that Dermot had no such
cowardice lurking inside of him.

The Little Bighorn loomed closer, now a only couple of
miles away. The wind burned his face and he could feel his
lips chapping. His mare began to tire and froth at the mouth.
He borrowed strength from Dermot, who showed no fear.

Into the valley of death.

The last two miles melted away. The Sioux camp was in
easy view across the river. There only appeared to be a few
women and children milling about. Where were all the warriors? Had they all gone to the south end of the camp to stand
against Major Reno's battalion?

Then the answer became clear: Five hundred yards shy of
the river, Sioux and Cheyenne warriors jumped out from behind bushes and trees, arrows nocked, and Winchesters
aimed directly at them. Before they could even rein in their
horses they were pelted with arrows and bullets. The warriors had been lying in wait. It was an ambush.

Brett pulled his horse up short, reached back and slipped
his already-loaded carbine out of its holster. He took aim at
the closest target and fired. The impact threw the Sioux warrior onto his back. His chest was torn open, exposing a rib,
and blood ran out and over his side; his arms shook from the
pain and shock.

While springing the trapdoor and ejecting the shell with
one hand, Brett snatched another cartridge from the ammunition bag attached to his belt with his other hand, popped in
the cartridge, snapped the trapdoor shut, cocked, aimed and
fired again all in the space of three seconds. Like all cavalry
soldiers, this was something he could do in his sleep. He repeated the process four more times, the only shot hitting its

mark being the first. He was peripherally aware of the carbine fire and blue smoke all around him as the other soldiers in the Gray Horse Troop did the same thing he was doing.

The Sioux warriors were temporarily stopped in their tracks and shrank back from the carbine-fire. Amid all the gunfire and Sioux war cries, Brett heard a voice shout from behind, "Fall back, boys, fall back!" He wheeled his horse about, and followed Lieutenant Smith back away from the river bank. Through the haze of blue smoke he could make out Custer and several troops retreating downriver and back towards the hills.

As soon as they put some distance between themselves and the ambushers, Smith called for a dismount. They nervously jumped down from the horses, knowing the Sioux might catch up with them at any moment. One man took the four gray horses and pulled them behind the skirmish line to hold them in safety. Daniel planted the guidon into the ground, and along with Brett and Dermot prepared for the onslaught, each going down on one knee and aiming their carbines toward the sound of approaching war cries.

As the whoops came closer, Brett stole a glance to his right at Dermot, who was frozen like a statue, the stock of his rifle near his cheek. A stream of sweat ran down his temple. Brett quickly looked to his left, where Daniel eagerly aimed, waiting for the warriors to come into range. His face showed the elation of a young boy about to fell his first buck.

The Sioux swarmed up the incline, some on ponies, many on foot. As soon as the enemy was within range, their troop commenced firing. Shot after shot, as quickly as they could reload, they aimed and pulled the triggers. Arrows whizzed by their heads, bullets sunk into the ground near their feet, and blue smoke soon obscured their sightline. Brett aimed at every moving target he could see. Ejected shells were clinking all around. It seemed that every approaching warrior he hit, twenty more he missed. Beside him Daniel cried out as though he were in the throes of ecstasy.

"I got another one!" he hollered. "Did ya see him go down?"

"Shut up and keep firing!" Brett had no patience for jubilation. There were too many. *By God, where are they all coming from?* In all the battles he had fought, never had he been so outnumbered. Already many had gotten by and were going after the battalions in the hills.

As much as the smoke hindered the troop from hitting their marks, it also screened them from Sioux fire.

"Yee-haa!" Daniel crowed. "I just got a big one! He might o' even been a chief!"

Two seconds later, a Winchester bullet tore through the private's skull. He slumped over. Brett nearly retched at the sight of brain-matter splattered all over the rocks. It was just the flesh and blood of another fallen soldier. He needn't waste time to even think on it for a moment. He fired off twenty or so more rounds at the warriors swarming around him. He and Dermot, enshrouded in smoke, were both standing now, firing round after round in all directions, with the serenity and precision of two well-trained troopers .

A very large Cheyenne warrior appeared though the smoke, and while Brett fumbled in his bag for another cartridge, the brave let loose his already-nocked arrow. It sunk deeply into Brett's shoulder. He was stunned as he looked at the feathered stick protruding out of his shoulder and wondered why he couldn't feel the pain. Dermot wheeled around and dropped the Cheyenne warrior with a bullet through his throat before he could nock another arrow.

"Brett!" Dermot called out. "Are you all right?"

"I can't feel it. What's wrong with me?"

Dermot ran towards Brett. Behind him was a wall of smoke. A shadow loomed darker in the smoke, rising behind Dermot until it became a Sioux on a black mount. He was decorated in full headdress; his long lean limbs, dark and powerful, were covered in sweat and dirt. Brett touched the arrow shaft in his shoulder, and its pain radiated into his thoughts, smearing and twisting them—the battle cries seemed far away now, and Brett believed the warrior was coming to help him. He would know how remove the arrow and fix the wound. The warrior came closer, lifting something over his head. It was very long and sharp. Brett watched dumbly, trying to understand how this tool would remove the arrow.

The object was a five-foot long lance. Fear breached his confusion, and Brett rushed into action, loading his carbine as quickly as he could, and then he aimed and fired into the warrior's chest. Too late. The warrior's hands were empty. The sharp end of the lance had suddenly reappeared on this side of Dermot's belly, pointing to the ground.

It felt like there was no air left in the world. Brett doubled over, full of Dermot's pain; they were both suffocating. There was movement and noise all around them, but he was barely aware of it. He wanted to move, to do something, but felt paralyzed. Dermot's face was a mixture of shock and torture. His body crumpled and fell to the ground, that horrific final expression of shock frozen on his face.

Brett's throat hurt. He realized it was raw from his screaming.

The Sioux warrior fell off his pony. Not even conscious of his actions, Brett reloaded and put another bullet into the warrior, this one taking out his throat.

Then it erupted in him. Pure, violent rage.

"DAMN CUSTER! DAMN HIM TO HELL!" He whirled around loading and discharging cartridge after cartridge. He had no inkling of how long he, all by himself, kept up that barrage of firepower. Very few of his bullets hit anything at all. He really wasn't even aiming. His mind had clapped shut and he felt no emotion other than rage.

His carbine was so hot that finally one of the copper shells jammed. He tried to eject the shell, but to no avail. He pulled his pistol out of its holster and fired it until it was empty. The smoke started to clear and behind him he saw most of the Gray Horse Troop slaughtered. Bodies lay in the sun, bristling with arrows, and bullet wounds oozing blood. Some of the warriors were hopping from body to body, stabbing them in the gut and taking scalps.

A young Sioux brave on a stolen gray horse rode straight at Brett. He had nothing to shoot him with. The brave passed him within inches, reaching out and brushing his hand across Brett's face, then rode off whooping. Counting coup. Brett began to run. He couldn't just stand there and wait to be killed.

Ahead of him another warrior on a pony was riding straight at a soldier. Brett recognized the hulking man but strangely couldn't recall his name. As the young warrior rushed past him, the soldier reached up, grabbed him by the arm and yanked him off the pony. The warrior hit the ground and rolled, ending up right at Brett's feet.

Brett raised the butt of his carbine and was just about to use it to crush the warrior's skull. He was only a boy, perhaps thirteen years old. He had a round face and full cheeks; his thin arms and legs were not yet fully developed. He stared up at Brett; his bright young eyes showed no fear as he bravely waited to die with honor. Brett froze, rifle suspended over his head. He couldn't bring himself to do it. He couldn't murder this boy. He also couldn't just stand there, he had to do something. So he kicked the boy in the stomach as hard as he could and turned and fled, leaving the young warrior struggling to regain his breath.

All around was despicable mayhem. Underneath the smoke of the battlefield lay his uniformed brothers in pools of blood, some already scalped. He tried not to look at the bodies as he avoided tripping over them. Tried not to recognize the faces. *Run! Survive!* His choice was to either stay and die like a brave soldier, or run like the coward he was. He made for the hills, passing fallen men of companies C and F, guidons trampled on the ground. As he ran up the hill, he saw to his left, high on a hill, dead horses dragged into a circle being used as breastworks. Behind them three or four men still stood, continuing to fire their pistols, in spite of the arrows lodged in their bodies. One of those men wore a buckskin jacket.

Custer refused to fall. Warriors bearing Winchesters and bows converged on the final stand and pummeled the colonel with arrows and bullets until finally, he fell. So the once-great man was dead. Brett couldn't feel his legs beneath him but knew he was still running. He ran on and didn't look back.

~~~

He met up with three other soldiers. They were screaming incoherently at each other and trembling as they fidgeted with their weapons as if they had no idea of the purpose they served.

"What company are you with?" Brett asked.

"Bloody Indians, everywhere." His eyes, unfocused, shifted back and forth.

"Where is your commander?"

The terror blocked his ability to comprehend. The three men looked at him like he was speaking another language. A small band of Sioux spotted them as the smoke cleared and started charging up the hill towards them. "RUN!" Brett screamed. "Run for your lives!"

Two of the soldiers took off in opposite directions. The one whom Brett had questioned just stood in a daze.

"Run, you fool. Can't you see they are coming?"

He looked Brett square in the eye, drew his pistol, placed the muzzle under his own chin and pulled the trigger. Drops of blood splattered across Brett's face and a large piece of the man's skull flew straight up into the air. His knees buckled and he fell, eyes open.

Brett ran for the hills, hoping to find refuge in one of the ravines. The band of warriors split up to chase them all down. Brett felt like he was running harder and faster than he had ever run in his life, but getting nowhere. He was just starting to become aware of the dull pain in his shoulder where the arrow was lodged. As he ran, fear gave him strength. He didn't look back out of a superstition that it would invite the Sioux to see him. He didn't want to know when he would be caught. *Let them catch me unawares. It's better to die without knowing it's about to happen.*

The war cries and gunfire began to sound more distant. Finally, about to drop, he slowed, and dared to look behind him. No one was there. Had the Sioux not chased him? In splitting up to chase the three soldiers had there not been any who had sighted him? He slowed to a walk, heaving like a spent racehorse but still moving. He was afraid if he stopped altogether, they might still come. Surely they would search the hills for every last soldier until all were dead. He must hide. He looked at the ground behind him, the tracks every-where. He must hide his tracks.

He soon came upon a small rocky creek. He dropped to his knees and scooped the cool water into his hands and gulped it down. He wrapped his fingers around the arrow and gave a gentle tug. Spasms shot through his shoulder. Too deep. The arrowhead was completely buried in muscle. He couldn't pull it out on his own, so he broke it off as close as he could to the wound. The blood had already started to clot around the wooden shaft.

Looking into the water, it dawned on him how he could hide his tracks. He jumped into the creek and began wading upstream. Even Sioux and Cheyenne couldn't track in the water. He felt like he was smiling, but he had nothing to make him glad.

~~~

He sloshed in the water for what seemed like miles, look-ing for cover. Finally he spotted a fallen tree lying on the bank, and its bark was peeling away from it in a large curved sheet. The sheet was nearly four feet long. Its highest point was little more than a foot off the ground. Could he hide un-derneath it? Not on the ground, it was too shallow. But in the creek, yes! Without getting out of the water, he reached over and dragged the bark so it was perched half on the bank and half in the creek. Underneath was a good ten inches of air. He could lie under it with most of his body submerged in the water and his knees drawn up and his head resting against the bank. If the Sioux did come this far they wouldn't see him unless they got down and looked under the tree bark.

He lay crunched in his watery shelter and waited. The sounds of battle had mostly faded. Distant gunfire still echoed in the ravines, though, and Brett wondered who was left alive to still be shooting.

He had no sense of time. He was too terrified to come out and look at the position of the sun. Then he heard voices, speaking Lakota.

He froze and scarcely breathed, fearing that the tiniest movement or sound would draw their attention. The trickle of the creak masked the sound of him turning his head to better hear. Of the voices that spoke he could make out at least three distinct ones. The discussion was calm, but he couldn't discern what it was about. His heart pounded in his chest and perspiration streamed down his face. The fear of discovery was so intense, he felt he might pass out. Time stretched and stilled. Would they ever go away?

Just as he thought he couldn't stand another minute of holding still, they were gone. If they had tracked him this far, they must have given up. He waited some more, until finally it began to get dark and he knew they wouldn't be back. For tonight at least, he was safe.

Only then did the reality hit him. Dermot was gone. Sarah was a widow and he had lost the one person in his life that meant everything to him. But his mind couldn't dwell on it. It hurt too much. He had to push it to the corner of his thoughts and lock it away to be examined later. Every other soldier in company E was likely dead as well. He'd seen Custer fall. He suddenly felt very lonely, like the last man on earth. By all rights he should be lying dead on that battlefield with all his comrades, not hiding like the sniveling, deserting coward that he was. Exhaustion began to set in and he felt himself start to drift off, but the image of a warrior slicing open a trooper's belly and pulling out his liver bounced around in his head and began to invade his dreams.

~~~

He woke suddenly, realizing it was pitch black and very cold. He had to get out of the water. He raised his head and listened. The gunfire had stopped, but there were other sounds that took its place—chanting and drums. He pushed the tree bark away and stood up, stepping out onto the bank. His legs were cramped and he shivered in the breeze as the water dripped from his clothing. He longed for a warm fire but knew it was impossible. He had no supplies and even if he did a fire would only alert the Sioux to his presence.

It was too dark to see anything, but the faraway sounds were distinct to his ears. The Sioux and Cheyenne were celebrating victory.

It went on for hours. The chanting haunted him. He wanted it to stop. It tormented him by constantly reminding him of the massacre. He sat huddled on the riverbank; the drums felt like his own heartbeat. At times it felt like the chanting was getting closer. In the blackness of the nearby bushes he imagined shapes moving toward him. He could feel breath on the back of his neck. When he whipped his head around, he realized it was only the wind. The throbbing pain in his shoulder seemed strangely in sync with the drums.

The wind and his body heat had dried his clothing and he began to warm up. His thoughts were a jumble of images and confusion. He couldn't sort it out enough to put together a plan of action. A piercing accusation kept surfacing—*You are a coward and a deserter.* Was he? What good would it have done to have stayed and died with the rest? Perhaps a couple more Sioux and Cheyenne may have been wounded or killed, but it would not have saved a single soldier's life.

He longed to be unconscious so he didn't have to think. After the celebrating quieted and morning drew near, he got his wish and fell asleep, lying on his side on the creek-bank.

June 26, 1876, Dawn

His dreams were of battle and echoing carbine-fire. He opened his eyes to a pale blue sky. The carbine-fire was *not* a dream. It was real—far off—but real. The realization that it was dawn and he was exposed out in the open jolted him awake. He sat up and groaned at the pain and stiffness in his wounded shoulder. He lowered himself back into the water and slid the tree bark back over himself. It was cold but his body quickly adjusted to the temperature.

He wondered whom the Sioux were fighting. Were there any soldiers in the battalions left alive? Perhaps Major Reno's troops, or Captain Benteen's? Or could it be that General Terry had finally arrived from the north?

The morning stretched on and still the fighting continued, sometimes in rapid volleys, and other times in spurts punctuating intervals of silence. The heat pressed on Brett's skin in spite of the cold creek. From under the tree bark he could see the noonday sun sparkling on the water.

He should be back down there in the midst of whatever skirmish was still going on. But he had seen the thousands of Sioux and Cheyenne warriors and knew that it would be impossible to get past them to return to whatever was left of the troops. He was reminded that he had no weapons. He racked his brain trying to remember what had become of his rifle. He must have dropped it at some point but he couldn't remember when. His pistol was still in its holster at his side, now hopelessly waterlogged and exposed to rust, having lost all its oil by now. The few ammunition cartridges he had left were also soaked inside the pouch on his belt. Returning would be suicide.

How were they holding out so long against such lopsided

odds? Unless reinforcements had arrived from both Terry and Crook...

The pain was getting worse in his shoulder. He could feel it swelling up, and it would soon fester. His stomach was crying out for food, too; he hadn't eaten in over a day.

As the afternoon wore on the gunfire volleys slowed. Longer and longer spans of silence separated them. It nearly drove him to insanity, not knowing what was happening. Were the Sioux winning? Had they nearly wiped out the rest of the battalions just like they had done the Gray Horse Troop? Or had the army regained control and driven them back?

Pretty soon the gunfire ceased altogether. As the sun sank and shadows crept over the ravine, he heard nothing but the trickle of water and the buzz of insects. When darkness finally obscured him, he came out of hiding to lie down on the bank once more. Every part of his body ached. He longed for a soft bedroll and pillow, but had to accept the ground. While he waited for sleep, he strained to hear. There were no drums, no chanting. Nothing but silence. He didn't know what it might mean. And not knowing only bred more fear inside him.

June 27th 1876, Dawn

Once again, he woke at first light. The dawning of a new day gave him new courage. There were no signs of fighting or for that matter, anyone at all. Without giving it a second's debate, he decided to return. He had to know what had happened. He pushed himself up and pain shot through his shoulder. He unbuttoned his coat and pulled up his shirt to examine the wound. All around the arrow, pus leaked from the infection. It felt tender and fevered to his touch. He splashed some cold water on it, closed his coat back up and started to retrace his way along the creek and through the ravine, returning to the hills above the Little Bighorn just as the sun rose over the horizon.

He wasn't prepared for what lay before him. Large dark mounds spread out haphazardly over the fields, along with smaller white ones. He didn't have to get very close before realizing the large mounds were the carcasses of the horses and small white mounds were the men, stripped naked and rapidly decomposing in the summer heat. He stopped. It was too much for anyone to bear.

But he forced himself to go on. He came to the first bodies. The Sioux had left them naked as the day they were born, mutilated with stab wounds and tomahawk chops. The skin, pink and baking in the sun. Flies covered the rotting flesh, maggots already squirming in the eye-sockets and carrion beetles eating away at the flesh. The scalps had been peeled off, leaving dark, dried blood on the bumpy white skulls. The bellies were bloated with expanding gasses and the odor of rotting flesh was so rank that Brett started to gag, but his stomach was too empty to be emptied further. Overhead vultures circled, some brave enough to land nearby and peck away at exposed organs. His impulse was to chase them away, but realized it would do no good; they would only return again.

He wandered from corpse to corpse, each seeming more atrocious than the last. The decomposition had rendered most of them anonymous. Until finally he came upon one he recognized—crudely scalped so that one sideburn was intact, and the other missing along with his ear. Brett recognized the face of Mark Kellogg in spite of the blackened, swollen skin. The reporter's thin body was stabbed and hatcheted and the only thing he was left with were his boots.

Nearby he spotted what he was seeking. The red hair was unmistakable. He turned away. He couldn't look. It hurt too much. But he had to. He gathered his courage and slowly approached the body. Lying on its side, naked and pink, a gaping dark hole in the stomach where the lance had gored him. A large circle had been cut out on the top of his head removing a section of his scalp. His face was purple and distorted from the swelling skin.

The knowledge that Dermot was dead and the grief he had been shielding from his consciousness suddenly broke free and he wailed out loud. Sobbing and crying, he wanted only to lie down next to the body and embrace it and hold it tight, but was repelled by the state it was in. He squatted over Dermot's remains, embracing his own arms as if trying to hold on to an invisible spirit, and rocked back and forth, crying uncontrollably.

"Why?" he cried, looking to the sky. "What possible reason did it serve for all to die? It's senseless! We did this! The army is responsible and I hate them for it!" He buried his face in his palms and cried until he had no tears left.

When he regained enough composure to limit himself to just a few sniffles, he looked around for something to cover Dermot's body. He couldn't leave it lying in the open for the vultures. He waded across the river into the deserted Sioux camp and found a wikiup with the stretched buffalo hide that had been left behind. He tore it loose and took it back to the body and carefully rolled Dermot inside of it. He hadn't the strength or the means to dig a grave, but gave a silent prayer over the body. *I loved you. As long as I live I will remember how dear you were to me and will guard my love for you against anyone who tries to take it away.*

Only then did he remember Sarah. He remembered the pledge he had made to Dermot. He thought about returning to Fort Lincoln with the news, and how broken she would be. If she did take him for her new husband, he would live in Dermot's shadow and she would forever be a reminder of what he lost. "Forgive me," he spoke to the covered form. "Please forgive me, Dermot, that I'm too weak to keep my promise. I can't face her. I can't go back to her without you. I'm sorry." Fresh tears streamed down his cheeks.

He looked to the north. Movement caught his eye. Miles away, across the river someone was heading toward him. He shaded his eyes and squinted. They appeared to be cavalry scouts. General Terry's troops were coming. He couldn't be discovered as the only survivor. Feeling faint and feverish, he made a snap decision. His name would die in honor on that battlefield with all the rest. He would leave the name Brett Price behind and start a new life in the west. Somewhere far from the army, where no one had ever heard of him. He leaned down and laid his hand on the hide-wrapped body. "Goodbye, my love." And as quickly as possible, he took off before the scouts could get close enough to spot him.

July 4th, 1876

Brett's eyes fluttered open. Above him was a ceiling made of dark, rough wooden beams. To his left was a window whose halfway-open shutters revealed a densely forested landscape. He appeared to be in some sort of a log house. The bed was soft and it felt like the mattress was stuffed with straw. The furniture was all very rustic and unfinished in appearance—a knobby rocking chair in the corner and a crooked little table beside the bed on which sat an oil lamp. He felt his face. What happened to his whiskers? Someone had shaved him clean. He looked underneath the covers and discovered all that he was wearing was a long white nightshirt.

"Hello?" he called out. "Is anybody here?"

Instantly a man appeared in the doorway. He was tall and had a close-trimmed beard and dark hair, roughly parted in the middle that flowed down to his shoulders. He smiled, and the crinkles around his pale blue eyes suggested he was around forty, or had spent most of his life in the sun and weather.

"Hello there, fella. I see you made your way back to the living. Before that fever broke a couple a days ago, I wasn't sure you was gonna make it."

"Where am I?" Brett asked. The man poured tobacco into his pipe from a little pouch, struck a match, and lit it.

"Don't you remember?"

The last thing Brett could remember was heading west from the Little Bighorn and then getting weaker and sicker as he traveled. He vaguely recalled eating a raw fish.

"I'm sorry, I'm afraid I don't."

"I was out hunting when you came stumbling by. Darn near shot ya. Thought you was a stag. You was in pretty bad shape. Not quite right in the head, all fevered up on account of that Indian arrow a-stickin' in ya."

Brett reached over to his shoulder and felt where the arrow had been. It was just a little bit sore, but now covered with a clean bandage.

"So's I brung ya here and fixed ya all up. Wasn't sure you was gonna make it 'til the fever broke. Then I just been a-waitin' for you to wake up so's I could find out yer name."

Brett stopped himself just short of blurting out his real name. He stared at the floor, afraid to look up into the man's eyes.

"It's okay, feller. You a deserter?" Eyeing Brett quizzically, he blew a stream of smoke at the ceiling.

"I beg your pardon?" Brett looked up quickly.

The man went to the foot of the bed and picked up the cavalry jacket from the top of a little wooden chest.

"They won't be looking for me," Brett said solemnly. "As far as they're concerned I'm dead."

"I see. You got a name, then?"

"Sam," he said, choosing the first name to pop into his head. "Sam Smith."

"Well, it's damned nice to meet ya, Sam. My name's Elijah. I think you and I ought to get along right fine."

The End

No Darkness

Jordan Taylor

1915, France, near the Western Front

"Lieutenant Darnell!"

"Sir?"

"Oh, there you are. Why are you skulking, man?" The red-faced, broad-shouldered platoon sergeant did not wait for an answer but plowed on before Darnell could even open his mouth, "Find someone to take with you down to the cellar. There should be half a ton of supplies in this bloody shack and no one seems able to find so much as a tin of jam."

Private Morgan stepped forward and saluted the sergeant. He had large front teeth and matching ears that reminded Darnell of a corgi.

"Sir," the private said. "Me and Stokes searched the cellar already. Nothing, sir. No sign anything's been in there for some time, sir."

The sergeant walked right past him as if he had neither seen nor heard the private. "Well, Lieutenant? What are you waiting for?"

Darnell turned on the heel of his mud-caked boot. He jogged down the back steps of the three-room farmhouse and out into the mud field that served as a lawn. He had no intention of finding a private to go with him to aid in the search. The whole platoon had already searched the house, barn, chicken coop and woodshed so thoroughly they could have drawn up perfect maps of the place.

They were supposed to meet a ration party at the farm, then travel with them back to the front. The platoon had arrived almost a full day later than expected and the rations were still not there. The sergeant ordered them all to search the place in case the party had dropped their supplies and retreated, though they knew the search was in vain before they had started an hour ago. Now most of the soldiers were standing around the barn and house, smoking and waiting for someone to tell them what to do next. They had pulled off their haversacks and unslung the rifles from their shoulders. Darnell resisted reprimanding them for this since he had left his own rifle and pack leaning against a kitchen wall of the small house.

He slogged through the mud to the cellar door, standing open from a previous search. The wood of the door was warped and beginning to rot; just like everything about this abandoned farm site; just like everything about this war. People back home were saying it would be over soon, Elizabeth had told him in her letter. Darnell gazed into the black pit of the cellar with a face so void of emotion it was almost unnatural.

"Lieutenant?"

Darnell whipped around. A very thin and wiry private stood there, the mud above his ankles, looking past Darnell into the black depths of the cellar. Darnell could not remember his name: Hogan. No, Howell. H-something. Darnell frowned.

The young man spoke, glancing up from the doorway to Darnell's face, "What are you doing, sir? We've already checked in there."

"Yes, I know that. But you need to check it again."

The private's eyebrows lifted. He looked alarmed.

"Is something wrong, Private?"

"No, sir."

"Then I suggest you start searching."

The young man nodded briskly and stepped forward. Darnell watched as he pulled a handkerchief from his pocket and pressed it over his nose and mouth before starting down the muddy steps.

Darnell followed. The smell was worse than the wet or cold or dark: A combination of mold, raw sewage and compost.

The private waved his free hand around the stinking cave-like room and turned back to Darnell.

"See, sir?" he said with the handkerchief still pressed over his mouth. "Nothing here but Mr. Tittles."

Darnell stared at him. "What?"

"Mr. Tittles." The private pointed at the far wall. Something chalk-white showed up on the ground in the dim light that reached it from the open door.

Darnell moved forward, stepping into a mound of loose bricks piled on the dirt floor and tripping over them. The private grabbed his arm to stop him from falling and Darnell rounded on him with such a furious expression that the younger man let go and took a few steps back.

"Sorry, sir," he said, his posture snapping to attention in an instant.

Darnell turned away, looking at the ground now, as he walked to the far wall and knelt to see what was there. He could just make out the almost intact skeleton of a cat, partially sunken into the soft floor.

"Bloody hell," Darnell said under his breath. "There's nothing here. It's a goddamn wasteland."

He stood up and turned to face the private. He was backlit from the light coming through the overhead doorway and Darnell could not see his face but could tell the private was watching him.

"Well?" Darnell snapped.

"Sir?"

"Why aren't you searching, Private?"

The young man hesitated, as if thinking Darnell might be joking, then turned and started walking the perimeter of the room, looking carefully into every corner. The whole space was about seven or eight yards square. Darnell sighed and glanced toward the ceiling where enormous wood beams stretched from one end of the room to the other, disappearing into the earth walls on either side. He imagined the sergeant above him in the farmhouse and mentally cursed him.

"There's still nothing here, sir."

Darnell looked around and saw the young man watching him again.

"Thank you, Private..." he trailed off, hoping he had not sounded like he had trailed off. The private did apparently notice however.

"Fisher," he said. "Private Fisher, sir."

Darnell grunted. Who was the H name? Why could he never remember names? Every time he heard one his brain turned into a sieve. He remembered faces. He always knew a face. As he looked at Private Fisher, he recalled the young man running into camp on the edge of a village three evenings before. He was flushed and laughing as he waved something over his head to show the rest of the privates.

"Look, lads!" he had shouted as he slid to a stop in front of them. "Some French chap at the inn gave 'em to me. There's enough here for everyone!"

There had been a scramble as the other privates grabbed for the cigarettes, grinning and thumping the hero on the back. He was grinning as well; dancing blue eyes, sandy hair and thin face.

When the sergeant had walked up to them, they all fell silent.

"Did you steal those, Private?"

He had stood at attention then, though he could not quite get rid of the smile on his face. "No, sir."

"Are you sure about that, Private?"

The young man did not waver. "Yes, sir! I am quite sure, sir!"

The sergeant had taken one from him, patted his shoulder like an approving father and walked away.

A pack of cigarettes but no food. They ran out yesterday.

No one minded since they would be meeting the ration party today. Or never.

"Sir?"

Darnell blinked. Fisher was still staring at him.

"Is there anything else, sir? Only, it smells worse than a piss pot in here."

Darnell shook his head and started walking toward the door, then stopped. A series of sharp cracking sounds came from outside. Men were yelling and screaming. There was an explosion and the ground beneath his boots shuddered. A shadow flashed past the open cellar door as someone raced away. Darnell turned to see Fisher standing in the same place he had been a moment before, looking toward the ceiling as though mesmerized.

"Private Fisher!"

The young man looked at him. Their eyes met for a moment. There was a sound like the world being kicked apart by a wrathful god. Then blackness.

~~~

Private Fisher lay on his stomach with the wind knocked out of him, fighting for breath. He dug his fingers into the earth floor beneath him, mouth wide open, though his face was also against the wet, cool dirt. Lights were popping in front of his eyes like tiny bombs. The pain in his back made him feel as if all his ribs had been broken off where they joined his spine. His whole body was shaking as he fought to suck air into his bruised lungs.

A full minute passed in which Fisher was aware of nothing but his own struggle to breathe, to be alive. At last he was inhaling and exhaling in fast, shallow gasps that drove most of the light bursts from his eyes and steadied his shaking hands. He tried to push himself up on his elbows but the moment he moved, pain shot up and down his back and through his ribs. The pain traveled like fire across his legs and arms and every toe and finger ached with it. Distantly, as if his own thoughts were coming from another person, he was aware of being grateful that he could feel his legs at all. That meant they were still there.

"Private! Private Fisher?" a voice called out through the haze of darkness and spotty lights.

He opened his eyes. There were no lights at all. He was lying in total darkness. The pitch black of a grave. The death of a grave. The stink of a grave. The smell came rushing back to him as if being struck in the face with it. Like whatever had hit him—ground shake, explosion, world falling in on itself. The ceiling. A beam from the underside of the house had collapsed in the explosion and smashed him to the ground.

"Private?" The voice was close, but Fisher could not think who it was coming from.

With an effort, he moved one of his feet, scuffing the toe of his boot across the ground. He could move his hands and feet, blink his eyes, open his mouth, and breathe. His back was not broken. He closed his eyes, turned his head sideways and rested his cheek against the cool ground.

He heard someone making a great deal of noise nearby; scrabbling, scraping, panting sounds. Like someone rearranging furniture in a great hurry. The image, along with his own whole-back prognosis, amused him and he chuckled.

The sounds stopped at once.

"Private Fisher? Is that you?"

"Me mum used to have a big fancy do every month or so," Fisher said, smiling into the darkness, eyes closed.

"Oh hell—I thought you were dead, Private." There was relief in the voice, bordering on hysteria.

"She'd redecorate the whole house, every time. Get me dad to move the couches and trunks and tables. And I'd have to help her put up new curtains and set the tables with brand new china."

"Were you hit on the head?"

Fisher chuckled again. "She wasn't throwing the china at me."

Something bumped against his knee, then a hand grabbed his calf. Fisher jumped.

"There you are," Darnell said.

"Don't scare me like that, mate."

There was a pause.

"Sir."

"What?" Fisher pushed slightly up onto his elbows, fresh pain racing down his back and through his whole torso as he moved. He lifted his head and looked in the direction of the voice, roughly two feet above his legs.

"I'm not your mate, Private. I'm your Lieutenant."

The image of his mother's elaborate, velvet-clad parlor vanished from Fisher's mind's eye so fast it was as if it had never been there at all.

"Yes, of course, sir. Sorry, sir."

"Are you hurt?"

"Something very heavy hit me, sir. I'm not sure how bad I'm hurt."

"A ceiling beam?"

"Yes, sir. Must've been, sir."

"You're lucky to be alive, Private."

Fisher grinned in the darkness. "Yes, sir, extremely. I can move my arms and legs and all. Just feel like my back's about split in two."

"Can you sit up?"

"I don't think so, sir."

Fisher heard the lieutenant rummaging in his belt pouches and pockets. Then he saw the glint of a spark as Darnell tried to strike a match. On the second attempt the spark took and the match burst into flame. He held it up and they both had a brief glimpse of the cellar, now thick with dust in the air and covered in debris. The beam that struck Fisher was not the only one to have fallen. The whole south and west sides of the cellar were caved in. The door was gone, replaced by a solid wall of rubble.

"How's Mr. Tittles, sir?" Fisher asked as Darnell looked around.

The match went out.

"The bones?"

"Yes, sir."

"Private, why are you calling a long dead and decomposed cat, Mr. Tittles?"

"Stokes named him, sir. Thought it was quite funny, he did."

"Is that so? I'll be having a word with Private Stokes."

"Will you hold a seance, sir?"

Silence.

"What?"

"A seance, sir. It's where a person—"

"I know what it is."

"Well, don't you think that's about the only way you'll be speaking to Stokes again, sir? I mean, sir, they can't have made it, can they?"

"What makes you say that?"

"Uh, the shells?" Fisher said hesitantly, as though he were being tested. "The bleeding big bomb that was just bunged into the house Private Stokes was in…sir."

"We don't know anything hit the house, Private. Chances are, it was just nearby. Everyone in that house could well have gotten out alive."

"How do you account for the floor collapsing in on our heads then, sir?"

"This place was so old and rotten, it could have happened without anything actually touching the house. We shouldn't assume the worst."

"They teach you to say that kind of thing to the lads, sir? Only, Lieutenant Hall was always saying the same thing. 'Rain'll stop by half of five, no question.' And 'Don't worry about that arm, Channing, you're right handed anyway, aren't you?' They reckon it'll cheer us up? We're not completely daft, sir."

Lieutenant Darnell struck another match and rummaged in the mound of rubble for a bit of wood. He lit the end of a stick and held it out from his face to look around. Fisher closed his eyes against the glare of the light.

Darnell crawled back to where Fisher was still lying.

"Do you have any matches, Private?" the lieutenant asked. "I'm almost out."

"Yes, sir. I nicked them from Bates this morning. Ran out of mine two days ago, sir."

There was a pause, then the lieutenant eased himself around to face Fisher without commenting. He held the light in Fisher's face while Fisher kept his eyes closed.

"You do have a cut on the head, Private."

"Do I?" Fisher was startled. He reached up and felt blood smeared across his forehead, though the cut itself, along his right temple, felt small. "That's nothing, sir. Must've hit it when I fell."

Darnell scanned the rest of him with the light. He was covered in dirt but did not appear to be badly injured or bleeding anywhere besides the one cut.

The lieutenant lifted the light again and looked around the little room. He stood slowly, watching to make sure his head would not hit the ceiling and avoiding the beam now facing diagonally down with one end still fixed at ceiling level. He walked to the mass of wood, rock, dirt, and mud.

"Come on, Private," he said, bending to set the half consumed burning bit of wood on a brick.

Fisher watched him, without moving, as Darnell began pulling rocks and splintered chunks of wood from the heap and tossing them back. After a moment, the lieutenant seemed to notice he was working alone and turned to look at Fisher.

"Well, Private? Get to work."

"But sir…"

"What?" Darnell's voice had become suddenly harsh and the single word was a snarl.

"Two things, sir. One, the door wasn't on that wall to begin with, it was over there. And two, I don't think I can stand up, sir."

Darnell raised his eyebrows. "What's wrong with your legs?"

"Nothing, sir. Not that I can tell."

"Then you can stand. As far as the door," he paused, looking around. "It was on this wall. I remember."

"With all due respect, sir, where you're standing now, you've got Mr. Tittles on your right. But when you come down through the doorway into here, he's just ahead. On the opposite wall."

Darnell looked around at the bones of the cat, barely visible in the dim light. "All right, the other one's the right wall." His voice was icy, but he stepped over to the other wall. "Now come on and help, Private. That's an order."

Fisher bit his lip, only to discover that his lip, along with the rest of him, was covered in a layer of dirt. He spat several times, then pushed himself up to his hands and knees. The pain that shot through his whole sternum was so sharp and intense he almost screamed. Like being run through by five bayonets at once. Like being run over by a train. Like a bomb going off inside his ribcage. He hissed his breath through his teeth and turned his head sharply to bite down on the fabric of his jacket sleeve, receiving a mouthful of mud.

Darnell was making so much noise, tearing through the debris, that he failed to notice. After a moment, resting on his hands and knees, with the sleeve between his teeth, Fisher felt ready for another effort at moving. He eased slowly upward, pulling his way up using the same beam that had knocked him down. The pain was like shock-waves, shooting through his body in agonizing bursts that took his breath and made his legs shake and head spin. Bright lights were popping in front of his eyes again. In color this time, green and yellow and red. Dancing white stars intermixed with them and the whole thing combined made him think of

Christmas. He smiled faintly as he paused again, gripping the beam with both hands, clutching as if it were a life-preserver.

"Private!" The lieutenant's voice cut into his mind and made him look up.

"I'm coming, sir. Just a moment. Need to catch my breath." Fisher could not see anything besides the lights going off in his head, but he could hear that the digging had stopped.

"What's wrong, Private?"

"Just a bit a pain where that beam knocked me, sir. My ribs...a bit banged up, I think." The words came out in gasps. The lights were starting to clear as he stood still, but he was having a much harder time getting his breath while upright than he had on the ground. Each time he inhaled it felt like every muscle from his collarbone to his last rib was tearing apart.

He watched the lieutenant walk over to him, facing him from across the beam.

"Are they broken?"

"I 'da know, sir. Never had broken ribs before."

"Well, sit back down and I'll look at them."

"Not so sure I can do that."

Darnell ducked under the higher part of the beam and walked around behind Fisher. He put a hand on Fisher's side to help him lower back down.

"Jesus Christ!" Fisher screamed at the touch. The pain from it was so intense he couldn't think for a moment.

Darnell jumped back, staring at Fisher as the younger man struggled to get his breath.

"Maybe I'll just stand here for a mo, sir," Fisher gasped out.

Darnell shook his head. "I don't think that's a good idea. You need to lie down."

"No, now I'm up, I don't want to be back down again."

For a minute they stood with only Fisher's ragged breathing breaking the silence. Then Darnell said, "Let's get you over to the wall. You can sit down there and lean against it."

It was a slow and painful journey, those two yards to the wall and then down to the ground. At last Fisher found himself still, leaning back on a basically flat surface. The pain began to ease. Darnell stood there, watching him, not speaking for a long time.

When Fisher's breathing slowed and his muscles had started to lose their pain-locked rigidity, Darnell spoke, "You may have a lung punctured by a broken rib."

"Do you have any medical training, sir?"

"No."

"Me neither. I always thought that'd be best, you know? I mean, say you could stand there and tell me exactly what's wrong with me. What good would it do? You going to fix me up? Bit of a joke really."

Darnell moved back toward the wall of rubble. "Just sit still. I'll see what I can do about getting us out of here."

"That's a bit of a joke too, of course."

Darnell stopped, turned and stared at him. "A joke, Private? You think us getting out of here is a joke?"

"No, sir. I think you, or even both of us, digging ourselves out is a joke, sir."

"Really? Have you ever done it before?"

"What?"

"Dig out of a place like this."

"No, sir."

"Have you ever failed to dig out of a place like this?"

"No, sir."

"Then what makes you think it's a joke?"

"Well, it's not just the ceiling, is it?"

"What do you mean?"

"It's the whole place, right? I mean, the farmhouse will be collapsed."

"Okay."

"So it's on top of us, sir. Even if you could dig through that rubbish there, by yourself, there'll be an entire house of rubbish to dig through after that. No offense, sir, but I don't suppose you can lift a house off this hole by yourself."

The lieutenant stared at Fisher for a moment. In the dim, failing light of the flame, Fisher could see his mouth was slightly open.

"Do you want to die here, Private?"

"No, sir. I don't want to die at all, sir. But I guess it'll happen at some point."

"So this is just as good a place as any to you?"

"No, sir. I'd rather die at home with me mum knowing where I was and what happened and me sisters knowing and all. You got any family back home, sir?"

"I…yes."

"Your mum and dad still alive?"

"My dad."

"You got school friends? I'm guessing you went to university?"

"What makes you say that?"

Fisher shrugged, but the pain of the movement made him gasp for breath again.

"Yes, I did."

Fisher nodded, still wincing. "That all?"

"I'm married."

"Married? I wouldn't have guessed that."

"Why not?" Darnell's voice had suddenly become sharp again, like a razor.

"No reason, sir," Fisher muttered in barely more than a whisper.

Darnell turned away.

"If you keep burning things in here for light, the smoke will kill us, sir," Fisher said.

"I know that, Private," Darnell snapped without looking around.

The lieutenant returned to his attack on the rubble pile and soon the bit of wood had burnt out and they were left in absolute darkness.

After a few minutes passed in silence, besides the shifting rubble, Fisher said, "You ever been bothered by small spaces, sir?"

Darnell did not answer him, though Fisher knew he had been heard because there was a slight pause in the moving earth sounds before they resumed at a faster pace than before.

~~~

"Someone will find us," Darnell said, leaning his head back against the damp earth wall behind him. "The sergeant knows there were men down here. He'll make sure the place is checked."

"And if they're all dead, sir?"

Darnell wanted to throttle Private Fisher. His hands practically trembled with the effort of holding them steady.

"If they're dead, then headquarters will send another platoon out looking for us and they'll find us."

"When'll that be, sir?"

"As soon as no one returns with the ration party."

"Do they have that many expendable platoons, sir? That they could just send one out if one didn't turn up on the nose?"

"They'll come soon."

"How long do you think the air will last, sir?"

"Bloody hell! Will you just belt up! What the hell are you getting from this? Huh? Sitting there talking about the overwhelming likelihood that you and I are both going to die in here and every single time you open your mouth that likelihood increases enormously. Is that making you feel better for some reason?"

"Sorry," Fisher muttered. "No, it's not making me feel better. But it's the truth. Why delude ourselves into thinking some brilliant solution will turn up?"

"It's not a delusion. It's a very real possibility that someone will help us out."

"Possible, I suppose. Anything's possible. There may be

some more enemy artillery out there right now getting ready to bung more shells that'll open a path right out of here."

"If they did that, it'd have to be such a strong blast it would bring the rest of the ceiling down on our heads. We'd never know if a path had been cleared or not."

Silence.

"Lieutenant?"

"What?"

"You don't really believe we're getting out of here, do you?"

There was another pause. Darnell sat with his eyes closed, pressing his bleeding hands into his filthy trouser legs. He did not know how long he had pulled at the rubble of the wall keeping them here. It could have been an hour, or five hours. He was lightheaded from hunger, weak with exhaustion, and there was nothing to be done for his torn and bloody fingers. The only thing that had improved about their situation rather than getting worse was that he no longer noticed the smell so much.

"I don't know," Darnell said at last. "I want to think so." He opened his stinging eyes and looked toward Fisher, sitting against the same wall, less than a yard away. But he could not see him. He only lit a match if he needed to confirm the location he was working on in the mound. Otherwise, they stayed in darkness. They each had partially full water bottles on their belts and Darnell still had his ammunition pouches. They had left the rest of their possessions; rifle, small kit and haversack, above. Darnell found himself wondering what would come first; death by suffocation or starvation.

He felt something crawling across his face, a spider probably, and jerked one hand up to brush it away. In the few moments his hands had been still they were already cramped. Between that and the dirt-filled open sores all over the palms and fingers, he winced in pain from the motion.

He wondered if any of the spiders around here were dangerous. Maybe a bite would finish him off and he would not have to worry about his hands anymore. The dirt and splinters in the wounds were causing them to itch and burn.

They had no weapons; not even a razor or a piece of rope. Only rocks and boards. And boot laces. Darnell found himself fingering the knot in his laces with his painful hands. How hard could it be? He pressed the back of his hand to his own throat. It felt soft and pliable.

"Tell me about your mum's parties," Darnell said.

"What?" Fisher sounded mystified. As though he did not understand what a mother or a party was.

"You said before…something about your mum throwing big parties when you were a kid. What were they like?"

"Oh, well, very fancy. Fancy enough that she broke me dad with 'em. See, we didn't 'ave a whole lot a brass to start with and she wanted folks to think we did. Also, wanted to make herself think we did, I reckon. I loved 'em. Used to run around and take all the ladies' hats and bow to them. Real little gentleman I was. Only, in truth, I just wanted to try 'em on."

There was a pause as Darnell gazed into the darkness in front of him, then turned his head to face Fisher. "The hats?"

"Yep. Loved trying on those hats. I'd stand in front of the mirror with me sisters and we'd all have to have a go with each one until we found what we liked best. Then we'd parade around the parlor in 'em while the ladies were eating in the dining room.

"I remember this one lady, Mrs. Bowne, who'd wear a brand new hat every time she came and with the most amazing feathers on it you ever saw. Her's were my favorites. She came in with one once that looked like it just about had a whole dead peacock on it. Biggest hat I've ever seen in my life. Well, a course me sister, Marie, wanted to wear that one. Got into a bit of a scuffle over it. I knew I wasn't to fight with me sisters, but I wanted that hat…" he trailed off, his tone of blissful remembrance.

Darnell waited a moment but Fisher did not speak again, apparently lost in thought.

"And?" Darnell asked at last, his voice impatient.

"And what?"

"What happened? Did you get the hat?"

"Ah, no. Marie gave me a black-eye and then me dad walked in and gave me a belting for fighting with me sisters."

"She gave you a black-eye and you got the belting?"

"Yeah, me dad had very vague ideas about how young ladies were supposed to behave, but very specific ones about young lads."

"Did he ever see you with one of the hats then?"

"Oh no, he wasn't often around while me mum was having one of her dos. We were just unlucky that one day. He saw me in me mum's wig once, but she was able to smooth that over; said I'd just been holding it for her rather than that I'd begged to try it on. Me mum didn't mind having a nancy boy for a son. I was just another one of her girls as far as she was concerned."

Fisher sighed. "He wanted me to play football. No one would let me on a team though. I was just too horrible at it. Did you ever play any sports?"

"Tried once or twice. Can't stand cricket, or football. Never could play either one. I like horses but I never learned to ride very well. Your dad must have been pleased you signed on."

"Yeah. He was real chuffed when they sent out the call for recruits. Wanted me to be first in line. Figured that would get me sorted. Make a man out of me. Keep me in line."

"Do you find that it worked?"

Darnell could sense Fisher's grin rather than see it.

"Seeing as I'm sitting here telling my superior officer about trying on a bunch'a ladies' hats and getting a shiner from me little sister, what do you think, sir?"

Darnell smiled as Fisher laughed softly beside him.

Darnell opened his mouth to ask how old the private was, then closed it again.

"What about you, sir?" Fisher asked.

"What about me?"

"Where'd you grow up?"

"Manchester. Didn't live much with my parents."

"Your mum die when you were little?"

"No."

"How old?"

"She died when I was sixteen."

"Then why…?"

"She was in prison at a women's labor camp while I was growing up. My dad left me at an orphanage."

Fisher did not say anything for a long time. Darnell listened to the sound of his own breathing, wondering how long the air supply would last.

"How come?" Fisher said at last.

"How come, what?"

"How come she was in prison?"

"She stole a blanket to wrap me in a few days after I was born. It was February."

Silence again. Darnell counted his breaths; in, out, in, out.

"You said you had a wife," Fisher said. "She back home?"

"In Oxford. We've got a little house there."

"That where you went to university?"

"Yes."

"She pretty?"

"She's beautiful."

"Is Oxford nice? I've never been."

"It's fine. She wanted to settle down and have a family."

"You didn't?"

Darnell hesitated. "I got her a puppy. Welsh corgi. Thought that might…"

"Keep her at bay?"

The silence this time was icy. Darnell felt his back go rigid as he glared in Fisher's direction.

"Not everyone is the same way you are, Private," Darnell said. His tone like a glacier.

"And what way is that, sir?"

Darnell did not answer. He eased onto his hip and pushed himself to his feet. His muscles ached and his hands throbbed.

Fisher was quiet as Darnell lit a match and held it toward the door-side wall. Once he had gotten his bearings on the place in the debris where he needed to work, he flicked out the match. As he started dragging rocks and splintered wood away from the mass, he tried not to think that the whole heap looked just as it did before he had started working on it.

~~~

Fisher was back in the parlor. He was clean and young and happy. The happiness filled him like drink, without sense of purpose. It was just there. Like the peacock hat on his head, huge and green and blue and gold, trailing feathers behind him like the robes of the queen herself.

He lifted his hands in front of his face and saw how clean and smooth and pink they were, like the hands of a baby. He touched his own face and felt that it too was smooth and clean. He smiled to himself as he heard the door open behind him. He turned to see his mother standing there, smiling like he was the embodiment of all her dreams come true. She dropped a curtsey and he bowed in return, sweeping the hat from his head with the feathers dragging across the plush carpet beneath their feet.

When he looked up, returning the hat to his head, his mother was gone. The door stood open just behind where she had been. He walked to it and looked through. Two men were lying on the floor in the kitchen. They wore the khaki uniforms of the British Army. Their bodies were covered in mud and filth, faces black with it, clothes caked in it. They were covered in wounds, blood smeared across their faces, their hands and backs. A great pool of blood seeped from under their bodies, spreading across the stone floor like a river. Fisher stepped closer and saw their faces.

He screamed.

"Private! Wake up!"

Someone was shaking him. Pain was shooting through his body like fire. Like death.

"Fisher, it's okay, wake up, man."

No, they didn't understand. There was no waking or sleeping, there was only pain. The pain was the universe. The pain was it.

"Stop it!" Fisher shouted and struck out at the same time. He hit something that was knocked away and the shaking stopped. The pain eased somewhat, though it still made him pant for breath. He opened his eyes.

By the dim light of a flaming wood chip that lay on the ground a yard away, he saw a man kneeling beside him. His body was turned sideways to Fisher, facing the wall. He was looking at Fisher with such hatred, Fisher tried to shift away from him but was stopped by fresh waves of pain.

"You bugger," the man hissed at him. "If you ever do that again I'll see that you're thrown in the stockade."

Comprehension of his surroundings and who the man beside him was came back in a rush as he watched blood streaming from Lieutenant Darnell's nose.

"Oh, sorry, sir," Fisher stammered, fighting to take slow, less painful, breaths. "I'm sorry. I didn't know what was going on. I didn't mean to hit you, sir."

"You fell asleep," Darnell said, twisting around into a sitting position beside him. "I'd have left you, only it didn't sound like you were having great dreams."

"No, sir. Thank you, sir."

Darnell pulled an already blood and dirt covered handkerchief from his pocket and pressed it to his nose. Fisher noticed his hands were also covered in blood. Darnell must have tried wrapping the cloth around them to protect them from the pile of rubble.

"Maybe you should try mine, sir." Wincing with the pain of moving, Fisher reached into his own pocket but found it empty. He looked around. Darnell watched him with the filthy handkerchief still covering his nose.

"Didn't you have yours out when you first came in here, Private?"

"What? Oh, yeah, the smell. Funny, I stopped thinking about it."

Darnell sighed. "I guess a man can only have so many miseries at one time."

Darnell prodded the bit of burning wood across the floor with the toe of his boot to help them see farther out.

"There it is," Fisher said, turning his head. "Still cleaner than yours."

Darnell stood up and retrieved the dusty cloth with his fingertips. He shook it off and dropped it in Fisher's lap on his way back to his place against the wall beside him. Fisher could see that, as gingerly as Darnell had touched the cloth, it still now bore a bloodstain the size of a shilling.

"You're the one who needs it," Fisher said.

Darnell shook his head. "It's just about stopped." As he spoke he removed his handkerchief from his face and blood ran down to his chin.

Moving slowly, Fisher picked up his own and held it out. Darnell reached to take it but Fisher shook his head. "You don't want to do that, sir."

Darnell stopped, his blood-caked, dirt-incrusted, torn, splintered, and swollen hand uplifted beside Fisher's dusty one. He lowered his hand and sat, motionless, as Fisher wiped the blood from his face, then held the handkerchief against his nose.

"I'm sorry," Fisher said again. He meant it. He felt a tightening in his chest at the sight of the blood on Darnell's face that had nothing to do with his own injuries.

Darnell did not respond, but sat staring at a point some

six inches to the left of Fisher's shoulder.

"How long do you guess we've been in here?" Fisher asked as he turned the handkerchief and reapplied light pressure.

"Ten hours? Fifteen? I don't know."

When Fisher felt Darnell's lips moving across his hand, with only the delicate cloth between them, he dropped his own gaze somewhere to the side of the lieutenant's shoulder.

"So it'd be quite late?" Fisher asked.

"I suppose."

"You should get some rest too. Have you been working on that wall all this time?"

"Not quite."

Very slowly, Fisher withdrew the cloth. "It seems to have stopped."

"What?"

"The bleeding."

"Oh, right. Of course."

Fisher had his eyes fixed on Darnell's when the lieutenant looked up and their gaze locked. For a second that was a lifetime and a single heartbeat, they stared into each others' eyes. Then Darnell blinked and looked away, turning his head and looking at the dying flame. He sighed and stamped it out under his boot.

In the sudden, all consuming darkness, Fisher felt an almost overwhelming urge to reach out and touch the man beside him. The inability to see that he was still there was terrifying but the thought of touching him was as frightening.

Desperate for something to say, something to make Darnell answer and therefore speak and be heard, Fisher spoke at random, "Have you made any progress?"

"No idea. Perhaps a little."

"What about headquarters?"

"What about them?"

"Sending someone. Do you still think they will?"

"I don't know." Darnell sounded exhausted, as if every

word was a great effort.

"Tell me about the house."

"House? What are you talking about?"

"In Oxford. You said you had a house."

"Oh, yes, it's just a tiny thing. A little cottage outside of town."

"What's it look like?"

"Why?"

"I just...wondered...sir."

Darnell sighed. "It's about thirty years old. Built in 1885, I think. Little stone path running up to the front door. Dry stone wall goes along one side. Roses growing all over the wall. That's why Elizabeth wanted it so much. Loved the roses. She has a big flower garden there beside the house."

"What color?" Fisher asked. He closed his eyes, trying to pretend he could open them and see Darnell's face whenever he wanted to.

"The roses?"

"The house."

"Oh, it's sort of a butter yellow."

"How long has it been since you've seen it?"

"I was only just deployed. It's been about three weeks."

"Was she sad when you left?"

"Of course."

Fisher caught the defensive tone and tried to think of something to change the subject. "What's the dog's name?"

"Fell. Elizabeth loves to go walking on the fells, gathering wild flowers in the springtime. So she named him Fell."

"Do you miss him?"

"The dog?"

"Yeah."

"Well, no, not really. He's a pretty nice chap but he was always her dog. She spoils him. Gives him three meals a day and lets him do whatever he wants."

Fisher tried hard to evaluate the tone of that last comment but was still unsure if there had been resentment in it or not.

"Do you miss her?" he asked after a pause.

"Yes."

Fisher waited, but no elaboration was forthcoming.

"No kids though?"

"No."

"Ever?"

"Do you have some personal interest in my family, Fisher?"

"Well, if I wasn't trapped with you in a two-man tomb I don't guess I would, but things being as they are, it's something to talk about."

"Talk about something else. Or, better yet, don't talk at all. I'm exhausted. Can you stay awake for an hour or so, just in case someone outside is calling out looking for us?"

"Sure. I can stay awake."

Fisher could hear Darnell shifting onto the ground. He opened his eyes, looking in Darnell's direction. He longed to lie down beside him but the pain in his ribs at the slightest movement was too intense to consider it.

"I'm sorry," Fisher whispered into the dark.

"What for?" Darnell's voice came from about a foot to his right at ground level.

"For being so nosy."

Darnell was silent.

Fisher waited, listening for his companion's breathing to become deep and regular, or for a snore, or some sign that Darnell was asleep. But the breathing never changed. At last, after an hour, or two, or three, he did not know, Fisher fell asleep, still leaning against the wall.

~~~

As time passed, Darnell found the work of clearing away rubble more and more difficult, not only because of his throbbing, burning hands, but because it had now been over thirty hours since he'd eaten anything. His brain seemed frozen, as dead as his mangled hands were becoming. His head throbbed almost as hard as his hands did. His back, legs, and shoulders were on fire. The muscles seemed to have reached some sort of maximum capacity he had not known they could. Sweat poured off him until it blinded him and he had to tie Fisher's handkerchief around his forehead. Or rather, Fisher had to. Darnell could no longer bend his fingers to anything so delicate and he had knelt beside Fisher to allow the young man to tie the cloth in place.

He longed to remove his uniform jacket and work in his shirt but so much debris cascaded down on him while he worked, he knew that would be foolish. He did not even take off the jacket during the moments he sat beside Fisher in the darkness, catching his breath and pushing his flaming hands into the cool ground. The bloody nose and the headband were bad enough but he could not stand the thought of having to get Fisher to help him with the jacket.

They had passed hours in silence, unaware of how long it had been since they were trapped. Their isolation felt complete without any outside sounds reaching them. The quiet and darkness hung on Darnell's shoulders like a physical weight, pulling him down.

At first he had felt panic, trapped, crushed, as if the room they were in was growing smaller and smaller. He had torn at the rubble wall in a frenzy at those times, hardly able to get his breath, wanting to see, to feel something other than blackness. Even the matches did not help much. When he lit one, though it forced back the dark, it made the incredibly small space all the more real. As time went on, he found that he was not thinking about it anymore. The exhaustion, pain and starvation fought with each other to be forefront in his mind. There was no room left for dwelling on the dark of the cage in which he was slowly dying.

And Fisher. He wondered if he would have kept trying to get out at all without Fisher there. The private could not get himself out even if he had wanted to. Darnell was their only option.

He was chopping upward into the mound, using a broken off board as a spade, when the ceiling shifted over his head. He jumped back as a cascade of earth and rubble fell around him. The dirt choked him, knocked him flat on his back, and fountained over him like an avalanche. Over the roar, he was aware of Fisher's voice yelling at him, though it seemed very distant.

There was a moment then, as the roaring in his ears faded, and his body was still under the pile of earth, that he felt content: It was over. He no longer had to worry about Fisher or himself or his hands anymore. He lay still, eyes closed, feeling the cool dirt and thinking about darkness.

But someone was shouting at him.

"Stop it, Fisher," Darnell said, lifting his head from the ground. "I'm fine."

He found that he was able to sit up quite easily. Dirt and bits of wood fell off him in a rush as he did. Only his legs were really covered. He started to brush them off, then stopped. If the ceiling had caved in…

He looked up so suddenly he felt a sharp jab of pain race down his neck. Nothing. All blackness.

"Blast," he whispered, feeling for his matches. "The whole bloody ceiling caves in and yet it's still there."

He could hear Fisher breathing hard behind him but the private did not say anything.

Darnell tried to strike a match. Nothing happened. "No, no, no, hell no," he hissed. The striking surface was covered in dirt. At last, after dragging the matchbox across his jacket several times, a match took and he held it up.

An area the size of half the overall ceiling space had caved in, leaving an inverse crater above them. But it was less than a foot deep.

Cursing, shaking out the light and kicking his legs, dragging himself out from under the mess, Darnell scrambled backward until he ran into something and heard Fisher gasp in pain close to his ear.

"Sorry," Darnell said. He pushed himself away from Fisher to lean against the wall beside him.

"That's quite all right."

"Did anything hit you? Are you okay?"

"I'm fine."

Darnell leaned his head back against the wall and closed his eyes. "Do you have any water left?"

"Yeah."

He could hear Fisher picking up the bottle and knew he was holding it out to him.

"Take it."

"No, that's okay. I just wondered."

"Do you hear something?"

Darnell sat still, listening hard, holding his breath.

"No."

"I think it's rain. Hard rain."

"That would be news," Darnell said.

They had been marching in rain and mud since Darnell had joined the platoon a week ago.

Fisher did not answer and they sat in silence for a long time. After awhile, Darnell thought he could make out the sound of pounding rain as well. Although it sounded as if it were coming from a great distance.

"I'm sorry, Fisher," Darnell said after another long pause. "For getting you into this."

"Getting me into what?"

"This pit."

"You didn't—"

"Yes I did! You needn't have come in here at all. You told me you'd already searched. Then, once we were down here, I made you stay and look around. I knew it was daft, but made you do it anyway."

"If I hadn't been down here, I'd probably be dead now."

"That's why I'm apologizing."

Fisher began to laugh, but Darnell could tell he was fighting not to. Darnell guessed it hurt his ribs.

"Did I say something funny?"

"You're not as bad company as you seem to think, Darnell," Fisher said, still chuckling. "Besides, it's not your fault. I assume the sergeant ordered you to look in here? You don't strike me as knob headed enough to want to come down for a kip. And think of the fun you would have missed if you'd been trapped without me."

Darnell smiled in spite of himself.

"You'd never have learned about Mrs. Bowne's peacock hat," Fisher said.

"And that would have been a terrible loss."

"Too right. And I haven't even told you about my music lessons."

"It's probably best that you don't tell me about your music lessons, Fisher."

"Why's that? I mean, say, just say for one fraction of one moment of one second that we get out a here. You wouldn't turn me in, would you?" Fisher's voice was light and cheerful, not sounding even remotely concerned by the possibility.

Darnell did not answer. Saying, no, of course not, would mean admitting that he knew what Fisher was talking about. And he knew perfectly well that was the only reason Fisher asked the question to begin with.

"They'll change the law of course," Fisher said. "Those bloody legislator bastards can't win forever."

Darnell turned his head to stare at Fisher in the darkness. "You think so? You're dead sure we're never making it out of here alive, but you think the legislators will back down? Where do you come up with your reasoning?"

"Well, it's just crazy, isn't it? It's like arresting someone for having green eyes or uneven teeth. You might as well sit around counting leaves on trees as try to arrest all of 'em in Britain."

"They don't see it like that. To them it's no different than arresting murderers and thieves. They may not get every one, but they'll do what they can."

"Like your mum? Guess it did the world a whole bleeding lot a good when they took her away from her baby."

Darnell turned his hands over, pressing the backs to the cool ground. He should be up working on the wall, he thought, now that there was less of it. When he shifted, leaning forward in order to stand, his head spun and for a moment he thought he might be sick. The hunger pains in his stomach were growing almost as strong as the pain in his hands. He felt disoriented and disembodied.

"I need to rest for a minute or two," Darnell said. "Then I'll get back to that wall."

"A minute or two?" Fisher said. "You don't think that's a bit of an understatement?"

Darnell did not answer. He curled into a ball on the dirt floor, eyes closed, trying to hold his hands so they would not touch anything.

"Tell me about your music lessons," Darnell said.

"Well, me sister, same one what gave me the shiner, and me, used to take piano. Me mum had this big old piano in the parlor and she played too, but not so well. She wanted us to have the best tutor there was, just like everything else she did. Had to be all the way or nothing. Well, one day, when Miss Rheese came for our morning lesson..."

Fisher went on, his voice drowning out the distant rain and soothing the throbbing of Darnell's seeping hands. His voice was light and musical, like the story he told, and Darnell thought he must have a good singing voice. A tenor probably. His voice went with his blue eyes and boyish face. Darnell wished he could see that face now, rather than having to imagine it. But he knew it would be following him to his dreams anyway.

~~~

This time Fisher was sure Darnell was asleep. The

breathing was deep and regular, an unbroken in and out, in and out.

Fisher lifted the jacket collar of his own uniform to his lips and bit down on it as hard as he could. Pressing both hands into the ground below him, he shifted forward, away from the wall. The scream of pain that fought to escape him as he slowly eased onto his back was stifled to a high-pitched hiss through the jacket collar.

After several agonizing minutes, he was lying on his back beside Darnell. The lieutenant's knees were touching his own legs and Fisher could feel Darnell's breath on his face. He wanted to touch Darnell's hand but knew what bad condition they were in. Instead, he lifted his own hand and, moving very slowly and carefully in the darkness, found one of Darnell's wrists. He covered it with his own fingers, then paused, holding his breath. Darnell had not stirred. Fisher closed his eyes, working hard to steady his breathing as his ribs screamed a painful protest at him. He tightened his grip very slightly on Darnell's wrist and was asleep in minutes.

He woke suddenly, aware of being intensely, overwhelmingly, cold.

The cold was in his flesh, in his very bones. The cold was so powerful he could not think, could not even understand for a moment that it was cold he was feeling. It was like a living force taking control of his body, weakening him, holding him immobile in a deathly grip like the heart of a glacier.

When thought returned, it was for his companion. Instinctively, he closed his hand and felt Darnell's wrist still there, in his grip.

"Darnell," he whispered the word, though he had not meant to. He had to cough and clear his throat for speech but the cough made his whole torso explode in pain. As he tried to catch his breath more pain seared through his body. He could not sit up, could not see, could not speak. His heart raced as his eyes stared desperately into the nothingness above him. A panic so powerful it drove both cold and pain from his mind took hold of him. It was a kind of blind, uncontrollable terror he had never felt before in his life.

"Darnell!" This time he shouted the word. The two brief syllables echoed in his ears like shells exploding at close range.

Beside him, he felt Darnell jerk awake and sit up in one fast, almost instantaneous, motion. The split second of relief Fisher felt to think that Darnell was awake and with him vanished as soon as the wrist was pulled from his grip.

"Christ! Where did all this water come from?"

Fisher made a blind grab and caught a sleeve of Darnell's jacket.

"Let go!" Darnell shouted at him from above his head. "We've got to get up out of it. Bloody hell! The whole place is flooded."

"I can't sit up," Fisher gasped, still clutching the sleeve as if it was his only chance at life.

"Well what the hell are you doing lying down in the first place? I thought you couldn't do that either!"

Darnell grabbed at Fisher's arms, felt his way up past his elbows, and pulled him into a sitting position.

Fisher screamed. The agony of being jerked so suddenly upright was almost beyond his mind's ability to take in. Explosions of light burst once more in front of his eyes. He could not sit up on his own and fell sideways. Darnell hung onto his shoulders to keep him up as he nearly lost consciousness.

"Dammit!" Darnell was still yelling, very close to Fisher's face. "Why didn't you wake me? There must be three inches of water in here."

"I—did wake—you," Fisher gasped the words out, fighting to stay conscious, clutching Darnell's wet sleeves. "Who do you think—that was—shouted…?"

"Feels like Greenland in here," Darnell said. He let go of one of Fisher's shoulders, scrambling for something in his pocket. Fisher heard a small splash as the matchbox plummeted into the water. Darnell swore as he turned to find it but Fisher clutched tighter to his arms.

"Don't let go of me!"

Darnell had already let go and was trying to push Fisher back. "Get off, Fisher! I've got to get them back."

"They won't work anymore."

"They might! Let go!"

"I can't stay sitting up on my own." Fisher's voice was choked. "Please don't let me fall back into it."

Darnell stopped fighting him. He stood still for a moment, panting, though Fisher could feel his arms shaking from the cold. Only then did he realize his own body was shaking.

Darnell took Fisher's upper arms in his hands. Fisher felt how weak the grip was. There was another splash beside him, then a thud just behind him. Darnell had lifted his foot from the water and kicked the wall to see how far they had to move.

"Okay," Darnell said, his voice now calm. "I'll get you back to the wall. You're going to need to stand up though, to get out of this water."

Sliding through the water with Darnell lifting and Fisher pushing with his legs, brought home for him how very wet it was. It wasn't just the paralyzing cold. It was like sitting in a shallow bath of just melted ice.

"You need to let go now," Darnell said once Fisher's back was against the wall. His face was very close to Fisher's as he bent over him. Darnell had already released his grip on Fisher's arms, but Fisher clutched Darnell's sleeves as tight as ever.

"Let go," Darnell repeated.

Fisher waited for the order, but it did not come.

"Fisher, you've got to let go. Let me get the matches. I'll be right here. Okay?"

Fisher slowly opened his fingers and Darnell stepped

away from him. Fisher listened to Darnell's boots sloshing through the water, then the splashes as Darnell searched blindly for the tiny box.

After a moment, he heard the muffled flick of a match across the box. Nothing happened. The sound came several more times, followed by splashing and swearing, then more flicks, then nothing. Those had been their very last matches.

Fisher listened hard to Darnell's ragged, somewhat frantic breathing. Then he heard Darnell's feet splashing through the water beside him and stop.

There was a pause, then Darnell said, "Feel the wall."

Fisher had his back against the wall but, unsure if this counted as feeling, he lifted his right hand to press it against the dirt above his right shoulder. The wall was soaked. It felt something like a sponge that had just been plunged into water than removed and left without being rung out.

"It's the rain," Darnell breathed. His voice was almost too soft for Fisher to hear. "The rain's in the ground. Once it's soaked the earth around here it has a nice little underground pond to drain into. How convenient for it." His voice rose toward the end and Fisher thought he sounded a bit mad.

~~~

Darnell worked on the rubble that blocked their way to freedom with a new intensity. He stopped periodically to soak his bleeding hands in what was now about seven inches of frigid standing water on the floor of the little room. He wrapped each hand in a wet, rung out handkerchief until both handkerchiefs were so shredded they didn't help anymore. He worked on and on as if driven by an outside force that had no relation to his own starved and battered body.

Darnell tried to make Fisher stand up, using the partially collapsed beam for support, but Fisher could not do it. In the end he said he would rather die of exposure than pass out from pain. Darnell had left him sitting against the wall.

Behind him, he could now hear Fisher shivering in the

darkness anytime he paused in his work. He tried to talk to the private to make sure he was staying conscious.

"How many sisters did you have, Fisher?"

"Still do."

"What?"

"They're still here. I didn't used to have 'em."

"Okay. How many?"

"Oh, three...?" Fisher said it like he was unsure, just guessing at the answer.

"Younger or older?"

"Did you ever see a fox get into a henhouse? Devilish clever, foxes."

Darnell wondered again if Fisher might have internal injuries, or if it was just the cold, as he pulled a two-by-four from the mass. Wondered too, if he would be too late even if he could get Fisher to a hospital right at this moment, as he dug a rock out of the earth and sent it rolling down the mound into the water.

"I grew up with about a hundred brothers," Darnell said after a silence.

"Your mum must have been exhausted. Your dad too for that matter."

The water level was rising so fast he had to force himself not to think about it. If he thought about it, he would panic. And he could not panic. He would freeze up and not be able to think or act. He had to work. It was all he could do to get them out.

"Did you get to eat the food at your mum's parties?" Darnell asked.

"What food?"

"How should I know? You were there. You said they ate in the dining room while you tried on hats."

"What'd you eat with all those brothers?"

"At the orphanage? Bread, porridge, soup. It all tasted the same. It all looked and smelled the same too."

"How'd they get bread to look like porridge?"

"Don't ask me. They must have worked hard at it."

Fisher chuckled. "Couple weeks back, I got some tinned milk in the rations. Sweet, you know? That was brilliant. You'd have liked that on your porridge."

"You're right, we never had that."

"Two older, two younger."

"What?"

"Me sisters. I'm the middle of five. Not a bad place to be."

"I thought you said you had three sisters."

"Did I? I told a lie. Have four. We get on great. Only me and Marie got into a bit of a scuffle now and again."

"So I heard."

"We never had any tinned milk though. Wish I had some right now. Wouldn't even say no to your bread what looked like porridge."

It was hours since they had first noticed the rainwater pooling in the cellar that Darnell at last stopped working. His body seemed to have reached some sort of breaking point and he simply staggered away from the wall and fell into the water. He crawled toward Fisher's anxious voice, calling his name as if from the other side of half a dozen brick walls.

When he felt Fisher's leg under his straining hand, he gave one last push forward with his legs through the water, and felt Fisher's hands grabbing his shoulders, pulling him the rest of the way. Fisher's hand was on his face, wiping water and sweat from his eyes. The fingers were very gentle, smooth and soft as rabbit's fur.

The pain and the water and the darkness disappeared.

Darnell was lying on his back in the sun on the campus grounds. Bird songs were in his ears and the smell of grass and flowers tickled his nose. The sun. The sun felt so good. He could not describe, not even to himself, how good the sun felt. It was like Sleeping Beauty waking with a kiss. And the sun was the kiss.

He was not sure how he knew, but somehow he sensed

someone approaching him. He sat up and smiled and saw a handsome young man dressed in a plain shirt and trousers, not a university lad. His sandy hair looked unkempt and his blue eyes caught the sun and danced with the light reflecting in them. He was grinning at Darnell with an expression that matched how Darnell felt; perfect: Happier than he had ever been in his life.

Darnell stood up, brushing grass from his trousers, and looked into those sparkling eyes. Fisher, still grinning, held out his hand for Darnell to take. Darnell lifted his own, reaching for Fisher's hand.

A glinting, silver handcuff was clamped around his wrist so quickly and unexpectedly, Darnell was unable to jump away. A faceless figure, dressed all in gray, gripped his other arm and pulled it around with fingers as cold and hard as the handcuffs they forced him into.

Darnell opened his mouth to cry out.

BOOM!

An explosion like all the sound in the world unleashed at once tore apart the silence in one deafening burst. Things were smashing into him, bits of wood and rock and dirt. Freezing water was sprayed into his face like a geyser. He could not see: Consumed by pitch darkness that swallowed his eyes like a living beast. Someone had their arms around him, pressing him back against a wall and down into more icy water. A searing pain shot into his arm like a thousand hot needles.

Then stillness.

Darnell opened his eyes to darkness. He felt Fisher's gasping breath on his face. His arms were around Darnell, forcing him back against the wall behind them. Something was falling, a thud here, a splash there, as if a child were tossing stones into a ditch.

He became aware of the terrible freezing grip of the water around him: Of Fisher's body shaking so violently, his arms were splashing water into Darnell's face: Of his own pounding heart and the pain in his upper arm.

"What happened?" Darnell whispered. When he opened his mouth to speak, he moved his head slightly and realized Fisher's forehead was touching his own.

"Shells," Fisher said through chattering teeth. "They've been getting closer and closer for a while now."

"So it hit just outside?"

"Must've."

"Are you hurt?"

"Apart from before, you mean?"

"Yeah, apart from before."

"A couple a rocks bounced off me. Didn't feel real great but I think I'm okay. The water took a lot of the debris force."

Darnell moved one of his legs and felt the resistance of the water as if he were in a pond.

"Are you all right?" Fisher asked.

"Something hit my arm," Darnell said, shifting for the first time to sit up, pulling his face away from Fisher's.

Fisher also tried to straighten up but Darnell heard him gasp from the pain.

Darnell tried to reach his left hand up to his right arm where he felt something sticking into his flesh, but his hand would not obey him. It was almost completely rigid. The fingers were stiff and so swollen they would not bend, the palms were so painful he could not stand the thought of touching anything with them even if he could grasp.

"Fisher," Darnell said, his voice weak and shaking. "You're going to have to see what's on my arm. I don't think I can use my hands."

Still shaking hard, Fisher lifted his own hand and touched Darnell's chest. He felt his way to Darnell's elbow.

"It's up by my shoulder," Darnell said. "Chip of wood or something."

When Fisher's hand hit the projectile lodged in his arm, Darnell swore and involuntarily jerked away.

"I'm sorry," Fisher said. His teeth chattered close to Darnell's ear. "It's wood. Scrap off a floorboard maybe."

"You'll have to get it out."

"I can't do that. I told you, I don't do medical."

"That's too bad for you," Darnell was panting from pain, shivering from cold. Sweat broke out on his forehead and he knew he had a fever. "It can't stay there and I can't pull it out."

There was a long pause as the two men shivered and tried, but failed, to catch their breaths.

"You ever thought about what might be floating around in this water with us?"

"Fisher, come on."

"Ever wondered how Mr. Tittles got here?"

"Fisher..." Darnell found the younger man's arm in the dark and clumsily pulled it toward his own arm with both of his mangled hands. "It's not that deep," Darnell said. "Just get it over with, right?"

"Right," Fisher muttered. He felt his way back to the wood fragment in Darnell's arm. "Kind of like a stake. If you were a vampire you may have been done for."

"Then I wish I were a vampire."

Darnell gritted his teeth, eyes tightly closed.

"What about leaving fragments behind?" Fisher said.

"Just pull the bloody thing out!"

The pain was far worse than when the wood struck him in the first place, like having a hot, rusty poker jerked out of your arm.

They sat in shivering silence until Darnell's breathing had returned to relative normal.

"Sorry," Fisher whispered.

"Don't be daft. You had to do it. I couldn't."

"Darnell?"

"What?"

"I can see your face."

"*What?*"

"Open your eyes."

Darnell opened his eyes and saw the very faint, very dark, outline of Fisher's head right beside his own. His brain raced to catch up with what he was seeing. Seeing. Light. To see you had to have light. Even if it was a tiny, minuscule pinprick of light. Somewhere in there, with them, there was light.

Darnell jerked upward, pushing off the floor, the wall, the water, scrambling, tripping, struggling to his feet. He half staggered, half ran, toward the area he had been digging at for so many hours. When he looked up, he saw a dim, gray hole at the top of the mound of rubble, about a foot across. The draft of fresh, rainy night air hit his face like the caress of a lover and he let out a cry that was part jubilation, part sob.

~~~

Before they could get out of their watery tomb, Darnell climbed the mound and cleared rubble at the top so they could both fit through. Fisher felt some of the excitement drain away when Darnell returned to stand next to him in the dark water.

"I can help you," Darnell said. "We'll make it."

Fisher closed his eyes, but nodded.

Darnell was somehow able to grip Fisher under the elbows while Fisher, in turn, hung onto Darnell's arms. It was not just pain now. It was the cold. Sitting in icy water past his waist for hours had numbed Fisher's body and mind until he almost could not lift one foot in front of the other. He found he could not support his own weight and clung to Darnell, terrified he would drop back into the water and never leave this pit.

As they started trying to climb out, with Darnell partly dragging him, the pain took over in his brain again. The popping lights had changed to one bursting ball of white, followed by pitch black.

When he opened his eyes, he was looking up into

Darnell's barely lit face. Darnell's hand, blood-caked and freezing as it was, touching his face while Darnell's worried eyes looked down into his own, made the pain almost worth it, at least for that moment.

"You blacked out," Darnell said.

"Are we out?"

Darnell glanced upward, then looked back at him. "We've only moved a few yards."

"Don't say that," Fisher said, struggling to get upright again with Darnell's help.

"I shouldn't have let you sit in that water for so long without getting up," Darnell said. His voice was angry but Fisher knew the anger was not directed at him.

"Let me? It wasn't really a choice of either of ours."

Darnell stared down at the rubble under their feet, panting as he supported Fisher.

"Why don't you go up?" Fisher said. "I'm out of the water here. Just let me sit back down on this pile and you go on. I can try again in the morning."

Darnell ignored him, did not even look at him. He took another step on the shifting mound of dirt, wood and rock, pulling Fisher with him.

Just at the edge, when Fisher could feel cold, fresh air on his face and see the nearly black night clouds above in the sky, they lost their footing. Both of them fell into the debris pile, sliding backwards. Through his own fresh bursts of pain that almost made him scream, Fisher was aware of Darnell's gasp beside him as he grabbed a splintered board in one hand and Fisher's arm in the other, keeping them from falling down the mound.

At last, after an hour, or three, Fisher could not tell, they reached the yard of the farmhouse. There was no moon or stars to see by, yet Fisher found that his light-starved eyes could see quite well. The house was gone. In its place was a huge jumble of broken bits of wood, ranging in size from splinters to a whole, intact quarter of a rear wall. There was mud along with metal, rock and plant bits mixed in with the mess. And human bits? Fisher wondered. He felt revolted as he sank to his knees in the mud and wood scraps. His mind was so overwhelmed by pain and cold and fatigue and hunger he could not think of anything clearly.

They both gasped in the new air, unable to get enough. Fisher was forced to breathe as shallowly as possible but he tried to compensate by taking the fastest small breaths he could, almost choking as a result.

Darnell lay on his side in the mud next to Fisher, one arm pillowing his head. He was smiling with the blissful look of a small child who has just won a game.

"It's not raining," Darnell said and Fisher smiled as well.

Somewhere, far back in Fisher's brain there was a warning going off, saying they should move, they should not stay out here in the open, the area was being shelled. But it was very far off and he was very tired.

Fisher opened his eyes to such overwhelming brightness he could not think. It was as if he was staring straight into the sun on the hottest day in August. He closed his eyes tightly and covered them with his hands.

There was pain throughout his sternum, but it was bearable. He was wet through, but not lying in a pool. He was tired, but awake. His mouth felt like old parchment and his stomach ached with hunger.

"Darnell?" Fisher said with his hands still over his eyes.

There was no answer.

"*Darnell?*" Fisher withdrew his hands and turned his head, squinting in the light, to look around him. No one was there. He looked the other way. Nothing but the debris field.

Fisher eased into a half sitting up position, pushing with his arms and moving very slowly. From there he looked around and saw the place in the mud where Darnell had slept beside him. There was a set of footprints leading away from the spot. None leading back and no other prints. He had gotten up and walked away, checking what there was to see.

Maybe looking for food or water or other soldiers. Fisher fought hard against the panic that was making his heart race and his breath come short.

As he looked around, he realized the day was in fact very overcast, with low, deep gray clouds, immobile overhead. The brightness had only seemed overwhelming. Remembering he still had a drop of water in his bottle, he unscrewed the top and swallowed what there was. Almost literally a drop, but it was something.

"Darnell," he called out, not daring to shout very loudly.

He closed his eyes. He had no idea if the territory he was in now was currently being controlled by friend or foe.

"Fisher." Darnell's voice came clearly to him from close by.

Fisher opened his eyes and turned his head to see Darnell picking his way carefully toward him over the debris. He was soaked and covered in mud. His right arm was smeared with blood near the shoulder. Under his left arm he carried a shiny metal tin. It was easy to see why he had the tin under his arm instead of in his hands. Darnell's hands looked like a raw steak a dog had chewed on, buried, dug up, and chewed on some more. They were red and black and yellow, swollen so badly it was impossible to tell where palm ended and individual fingers began. Blood and yellow-brown pus oozed from open sores. The sores covered every inch of skin from his wrists down.

Fisher looked away, fighting the urge to retch, as Darnell approached him. He felt so sick he was glad there was nothing in his stomach.

"I think I found something to eat," Darnell said. "But I couldn't get the tin open."

"Can't think why," Fisher said under his breath, still not looking at Darnell.

"What?"

"Good morning." Fisher turned his head and looked up into Darnell's brown eyes. "I wondered where you'd gone."

"Just walking around the farm. All of the buildings are flattened. There's a bit of a wood about a quarter of a kilometer away where we could rest up. We shouldn't stay out here."

"Sure. Do you know how long it will take me to walk that far?"

"We'll do the best we can." Darnell carefully lowered himself onto his knees beside Fisher and dropped the tin in the mud.

Fisher picked it up. "This was Bates'. His mum sent him biscuits. We all gave him a lot of grief for it." He looked up into Darnell's face. "They're all dead, aren't they?"

"As far as I can make out, yes."

The morning air was cold and damp but Darnell's face was covered in sweat. His hands and arms were trembling.

Fisher reached up to touch his forehead. Darnell jerked his head away. "Don't. Just open the tin."

Awkwardly, one-handed, so that the other could keep him propped up, Fisher pried the lid off the silver tin. Inside were three large, oatmeal biscuits.

Fisher closed his eyes. "Thank you Bates, for not being the gluttonous bastard we all said you were."

He looked up at Darnell. There was no way to hand-feed another adult without it being either very intimate or very condescending, Fisher thought. Alternating images of strawberries dipped in chocolate fondue and vegetables boiled until they were mush, drifted into his mind.

In the end he just held up a biscuit and Darnell took a bite of it. Fisher sighed as he bit into his own biscuit. Not everything had to be as complex as his mind tried to make it.

Darnell wanted to save the last one but Fisher beat him down on the grounds that if they were saving it in case they got more hungry, without being dead, there just wasn't any logic to it. They split it. Then Darnell indicated the new water bottle he had found to replace his own. It was almost full.

After the stale biscuits, which somehow tasted like individual squares of heaven, and mildewed smelling water, they sat side by side, looking toward the destroyed barn and fields beyond. A bird called from somewhere nearby, otherwise the silence stretched on unbroken for many minutes.

"I never thought we'd get out of there," Darnell said at last.

Fisher looked at him. "Seriously? What about all that 'They'll find us' rubbish?"

Darnell shrugged. "I felt like I should say it. I didn't really believe it. I thought we'd both die in there as soon as I realized what had happened."

"That's what I said I thought you were doing."

Darnell smiled.

"Well, I didn't really believe what I said either, that there'd be another explosion and it'd open something up."

"We better get going if we want to reach those woods before dark."

"What about finding more supplies around here first?"

"I can come back. I don't have any trouble walking."

"You've got a high fever and you're just about starved. How many trips back and forth do you reckon you'll be able to make?"

"Enough trips. Come on, I'll help you up." Darnell got to his feet without letting his hands touch the ground. "Take my arm."

They made it to the scrubby patch of woods before dark and settled themselves in the lee of a small boulder Darnell found for them. After he caught his breath, Darnell straightened up to return to the farm site.

"Don't go back," Fisher said, watching him with round, frightened eyes.

"I've got to. There'll be things there we can use."

"It'll all still be there in the morning."

"Matches, food, a weapon. We need provisions, Fisher. I'm going back now."

"Don't, please. First thing in the morning. I can go with you."

"Hell, Fisher, I'm not going away forever. I'll be right back."

"What if something happens?"

"Such as?"

"What if there're still enemies out there?"

Darnell shook his head and turned away, starting to walk back toward the farm.

"Darnell," Fisher said desperately behind him.

Darnell did not answer or look around.

Fisher watched him walking away with a horrible nauseated feeling in the pit of his stomach.

As darkness began to fall so did the rain. Gentle sprinkles at first, then more, until it was a steady, if not torrential, shower. Even when night had fully covered the countryside, it was nothing like the pitch of the cellar. Fisher sat in the dark with his back against the rock and wondered if he was really any better off now. They had avoided certain death by escaping that grave, but now what? They had no means of communication. No food. No shelter. They were hurt and weak and starving. They did not know where allied forces might be. They knew to travel east to reach the trench and their own men, but clearly the trench had been breached. Even though it seemed likely that the breach was an isolated incident, they could not be sure. And, regardless of the direction they chose, how could they travel in the condition they were in?

And now he was alone. Darnell had always been there in the darkness of the cellar. Now Fisher found the aloneness worse than the pitch black, worse than the water, worse than the physical ache of his own body, worse than being trapped. Solitude was a trap in and of itself. After an hour of sitting alone against the rock, he was so desperate to hear the sound of Darnell's voice, he tried to pull himself up the rock where he would call out to him, dangerous or not. The pain stopped him and he sat back, hissing out his breath and closing his eyes on tears of self-pity.

When the pain subsided he became aware of how much he needed to pee. Moving as slowly as possible, he struggled to his knees. How, he wondered, undoing his trouser buttons, was Darnell managing this now? He discarded the idea of asking. There did not seem to be any way of inquiring if Darnell needed help getting his pants off without it being taken badly.

The darkness grew heavier as the minutes passed. What if Darnell did not come back at all? His breath quickened as his heart rate did. The pain of taking deeper breaths made him pant even more and he moaned aloud. He dug his fingers into the soft ground beneath him and counted, very slowly and quietly, out loud. When he reached one hundred he started over. After three more times he stopped and listened. He could still hear nothing but the rain.

He'll be back soon, just a few more minutes, Fisher told himself. A few more. A few more. A few more. He still was not back.

Fisher twisted around, gritting his teeth and grabbing the wet rock behind him. He had to stand up, had to look and call out. His hand slipped on the wet surface and he fell onto the sodden ground. His cry of pain was muffled by the patch of moss his face smashed into. He swore and hissed Darnell's name over and over in a whisper as he pushed himself back up off his chest.

Sitting up once more, leaning back against the rock and trying to think of nothing but his own breathing, he heard footsteps approaching through the rain. His heart leapt as he opened his eyes and turned his head. He could see only very dim shapes of trees and brush.

"Fisher?"

"Over here." His voice was hoarse. He wanted to run to Darnell, to cry out, hug him, thank him for coming back, for being alive. Instead he said, "Found anymore matches?"

"Some," Darnell said.

Fisher could hear him very close now and saw his outline

as he stepped around the rock to face Fisher.

"You okay?" Darnell said.

Fisher thought this an odd thing to ask of someone who had been sitting around doing nothing for hours while the questioner had been doing all the work.

Fisher just grunted.

Darnell had what looked like a parlor rug draped over one arm. It turned out to be a very old, well used, horse blanket. He had also found a bedroll into which he had been able to stuff matches, a water bottle and a rifle. Everything was wet.

The platoon had not had any food when they arrived at the farm and Fisher did not ask if Darnell found any. The biscuits had been more than they could hope for.

"No sign of anyone alive," Darnell said as he dropped the bedroll into Fisher's lap. "I'll look again tomorrow. If we could manage to gather any wood we could start a fire."

"What if the wrong buggers see the smoke?" Fisher set the water bottle and rifle beside him and tucked the matches under his jacket, hoping there was some chance they'd be dry enough to use.

Darnell ignored him. "With a fire and the rifle, maybe we can get something to eat."

"Like a little rabbit?" Fisher said, unrolling the sodden blanket. "Do you realize how fast and small those things are? I couldn't hit the biggest target on the range from thirty yards. And I don't think you're going to be pulling a trigger anytime soon."

"You can't hit anything with a rifle?"

"Never could."

"Well, hell, Fisher. How'd they let you pass training?"

"Needed more blokes out here, didn't they? Didn't seem to bother 'em too much to be perfectly honest. Did you ever get the hang of it?"

"I was pretty good. When I had fingers."

"Ever shoot at a man?"

"No."

"They never act like there's any difference. You shoot a block a wood, you shoot a man. Same thing. Bloody stupid, the men running this thing."

Darnell did not ask what he meant by "this thing."

They somehow managed to drape both the heavy horse blanket and the bedroll over themselves. Darnell remained sitting up, close against Fisher, rather than trying to lie down on the drenched ground. The blankets may have been wet but at least they trapped body heat. Even as Fisher began to warm up, he could feel Darnell shivering uncontrollably beside him. Fisher fumbled his hand through the blankets pressing down on them and touched the backs of his fingers to Darnell's forehead. He almost gasped aloud: The skin was on fire. It was so hot it felt as if it should be blistering.

"We need to find something to clean your hands," Fisher said.

Darnell gave a dry chuckle near his ear. "I'd say it's a bit late for that."

Fisher did not say anything, too afraid his voice would break if he tried. He wished Darnell would lean his head against his own but Darnell lowered his chin to his own chest. They sat in silence as the rain beat steadily down on them. Many things ran through Fisher's mind that he thought of saying, or asking. About what they were going to do. About the possibility that they would be discovered by the wrong people. About how long they had been down in the cellar. Long enough that something had changed about who controlled the surrounding countryside?

But he said nothing. He sat with his eyes closed, listening to Darnell breathe, feeling his constant shivers, along with such intense guilt it almost made him physically ill.

"Did you ever go to the seaside when you were a kid?" Darnell said.

Fisher opened his eyes and stared at the dark blanket hanging in front of him. He turned his head to look at

Darnell, though this did not really do anything as far as see-ing went.

"Where'd that come from?" Fisher asked.

He felt Darnell shrug against him. "Just wondered. I went a few times."

"Yeah? Who with?"

"My dad came and got me from the Manchester orphan-age once I was a bit older. He took me to the sea for the sun. That's what he said."

"Why was it really?"

"Well, there were so many people there. Very hot. It was August. Lots of folks on holiday. People leaving things lying around. He pointed out this one lady's handbag she'd left in the picnic basket while she splashed in the water with her little girls. Then he walked up and nicked it, easy as any-thing. Came back to me and said, 'Now you have a go. See the chap over there with the cane?' And I asked him what the hell he was playing at. They got Mum over a blanket and he was out there knocking off wallets."

"You wouldn't do it?"

"No. Told him to go to hell."

"What'd he do?"

"Punched me so hard in the jaw it knocked out one of my back teeth. I'd only just got in all my grown ones too."

"There on the beach?"

"Sure. Didn't bother him."

"Did anyone do anything?"

"Nah. Problem was, then he left. Got a cab back into town and left me there."

Fisher did not speak, unsure if Darnell wanted to go on or not, but not wanting to press him.

After a moment, Darnell said, "When I got back to his place, he told me he didn't want me there. To pack up and return to the orphanage if I couldn't do as he said. So I told him I'd do it to stay."

"Did you?"

"Stay?"

"Do as he said."

"For a week. Must'a nicked about a hundred shillings: Race tracks, beaches, train stations. Wasn't half bad at it. Then I went back to St. Mary's."

"Why?"

There was a long pause before Darnell spoke again. "Because I didn't know who they were. That sounds terrible, you know? 'Cause it shouldn't matter who they are. But I kept thinking about my mum and us not having anything. What if what I took at the station was from a bloke who didn't have anything else? What if he had just enough to get a ticket home to see his dying mother? What if he had just enough to pay the rent so his kids had a roof over their heads? I couldn't sleep at night."

Fisher was silent. He could not think of anything to say. Darnell was still shaking. The rain fell around them without change in speed or rhythm.

Fisher so desperately wanted to put his arms around Darnell, he had to dig his fingers into his own trouser legs to keep them still. He closed his eyes, trying to take steadying breaths. His face was still turned toward Darnell and the effort of not moving it closer was more than he could handle. He bent his neck until his forehead was resting against Darnell's hot temple. Apart from the shivering, Darnell did not move.

Turn. Turn your head to face me. All of Fisher's thought and energy, all of his life and soul, went into the plea which he did not speak aloud. Over and over he begged, so focused on his request that his ribs stopped aching, his body became dry, his stomach became full, his mind became rested. There was nothing else in the world, in the universe, besides Darnell needing to turn his head.

But Darnell either did not get the message or was unwilling to comply. Seconds passed, then minutes. Minutes in which Fisher's mind gradually remembered that he was cold, wet, starved, hurt, and tired.

He opened his mouth, but words would not come to his throat. He could no more say what he wanted to than force Darnell to move by the will of his own mind. So, like his request, he said the words only inside his head. Over and over, a hundred, or a thousand times, until he fell asleep.

~~~

When Darnell opened his eyes, he thought he was still in a freezing, dark, flooded grave. He was drenched, though he did not feel at all cold, rather as though his internal organs were being cooked over an open fire. He could see only darkness. Then a shiver he barely realized was coming from his own body, shifted the blanket over his face enough that he could see some light through the folds.

He raised his head, surprised to find that it had been against the shoulder of the man beside him. He lifted his hands to push back the blanket. Pain raced from his fingertips to his shoulders so fast and hot and sharp, it took his breath away. He gasped and swore, dropping his hands back to his lap.

Fisher stirred beside him.

"Was wrong?" he mumbled without opening his eyes.

"Can you get these blankets off our heads?" Darnell said. He had not meant to sound as angry as he did.

Fisher, sitting up straighter and blinking several times, reached up and pushed the heavy, sodden layers away.

Sunlight hit Darnell in the face like a fist and he turned his head. When he opened his eyes it was to see Fisher's face very close to his. The young man was dripping water, pale as death, face smeared with mud, a streak of blood still across his right temple, and grinning like a crazy person.

"Sun's out," Fisher said through his grin, which was so broad it looked impossible, like his face would split apart.

"I can tell," Darnell said, looking into Fisher's eyes. They were exactly the same color as the clear sky visible over his head. Darnell found it impossible not to smile when looking at that face.

The sun was so real, so plentiful, so alive. It was like seeing laughing children or frolicking kittens. Like a hot meal by a pleasant hearth. Or the embrace of a mother to her child.

The sun-haze that had seized his brain was interrupted by the thought of how close Fisher's face was to his own, with his eyes, unblinking, locked on Darnell's. Darnell blinked and jerked his gaze away, turning his face upward, closing his eyes, still smiling.

"How do you feel?" Fisher asked.

"I feel..." The smile spread farther across Darnell's face. "Alive."

They pulled the bedroll and horse blanket over the rock at their backs and propped the wet riffle against it. It took them half an hour to get off their uniform jackets and hang them up as well. They were both panting afterwards, Darnell leaning against the rock, weak and shaking, and Fisher sitting on the ground, holding his ribs.

"You know what we need?" Fisher said once he had caught his breath.

"A phone line, a roast chicken, some mince pies, strong whisky, a whole lot of antiseptic, dry clothes, warm beds, a bath and a shave?" Darnell asked.

"Apart from those things, I mean. That's just fancy stuff. What I was thinking was a fire. The sun's brilliant an' all, but we'd be a lot better off with a fire."

"What about getting the wood?"

Fisher waved his hand around. "It's all here."

"Right, well then, I'll just grab up some branches with my teeth like a dog and bring them to you."

"I could get it. Just give me a minute." Fisher was still holding his ribs.

Darnell shook his head. "Everything's wet anyway."

"How are we going to cook that rabbit I'm going to shoot then?"

"How are you going to shoot a rabbit if you can't hit any-thing?"

Fisher reached out and pulled the rifle toward him. He opened the chamber and looked inside.

"It doesn't matter," Fisher said. "You couldn't shoot one either. This weapon's not loaded."

Darnell chuckled.

Fisher shifted around to look at him. "Was that amus-ing?"

"Fisher, do you ever feel like, no matter what you do, you're going to lose? Like you're just taking blow after blow and never landing one yourself?"

"Sure. I always felt like that fighting with Marie."

Darnell laughed and Fisher grinned at him. "I thought you still had your ammo pouches?"

"I did until I was trying to drag you out of that pit. Left them there. Too heavy."

"You suppose those matches are dry at all? I'm going to get us some wood."

By moving slowly on his knees and using a heavy stick as a sort of crutch to keep his upper body as still as possible, Fisher inched his way around the nearby brush and thin, scrubby trees. He managed to accumulate a small pile of firewood and kindling which he spread in the sun beside their rock as he returned with them. Darnell kicked out a chunk of earth to make a small fire pit and pushed some kin-dling in with his foot.

Neither of them mentioned the possibility of an enemy seeing the smoke as Fisher tried over and over to light the damp twigs and grasses with the mostly dry matches. Darnell was beyond caring who saw it.

It took Fisher forever, about twenty minutes, to get a spark to take in the finest grass stems. At last a tiny flame spread up its length, migrated to another and then a twig. Gazing at the flames with intense concentration, as though they might go out if he looked away, Fisher grabbed more wood and slowly added it in.

Darnell, who had been leaning on the rock, facing into the sun with his eyes closed, walked over beside Fisher.

"I would applaud you, but, well..." Darnell shrugged.

Fisher gingerly pulled off his gray shirt and held it so close to the fire, Darnell was surprised it did not ignite. When Darnell looked down at Fisher's bare torso he saw a mass of purple, red and black bruising covering his back and blotched over his chest and sides. He looked away, not saying anything. Fisher slowly turned the shirt so the heat could reach every angle. It was already almost dry from being in the sun for so long and soon Fisher was pulling it back on.

Darnell clumsily brought him the uniform jackets and he held those up as well, both partly dried, until they were stiff and warm through. Darnell stood very close to the flames, trying to dry his trousers. Standing without support made him feel lightheaded and dizzy so he had to kneel, turning his head away from the intensity of the heat. The fire was beginning to die down by then. It had already consumed almost all of the wood Fisher had managed to gather.

Fisher looked up at Darnell. "We need to go back to the farm while the sun's out and see what we can do about those mince pies and antiseptic."

Darnell glanced toward the farmhouse wreckage, not visible beyond a small roll of hill. He did not say anything. The truth was he did not think he could make the walk back. He felt so weak he could hardly stand on his own for ten seconds. Walking a quarter of a kilometer might as well be a thousand kilometers. He looked into the dying fire, feeling Fisher's eyes on him.

"Can you walk?" Darnell asked.

"I can try." Fisher smiled at him.

Darnell leaned his head back again and felt the sun on his face. This time its warmth failed to penetrate his skin. He felt a terrible, powerful cold right down through his bones. He opened his eyes and looked at Fisher, seeming to see him through a red mist.

Once they both had their jackets back on, the fire had died to embers. The sun reached its peak in the sky as the two men started back toward the farm. Darnell understood how weak he really was when he realized Fisher, face screwed up in pain, was supporting him more than the other way round. They spoke very little as they moved over the pitted ground toward the farm. They had just crossed the hill and were standing slightly above the site when Fisher stopped.

"Look," Fisher said, indicating only with his eyes.

Darnell looked but his vision was blurred and he shook his head. "What is it?"

"Bodies. But it's not our men. Looks like Germans."

"Then it's a good thing they're bodies," Darnell said, closing his eyes and opening them again with the hope of being able to see more clearly.

They made their way across to what was indeed two dead German soldiers. Darnell's stomach churned. Fisher looked away, breathing hard through his mouth. The recent weather had been unkind to the already decomposing soldiers.

Darnell sank to his knees, shaking and sweating, while Fisher eased carefully onto his own knees and inched toward the corpses.

He stopped, staring at the ground. "I don't think I can do this."

"Do what?"

Fisher looked back at Darnell. "You know, search them. It's not right."

"What if they have food?"

"That wouldn't affect it being right, would it?"

"Fisher, where do you think I got the biscuits and matches and rifle?"

Fisher did not reply. He glanced at the bodies, then out across the field beyond.

"They don't need those things anymore," Darnell said.

"I'm not saying it's right either, but it's all we've got."

Still not speaking, Fisher pulled the collar of his jacket up to cover his mouth. It would not reach as far as his nose. With his right hand, he pulled a rifle and ammo bag from one and flipped up the tops of the pouches on their belts and packs on their backs. They were even more ill equipped than the platoon had been. But they had food. Each had a small linen bag with wet, slightly moldy crackers still in them and a tin of bully beef.

Darnell watched Fisher pull out each item from the bags, then condense what he wanted into one pack plus the rifle. He drug the bag and weapon across the ground behind him as he crawled back to Darnell on his knees, not looking at him.

"Let's go back," Darnell said. "This is enough."

Fisher looked down at the bag in his hand. "They don't have any medical supplies. We should—"

"Fisher, where are we going to get antiseptic? We didn't have any. They don't have any." He glanced at the two bodies. "What we really needed was food. And we found some. Let's go back."

By the time they had returned to their camp the sun was getting low in the sky. They ate the moldy crackers and Fisher managed to gather some more wood which they made stretch by having only a tiny fire. The tinned meat was the real delicacy which they savored, opening only one tin with the point of the bayonet from the British rifle. The two men sat close together, by the fire, alternating bites as Fisher fed them both. Darnell found that he did not mind much having to let Fisher hold the spoon for him. The taste of the meat and the feel of eating something was so good, so incredible, he did not really care how it was happening.

Fisher closed his eyes at the first bite and chewed slowly. Then he swallowed and said, "This is the best thing I've ever eaten in my life."

When the tin was empty it took all their willpower not to

open the other one.

Darnell was so weak he could not stay sitting by the fire, even leaning against Fisher. He slumped onto the damp ground, smiling as the sun's afternoon rays played across his face. A moment later, Fisher was touching his head and saying, "Sit up."

"Can't," Darnell said.

"Just for a second," Fisher said.

Fisher held the now almost completely dry horse blanket and bedroll. Darnell sat up and Fisher spread the horse blanket on the ground. Darnell lay on it and Fisher covered him with the bedroll, then folded the extra part of the blanket over the bedroll. Darnell closed his eyes. Somehow having food made him more aware of his other discomforts. Having to think less about the terrible ache in his stomach brought his throbbing, burning hands and aching body into sharper focus. His skin was covered in sweat, though he shivered with cold. The agony of his festering hands was so strong it was as if they were not his hands at all, but a malevolent force that had attached itself to him.

He started when a cool, damp cloth was pressed to his forehead.

"What's that?" He opened his eyes but could not focus them. He only remembered the handkerchiefs had been shredded.

"One of my socks," Fisher said.

Darnell smiled. He could tell the thin fabric was no sock but he did not argue.

"How much daylight do we have left?" Darnell asked.

"Oh, maybe half an hour."

"Do you have enough wood to keep the fire going for a bit? You should get some more if you can."

"I've got extra."

"I'm sorry, Fisher. I wasn't a very good leader. Never wanted to be an officer in the first place to be honest with you."

"You're a great leader. And it didn't matter if you wanted to do it or not, you're good at it anyway."

"I thought, once we got out, that would be enough. We'd find our way to allies."

"Yeah. I guess I thought they'd find their way to us. But who knows what's going on now with them fighting this side of the trenches. No German ever should have gotten this far in."

"I doubt there are more. We'd be in the middle of it if there were."

"Darnell?"

"Yeah?"

There was a pause, then Fisher said, "Nothing."

Darnell opened his eyes and tried to focus them on Fisher. The sun, perched on the edge of the horizon, illuminated one side of his face. He looked so drawn and sad, Darnell wanted to reach out to him, to take his hand or squeeze his shoulder and tell him they would be all right. But even the thought of moving his hand was agony. He closed his eyes again.

"I'm sorry I didn't help dig," Fisher whispered.

"Not didn't," Darnell said. "Couldn't. It wasn't your fault."

"In the morning, I'm going west to see if I can find anyone," Fisher said.

Darnell shook his head. "How far are you going to walk on your own? You'll end up killing yourself if you keep trying to do so much."

"It doesn't matter, does it? We can't just stay here."

"Tell me about Marie."

"Marie?"

"Your sister. Where is she now?"

"She's still with me mum. They're in London now though. The two of them and our youngest sister. In a flat by the Thames."

"Did your dad enlist?"

"Yep. Yours?"

"No idea."

"You think they'll start conscription?"

"I don't know. You'd think they've got enough volunteers."

"Why'd you volunteer?" Fisher asked.

"I felt like I needed to, I guess. It's a funny thing: I've never even been on a trench line yet and I still think the whole thing's a bloody mess."

"You don't want to be on one. Believe me."

"How long have you been out, Fisher?"

"Three months before you got here. After Lieutenant Hall was killed, we didn't think they'd send us another lieutenant. Figured they'd let the platoon sergeant handle everything. I bet you wish they had."

"No. I don't wish that. They'd have sent me somewhere. I'm glad it was here."

"Just because you weren't pushed right into the trenches," Fisher said, chuckling a little.

"No," Darnell said. "Not just because of that."

Fisher did not reply. The last edge of the sun vanished below the horizon and a lavender gray twilight settled over them.

After some time, Darnell opened his eyes, looking into Fisher's face. "I don't think we've been properly introduced," he said. "My name is Lewis. Lewis Darnell. I'd shake your hand but... perhaps another time?"

Fisher grinned. "Another time then." The grin faded and Fisher jerked his head in the direction of the farm. "Do you hear something?"

"No," Darnell said, his voice hushed. "What is it?"

"Someone's coming toward us."

Adrenaline flooded Darnell's system so fast he was not aware of the effort it took to throw the blankets off himself and get to his feet. Fisher was also moving with startling speed, standing up and grabbing the German rifle before

Darnell was fully upright.

"Is that one loaded?" Darnell whispered, not looking at Fisher but over the top of the boulder that lay between them and the farm.

Although they had retrieved ammo with the rifle, neither had thought to check that it was already loaded after the excitement of the food. Fisher pulled open the chamber as quietly as he could and looked inside.

"*Bloody hell,*" Fisher hissed the words out like a cat, whether out of anger or pain Darnell was not sure.

Fisher looking frantically around for the ammo bag on the ground. Darnell walked to the large rock, with it between himself and the farm site, staring hard into the fast growing gloom.

"I can see them. Fisher, look. I think it's our men."

Fisher stepped up beside him, holding the rifle limply in his right hand.

"It's another platoon," Fisher breathed. Then he yelled, waving his arm over his head, "Over here!"

Darnell, calling out his and Fisher's company name, stepped around the rock toward them—but he stopped halfway. Something slammed into his chest with enough force to throw him to the ground at the same instant his ears caught the sound of a rifle crack. There was another crack followed immediately by shouting; men's voices, one very close but the rest coming from some distance.

Fisher was screaming that he and Darnell were British soldiers. A large number of men were running toward them. Darnell could feel the vibrations in the ground beneath him. A deep-voiced man was yelling, "Hold your fire! Hold your fire!"

Now the voices were close. Fisher was still yelling at them and the deep-voiced man was yelling back, "Get a hold of yourself, Private! It was an accident. My men weren't expecting a couple of shadows to jump out at us. We only just got the last of the bleeding trench breachers beaten back.

Didn't think there was anyone left out here alive."

Darnell stopped listening as he became aware that he had not taken a breath since he hit the ground. He tried to inhale and felt thick, hot liquid bubbling up his throat and into his mouth and nose. He could not think where it was coming from. The sky over his head was a pale purple rose that made him think of Elizabeth's favorite dress.

Then Fisher's dirt-smeared face was directly over his, staring down into his eyes. Fisher's cheeks were streaked with tears. More of them fell from his sky-blue eyes as he looked into Darnell's own eyes.

Darnell remembered the ocean in those eyes. Had Fisher been with him then? When he raced along the beach under the hot July sun, his feet just touching the edge of waves. It seemed like Fisher must have been there: He had always been there.

"I'm so sorry, Lewis," Fisher whispered, his voice choked with sobs.

Something wet touched his face—sea spray...no...Fisher's tears dropping on his own cheeks. He wanted to reach up and take Fisher's face in his hands and tell him everything was okay. He wanted to hold him close against his own body and tell him nothing bad would happen anymore. No cellar. No pain. No war. No darkness.

"It's okay," Darnell said. His words were muffled through the liquid filling his mouth. "It's okay, Fisher. Not your fault. Sorry it wasn't...different...time and place—for us."

"Me too," Fisher whispered the words so softly they made Darnell think of butterfly wings. He imagined the words flying gently around his head like tiny, visible sparks; light and friendly. The same color as Fisher's eyes.

"William," Fisher said, just as softly. "My name is Will Fisher."

Darnell smiled and closed his eyes. He wanted to say the name back but he had no air and his mouth was now full of the hot liquid. He moved his lips, soundlessly forming the words, "Will Fisher."

~~~

Fisher got off the train in Oxford with a scrap of paper in his hand and just enough money in his pocket to get back to London. The blinding March sunlight had brought children outside to play and the streets were too busy and too loud and too bright. He slipped off to a side-street and hailed a passing coal cart. He showed the man his bit of paper and was pointed on down the street.

During the half-hour walk his mind was blank. He did not think of what he was going to do, or where he was coming from, or why. He thought of nothing but the cobbles under his feet, the weeds by the roadside, the tabby cat sitting on a wall he passed.

The city faded away and smaller cottages and larger gardens began to emerge around him as he walked. When he at last stopped, he did not need to double check the paper in his hand. He stood and stared at the little house for several minutes without moving. Red roses were blooming along a dry stone wall. They hummed with bees whose yellow bodies were only slightly brighter than the creamy yellow of the paint on the small house. A flower garden ran all along one side. So many colors and patterns burst from it they were hard to take in.

As he stood there, staring around with dazed eyes, Fisher heard a click. He blinked and looked at the door where a young woman was now standing, watching him.

"Can I help you?" she asked.

Her auburn hair caught the sun and sparkled like stars. Her face was as smooth and soft looking as fresh cream. Her eyes were very large and pale, liquid green. Her black dress contrasted violently with her shimmering surroundings.

"Private Fisher, ma'am. I served with your husband—"

"They already told me. Over three months ago now."

"Yes. I'm not here on official business. I just wanted to

meet you. See, I would have come as soon as they brought me home but I've been in hospital. Had nine broken ribs and then I punched the platoon sergeant who...well, I didn't think I'd be coming home at all, but..."

She tilted her head to the side. "Come in. What is it you'd like to talk about?" She stepped back, holding the door open for him.

Fisher walked up the stone path to the front door and stepped inside feeling suddenly uncomfortable. The ceiling seemed to be pressing against him and he felt that the bright foyer was the size of a loaf of bread.

"Please have a seat," she said, indicating the room to his right. "I'm just getting tea."

"No, ma'am, that's all right. I'll only be a minute. I need to get back to the station soon anyway. I'm going back out tomorrow."

A short-legged dog with a brindle and white coat and huge, upright ears, trotted into the foyer. He was wagging his tail and went up to Fisher, sniffing his trouser legs. The woman ignored the dog, facing Fisher, gazing into his eyes as though wishing to read his mind. He looked away, glancing down at the dog, then back to her face.

"I wanted you to know how brave Le—Lieutenant Darnell was. He saved my life. And he endangered his own life to do it. I've never met anyone else like him."

"Thank you for that," she said, still watching him steadily. "Lewis was a very kind person. I know he would have wanted to do everything he could for his friends." He noticed that she did not say "troops" or "soldiers."

"I'm sorry...about what happened."

She nodded. "No one expected it, of course. When you all weren't even out at the front, to be attacked like that."

Fisher blinked. He again looked down at the dog, who was standing in the open doorway, looking outside with only mild interest.

"No, we didn't. It was at a little abandoned farm—"

"They told me about the explosion there."

"And what happened?" Fisher shifted his gaze back to her face.

"Yes. That the cellar caved in. You were the one survivor, weren't you?"

"Yes, ma'am. But your husband didn't die in—" he stopped. He looked around the little foyer and sitting room, carefully decorated with bright, flowery fabrics. He looked at the beautiful woman dressed all in black in front of him.

"Vain," he said. "He didn't die in vain."

She nodded but for the first time looked away. "Isn't war in vain, Mr. Fisher?" she asked, moving her eyes back to meet his as she spoke.

Fisher dropped his gaze to the frayed rug. "As far as I can make out."

"Won't you stay for tea?"

"No, thank you. I best be off."

She nodded and smiled a smile that did not reach her eyes.

Fisher stepped around the dog, back to the stone path outside.

"Thank you for stopping by, Mr. Fisher," she said, walking to the doorway. "I'll be sure to let Dr. Aldridge know you came. He was a very dear friend of Lewis."

"Dr. Aldridge?" Fisher gazed blankly at the roses.

"Yes, do you know him? He's one of the only doctors left in Oxford since conscription. He went to university with Lewis."

"But Lieutenant Darnell wasn't—"

"Oh, no, Lewis studied history. He was very interested in the Renaissance, but he used to play cricket with John Aldridge every Saturday. Aldridge was devastated when he heard what happened."

Fisher looked at her. He could not read her sea-green eyes. Could not see her feelings in them or know her thoughts.

"Is that so?" he said after a pause in which they stared into each other's eyes.

"You could go and meet him if you like. He'll be at the hospital. I suppose it's only a matter of time before they need to take every last man and we'll be left without doctors for civilians."

Fisher nodded, not hearing what she said. "Goodbye, Mrs. Darnell. It was very nice to meet you."

"Goodbye, Mr. Fisher. Safe journey."

Fisher turned and walked down the path. He went along the road toward the heart of the city until he reached a busy intersection and found someone to ask which way to the hospital. He did not flinch when a carriage almost ran into him on the street. The driver cursed and yelled epithets after him but he did not hear.

Standing on the front steps of the hospital, he looked up at the double doors, gazing unblinking and unmoving for a long time, as he had done at the house. After several minutes passed, Fisher lifted one foot, as though to place it on the next step, then turned and went back to the street.

He walked along the cobbles to the train station, staring straight ahead. From there, he returned to London. From London, he returned to the front.

Our One and Only

E. N. Holland

Dedication

To Chrissi, with great love and affection.
Thank you for taking me on my own personal pilgrimage,
which inspired this story.

PART I: THE NEWS

Baltimore, Maryland, October 1944

The knock on the door sounded surprisingly loud.

Audrey Fiske plunged her hands into the soapy water. "Who can that be?" she said to herself.

There was a second knock, as loud as the first.

Audrey turned to her son, sitting at the kitchen table, absorbed in the morning paper. "George, dear…can you please answer the door?"

Startled, he looked up. "Mother?"

She nodded towards the front door. "Someone is pounding on the front door, and I am up to my elbows in soapsuds. Can you answer it, please?"

"Oh, yes, of course. Are we expecting anyone?" Audrey shook her head no.

George Fiske rose quickly from his seat and moved through the kitchen. At the door, he paused, then pushed back the curtain on the window and glanced out, hoping to see who was on the step. His heart skipped a beat when he saw the black and yellow Western Union bicycle parked at the curb.

"Mother," he called into the kitchen. "I think we're receiving a telegram."

Audrey froze, then quickly rinsed her hands under the faucet, drying them on her apron. "I'll be right there," she said. She walked towards the door, reflexively smoothing her hair as she passed the hall mirror.

"Do you want to answer it?" he asked.

231

"No, you go ahead." She glanced at the two flags hanging in the window, each one with a blue star. She felt a sense of dread rush through her.

George opened the door and saw a Western Union delivery man waiting patiently on the stoop. "Telegram, sir. Is this the Fiske residence? It's addressed to Mrs. Harold Fiske." He offered a pale yellow envelope.

"Yes, we're the Fiskes." George signed the receipt and dropped a few coins into the man's hand. "Thank you."

The man tipped his cap and nodded, then turned and headed to the curb where his bicycle stood waiting, a silent sentry.

George quietly closed the door. His mother had moved to the living room and now sat on the couch, her face in her hands. He held out the telegram to her.

"No." She shook her head. "You read it, please."

George nodded and gently slipped his finger under the flap of the envelope, loosening the glue, then pulled out the thin yellow paper. Teletype words were pasted across the page. He read it quickly and as the words became meaningful he felt dread in his heart. "It's Eddie, Mother," he said softly.

"He's been injured?" she asked, looking up, a hopeful note in her voice.

"No, Mother, he's been killed. September twenty-first. In France."

Audrey's face crumpled in grief, a loud keening wail coming from her lips. "Not my baby," she sobbed. "It wasn't supposed to happen this way!"

George stood there, feeling awkward in the face of his mother's grief. He was twenty-six years old and had seen his mother cry plenty of times, but had never seen such a look of raw pain as he saw now. He wanted to cry but held back his tears. He had the foolish thought that if they both started crying, they might never stop.

After a few minutes that seemed like hours, he sat next to

his mother on the couch, putting his arm across her shoulders. He sat in silence, listening to his mother's sobs that eventually subsided to an agonized weeping. He offered her his handkerchief and she accepted it, wiping the tears from her face. Her cheeks were blotchy and red, her eyes dull and wet. She cast her glance around the room. George had the feeling she was looking anywhere but at his hand, where he still clutched the yellow telegram. "I think I'm going to go lie down for a bit," she said. "I don't feel so well."

"Of course. Let me help you." George stood and offered her his hand, folding the telegram and stuffing it in his pocket. His mother's face looked as if she had aged ten years in the space of an hour. If he had ever wondered what a broken heart looked like, he was seeing it now. "Would you like me to call Father O'Malley?" he asked. "Perhaps he could come and sit with you."

"No." She shook her head. "I just want to be alone right now." George nodded. "Maybe tomorrow...we could go to Mass in the morning. If I feel up to it, that is."

"Yes, of course." He helped his mother up the stairs, then walked with her to the master bedroom at the front of the house. He pulled the shades on the windows. "Would you like me to turn down the blanket?"

She shook her head no. "I'll just rest here," she said, tears once again filling her voice.

George nodded, backing towards the door. "If you are all set, I think I'll go down to the office," he said. "Someone needs to tell Phil."

"Yes..." Her voice trailed off. "In person is best. Don't call him on the phone."

George nodded, patting his mother's shoulder one more time. "Okay, then. I'll be back in a little while." He exited the room, closing the door softly as he left.

~~~

Back downstairs, he paused for a minute. It was a thirty minute walk to the office, fifteen minutes by streetcar—but on this occasion, George decided to take the car. He hadn't been using the car much as gas was strictly rationed, but he thought it might be best in case Philip needed a ride home. He had a feeling he wouldn't be in the mood to ride the trolley.

He backed the car out of the driveway and drove through the quiet neighborhood, then turned left onto Frederick Road. Traffic was heavier but it was still relatively quiet, given the day and time. As George pushed on the accelerator, he had a momentary wish to just keep driving. Away from Baltimore, away from his mother's grief, away from the task that now awaited him. But he knew that was irrational and with a deep sigh, pointed the car towards the Fiske Insurance Agency.

Five minutes later, he pulled up in front of the office, relieved to find a parking place right on the street. He wondered, as he always did, if it was bad for business not to have a parking lot. *Maybe when the war is over. When will this damn war be over? It seems like it has been going on forever. If it ended last month, Eddie would still be alive...even last week.* He sighed, again holding back tears. Just like he needed to be strong for his mother, he needed to be strong for Philip. Sometimes he hated being the oldest.

He pushed open the glass door, the small bell tinkling and announcing his arrival. Philip Cormier looked up from his desk and smiled. "Hi George. What are you doing here? I wasn't expecting to see you today. It's Wednesday, you know—day off for the boss."

"I know it's Wednesday. I, um..." he paused, looking at Philip's happy, guileless smile. He knew in a minute that smile would be gone. He wondered when he would see it again.

"Yes?" asked Philip, expectantly.

"Phil, I have some bad news. Mother and I received a Western Union this morning. It's Eddie. He's been killed in France." He blurted it all out, wondering if it was better that way. Or maybe he should have broken the news into bits. Too late, now. The words were out, hanging in the air between them.

Philip looked at him. "Eddie? Killed?"

George nodded yes.

"There must be a mistake. I would've known if something had happened to him."

"What do you mean?" George asked, puzzled.

"Eddie is with me all the time," said Philip simply, as if he was explaining a math problem. "I would have known if something had happened to him. I would have felt it in my heart. Maybe he was injured, but he's not dead."

George moved to the desk, wondering if he should show Philip the telegram, offer him tangible proof of Eddie's death. "Philip," he said softly, "I don't think the US Army makes mistakes when it comes to telling families that their loved ones have died. The telegram was very clear. Eddie was killed in France on September twenty-first."

Philip looked up at the man standing next to him. "You're serious?" he asked. "You're not making a joke?"

"I would never joke about such a thing, you know that. He's my brother and I love him as much as you do."

George looked at Philip, watching the emotions play across his face. A flash of anger, then puzzlement, and then, grief arrived. Tears welled in Philip's eyes and ran down his cheeks. "No," he said, "no, it can't be...."

And with that, Philip slumped down in his chair, dropping his head onto his arms folded on the desk. George watched his shoulders shake and once again, he felt awkward and out of place. He bit his lip, for the third time holding back his own tears. "Philip," he said, touching him lightly on the shoulder. "Come with me. We can sit on the couch in my office."

Philip stood mutely, letting himself be led into the other room. On the couch, he fell against George's chest, and this time, he really started to cry, his tears soaking through the thin fabric of George's shirt, feeling hot against his skin. George embraced him gently, rubbing his hand in circles on Philip's back. "I'm so sorry I had to tell you this," he murmured. "I prayed that this day would never come. I know how much you cared about him."

As he had done with his mother, George sat with Philip for a long time and Philip's tears flowed freely. Eventually his sobs gave way to a gentle weeping. George pulled a large handkerchief from his pocket and offered it to Philip who took it and blew his nose, hiccupping slightly.

"I don't think I can keep working today," he said, almost apologetically.

"Of course you can't," said George. "I'll close up for the day. I brought the car—I can give you a ride home."

Philip looked at him, surprised. "Thank you, George. That's…that's very considerate of you."

"Philip, it's hard for me to say…but…I know what you and Eddie meant to each other. I…well, being considerate is the least I can do."

"I love him," said Philip simply.

George nodded. "I know you do," he said, feeling a slight flush rising in his cheeks. While he understood his brother's relationship with Philip, the topic was still awkward for him to discuss.

"He means more to me than anyone, and you're the only person I can say it to," Philip continued. "I can't talk to my parents, I can't talk to your mother. At least I can be honest with you."

"Yes, of course you can, Philip," he said, suppressing his discomfiture. "Come on." He stood up, reaching out a hand. "Let's get you home."

~~~

They walked up the steps of the brick rowhouse and

Philip put the key in the door. "Don't be surprised if Mrs. Washburn greets us," he said, and no sooner were the words out of his mouth when his landlady appeared in the doorway.

"Philip, you're home at a funny time. It's the middle of the day."

"Hello, Mrs. Washburn. You know my boss, George Fiske."

"Yes, of course, Philip," she said, acknowledging George. She touched Philip's hand. "Is something wrong? Is someone ill?"

Philip shook his head and George noticed the tears beginning to well in his eyes again. "Let's get you upstairs," he said, pointing to the stairs. Philip nodded, mute. George turned back to Mrs. Washburn. "It's my brother," he said. "We got a Western Union this morning."

"A telegram? Has he been injured?"

George shook his head no and Mrs. Washburn's hand flew to her mouth, her face registering understanding. "Oh my God, he's been killed?" she exclaimed but her voice was still questioning.

George glanced at the stairs, grateful that Philip was out of earshot. He nodded yes. "I really can't talk about it right now."

Mrs. Washburn reached for his arm. "Go, go comfort your friend. I know how close Philip was to your brother."

George gave her a thankful smile and quickly walked up the two flights to the small apartment on the top floor of the house. It was unusual, Philip living alone like this. Most men tended to stay at home until they got married—or drafted. But one night when they were out together, after a few too many beers, Philip had confided to George why he had an apartment. "When Eddie gets home," he said, "I'll have a place for him. We're going to move in together. Two old buddies, sharing the rent." He paused, then, "I don't think Mrs. Washburn will realize she has two queers living in her attic. Or if she does, she won't care."

"Is this what Eddie wants?" George asked.

"Yes, it is," said Philip. "I know it is. We want to be together, come hell or high water."

George sighed as he reached the landing, watching as Philip slowly unlocked the door. *Hell has come. And Eddie isn't coming home.*

~~~

They stepped into the apartment. George glanced at the immaculately clean living room. He knew Philip was neat and precise from his work at the office, but this was even more extreme. It looked like Philip had put his life on hold, waiting for Eddie to return from the war. The room was expectant and vacant, waiting for something—or someone—to fill the space.

Philip closed the door, then went and sat on the couch, and on his face George saw the artifice of sociability crumbling into grief again.

"Can I do something for you?" Once more, George reached for his handkerchief and offered it to the anguished man. "Make you some lunch?"

"No." Philip shook his head. "To be perfectly honest, I'd like to be alone. I'm sorry, George, I'm not trying to kick you out…"

"Of course not," George answered quickly. "I understand." He started to move towards the door. "I'll just be leaving then…"

"Wait," said Philip, suddenly. "Just one thing. You said you got a Western Union?"

George nodded.

"What did it say?"

"I actually have it with me." He pulled the telegram out of his pocket. "If you feel up to reading it."

Philip nodded. "Yes. I want to see it."

George handed him the flimsy yellow paper, which Philip smoothed gently as he unfolded it on his knee.

WASHINGTON DC 321 AM=

MRS. HAROLD FISKE=

2308 GREENLEA RD BALTIMORE MARYLAND=

DEEPLY REGRET TO INFORM YOU THAT YOUR SON PRIVATE FIRST CLASS EDWARD GABRIEL FISKE USA WAS KILLED IN ACTION 21 SEPTEMBER 1944 IN FRANCE IN THE PERFORMANCE OF HIS DUTY AND SERVICE OF HIS COUNTRY. THE DEPARTMENT EXTENDS TO YOU ITS SINCEREST SYMPATHY IN YOUR GREAT LOSS. ON ACCOUNT OF EXISTING CONDITIONS THE BODY IF RECOVERED CANNOT BE RETURNED AT PRESENT. IF FURTHER DETAILS ARE RECEIVED YOU WILL BE INFORMED. TO PREVENT POSSIBLE AID TO OUR ENEMIES PLEASE DO NOT DIVULGE THE LOCATION OF HIS BATTALION OR POSTING.

PAUL W. BAADE MAJ GENERAL 35TH INFANTRY DIV USA

"That's it," said Philip, refolding the paper and handing it to George. "A life summarized in three lines of teletype."

George nodded. "I can't believe it. It doesn't seem real."

"Maybe it isn't real. Maybe they made a mistake."

"I don't think we can hope for that, Phil," said George, his voice soft.

"No...but maybe right now, it gives me some comfort." He gave George a crooked smile, then rose from his chair and pulled his friend into an awkward embrace. "Go home to your mother," he said. "She needs you now."

"And you?"

"I'll call you if I need anything." He paused. "Don't worry...I'll be okay."

"You're sure?"

Philip nodded. "I'm sure."

"All right, then. I'll talk to you later."

~~~

Philip spent a long time sitting in his living room, not moving. He could feel his grief inside him, as if it was a living thing, taking shape, filling all the spaces in his body. It covered his heart in a black shroud, moved through his organs like a miasma, sucking the joy out of him. He wondered if he'd ever feel happy again, if he could ever laugh and feel carefree. Or was he doomed to a life where he was filled with a black cloud of grief?

Late in the day, he finally found the energy to move a little bit, and pulled a small photograph album out of the drawer in the end table next to the couch. He flipped it open, looking at the black and white photographs. *My Eddie pictures*, he thought. He actually had a sizable collection; his father fancied himself an amateur photographer and since he and Eddie had been inseparable from the time they were in fourth grade, it wasn't surprising that they both showed up in countless photos. Philip quickly flipped past the pictures in front of the church, on the playground, and at school recitals—he wanted to look at the ones at the back, the last time they were together.

Ocean City, Maryland, July 1943

"Here we are!" crowed Eddie. "Mrs. Bellingham's boarding-house. Recognize it?"

"Of course I do, you nitwit," said Philip. "I came here enough times with you and your family."

"I wonder if Mrs. B will recognize *me*." Eddie flexed his muscles in a boxer's pose. "I'm all grown up." He laughed and Philip poked him in the ribs.

"You think you're all grown up but remember which of us is older," countered Philip, with a chuckle.

"Yeah, but I'm the tough guy and you're the ninety-eight pound weakling," Eddie grabbed his duffle from the trunk of the car. "Come on, let's see if she has a room for us."

He bounded up the steps, full of restless energy and laughing confidence. Philip followed behind, shaking his head in appreciation at the man he adored. He sent up a silent prayer, thanking God that Eddie adored him back and that they both knew it.

They entered through the large doorway, standing in the quiet entry. "Anyone home?" Eddie called, and waited for an answer.

In a few seconds they heard the sound of footsteps and an older gray haired woman hurried towards them from the back of the building. "I'm coming, I'm coming," she called. "I wasn't expecting anyone." She stopped short at the sight of the two young men in front of her. "May I help you?" she asked.

"Hey, Mrs. Bellingham, how are you?" Eddie reached out a hand.

"Do I know you, young man?" she said, adjusting her glasses.

"Yes, I'm Eddie," he said. "Eddie Fiske! I know it's been a few years but I hope you haven't forgotten me."

"Oh my goodness, Edward!" She reached for his hand and then pulled him into an embrace. "It's been so long and look at you, all grown up." She held him by the shoulders and gave him a thorough once-over. "How are you, anyway? How's your family?"

"My mother's good. My father died four years ago, which is why we haven't been to the shore in awhile. Well that, and the war."

"Oh, I'm so sorry to hear that. Was it sudden?"

Eddie nodded. "Yes, he had a heart attack, died in minutes. Probably a blessing, as Father O'Malley keeps trying to tell my mother. He never knew what hit him."

"You have my sympathy, even belatedly. I always thought your father was a wonderful gentleman." She paused. "And you? And your brothers?"

"George is in Baltimore, running Dad's insurance business. John is in the Army, stationed out in California. And me...well, I've been drafted too. I've got another week of freedom and then I head to Fort Meade."

"You don't look old enough to be in the Army, Edward."

"I'm nineteen, Mrs. B. Old enough to kill Japs or Germans, whichever place they send me to." He paused for a moment, the reality of the war intruding on his holiday spirit.

"And you, young man?" she said, turning to Philip.

"I'm Philip Cormier." He extended his hand. "We've met a few times—I came with the Fiskes on vacation. I can imagine you don't remember me, though. I was always the quiet kid."

She smiled. "With Edward around, everyone else always seemed quiet by comparison." She gave Eddie a smile. "So, how can I help you today?"

"Phil and I decided to take a short vacation before I leave and thought the shore was the place to be—and of course, there's only one place to stay in Ocean City." He gave Mrs. Bellingham a little wink.

She smiled at him. "I guess that means you are looking for a room." She pulled the register out of the desk drawer and looked through the entries. "How long do you think you'll be here?"

Eddie shrugged. "Three days? Maybe four? Depends on the weather."

She nodded. "I have a family room on the third floor…if you don't mind the stairs. And the bathroom is on the second floor which some people don't like. But I can let it to you for ten dollars for four days."

"Family room?" asked Philip, not understanding.

"Yes, it's a single room with a double bed and a single bed—suitable for parents with a child. If you don't mind sharing a room…"

"We don't mind sharing at all," said Eddie, giving Philip a surreptitious wink. "Here, let me fill out the register." He scribbled his name and address and pulled out a ten dollar bill from his wallet, sealing the deal before the owner had a chance to change her mind. "Ready, Phil?" He grabbed his bag. "Let's go get settled and then we can hit the beach."

~~~

In their room on the third floor, Eddie slammed the door behind him. "I can't believe she gave us a room with a double bed!" he crowed. He grabbed at the waistband on Philip's pants and pulled him towards him. "C'mere, you. I need a kiss."

"Eddie!" Philip whispered. "Shh! Someone might hear us."

"No one's going to hear us, we're on the third floor. Besides," he added, "everyone is probably at the beach."

"Which is where we should be," Philip twisted slightly in

Eddie's embrace but then relented, as he always did, melting into his lover's arms.

"Don't worry, we'll get there. I just need a little indoor recreation, first." He winked as he pushed Philip back on the bed.

Philip let his mind linger on the memory. When they first realized their feelings for each other, their lovemaking had been artless and awkward, shaped by their innocence and inexperience. But as they learned to listen to their bodies, they discovered what they enjoyed and how to please each other. Eddie was a tender and gentle lover, who liked to pleasure Philip to the point where all he could do was cry out, incoherent in his passion. Philip responded in kind, allowing his inhibitions and shyness to melt away when he was in the cocoon of his lover's arms.

~~~

They spent four days in Ocean City. Eddie wanted to stretch it to five and Philip was tempted, but common sense prevailed—Eddie still had packing to finish as well as loose ends to tie up before he left for Fort Meade. Philip couldn't be selfish; he knew Eddie needed to spend time with his family, especially his mother, before he left.

They spent their days at the beach, venturing into the ocean to swim and retreating back to their blanket and big umbrella to dry off. Philip would lie on his side, propped on his elbow, staring at his lover. He had never realized how *sensuous* the beach could be. "You were a genius to think of this," he commented one afternoon.

"Think of what?" asked Eddie.

"Coming to the shore. It's brilliant."

"Not so brilliant, we've done it all our lives."

Philip chuckled. "Yes, but now I like to look at you in ways I didn't know before and this gives us a legal excuse to lie around half-naked."

Eddie grabbed a towel and wrapped it around his shoulders. "You shouldn't be staring at people in public!" he laughed.

Philip pulled at the towel, bunching it up and throwing it aside. "I'm not staring at *people*," he said. "Just you. You know I think you're gorgeous."

Eddie blushed at the compliment. "You're a pretty fine specimen yourself, you know."

"Nah, I'm skinny with ordinary brown hair. You're the good looking one…" and as he said this, he reached out for Eddie's cheek, touching it lightly with his fingers, looking at the lashes feathered on his cheek, the shock of dark hair falling on his forehead. Philip leaned in as if to kiss the other man, then recoiled and glanced around, wondering if anyone had seen the intimate gesture.

Eddie caught Philip's fingers and twisted them in his, nodding his understanding. "It's okay," he said softly. "No one is paying any attention to us."

Philip paused, realizing this was probably true. Even at the height of summer, the number of people on the beach was just a fraction of what it would have been in the pre-war days. Blankets and umbrellas were spread out far along the sand. Everyone seemed absorbed in their own world; no one was noticing the two young men who kept to themselves.

"There are probably people here just like us," Eddie said and Philip looked puzzled.

"What do you mean?" he asked.

"Couples spending a few last days together. Girlfriends, boyfriends, fiancées…we're not so unusual."

"Father O'Malley says we are. In fact, he says we're sinners."

Eddie snorted. "Father O'Malley doesn't have sex. How the hell a priest is supposed to advise couples about what goes on in their intimate lives is a mystery to me."

"If you want to know the truth, I've kind of wondered about that too."

"Trust me, sweetheart," said Eddie, reaching again for Philip's hand. "We're not unusual."

"No, we're not," answered Philip, finding strength as he

clasped Eddie's hand. "Just two people who love each other, struggling with good bye."

~~~

In the evenings, they ate an early supper and went back to their room. All the lights were extinguished along the Boardwalk and Trimper's Amusement Park was closed—it was too dangerous to have lights acting as a beacon for German U-boats that might be lurking off shore in the Atlantic. While many beachgoers complained about the blackout, Eddie and Phil didn't mind. They'd buy a few bottles of beer to enjoy in their room, pull the blackout shades, and luxuriate in their time alone.

On their last day, they splurged on steamed crabs, sitting for hours at a picnic table on the deck of a rundown crab shack, hammering the shells with wooden mallets and picking out the morsels of meat with their fingers. The owner had the All-Star game on the radio and when they finished their meal they stayed until the end of the game, drinking beer and listening to the crack of baseballs from Shibe Park in Philadelphia.

That evening, in bed, Philip took the lead. Eddie seemed lazy and sluggish, probably from the combination of rich food, beer, and sun. Philip could feel him surrendering to his kisses and caresses, limp and pliant in his arms. Philip let his passion guide him, using his tongue and hands to touch his lover all over, wanting to remember his taste, his scent.

They dozed, then woke up and made love again, not wanting to waste their last hours together sleeping. At one point, Philip got up and raised the shade, letting the silver moonlight slant into the room and across the bed.

"Look at you." Eddie watched Philip as he stood silhouetted in the window, the light shining over him. "You look like David."

"David?" asked Philip. "David who?"

"David of David and Goliath," answered Eddie. "The statue in Italy. The one carved by Michelangelo." He paused and Philip could feel Eddie's eyes on his body, traveling over him as if to memorize every curve. He had never felt so loved. "The moonlight makes you look like marble...like the statue. All white and milky."

"I've never seen it," said Philip. "I've never been to Italy."

"Neither have I, you numbskull!" Eddie laughed. "But I've seen pictures. He's a fine looking man, just like you are."

Philip turned in the window and affected a rakish pose, his hand on his hip. "Fine looking, huh?"

"Tell you what," said Eddie. "Someday we'll go to Italy and I'll stand you next to David and then we can do a side-by-side comparison."

Philip nodded. "That sounds good. Let's make a date." He turned back to the window and looked out, the silver crescent of the moon high in the sky. "Eddie, promise me something."

"Sure, what?"

"Promise me that when you look at the moon, wherever you are, you'll think of me."

Eddie rose up off the bed, crossing to the window and pulled Philip into his arms. "That's an easy one," he said. "I'll be thinking of you all the time, anyway, so adding in the moon will be simple."

Philip nodded, then suddenly felt a crushing sadness. Tears sprang to his eyes and he screwed them shut, trying not to cry. He had promised himself he wouldn't cry, wouldn't be weak in front of his lover—but his willpower was not great enough to prevent a few tears from slipping down his cheek.

Eddie wiped them away, then kissed the spot. "I love you, Phil," he said softly.

Philip nodded. "I know. I love you too."

Eddie released him from his arms and took Philip by the hand. "C'mon, let's go back to bed. We have a few more hours before the sun comes up."

They lay back down together, Eddie pulling Philip close and dragging the thin sheet up over their shoulders. Philip felt vulnerable and frightened and he could tell that Eddie was trying to reassure him, kissing him lightly in his hair, on his forehead, murmuring gentle words of love. Philip relaxed a bit under his ministrations, then turned onto his back, heaving a big sigh.

"I just wish you didn't have to leave," he said. "Or that I could be going with you. My damn heart."

"Don't blame your heart," said Eddie.

"Why not? It's what kept me out of the Army. Stupid heart murmur."

"That stupid heart murmur is what brought us together in the first place, don't forget that."

Philip gave a soft laugh. "Yeah, I suppose you're right."

"I am right. If you hadn't missed a year of school being sick, we would have never gotten to be friends. Fourth graders don't hang with fifth graders, you know how it works."

"Pretty rigid class system back then in elementary school," Philip commented, with a wry chuckle.

"There sure was. And there's a rigid class system in the Army, too. Don't kid yourself, Phil. It's better this way. If you had been drafted, too, we wouldn't be together. We'd still be apart—the only difference would be that we'd both be in danger. This way—well, you'll be home, safe, waiting for me."

"I just wish—I just wish I could be with you, to protect you."

"You can protect me with your love," said Eddie. "Promise me you'll never stop loving me. That will keep me safe."

"You know I'll love you forever," answered Philip.

Eddie nodded. "Yes, I know."

Philip suddenly reached for the crucifix that hung on a silver chain around his neck. He slipped it over his head and reached for Eddie. "Here, take this," he said. "Wear this for me. It will remind you of tonight—of our promises."

"I can't take that," Eddie protested. "Your grandmother gave it to you for your Confirmation. I remember when you got it."

"I know, but I want you to have it. Come here." Eddie bent his head while Philip slipped the chain around his neck. He touched the crucifix where it now rested on his lover's chest, feeling the familiar contours of the metal Jesus nailed to the cross.

"I'll bring it back to you," said Eddie, softly. "You'll have it back, along with a ring."

"I don't need a ring."

"I know you don't need one, but I want to give you one. If I had something now…" He held up his hands, bare of all jewelry. "If I had something now, I'd give it to you, but it will just have to wait until the next time we're together."

"Okay," said Philip, nodding. "I'll wait for that."

Eddie wrapped his hand around the crucifix, then held it up. "Thank you for this," he said, and Philip leaned in and kissed it, then kissed Eddie's lips.

"Jesus will keep you safe. What my love can't do, He will."

~~~

Philip closed the photo album, tears now dripping freely on the cover, his grief overtaking him again. *So much for the power of love. So much for the protection of Jesus.* And as he licked his salty tears from his lips, he felt his heart breaking into a million pieces in his chest.

Field Headquarters, 35th Infantry Division, St. Avold, France, November 1944

Captain John Sheridan stood in the doorway and saluted his commanding officer. "Good afternoon, General Baade, sir!"

"Good afternoon, Captain." The General returned the salute. "At ease." He nodded towards a chair in front of the desk. "Have a seat, Sheridan. What's on the agenda for today?"

"I have completed my investigations into the deaths of ten soldiers killed in September, sir, and have written more detailed letters to the next-of-kin for your signature."

"Excellent," said General Baade, reaching for the folder. "All these men are heroes?"

"Yes, sir. No untoward deaths or accidents in this group. All died at the hands of the Germans."

Baade sighed as he opened the folder. "I assume you've processed the paperwork for Purple Hearts for all of them?"

Sheridan nodded. "Yes, sir, I have."

"Any who should receive the Bronze Star?"

"I've made a few suggestions, sir. You can decide if you agree or not."

"All right then, let's begin." Baade picked up the first letter in the stack. "Private First Class Jones."

"Yes, the first three in the group: Jones, Callahan, and Spinoza, were all killed together when they stepped on a land mine."

"Damn," said Baade softly, under his breath, as he looked at the letters. "Jones and Callahan were privates..."

"And Spinoza was a sergeant. He was the oldest of the three and the only married man. You'll see there is a letter for his wife as well as his parents."

Baade nodded, studiously reading the letters. He picked up his fountain pen and carefully filled it with ink, then signed each letter above his typed name.

Together, they worked through the pile of letters, Baade asking questions about each man. Sheridan had their personnel folders and relayed what information he had, showing his commander photographs and commenting on their role in the battalion.

"All these replacement soldiers," Baade said at one point, his voice a growl. "I feel like I don't even know the men under my own command!"

Sheridan paused, not sure what to say.

Baade eyed him, then picked up the last letter in the folder. "Private First Class Edward G. Fiske," he read. "Tell me about him."

"PFC Fiske was from Baltimore, sir. Drafted last year, stationed at Fort Meade for six months, shipped out to England in December. He arrived here in France in mid-July." Sheridan passed a photograph across the desk and Baade picked it up, studying the face in the grainy image.

"He looks so young," he commented.

"He was twenty, sir. Very well liked among the men. He had a good sense of humor."

"Did you know him?"

"Yes, sir, I did. He was outgoing—hard to miss, even in a crowd."

"How was he killed?"

"A sniper, sir."

"A sniper? When did the Germans start wasting sniper bullets on privates?"

"Well, sir, he was actually aiming for an officer..."

Baade raised his eyebrows. "Oh? Who?"

"Me, sir," said Sheridan softly.

Baade looked puzzled. "Go on..." he said, motioning for the personnel file that Sheridan held in his hand. "Tell me what happened."

Sheridan took a deep breath. "I was with Lieutenant Stoner, PFC Fiske and two other men. We suspected there was a German patrol near us and I was scanning the trees with my binoculars."

Baade opened the personnel folder but at the same time, nodded at Sheridan, encouraging him to keep talking.

"Foolishly—I rose up out of my crouch. I don't know what I was thinking, sir. I was so intent on seeing the enemy in the trees."

He paused, taking another breath, finding the fortitude to continue. "Stoner was tugging at my pants, trying to pull me back down to safety. All of a sudden, Fiske leapt up, and jumped over Stoner, landing on my back and pushing me into the dirt."

"Then what?"

"The bullet that was intended for me hit Fiske and killed him, instantly."

"Where was he hit?"

"Right between the eyes, sir, as they say in the movies."

"Was he wearing his helmet?"

"Yes, sir, but it appeared to have been knocked askew from the force of him jumping on me."

Baade nodded. "Then what happened?"

"Lieutenant Stoner picked up his weapon and shot the sniper. There was an exchange of gunfire and two other Germans were killed. We didn't lose any other men."

"And you?"

"I lay where I was, under Fiske's body. Eventually the others moved him, and I could get up."

Baade gave him a look that was unreadable, then picked up a letter from the file folder and read it quickly. "This is addressed to his mother..."

"Yes, sir. His father is dead. Died in '39 when Fiske was fifteen."

He read it again. "You have only the barest details of what happened." His voice was icy.

"I thought...I thought that would be classified information, sir."

Baade looked at the captain carefully, noting the flush in his face. "Let me read between the lines," he said slowly. "Are you telling me, Captain, that a man gave his fucking *life* for you and you are too embarrassed to write a letter that tells his mother this little tidbit of news? That tells his mother just how much of a hero her son really is?"

Sheridan reached for the letter. "I'm sorry, sir. Give me the letter and I'll re-do it."

Baade snatched the letter away. "No, goddammit, I'll do it myself." He set the letter aside on the desk. "What the hell were you thinking, Sheridan? Standing up in the line of fire?"

"I told you, sir. I wasn't thinking. It was a stupid mistake."

"Stupid doesn't begin to characterize it. You are an officer, Sheridan. A *captain*." He paused, looking at the man in front of him, noticing the insignia on his combat fatigues. "Goddammit, Sheridan, if I could bust you to private I would...fucking UCMJ..."

Sheridan blanched. "Sir?" he said, his voice soft.

The General looked at him through narrowed eyes. "I can dock your pay for the next month. Maybe that will teach you not to act like an asshole in the heat of battle."

Sheridan didn't say anything, just looked numbly at his commanding officer.

"Yes," said the General, nodding, thinking out loud. "Effective immediately, for a month. You can draw up the paperwork."

Sheridan bowed his head. "Yes, sir," he said softly, emotions roiling in his gut.

"And spend some time considering how to save a soldier's life...not sacrifice one of your men to save your own fucking skin."

"Yes, sir," he answered, his voice wooden.

They sat for a minute in silence, Baade letting his anger subside. Maybe he was being too harsh, taking it out on Sheridan, but it seemed so pointless. He picked up the photograph of Eddie Fiske, again, looking at the smiling face, the laughing eyes. *So many young men killed...on my watch.*

"Are we done sir?" asked Sheridan.

"You tell me. Are we? Any other letters? Did Fiske have any other next-of-kin? Girlfriend, fiancée?"

"No, sir, but..." Sheridan paused.

"Yes?" prompted the general.

He motioned to the personnel folder and Baade passed it to him. Sheridan opened the file. "Among his personal effects we found these two letters. I wasn't sure what to do with them." As he had done with the photograph, he passed the envelopes across the desk.

General Baade picked the first one up and looked at the address. *Phyllis Lord, Noctorn Manor, Dartmouth, Devon, England.* "Do you know this woman?"

"No sir, I don't. But one of the men told me that Miss Lord and her mother were frequently at the base, volunteering. Handing out donuts, rolling bandages. Mrs. Lord often spent time in the sick bay taking dictation and writing letters for the injured men."

Baade nodded and slipped the letter from the envelope. He quickly scanned the words.

Dear Phyllis,

If you are reading this, then the thing we talked about has happened. Please keep your promise to me and write Phil. It means a great deal to me.

Thank you for being a friend when I really needed a friend.

Love,

Eddie

"Love, Eddie?" asked Baade. "Was she a girlfriend?"

"I don't think so, sir. According to the man who knew Fiske, he said that they were close friends. They were often seen together when she volunteered and also at the Canteen dances. And...they went to church together a few times."

"Church?"

"PFC Fiske was Catholic, sir. Apparently Miss Lord is too."

"I am assuming 'the thing we talked about' is a euphemism for getting killed."

"Yes sir, I think that's correct."

"And so, who's Phil?"

Sheridan nodded towards the desk. "Please look at the other letter, sir."

Baade picked up the second envelope, once again studying the address. He pulled the thin paper out and unfolded it neatly on his desk.

September 19, 1944

Dear Phil,

I've been thinking a lot about baseball and remembering listening to the All-Star game with you last summer. What I would give to be able to have a Natty Boh right now! Along with a few steamed crabs and some sunshine. We don't get the ball scores very often here, although once in awhile they make an announcement in the mess tent. Promise me that one of the first things we'll do when I get home is go to a game—well, after our welcome home reunion, that is.

He looked up. "When was Fiske killed?"

"September twenty-first, sir."

Baade nodded, tapping his finger against the letter, lost in thought. Then, "Captain, do you have a piece of stationery with you?"

"Yes, sir," he said, pulling out a paper. "Would you like to dictate something for me to type?"

Baade shook his head. "No, this one is off the record." He dipped his fountain pen in the ink bottle and pulled the lever to fill it, then began to write.

9 November 1944

Dear Mr. Cormier,

The enclosed letter was found among the personal effects of PFC Edward G. Fiske who was killed in action on 21 September 1944. An investigation into the circumstances of his death found that he was shot and killed by a German sniper bullet. He saved an officer's life in the process. He died a hero in service to his country and will be awarded the Purple Heart and a Bronze Star for his bravery.

I extend my deepest sympathies to you on the loss of your friend.

Yours sincerely,

Paul W. Baade

Commanding Officer and Major General, 35th Infantry Division

He folded the letter and put it together with the other one, then inserted both in the envelope. "Please type up an envelope for these and send to Mr. Cormier. Also, send the letter to Miss Lord but include a typewritten notification of Private Fiske's death. Use a variation on the girlfriend/fiancée letter."

"Yes, sir," said Sheridan, taking the envelopes and the stack of signed letters. "Should I sign the letter to Miss Lord?"

"No, bring it to me when it's ready. I'll sign it."

"Yes sir." Sheridan began to rise out of his seat. "Is that all for today?"

"Yes, I think so."

Sheridan stood and saluted the General, who returned the salute. "Dismissed, Captain."

PART II: THE AFTERMATH

Baltimore, Maryland, June, 1954

Philip lifted the heavy brass knocker and brought it down on the door, feeling it vibrate in his hand. "I'll be right there!" he heard a voice call, and seconds later, the door opened, framing Audrey Fiske. "Prompt, as always," she said, with a smile.

"Hi, Mrs. Fiske. Ready to go?"

"Just give me a second to fix my hat." Audrey looked at herself in the mirror, wiping off a smidge of lipstick with the edge of her finger. She picked up her purse and gloves. "Do I look all right?" she said, turning to Philip. "I wasn't sure what to wear."

Philip nodded. "Yes, that's a lovely dress." He noticed the gold star pin affixed to her collar. He realized that Audrey Fiske was an attractive woman and wondered why she never remarried.

"I chose navy instead of black," she said. "I'm sick of black. It's been ten years."

Philip nodded, holding the door open, letting Audrey pass. "Navy is a good choice."

"By the way, I like your tie. You look very nice, too." She smoothed the lapel on his jacket and removed an imaginary piece of lint from his shoulder.

Philip smiled to himself. He remembered that she did the same thing to Eddie—it was as if she had transferred her mannerisms for her son to the next most convenient man— her son's lover. "Thank you, Mrs. Fiske," he said softly. He

257

wished in that moment he could call her mom.

She stopped on the sidewalk. "That reminds me," she said, as Philip opened the car door. "I've been meaning to suggest this—I think we are at an age where you can start calling me Audrey. You're not a teenager anymore."

Philip was surprised—he felt as if she was reading his mind. "Mrs. Fiske—Audrey...I'll try," He smiled at her. "Old habits die hard, you know."

"It would make me happy. I often think of you like a son." Her words gave Philip a pang. He wished he could be a son, too—or husband, or lover, or something. Mostly he wished that Eddie was still alive.

She slid into the car and Philip closed the door gently, then walked around to the driver's side, settling in behind the wheel. He nosed the car away from the sidewalk and started driving down the quiet street.

They were silent for a few minutes, then Audrey turned to Philip. "Thank you again for doing this. I appreciate you going with me."

"No thanks needed, Mrs. Fi—Audrey," answered Philip. "I'm honored that you invited me."

"It's not a chore?" she asked.

Philip shook his head. "Not at all."

"I asked George..."

"But George is busy with the baby." Philip laughed. "He has hands full. Every time I see him he has big bags under his eyes."

"Three little ones under the age of six! I remember it well. Although Eddie was always such a good baby..."

Tell me about Eddie when he was a baby. Tell me everything you know. Instead, he said, "I was honored that George and Betty asked me to be Taryn's godfather."

"Yes," said Audrey, patting his knee. "I encouraged him to ask you. He was thinking about asking his brother John—again—and I said, pshaw to that. John's gone off to California and forgotten about us."

"I don't think he's really forgotten..."

"Some days I feel like it." Audrey had a trace of bitterness in her voice. "He married that girl and she has him in her clutches—all her family, brothers, sisters, aunts, uncles, cousins—I couldn't keep track of them at the wedding."

Philip smiled to himself. He'd heard it all before. Audrey could never accept that John decided to settle in California, where he had been stationed, after the war. When he cemented that decision by marrying a third generation Californian, Audrey seemed to write him off completely.

"So I guess you didn't ask him about coming for this ceremony today?" Philip asked.

Audrey looked at him, her expression clear. "Of course not. He didn't show up for three different baptisms of his brother's children, I certainly don't think he'd make time for a military ceremony honoring his deceased brother."

"Well, we all have our priorities..." said Philip, and Audrey smiled at him.

"You are such a peacemaker, Philip. That's what I like about you." She turned and looked out the car window again. "I still don't understand why *I* was invited to this event. Eddie wasn't killed on D-Day, after all."

"They call it the second round of D-Day," Philip replied. "D-Day wasn't just June sixth. It went on for months."

"I know, but..." she shrugged. "Eddie was from Baltimore, and was just a Private First Class. To be invited to a D-Day ceremony at Arlington National Cemetery? With the President in attendance? I don't understand it."

"Of course President Eisenhower will be there. He was the general who ran the whole shebang. As for your invitation...take it at face value. Eddie gave his life for his country and you get to be honored."

"I suppose," she said, still uncertain. She was silent again, watching as they merged in with the cars on the Baltimore-Washington Parkway. Philip pressed the accelerator and moved into the flow of traffic.

"So, tell me what's new with you, Philip." Audrey settled back and adjusted her skirt over her knees.

"Nothing much. Same old, same old. I've been busy with work since George has been taking some time off."

"And he appreciates your help," said Audrey, nodding.

"That's what I'm there for." Philip shrugged.

"What about you, Philip? When are you going to settle down?"

He chuckled. "I think I am pretty settled down. Did you hear? I'm talking to Mrs. Washburn about buying her house. She wants to move to Florida."

"Well, that's wonderful," said Audrey. "But you know what I mean…when are you going to get married?"

"I'd have to meet someone before I could get married," said Philip carefully.

"Are you doing anything to meet anyone?"

"Not really. Maybe…maybe I'm not meant to be married."

Audrey gave him a stern look. "What sort of foolishness is that?" she said. "Of course you are meant to be married. You're attractive, you have a good job, you're buying a home…in my time, you'd be known as 'a catch.' I don't think the world has changed that much—you're still a catch, for the right girl."

"Well, I haven't met her yet." Philip felt a twinge of anxiety. This wasn't the first time they'd had this conversation and he never enjoyed it. He knew in his heart the chances of his marrying a woman were next to nil.

"I wonder who Eddie would have married," she mused, looking straight ahead. "I wonder if he would have had children by now. One thing I have discovered," she said, looking at Philip again and patting his knee, "I really love being a grandmother. It would have been a blessing for Eddie to have kids."

Philip felt a lump in his throat and worked hard to control his emotions. "Yes," he said, trying to keep his voice neutral.

"Children are special."

He reached for the radio and snapped it on, fiddling with the dial, searching for WBAL. "Do you want to listen to some music?"

"If you don't want to talk…"

"I need to concentrate on the road." He pointed to the highway. "There's a lot of traffic." There wasn't really, but Audrey didn't drive much and he was hoping she'd believe his fabrication. He hated the marriage conversation.

"Oh yes, of course." Audrey folded her hands in her lap. "I'll just watch the scenery."

~~~

An hour or so later, they pulled into the parking lot of Arlington National Cemetery. A Marine corporal was waiting to greet them, clipboard in hand. "Welcome to Arlington," he said, as Philip rolled down the window. "You're here for the D-Day Memorial?"

Philip nodded. He gave their names and the Marine consulted his list, checking them off. "You can park anywhere. There are other soldiers stationed on the path to direct you to the ceremony." He glanced at his clipboard again. "Ma'am, there's a note here that Colonel Sheridan wants to talk to you."

"Colonel Sheridan? Do I know him?"

"I wouldn't rightly know, ma'am, but I suspect he'll be looking for you. I saw him earlier, I know he's here." He waved them on in dismissal and Philip drove away, pulling into an empty parking space.

"I wonder what a colonel wants with me?" Audrey mused, and Philip smiled.

"I wouldn't have a clue, but I am sure we'll find out."

They got out of the car and started walking along the path to the amphitheater, hundreds of graves flanking them on either side. "It gives me chills," said Audrey, looking out at the massed white crosses. "Thinking that under every one of those gravestones is a young man."

"I know. When was the first soldier buried here? Do you know?"

"The Civil War, I think. It was for the Union soldiers, at first. Now it's for everyone." She suddenly stopped abruptly on the path. "Eddie could have been buried here, you know."

"He could?" said Philip. "No, I didn't know."

Audrey nodded, and they resumed walking. "I got a letter a few years after the war ended. If I wanted his body sent home, I could have had that done. He could be buried here, or at a cemetery in Baltimore—or anywhere, really."

"But you didn't…"

She shook her head. "No. I thought it was better that he not be disturbed. He's buried in France with all his fellow soldiers."

"In Normandy?"

"No, the other side of the country—near Germany. It's called the Lorraine American Cemetery."

"I wonder what it looks like," said Philip.

"Like this, I suspect." Audrey fanned her hand at the graves that surrounded them. "I don't think the military has much imagination when it comes to cemetery design."

"Have you ever thought of visiting?" Philip asked, and Audrey nodded.

"I have—I've asked George about taking me. It's an awfully long journey, but maybe someday."

They had arrived at the amphitheater and were greeted by another Marine. Noticing Audrey's gold pin, he said there was a special section for Gold Star mothers and loved ones, and escorted them to the bench.

Philip watched as people streamed in: women, men, children, babies carried in their mothers' arms. He glanced at the faces, wondering if there was another person like him in the crowd—a lover, lost and bereft, mourning silently, no one to talk to.

The ceremony began promptly at two. Philip hadn't known what to expect and was dreading it a little bit—he always thought war was sort of pointless and his feelings only sharpened after Eddie's death. He was glad for his heart murmur and 4-F classification that had kept him out of Korea. He was young enough, still, and men were being drafted.

To his surprise, however, the ceremony turned out to be pleasant—well, if not pleasant, at least appropriately moving. There were a few speeches, a military band that played hymns and marches, a wreath laying ceremony on the Tomb of the Unknown Soldier. It finished with a twenty-one gun salute and a military flyover. Philip was impressed. More than once he had to keep himself from crying. He noticed Audrey dabbing at her eyes and he rested his hand lightly on her knee, hoping to offer her a small measure of comfort. *God knows, we both need it.*

When it was over, they stood to leave, the crowd moving slowly out of the amphitheater. "I could probably drive the car closer to pick you up. If it's too long a walk to the parking lot."

"Oh, Philip," Audrey replied. "I'm not that old, yet."

They noticed an officer in dress greens threading his way through the crowd. It appeared that he was heading towards them. "Could that be Colonel Sheridan?" Philip asked. Sure enough, he was right.

"Mrs. Fiske?" said the man as he reached them. "Corporal Baker told me he greeted you at the gate and that you were wearing a blue dress—a lovely dress, if I might add."

"Oh!" Audrey shook his offered hand.

"Do you have a minute to talk?" He looked from Philip to Audrey.

"Yes, of course. We're not in any rush, are we, Philip?"

Philip shook his head no.

The Colonel pointed to the bench, inviting them to sit down. "I am very happy you were able to make it today, Mrs. Fiske. The invitation was sent on my request."

"Ah, well that clears up one mystery. I was wondering why we were invited."

"You were invited because your son was a hero. He deserves to be recognized and I am long overdue in sharing this information with you." He paused, running his finger along the sharp crease in his pants. "Mrs. Fiske, your son was killed in the process of saving another soldier's life—my life, as a matter of fact."

Audrey's eyes widened. "He did? No one has ever told me..."

"Yes," he said. "And that's the part of why I am here: to explain what happened and apologize. The process, during the war, was to send out personal letters, after the telegram notification, explaining to loved ones the circumstances of a soldier's death, when the circumstances were known. Unfortunately, in the case of your son, the proper letter never got sent."

"Is there a reason why?"

"It was—to use an Army term—a SNAFU. I assume you know what that means?"

"Yes, I do. But I am not going to say it in this sacred place."

The colonel smiled at her. "That's probably best. Anyway, when the war ended, I had the opportunity to review some files and realized that an error had been made. I've been trying to figure out a way to meet you in person for at least seven years so I could share this information."

"And what exactly happened?" Audrey asked softly. "When Eddie was killed, I mean?"

"A sniper was aiming at me. PFC Fiske realized what was happening and pushed me down in the dirt. Unfortunately, then he was exposed and killed by the bullet that was intended for me."

Audrey reached for Philip's hand and squeezed it. He squeezed it back.

"Your son was very brave. He acted in selfless and heroic manner. He was a true soldier."

Philip looked at Audrey and could see her eyes were

moist. He handed her a handkerchief and she gave him a grateful smile. "Have you ever seen his grave?" she asked softly.

"Not the permanent one. The men who were killed were buried in temporary graves after the battle. I haven't had a chance to get back to France since 1946."

She nodded. "Thank you for telling me this." She paused, then touched his hand. "Now, tell me about yourself. Obviously, you are still in the Army."

"Yes, and that is also because of your son. I was planning on getting out at the end of the war, just like everyone else. But, because of what he did...I decided to stay in and see if I could save a few soldiers' lives, too."

"And have you?"

He nodded. "I was in Korea for two years. I like to think I made a difference there. Nothing quite as heroic as your son, but I've done my duty."

She smiled. "When will you get discharged from the Army?"

"I'm looking at seven years. Assuming we manage to keep peace with the rest of the world."

"Are you married?"

He nodded. "For six months. My fiancée—well, now, wife—wanted to wait until I was home from Korea."

"I wish you much happiness," said Audrey. "I hope you have a little boy and that he never has to go to war."

"I hope that too, ma'am. You don't know how much I pray for that." He reached into his pocket, extracting a heavy vellum envelope. "There's a small, invitation-only reception that will be held at the Mayflower later this afternoon. If you'd like to attend, I was able to secure an invitation for you. The President will be there."

"Oh my!" said Audrey, taking the envelope. She looked at the invitation, reading the heavy engraved letters. "What an honor!"

He stood up, smoothing his jacket. "Now, if you can excuse me, I need to be going. I'm glad we had this chance to talk."

Philip stood, extending his hand. "Thank you for talking to Audrey and delivering this most overdue news." He had an edge to his voice.

The Colonel looked at him, puzzled. "I'm sorry. I've been terribly rude. Your name is..?"

"I'm Philip Cormier," Philip said simply.

"PFC Fiske's brother...relative...?"

"Friend," Philip said shortly. "Close family friend."

"Ah," he said, nodding. "Well, thank you for coming. I hope to see you at the Mayflower. Of course, Mr. Cormier, you are invited too."

He turned and left, Philip watching his broad shoulders as he walked away from them. He realized he had never felt so invisible in his life.

~~~

"Isn't that amazing?" said Audrey, as she watched the Colonel walk away. "Eddie saved his life. I can't believe no one ever told me. Would you have ever guessed, Philip?"

"Actually, I knew," he said slowly.

"You knew? How?" Audrey didn't even try to conceal her surprise.

"General Baade wrote me, too. Apparently, Eddie had a half-finished letter to me in his pocket. The General wrote a note expressing his sympathies and said that Eddie had saved an officer's life. That's all," he added hurriedly, realizing suddenly how awkward this was. "Not as much detail as Colonel Sheridan just gave us."

If Audrey picked up on his confusion, she gave no hint. "Oh, my," she said, patting Philip's arm. "The General took time to write my son's best friend a note. That's sweet." As she said this, she used the handkerchief she was holding to dab at her eyes.

Philip hesitated. "Audrey, I..." he paused.

"Yes?" she asked, expectant.

Audrey, I...I was more than Eddie's best friend. I was his lover and soulmate and I loved him with an intensity and passion that was...is so strong it hurts—I feel it every day in my entire being—and it hasn't diminished one iota in the decade since his death.

He looked at her face. *Do I tell her? Do I tell her the truth? That her darling son was a wonderful man who gave his heart and his love freely—so completely to me and all he came in contact with that his loving, generous heart allowed him to sacrifice his life to save someone else? Or would the knowledge that he loved a man—he loved me—destroy her memory, her image of her son and turn him into someone she would see as disgusting and filthy...a pervert, a queer...a sodomite?*

"Philip." She touched his arm again. "Are you all right?"

He started. "Yes," he said, shaking his head and clearing his thoughts. He looked at Audrey's blue eyes and realized they were the exact same shade as Eddie's. Her face had an open look of love and he realized that for Audrey, the pain of losing her son hadn't diminished either. *No need to add to her burden.* "I was just going to say that I agree with you...it's amazing that in the midst of a battle with men being killed, a general would find the time to write to one of his soldier's friends. I've always treasured that letter."

"Maybe you can show it to me some day." Her voice was soft.

"Of course. I know right where it is." Philip offered her his arm and they started walking up the path leading away from the amphitheater and back towards the entrance to the cemetery. "Do you want to go to the reception at the May-flower? It's really not a problem for me to drive into the city."

Audrey shook her head. "No." She looked at Philip closely. "I have a feeling you don't want to go," she said.

Philip looked at her, not sure of her motive. "You know I'm not one for socializing," he said. "But the President will be there. I am your chauffeur for the day."

"No...no. I really don't want to go. I've had enough with painful conversations for one day. Let's go home."

Philip nodded, thinking that painful conversations would turn into painful memories, which would invade his dreams and rob him of sleep, as they had so many times before. He sighed, wondering if grief had a timeline and if it did, if he'd ever figure out where on it he was.

The Roosevelt Hotel, New York City, New York, September 1964

Philip slid into the chair at the small round table, looking around at the smoky, crowded bar. A waitress was moving through the tables and within a minute or two was at Philip's; she set down a napkin and bowl of mixed nuts. "Welcome to the Madison Club," she said. "Can I bring you something from the bar?"

Philip nodded. "A gin and tonic, please."

"Sure," said the waitress. "Any special brand of gin?"

Philip glanced at the bottles stacked up behind the bar. He saw a familiar green one on the top shelf. "Tanqueray...with a lime. And Schweppes tonic."

"That's all we serve." She smiled at him. "Tanqueray and tonic, coming right up."

She disappeared back into the crowd and Philip felt a rush of excitement in his chest. *This is fun...something different. Getting away from Baltimore—having an adventure.* He popped a few nuts in his mouth and settled back in his chair, ready to enjoy the evening.

The waitress returned, putting the drink down on the table in front of him. He looked at the tall glass with the bubbles rising to the top, the bright green lime and the red cocktail stirrer. Something about it all seemed so perfect. He felt another tremble of excitement.

"Two-fifty for the drink, but I can run a tab if you like."

"Oh, great. Can I charge it to my room?"

"You're staying here? Sure, no problem. Room number?"

"903."

She scribbled it on the paper. "You're all set," she said. "Enjoy your evening."

Philip sipped his drink as he scanned the room again. He looked at the knots of people and wondered who they were. Folks stopping for a drink on the way home from work? Having a drink before going to the theater? He frowned. He realized he had no idea what time the theater started in New York. Eight? Nine? He glanced at his watch. Eight-thirty. Maybe it was too late for a show. Perhaps they were all going out to dinner.

"Mind if I join you?"

Philip looked up, startled at the voice. "Excuse me?"

A young man was pointing to the empty chair at Philip's table. "Mind if I join you?" he repeated. "It's crowded, not too many empty seats and you look like you could use some company."

"Oh!" Philip was surprised, but also intrigued. He nodded. "Sure. Have a seat."

The man slid into his seat and Philip gave him the once-over. He was handsome, in a California surf bum sort of way. Blond hair slicked back, tan, madras-plaid shirt, white denim jeans. He couldn't see his feet but Philip suspected he was wearing black penny loafers, no socks. Philip guessed he was in his early to mid twenties.

"I'm Jeff, by the way." He extended his hand. "Jeff Hunter."

"Philip," he replied, shaking the offered hand.

"Just Philip?"

"For now," said Philip, with a small smile. He wasn't sure why he was being cautious.

Jeff smiled in return. "Sure enough. Do you live here in New York or are you visiting from out of town?"

"Visiting. I live in…Philadelphia."

"Ah." Jeff leaned back in his chair. "The city of brotherly love."

"That's right. And the Liberty Bell."

The waitress reappeared at the table. "Can I get you something?" She put another napkin down on the table.

"Sure." Jeff looked at Philip's glass. "I'll have what he's having."

"Tanqueray and tonic?" asked the waitress and Jeff nodded. He gave her a little wink. "That sounds great."

Philip looked at his glass and noticed it was almost empty. "I'll have another, too," He drained the glass and handed it to the young woman. He felt reckless, slightly out of control. He realized he was having fun. He was surprised this handsome stranger wanted to talk to him.

The waitress left and reappeared in what seemed like seconds, putting both glasses down on the table. "Shall I put these on your tab?" she asked and Philip nodded. "That would be fine."

Jeff lifted his glass in a toast. "Why, thank you, Phil. Here's to."

"Here's to," said Philip. "And it's Philip," he added.

"Not Phil?" Jeff raised an eyebrow.

"Only to my closest friends." Philip gave him a small smile.

"Oh," said Jeff, drawing out the word. "Maybe we'll get to that point." He lifted his glass and took a sip, and gave Philip a wink as he looked at him over the rim. Philip felt a shiver run down his spine.

Jeff put down his glass and reached into his pocket, pulling out a pack of Marlboros. He opened the box and offered it to Philip, who shook his head. "No thanks. I don't smoke. But you go ahead," he said, noticing the book of matches in the ashtray on the table. He picked them up and lit Jeff's cigarette and watched as the tip glowed orange, Jeff inhaling deeply. He exhaled smoke through his nostrils, the plume wafting lazily upwards, over their heads. Philip wasn't much for smoking, but at times he thought it was sexy. This was one of those moments. He felt another tremble of excitement.

"So, what brings you to New York?" asked Jeff. "Business?"

"No, actually, I'm meeting a friend and we're going to the World's Fair."

"Oh, cool. I haven't been yet, but I am hoping to go soon. Make sure you see the Pepsi exhibit. I've heard it's terrific."

"Yes, that's what people have told me. And the GM one, too."

"So this friend of yours…he? She?"

"She," answered Philip. "With her family. They're visiting from England."

"Oh, wow!" said Jeff. "All that way to visit the World's Fair. Mayor Wagner will be thrilled."

Philip chuckled. "Well, it is the *World's* Fair. There should be some international guests."

"So, this friend…you see her very often? Have you ever been to England?"

"To be perfectly honest, we've never met in person. I guess you could call us penpals, if that's not too corny."

"Don't tell me you started writing each other in high school or something."

"Not quite, but it has been twenty years. I'm excited to finally meet her."

"Twenty years! You've got to tell me how that happened." Jeff gave him another inviting smile. Philip felt himself being sucked in by his charm.

"Well, um," Philip spoke slowly. "I had a friend who was killed in the war. She wrote me a letter to tell me."

"Shit, that's hard. Which war? Korea?"

"No," answered Philip. "World War Two. Korea wasn't quite that long ago."

"Damn, you don't look old enough to have known guys in World War Two."

Philip wondered if the flattery was an act, or sincere. He realized he didn't care. "We were very young," he said softly. "He was just twenty."

"Well, damn, that is hard. I'm sorry to hear about your friend."

"Thank you," said Philip. "It's been twenty years but I still miss him."

Jeff paused. "So this woman...your penpal..."

"Phyllis met Eddie when he was stationed in England. He asked her to write me if anything happened. I'm not a member of his family, you see. He was afraid I wouldn't get a personal letter."

"Well, it's good that he was thinking ahead. Sad, though."

"Yes, it is."

"You must've been really good friends," Jeff added.

"We were," said Philip. "Very close."

Jeff looked at him and Philip could tell he understood his meaning.

They finished their drinks. "Another round?" asked Philip.

Jeff nodded yes. "Sure. I'm enjoying talking to you." He motioned for the waitress and before five minutes had passed, refills were on the table in front of them.

"So tell me about yourself," said Philip. "What do you do? Go to school?"

"No, right now I'm a courier," Jeff answered. "But I'm hoping to break into modeling."

"Courier?"

"Fancy name for a delivery boy." Jeff gave him a wry smile. "I ride around midtown on a bike, delivering letters from one business to another. The guys in the corner offices need something to read, you know."

"Ah," said Philip. "I see."

"Don't tell me you're a guy in a corner office. Hope I didn't insult you."

"Hardly," answered Philip. "I'm just a lowly insurance salesman from Baltimore."

"Baltimore? I thought you said you were from Philadelphia."

Damn, thought Philip, feeling a buzzing in his head. "Sorry," he said. "That was a little fib."

"Okay. And your name isn't Philip?"

"No, that's my name. And I'm really here for the World's Fair, too."

"You're sure, now? You're not a closeted guy with a wife and kids out on the island?"

"Huh?" Philip felt stupid. He had no idea what Jeff was talking about.

"I've met a few guys who come to New York for a little action. Pretty common phenomenon, actually. Living on the down low."

"No." Philip was still not entirely following the conversation. "I've never been married."

"But you were close with your friend Eddie," Jeff said.

"Yes. That's what I said. Very close."

Jeff pulled out another cigarette and Philip lit it, again watching the smoke drift between them.

"You like being a courier?" asked Philip, and Jeff shrugged.

"It's okay. Riding a bike all day keeps me in shape. Good for my modeling career." He winked again.

"You keep winking at me." Philip suddenly felt a little tipsy.

"That's because I think you're cute," answered Jeff, winking yet again.

"I'm too old to be cute," said Philip archly. "In fact, I'm not sure I was ever cute."

Jeff laughed. "Okay, good looking then. You're a decent looking man."

"Well, thank you for that. I'm not used to compliments."

"You don't have a boyfriend?" asked Jeff, softly.

"Someone to say nice things to you?"

"No." Philip felt a flush rise in his cheeks. *Boyfriend. Such an intimate word.*

They finished their drinks and Jeff held his up, looking at the glass. "What do you say...we can buy another round and take them up to your room—I assume you're staying here at the Roosevelt?"

"Yes, I am." Philip felt his cheeks redden even further.

"We can go up to the room and be a little more...private. I can give you a few more compliments."

Philip felt the heat of desire pool in his groin. "We can do that," he said slowly, "but we don't need to buy any more drinks. I've got a bottle of bourbon in my suitcase."

"Oh, isn't that convenient," said Jeff, his wry smile flicking across his face again.

"Sometimes I like a nightcap, especially when I'm traveling. I don't sleep very well in hotels."

"Ah," said Jeff. "I have a cure for that, too."

"I'm sure you do," said Philip, feeling a trill of anxiety mixed with excitement rush through him.

Jeff caught the waitress's eye and they settled the bill. Philip rose from the table, feeling a little woozy. How many drinks had he had? Three, four? He couldn't remember. As they left the bar, Philip said, "Maybe going to the room is a bad idea. I think I've had enough to drink."

"Oh, come on," said Jeff softly, holding his elbow. "You don't have to drive or go anywhere. What does it matter if we both get plastered? That's part of getting acquainted."

They walked to the bank of elevators and stepped into an empty one. Philip pushed the button for the ninth floor and as the door closed, Jeff pushed Philip against the wall, grinding his hip into the other man's crotch. "You like that?" he asked, his lips close to Philip's ear.

Philip felt a wave of desire sweep over him. "Yes," he said, "I do."

The elevator door opened and Philip was thankful there

wasn't anyone standing on the landing. "Let's go." Jeff pulled him by the hand, heading down the hall to room 903. Philip fumbled with the key, managing to get it into the lock and opening the door. In the room, Jeff slammed him against the wall again, this time grinding more forcefully, nipping at Philip's ear with his teeth.

"Do you want a drink?" squeaked Philip, helpless under the onslaught.

"Later," said Jeff. "I want to get to know you, first."

Jeff pulled at Philip's clothes and Philip felt Jeff's hands hot on his skin. This was sex, pure and simple. There was no intimacy, no love, but it quelled a desire and filled a need that Philip had let go too long unfulfilled.

They tumbled on the bed for a coupling that was quick and fast; the combination of being slightly drunk and a ravenous craving for physical touch meant that Philip was not able to hold back his release. "Sorry," he said, when they finished, lying panting on the bed, a single bead of sweat running down Jeff's chest. "I'm like an overexcited teenager."

"Not a problem," answered Jeff with a wink. "Fast and furious is sometimes fun, too." He pushed himself up off the bed and went into the bathroom, returning with a towel which he used to wipe them both off. "Now, what about that drink?"

"Sure," said Philip, "I'll get it." He started to sit up, then flopped back against the pillow, his head spinning. "Actually, you can do it. The bottle's in my suitcase." He pointed to the small overnight bag on the luggage rack.

Jeff opened the case and pushed among the shirts and underwear, pulling out a fifth. "Ah, Jim Beam. That's what my dad drinks." He rummaged around a bit more, pulling out a black leather case. "What's this?"

"My camera," answered Philip. "Please leave it alone."

But despite his request, Jeff was opening the case, taking out the camera and looking at it. "Nice," he said. "A Leica."

"It was my father's. Put it back in the case, will you?"

Jeff held it up to his face, looking through the view-finder. "I told you, I want to be a model," he said. "I'm into cameras." He focused it on Philip, sprawled on the bed. "We could take a few art shots."

"I asked you nicely." Philip was starting to feel annoyed in spite of his post-coital haze. "Please put it away. It's old and I don't want anything to happen to it."

"Okay, okay." Jeff put the camera back in its case and closed the suitcase. He picked up the bottle of bourbon. "Do you want to drink from the bottle?"

"There are glasses in the bathroom. Even though we just had sex like savages, we can still drink like civilized men."

Jeff went into the bathroom, coming back with two glasses in his hand. "I think you have a sense of humor, Philip," he said with a wink.

"I have my moments." Philip took one of the glasses and Jeff poured a splash in it. "Cheers," he added, downing it quickly.

The liquid burned his throat but it tasted good, numbing the ends of his nerves which felt like they were on fire. Jeff slid into the bed next to him, propping the pillows against the headboard and sipping at his drink. "Mind if I smoke?"

"Go ahead," said Philip. "Use the ashtray, though."

Jeff reached down next to the bed and picked up his shirt, rummaging in the pocket again. But instead of pulling out the box of Marlboros, he pulled out single...something. Philip looked at it, puzzled. "What's that?" he asked. "A homemade cigarette?"

"It's a joint," said Jeff. "You've never seen one?"

Philip shook his head no. "A joint?"

"You know...marijuana. Just what we need to keep this little buzz going."

Philip sat up abruptly. "Marijuana!" he said. "You can't smoke that in here...it's illegal!"

Jeff gave him a baleful glare. "Hate to break it to you

buddy but…what we just did is illegal. They still have anti-sodomy laws on the books in the state of New York. A little dope is the least of your worries."

Philip fell back against the pillow. "Good God."

"Oh, come on. Stop being such a worrywart." Jeff stood up and took the towel off the end of the bed and tucked it against the bottom of the door. "There. That should block any telltale evidence."

Jeff came back to the bed and climbed in, then lit the joint and took a long, deep inhalation. Philip watched him as he held the smoke in his lungs, then slowly exhaled. "You want to try?" he asked.

"I don't think I should."

"I promise not to tell your mother," Jeff said, with another wink.

Philip looked at him, then laughed. "I guess I am acting like a little old lady, aren't I?" he said. He reached for the joint. "Okay, I'll try it," he said, putting it between his lips.

"Inhale and hold it," said Jeff. "Then exhale slowly."

Philip did as he was instructed, coughing a little, but mostly managing not to embarrass himself as an amateur smoker. He remembered the one time he and Eddie had tried smoking together, buying a pack of Camels from the grocer and hiding behind the school gym to smoke them. Philip hated the taste and ground out his cigarette before he had even smoked it all the way down. Eddie didn't seem to mind as much. Philip wondered if Eddie had started smoking in the Army. So many men did.

"Still with me?" Jeff passed the joint back to Philip. "You seem a million miles away."

"Sorry. Just thinking about some old memories."

"First sign of getting stoned—reminiscing."

"Is it really?" said Philip, surprised.

"I don't know," Jeff laughed. "I'm just making shit up." He took another sip of bourbon and handed the glass to Philip. "Now, isn't this fun? A little party?"

Philip nodded, his limbs feeling heavy and immobile against the smooth sheets of the bed. He began to think he had never felt sheets that were so smooth in his entire life. *Maybe I can ask at the front desk where they buy them*, he thought. *I'd like to get a set for my bed at home.*

Jeff's hand reached under the sheet, running along Philip's thigh, brushing over his hip. "Ready for round two?" he asked, turning on his side, bringing his lips close to Philip's cheek.

"Yeah," said Philip softly, his eyes unfocused and head spinning. "Except I don't think I can get it up again."

"Don't worry about that." Jeff's hand was becoming more insistent, sliding inward, fingers twisting in his pubic hair. "I'm a pro. I've got my methods."

Those were the last words of the evening that Philip remembered.

~~~

Philip woke the next morning, bright sunlight shining through a crack in the curtain. "Oh God," he moaned. His head was pounding and his tongue felt thick and furry and too large for his mouth. The light seemed impossibly bright and he felt as if it was searing his eyeballs, which in turn felt coated with sand.

He wondered what time it was and reached across to the bedside table, fingers seeking his watch. Nothing. He sat up, puzzled, but realized that sitting up too fast was a mistake. A wave of nausea rolled through him and he dashed into the bathroom, vomiting into the toilet. "Oh God," he moaned again, clutching the porcelain commode as if it were a life raft.

He knelt for a few long minutes, waiting for his head to clear. It suddenly dawned on him that he had no idea what time it was. *Damn. I'm supposed to meet Phyllis at ten.* He had this horrible, sinking sensation that she was in the hotel lobby, anxiously waiting for him, while he was up in room 903 puking his guts into the toilet.

280 E. N. Holland

He stood up, feeling shaky and lightheaded, and splashed some cold water on his face. He poked through his toilet kit and found a bottle of aspirin, shaking four of them into palm. *Desperate situations call for desperate measures.* He washed the pills down with a glass of water.

He looked at the glass which he had picked up from the bathroom shelf. There was a second one, clean and turned upside down. *Wait a minute. Wasn't I drinking last night?* He looked around the bathroom. Everything was neat— towels folded on the rack, glasses in their place.

He returned to the bedroom. His clothes were folded neatly on top of the suitcase and his jacket hung from the back of the desk chair. *Maybe I dreamt the whole thing.* But he remembered Jeff riding him, pounding his ass into the mattress. He touched his throbbing head again and realized that his memory of the evening was very definitely real.

He looked for his watch again, puzzled that it wasn't on the bedside table. He remembered taking it off. He *always* took it off before he went to bed. He got down on his hands and knees and looked under the bed then reached under the night stand. Nothing.

He sat on the edge of the bed, realizing again he had no idea what time it was. He picked up the phone and dialed zero.

"Hotel operator," came a voice. "How may I direct your call?"

"Please," said Philip, his voice sounding unnaturally loud in his ears. "Can you tell me was time it is?"

"Nine-thirty a.m., sir," said the operator. "It's Saturday morning, September nineteenth."

"Okay, thanks." He hung up the phone.

Philip had thirty minutes. He wondered if he could pull himself together in that amount of time. What he really wanted was to go back to bed and sleep for about four more hours, not get on a train and head to Flushing Meadows. *Maybe a hot shower will do the trick. A hot shower and a cup of coffee from the coffee service in the lobby.*

He stood up and walked to his suitcase, opening it to get a clean pair of boxers. As he looked down, he realized something was amiss. He frowned, pushing his hand among his clothes. The bottle of Jim Beam was missing. And...*Fuck! My camera!* He started pulling out his clothes, but realized the camera case was too big to be hidden under his pants or socks. He had a horrible sinking feeling. *Oh good Lord. My camera...my watch...*

Suddenly, he whirled around, grabbing his jacket from the back of the chair. He stuck his hand in all the pockets—nothing. *No, no, please,* he prayed. He grabbed his pants and felt through all those pockets, then his shirt. Nothing.

He sunk down on the side of the bed, his head in his heads. "Goddammit!" he said aloud, once again, his voice pounding in his ears. "He stole my fucking wallet! And my camera! And my goddamn fucking Timex!"

Philip trembled a bit. He was so angry with himself he wanted to hit something while at the same time he wanted to cry at his own stupidity. *Bringing a stranger to the room! What the hell was I thinking?* But he knew the answer to his own question. He wanted to get laid, and he did, and now he was paying the price.

He groaned again, then looked at the phone. He realized he needed to deal with his wallet, but he had a more immediate concern. He picked up the receiver, once again dialing zero.

"Hotel operator," came the voice again. "How may I direct your call?"

"What time is it?" he asked, feeling like an idiot.

"Nine-thirty-seven, sir," said the operator. "It's Saturday, Septem..."

"Yes, yes, I know," he said, interrupting. "Listen, I need to get a message to a hotel guest. It's urgent."

"Certainly, sir. What is the guest's name? I can connect you to the room."

"No, no, I don't want to talk to her. Just let me give you the message. Can someone deliver it?"

"I can try, sir, but I can't guarantee receipt. It's better if you call."

"I can't. I don't have time. Okay, here's the message." He dictated quickly. "Phyllis, so sorry. A family emergency has come up and I must return to Baltimore immediately. I am so sorry to ruin our plans. I'll be in touch when you get home to England. Have a great vacation in New York. Philip. Read it back to me," he snapped, and the operator did so. "Okay, can you please see that gets to Phyllis Hastings *immediately.*"

"We can try, sir. Hastings…in room eleven twenty-three."

"Thank you." Philip sighed, annoyed again at his stupidity. "You've been very helpful."

"You're welcome, sir. Have a nice day." The line clicked dead.

He hung up the receiver and groaned again. It was starting to sink in—he had no money, no license, his train ticket was gone—his one and only credit card, American Express—gone. No watch and his father's beloved camera—gone forever. He felt tears pricking at the edge of his eyelids. He had never felt so stupid in his life.

He stood up and went back to the bathroom, drinking another glass of water and looking at his bleary reflection in the mirror. *What a sad sack I am.*

In the room, he crossed to the window, pulling the curtain closed tightly and blocking out the sunlight. Then he crawled back into bed, pulling the sheets up over his head. He wasn't sure how he was going to deal with everything, but he knew he'd be better able to cope after a few hours of sleep—and that became his only, and most immediate, plan.

Baltimore, Maryland, June, 1974

Philip lifted the latch on the gate on the fence and slipped into George Fiske's backyard, unnoticed. He glanced around at the group of people scattered across the lawn, looking for familiar faces. Philip always felt awkward in the first few minutes at a party. The guests tended to be couples with lots of children running around. He was invariably the only single man.

He scanned the group and saw his goddaughter—the guest of honor—making her way around the yard, shaking hands and hugging her friends and relatives. Philip sighed, watching her. Of George's three children, Taryn was the one he considered to be most classically "Fiske" in her looks: smooth dark hair, blue eyes, a straight nose over a broad smile of white teeth. She reminded him so much of Eddie that sometimes it pained his heart to look at her.

She turned in his direction and saw him instantly, waving and calling out, "Uncle Philip! You're here!" She hurried to his side and Philip pulled her into a big hug. "I'm so glad you came."

"I wouldn't have missed it for the world, sweetheart. It's not every day that my goddaughter graduates from college."

She smiled at him. "I know. I can't believe this day is here. Four years sure went fast, didn't it?"

"It sure did. Now that you are graduated, are you officially a nurse?"

"Not quite. I take my boards in July. I'm a graduate nurse

283

until the results come back."

"Ah," said Philip. "And when do you start your new job?"

"A week from Monday. I move next weekend. Tim is helping me."

"I can't believe you're moving to DC. We have good hospitals here in Baltimore." He smiled at her. "You could work at Johns Hopkins."

"Oh, I know we do!" Taryn laughed. "I did clinical at most of them. I just wanted to have a change, really break free. Maybe I'll end up moving back but for now..." Her voice trailed away.

Philip patted her on the shoulder. "But for now, you're young and you should see the world. If I had my life to do over, I'm not sure I'd stay here either."

"Oh, Uncle Phil..." she said, frowning.

"Don't feel sorry for me," he said with a wink. "I'm old and you're young. You have your whole life ahead of you." He reached into his jacket, pulling out an envelope from the inside pocket. "Here's a little something for you that I hope will come in handy."

She took the card, slipping her finger under the flap on the envelope. "You didn't have to do this," she said.

"I know I didn't *have* to, but I wanted to," he answered, with a smile.

Taryn pulled out the card and opened it. She laughed. "A gift certificate...from Sears!"

"I hope it's not too boring. I was trying to be practical. I was thinking back to my first apartment and remembered buying all sorts of things I never expected to buy...a mop, a broom, even an ironing board." He chuckled at the memory.

Taryn kissed him on the cheek. "It's wonderful. I like practical and I know I'll need tons of stuff. Thank you so much."

He smiled. "You are very welcome. Now," he said, pointing to the guests, "I shouldn't keep you from your party. I see your father over by the beer. Maybe I'll go join him."

"Okay, Uncle Philip. Thank you again. She spied another group of friends coming through the gate in the fence and hurried off to welcome them.

Philip ambled across the grass, heading towards the table with beverages and drinks. "Hey George," he said, raising his hand in greeting.

"Philip! Good to see you." He stuck out his hand and Philip shook it, no longer surprised at the formality of the gesture. He could remember exactly one time in his life when George hugged him—the day in the office when he told him about Eddie's death. Philip realized that this was a difference between the brothers: Eddie was always outgoing and demonstrative; George was stiff and reserved. He wondered if George was affectionate with his children.

"Thanks for coming," said George.

"Lovely day, isn't it?" Philip said. "Makes me think about summer."

"Sure does. Want a beer?"

Philip nodded. "That would be good. Thanks."

George reached into the cooler and pulled out a brown bottle of National Bohemian. Twisting off the cap, he handed it to Philip. "So," he said conversationally, "speaking of summer...have any plans? Vacation?"

Philip took a swig of the beer. "I'm thinking of going to Fire Island again. I put down a deposit on a quarter-share of a house for two weeks at the end of July."

George shook his head. "Why go all the way to New York to go to the beach? What's wrong with Ocean City?"

"Ocean City is all about condos, kids, and crowds," said Philip. "Fire Island is quieter—more pleasant. Sort of like Ocean City in the old days. You still have to take a ferry to get there."

"I hear that Fire Island caters to a more *adult* crowd."

Philip shrugged. "There are plenty of families with kids

on the ferry but at the Pines—you're right. It does seem to be a predominantly single male bunch. That's why I enjoy it."

"I hear that there are people having sex in the dunes."

Philip looked at him, raising an eyebrow. "You hear all sorts of things, don't you?" He shrugged again. "I wouldn't know about the sex. They do have nude sunbathing, though."

"Do you do that?"

"Sure, why not? When in Rome..."

"I can't believe it," said George, scorn in his voice. "When did you turn into an exhibitionist?"

"Oh for Pete's sake, George," answered Philip. "When did you turn into a prude?"

They locked eyes, each sipping their beer. *Stiff and reserved. Eddie would have gone nude on the beach.* The thought made him smile.

George turned to walk away but Philip reached out, grabbing his elbow. "I could change my plans," he said. "I've only paid the deposit."

"Change your plans to what?" asked George, turning back towards Philip. "Go to Ocean City?"

"No. The trip we've talked about—going to France to visit Eddie's grave."

George sighed. "Are you bringing that up again?"

"Sure, why not? Your excuse has always been the kids. But now that Taryn has finished nursing school and is moving out on her own, no one is left at home. Maybe this is the time."

George hesitated. "How can we go, Philip? France is so far away."

"Not that far. Just get on a plane and go. They have direct flights from Friendship Airport to Paris. I checked."

"But I don't have a passport. I probably couldn't get one in time."

"It doesn't take that long. If we plan to go in September, they'd have plenty of time to process it."

"Why September? I thought you said July."

"Well, September is the thirtieth anniversary of his death. Might be a fitting time to make a visit."

George sighed. "The business. I can't leave the business for three weeks."

"Who said anything about three weeks? We could go for a week. Make it a short trip."

George shook his head. "All that way for a week? Seems foolish to me. Besides Betty doesn't like flying. How can I go gallivanting off to Europe without her?"

Philip looked at him. "Jesus Christ almighty," he said. "You're the man with a million excuses, aren't you? It used to be kids and money. You couldn't afford to get away, you needed to save your vacation time to do things with them. Now the kids are grown and gone, you've got plenty of money but you still have excuses: passports, work, your wife doesn't like to fly. Why don't you just be honest with me and say you don't want to go and see your brother's grave?"

"I didn't say that…" George protested.

"Not in so many words," retorted Philip. "But it's pretty obvious that you don't want to go. You know, you broke your mother's heart over this. She begged you to take her and you never did. I should have just stepped up to the plate and done it when I had the chance."

"Then why didn't you?" said George, his eyes flashing.

"You know why. She wanted to see her son's grave with her *son*, not her son's *lover*."

"She didn't know you were his…lover." George grimaced as he said this and Philip fixed him with a stare.

"I know, which would have made the trip even more pointless. Why should a Gold Star mother be traveling with her son's childhood friend?" He paused. "You didn't do the right thing, George. Admit it. And it's probably the guilt that you're feeling that won't let you go now."

"I'm not guilty," said George angrily. "Don't try to tell me what I'm feeling."

Philip looked at him, shaking his head. "Forget it,

George. Forget I brought it up. I'll just go to Fire Island Pines, like I planned." He set his empty beer bottle down on the picnic table. "I think I'll be heading home, too. Where's Betty?" he scanned the crowd of people, looking for his hostess. "I need to say goodbye, thank her for the party." He saw her coming out of the back door of the house, a large platter of sandwiches in her hands.

"You don't need to leave," said George, weakly, but Philip ignored him, turning on his heel.

He walked over to George's wife. "Betty, let me help you with that." He took the tray from her hands.

"Thank you, Philip." She smiled warmly at him. .

"Thank you for the party, too. I think I'm going to be heading out."

"Heading out? But you just got here…and we're just getting started with the food! I have a very special cake that I baked."

"No, really, I need to be going."

She patted his elbow, looking over towards her husband. "Did you and George have a tiff? Don't let him drive you away. He's been such a pill for days."

Philip chuckled. "Pill. That's a good word for it."

"I think he's a little emotional about his youngest graduating from college and moving away. It's reminding him how old he is. Not that he's really that old—but he thinks he is." Betty picked up a paper plate and put a few sandwiches on it, handing it to Philip and motioning him towards the bowls and platters of food on the table. "Help yourself to some salad. Find someone else to talk to. You really want to stay and have some cake."

Philip hesitated, looking at the plate in his hands, then sighed, picking up the spoon to serve himself some coleslaw. He realized he was tied to the Fiskes, unable to break away, unable to leave. *This party is a metaphor for my life. Bound to a family by a lover dead for three decades. Will I ever grow up and be able to move on?*

He took a few bites of the coleslaw, then set the plate down on the table. He walked over to George, still standing near the cooler of beer. "Give me another one?" Philip asked.

"I thought you were leaving."

"Your wife talked me into staying," Philip replied. "She bribed me with the promise of a slice of her home baked cake."

George smiled. "Always impossible to resist." He paused, then, "Listen, I'm sorry. I shouldn't have blown up like that. I've been a little on edge."

Philip nodded. "I'm sorry too. I shouldn't have said those things about your mother."

"We'll make that trip, one of these days. I promise."

"Really? You mean that?"

"Yes, I do. He was my brother, you know, and I loved him too. You don't have a monopoly in the love department."

Philip smiled. "Well, okay then." He took a sip of his beer, hesitating. "But not this year, I guess? For the trip I mean."

"No. Go ahead with your rental at the beach. Maybe next year. It'll give us some time to plan…we can make it special. Maybe I can even convince Betty to get on a plane."

"It's a deal." Philip held up his beer in a simple toast. "Next year."

"Yes," said George. "Next year."

Baltimore, Maryland, September, 1984

Taryn stopped the car at the curb. "Here we are!" Her voice was bright.

Philip smiled at her. "Thank you for the ride. I appreciate it."

"Not a problem, Uncle Phil," she replied. "Anytime."

"Would you like to come in for a drink? I made a fresh pitcher of iced tea this morning."

"No, I probably should get back to the family."

"Well, okay then," said Philip, his hand on the latch.

She looked at him, then abruptly put the car in park, taking the key from the ignition. "As a matter of fact, iced tea sounds good. I need a break from Mom and all the mourning relatives."

Philip smiled again. "Well then, let's go." He opened the door and waited for her to get out of the car.

Philip unlocked the front door and held it open, ushering his goddaughter in. "Anything new since the last time I was here?" she asked.

"I don't think so. I'm thinking of buying a new couch but I'm not sure I really need one."

He opened the hall closet and hung up his jacket, then loosened his tie. "Give me a minute to get the tea. Make yourself comfortable." He pointed to the living room and Taryn nodded.

He came back five minutes later with a tray, laden with a pitcher and glasses and a plate of Pepperidge Farm cookies.

"It's all I had." His voice was apologetic.

"It's perfect," said Taryn as she picked up a Milano and took a bite. "I associate you with these kinds of cookies." She smiled at him and he smiled back. She pointed to the mantel. "That picture's new."

"Not really new, but new to me," Philip answered. "Your father gave it to me a few weeks ago."

"That's his brother, right?" Taryn said. "My Uncle Eddie? He used to have that picture on his dresser. I remember it from when I was little."

Philip nodded. "It's the only picture any of us had of him in uniform."

Taryn picked up the framed photo, studying the grainy image. "It's so hard to tell what he looked like."

"He was very handsome," Philip replied. "You remind me of him, actually. Same black hair, blue eyes. I think of it as the Fiske gene."

She smiled. "Do you have any other pictures of him?"

He nodded. "I do." He crossed to the bookcase and pulled out a photo album. "Careful. It's old and sort of delicate."

Taryn sat down on the couch and Philip sat next to her. She paged through the album, smiling at some of the pictures. "You did a lot of church things, didn't you?" she said, pausing at one of Eddie and Philip in their altar boy robes.

"Oh, we sure did. St. Bridget's was our second home."

She smiled and continued to flip through the book. The last picture was a snapshot of them on a blanket, wearing bathing suits. Eddie had his arm around Philip's shoulder and Philip's hand rested lightly on Eddie's knee. "Where is this?" she asked.

"Ocean City. That was the last time I saw him. He was mustered off to Fort Meade a week later and never came home."

Taryn paused, studying the picture. "Who took this?"

"A woman who was sitting near us on the beach—she

was there with her kids. Her husband was in the Navy, I believe. On a destroyer in the South Pacific. She saw us taking pictures and offered to take one of us together."

"That was nice of her," said Taryn. She looked at the picture again, then looked at her godfather. "You cared for him very much, didn't you?"

Philip nodded. "I did," he said softly. "Not a day goes by that I don't think of him."

Taryn closed the album and set it on the table, picking up her iced tea and taking a sip. "World War Two seems so far away to me. Do you realize it was over for almost ten years before I was even born?"

"I know. Some days it seems like yesterday—friends getting drafted and being shipped out. Other days—it seems like it happened in a different life. I have a hard time reconciling it."

"What was he like?" Taryn asked, abruptly.

"Who?" asked Philip, confused.

"My uncle."

"Eddie? He was a great guy. Kind, generous...great sense of humor..."

"You sound like my father," she said. "He always spoke of him in such glowing terms."

"Well," answered Philip, "that's what happens when you get killed so young. You don't have time to develop bad traits like all the rest of us."

Taryn smiled. "You think so?"

Philip shrugged. "Either that or our memories soften with age. We remember the good stuff but the bad stuff fades away." He paused. "Do you think it's a remarkable coincidence that your father died on the exact same day, forty years later?"

Taryn looked at him. "Yes and no. I've seen it happen with some of my patients. They have certain anniversaries, or dates in mind, I think. They set their mind to dying on a certain day."

"Do you think your father did that?" Philip asked.

"I'm not sure," she replied. "I've thought about it. One of the other nurses on the unit describes it as the angels bringing their loved ones to them—maybe that's a little too far-fetched, though."

Philip took a breath, feeling a shuddering in his chest. "If Eddie was bringing a loved one home, I wish he had picked me."

Taryn rested her hand lightly on Philip's. "Obviously, it wasn't your time, Uncle Phil." Her voice was soft.

"I know," he replied. "But some days it is just so hard...George's death isn't helping things, either. It's a little bit like rubbing salt into an open wound."

Taryn looked at her godfather. "Forgive me in advance if I'm being too blunt, but I think you need some closure. It has been forty years, after all."

Philip shook his head. "Darling, you don't know how often I think the same thing. I feel like I'm trapped in a maze and can't find my way out and I keep going around in circles." He looked at her. "Do you have the secret? A magic closure pill?"

Taryn smiled ruefully. "Unfortunately, no. For my patients, their families, we suggest grief counseling. That seems to help."

"I don't think that had been in invented in 1944. Besides, no one would think to offer it to the invisible lover."

Taryn nodded, then paused. She took a breath. "Have you considered visiting his grave? We don't have cemeteries for the dead people, you know. They exist for the loved ones left behind."

"I've talked about going to see his grave for years," Philip replied. "I always wanted to go with your father. I actually thought we were going to make it a few years ago, then he got sick." He shrugged. "I don't think it will happen now."

"What about my Uncle John?"

Philip shook his head. "No, John's not interested. Besides," he dropped his voice as if he was telling a big secret. "I never really liked John. I always thought he was a bit of a jerk—seeing him at the funeral today reminded me that he really hasn't changed at all."

Taryn smiled. "I don't really know him. But he did seem rather pompous, didn't he?"

"You're kinder than me," Philip said. "I'd call him an ass."

Taryn laughed. "Well, okay, so I guess you won't be traveling with him. What if you just went by yourself?"

Philip looked at her, his brow creased. "Seriously, does that sound like fun? If I wanted to go alone, I could have done it years ago."

"What if you went on a tour? You'd meet people that way…"

"I doubt they have tours to the American cemetery in France. Normandy, maybe, but Eddie's buried in the other one, on the other side of the country."

"What if you took a tour to Paris and then made a side trip? Do you know how far away it is from Paris?"

"A few hours. I've looked it up on a map." He picked up his iced tea and drained the glass. "Listen, Taryn, you're very sweet to make all these suggestions, but believe me, I've thought about these options for years. Your dad was my only realistic traveling companion and now that he's gone…" he shrugged. "It looks like I'll be staying home."

Taryn stood up, picking up the tray of glasses and cookies. "It just seems to me that there must be *someone* in your life who would be interested in traveling with you. You've pinned all your hopes on my father and now…if I can give you my opinion…you're using him as an excuse."

Philip blinked. "Excuse me?" he said.

She put the tray down and sat back down again. "I'm sorry. I don't mean to be unkind. It's just that…" she reached for the photo album and flipped it open to the last page.

"Some woman on the beach was willing to take this picture for you. She didn't know you from Adam. I'm sure there's someone else out there in the world who would be willing to travel with you. That's all."

"Taking a picture on the beach and making a journey to France are two very different things," Philip said, trying to keep his voice under control.

"Is it? Really?" She stood up again and picked up the tray, walking into the kitchen. Philip could hear her opening and closing the refrigerator, putting the glasses in the dishwasher. She came back in the living room and stood in front of him, her hand on her hip. He smiled in spite of himself. It was such an Eddie pose.

"Uncle Phil," Taryn said, looking directly at him. "Of all my relatives and family friends, you're the one I love the most. I've always loved you. But I've always sensed that there's some sort of unhappiness there...It would make me happy if you could find a way to make yourself happy."

He smiled at her. "So it's all about you, now? You need to be happy?"

"Well, if that's what it takes to convince you, yes..."

He stood up and moved to her, kissing the top of her head. "I'll think about it. I promise."

"Well, all right then," she said. "I guess that's all I can ask." She picked up her purse. "I'll probably be coming up from DC a little more often than usual. I want to spend some time with Mom. Maybe we can get together, too. Have lunch or something?"

"That would be nice." Philip escorted her to the door. "Just call. My schedule is pretty flexible now that I'm retired."

"I've always heard that people get busier when they retire."

"Really?" said Philip. "That's not true for me."

She gave him a quick peck on the cheek. "Think about what I said. It's important." With that, she dashed down the steps, waving as she got into the car. Philip waved back, feeling the familiar ache once again filling his chest.

He closed the door and turned back into the house, picking up the Mass card from the funeral. He looked at it, reading the date. *September 21, 1984.* He sighed, feeling old and alone.

He sat down at his desk, turning Taryn's words over in his mind. *Maybe a tour is a possibility,* although he had no idea about how to go about it. *Find a travel agent, I suppose.*

He opened the drawer and pulled out a piece of heavy stationery. *First things first. I need to write Phyllis and tell her about George.* He looked at the Mass card and decided he would send her that, too. *She's a good Catholic. She appreciates the rituals.*

He picked up his pen and began to write.

PART III: THE JOURNEY

St. Avold, France, March 1985

Philip stepped off the train and reached out a hand to help the woman who followed him. "Let me take your bag, Phyllis," he said, and she smiled.

"Thank you, Philip. You're such a gentleman." She buttoned up her coat and pulled out a pair of gloves from the pocket. "Even though the calendar says it is spring, it's still chilly here, isn't it? Do you have a hat?"

"I'm fine," answered Philip.

"Listen to me, I sound like such a mother hen!" she said with a laugh. She paused on the platform, looking around. "I think we can probably get a taxi and check into the hotel. Then, after we get settled, have some lunch? Maybe visit the cemetery in the afternoon if you are up to it."

"That sounds good." Philip nodded. He appreciated her take-charge attitude and ability to speak passing French. Two days alone in Paris had made him feel like a completely inept traveler. He realized that reading guide books for six months did *not* prepare one for a European trip, Mr. Frommer's and Mr. Fodor's opinions notwithstanding.

"We could rent a car, you know," Phyllis was saying, pointing to the large yellow and black HERTZ sign that was hanging in front of them. "Then we wouldn't have to rely on cabs."

"A car? I can't imagine driving in France."

Phyllis laughed. "It's not like Paris—I can't imagine driving there, either. St. Avold is a much smaller city and the

297

cemetery is a few miles out of town. It might save us some money."

"Don't worry about the money, Phyllis. I've saved up for this trip for forty years. I'll happily pay all the cab fares."

"Well then, I guess it's settled. We can always come back later if we change our minds."

They walked through the train station and found a cab waiting at the taxi stand. "Le Novotel Hôtel, monsieur," Phyllis instructed, and the driver nodded.

The taxi drove quickly through the city streets which, Philip noted, had far less traffic than Paris. Still, cars were turning quickly and darting every which way and he couldn't quite picture himself at the wheel.

He looked at the buildings of the city as they passed through the streets. "It's not quite what I expected," he said, gesturing at a non-descript office park on their right.

"What do you mean?"

"I always imagined France as—well, quaint. Pretty. This could be an American city anywhere."

"If you want pretty, you need to go to Provence and see the olive trees. Or the Dordogne for medieval walled cities and prehistoric treasures. This," she gestured out the window, "is the industrial heartland, crossroads of Europe. The German border is just a few miles away, as you know."

"Yes, of course," Philip answered slowly.

"Keep in mind why Eddie was fighting here. Olive trees aren't much use to the war effort, now, are they?"

Philip chuckled. "Good point. I should have thought of that."

Phyllis nodded. "On top of that, this area was pretty well destroyed in the Great War. They spent twenty years rebuilding, only to have it be destroyed a second time. I imagine the architects in the fifties were more focused on expediency versus style the second time around."

"Yes…and fortunately, we've managed to go forty years this time without a war—in this part of the world, at least."

"And let's hope it stays that way."

As they continued to drive, Philip realized they were leaving the city center. Five minutes later, they pulled up in front of a modern building, nestled against an expanse of trees. "L'hôtel, Madame," announced the driver. "Cinquante francs, et vingt francs pour les valises."

Philip pulled out his wallet and extracted a one hundred franc note. "Is this enough?"

"It's more than enough." Phyllis handed the driver the money, speaking quickly in French, and received twenty francs in change.

They got out of the car, Philip casting an eye around the parking lot. "This is even less what I was expecting."

"I hope it's all right." Phyllis had a note of apology in her voice. "There aren't many hotels in St. Avold and this one got a good rating. We could have stayed in Metz but that's 28 miles further west. I thought you wanted to be near the cemetery."

"Oh, I'm so sorry!" exclaimed Philip. "I sound like an ungrateful bastard, don't I? This is wonderful and I appreciate all that you have done."

"Well, then, good." Phyllis led the way into the lobby and Philip followed with the suitcases.

~~~

Sixty minutes later they were in the hotel restaurant, Philip carefully studying the menu. "I could ask if they have one in English," Phyllis offered, but Philip shook his head.

"No. I'm determined to figure this out. I feel like such a country bumpkin."

"You haven't traveled much?"

Philip shook his head. "No. To New York a few times, the shore. A couple of business trips to Chicago. That's about it." He paused. "George and I often talked about making this trip, but…" He shrugged.

"Has anyone from the family ever visited Eddie's grave?"

Philip shook his head no. "It's sort of sad, isn't it? No one ever came to lay a flower or a wreath for him. At least I'm finally here to set things right." He reached out and touched Phyllis's hand across the table. "Thank you again for coming with me."

Phyllis smiled. "Thank you for asking me. It's an honor."

A waiter appeared at the table. "Monsieur? Madame?"

"Have you decided, Philip?"

He nodded and they placed their orders. "Shall we have some wine?"

"Wine would be lovely." Phyllis turned to the waiter and spoke quickly in French.

"Mais oui, bien sûr, Madame," he said, turning on his heel and departing.

"I hope red is alright with you?"

"Red is perfect, since I think I ordered the French equivalent of beef stew."

"*Boeuf bourguignon*, yes, you did," said Phyllis. "And I suspect it will be excellent."

The waiter returned with a bottle, which Phyllis inspected and then nodded her approval. He poured a taste for each of them and then filled the glasses.

"To Eddie." Philip raised his glass in a toast.

"To Eddie," answered Phyllis.

They chatted for a few minutes, talking about the trip and their rooms, sipping their wine and picking at the *crudités* that the waiter had placed on the table. Then, abruptly, Philip said, "May I ask you a personal question?"

"Well, I guess." Phyllis looked slightly taken aback. "As long as I have the right to refuse to answer."

"Oh, I'm sorry, I'm being rude."

"No, go ahead…as long as it's not about either of my husbands." She smiled, trying to ease the frisson of tension in the air.

"Were you in love with Eddie?"

Phyllis paused, running her finger along the crease in her

napkin. She wasn't really surprised at the question nor was it unexpected, but she wanted to answer it the right way. It seemed that a great deal hung in the balance. "I suppose I was a little in love with him. Or maybe 'smitten' would be a better word. I was very young—just seventeen. Can you fall in love at that age?"

"I think so. I did. In fact, I was sixteen. There was no doubt in my mind what I was feeling."

"Ah," said Phyllis, "I was a little less sure. So maybe it wasn't love. But I was certainly very fond of him, and very attracted to him, too. He was such a handsome man."

"Wasn't he? I used to tell him he was gorgeous." He blushed at this, wondering why he was sharing so much with a woman he barely knew. But that wasn't true—they'd been corresponding for forty years. She was as close a friend as George had been. Maybe even closer.

"Philip, just so you know..." This time, it was Phyllis who reached across the table and touched Philip's hand. "He was always a gentleman with me. He never made any advances. I'm not sure he ever even touched me."

"Never?" Philip raised an eyebrow but smiled. He was trying to keep the tone light.

"Well, he held me when we went dancing, of course. But never any...necking." She smiled, a flush creeping into her cheeks.

"Dancing?"

"Oh yes, many times. They had dances at the Canteen almost every weekend. I loved it. Eddie was a wonderful dancer."

"He was?" Philip was truly surprised at this revelation.

"Oh, yes. I always felt as light as a feather in his arms."

"I wonder where he learned that," mused Philip. "I didn't know he knew how to dance."

"Basic training?" she said, and they both laughed.

The waiter reappeared, this time with two salads. They paused while he served them, then once again, he silently disappeared.

"What sort of things did you and Eddie like to do?"

Philip ate a forkful of lettuce. "The usual. We went to movies, played ball with our friends. My dad collected model trains—we spent hours playing with those." He paused. "Once we started...being intimate...we mostly wanted to be alone." Philip felt his cheeks turn red. *How on earth did that ever slip out?*

Phyllis looked at him, her expression conveying nothing. Philip picked up his wine glass and took a large sip. "I'm sorry. That was an embarrassing thing so say. I'll shut up now."

She shook her head. "No, please don't. I understand the relationship you had with your...*lover*." He sensed that her choice of words was deliberate. "You've probably never talked about this with anyone, have you?"

Philip shook his head no. "George knew, but he never said much. With him, it was a 'hear no evil, speak no evil' sort of attitude."

"So, maybe, after forty years, you need a confidante."

"Maybe I do." Philip was slightly embarrassed at the direction in which the conversation was heading. But Phyllis was right—he wanted to share memories of Eddie and at last, here was the one person in the world who seemed to understand how he felt—probably because she felt the same way, too.

"So, tell me the story."

"What story?" said Philip, feeling slightly confused.

"How do two young men figure out they are in love? Lord knows, I had a hard enough time figuring it out for myself and I was doing it in the expected and usual way."

Philip smiled, then ran his finger around the base of his wineglass, smearing a drop of wine that had splashed there. "Ah, well, let me think..." He paused. "Eddie and I were pretty much inseparable from the time we became friends in fourth grade. We did everything together—school, church, baseball, Boy Scouts. You name it. In the summer of '39, we had outgrown a lot of those activities—too old for Little League, past our prime to be altar boys—so we spent hours just hanging out, talking about stuff, like boys do."

Philip looked out the window, seeing the image as clear in his mind's eye as if it were yesterday: Eddie sprawled on the bed, Philip sitting on the floor, the baseball game playing on the radio.

"Are there any girls you like, Phil?"

Philip shrugged. "I don't know. I haven't paid much attention. Delores Martin is sort of cute."

Eddie rolled back on the bed, hands behind his head. "I have my eye on Anne Haskell, myself."

"She's okay, if you like blondes. I like dark hair. Like yours." Philip gasped as he said this. He had no idea where that comment had come from or why it had come out of his mouth.

Eddie smiled at him, that wry smile he always gave everyone. "You like my hair, huh? And my blue eyes? You like them too?"

"Yes, and your blue eyes." Philip looked down, knowing his cheeks were likely as red as tomatoes.

"You ever kiss a girl, Phil?"

"I just told you, I've hardly paid attention to girls. How can I be kissing one if I'm not even looking at them?" He paused, annoyed. He wasn't sure why Eddie's comment bugged him so much. "What about you, Romeo? Have you kissed any girls?"

"Not yet, but I've been wondering about it. Must be kind of exciting. The grown-ups sure get all het up about it."

He rolled over onto his stomach, shifting on the bed so his face was close to Philip's. "I was thinking...maybe we could practice, so when the time comes to kiss someone, we'll know what we're doing."

Philip felt his heart thumping in his chest. Kiss Eddie? His best friend? The idea was vaguely disquieting, but at the same time exciting. He felt a stirring in his pants.

Before he had a chance to answer, Eddie reached out and pulled Philip's face towards his, pressing their mouths together. Philip had the sensation of Eddie's lips being very soft, his mouth opening slightly. He could taste the tang of the Pep-O-Mint Lifesaver Eddie had been chewing on just moments before.

Philip broke away, breathless, but Eddie didn't relinquish his grip. "Eddie...I..." he stammered.

"We're just practicing," Eddie said. "It's not for real." And with that, he leaned in and kissed him again. Philip surrendered to him, letting his mouth open, their tongues lightly touching, darting back and forth.

This time, when they broke apart, it was Eddie who was breathless. "If we're going to practice," said Philip, "I think we should get in the right position." And he scooted up on the bed, pulling Eddie into his arms, twisting his hands into his hair, and they kissed for a third time.

Philip shook his head, bringing himself into the present. "We were talking about girls and we decided we needed to, um...practice kissing."

Phyllis laughed, but it was a kind laugh. "Practice kissing?"

"Yes. Well, we both realized we had no experience with girls and we wanted to know what to do when the time came. We were both interested in girls, you see...or at least, at that time, we were still kidding ourselves that we were interested in girls."

"I see. It makes sense."

"You never had a practice kiss with anyone?"

Phyllis shook her head. "No...just the real thing. Since we are being honest with each other, I'll tell you that I wished that initial kiss had been with Eddie. Instead it was the man who became my first husband. But that's a different story for another day."

The waiter appeared at the table with their meals and they paused while he served them, refilling their wine glasses for a third time. The bottle was empty. "Un autre, Madame?" he asked.

"Would you like another bottle of wine, Philip?"

He paused. He rarely drank in the middle of the day and never two bottles of wine! "Sure," he said, casting caution to the wind. "Why not? I am in France after all."

The waiter nodded and left, returning quickly with the second bottle of wine, this time simply opening and pouring, without any preliminaries.

Philip took a bite of his *boeuf.* "This is delicious," he said. "As you predicted."

"Excellent. My *brochette* is quite tasty, too." She paused. "Do you want to continue with the story?"

"Right." Philip took another sip. "Where was I?"

"Kissing practice."

"Yes, kissing practice." He paused.

"So, was that it? Practice kissing led to love?"

"Well, not exactly."

Oh, yes exactly. They practiced for hours, becoming more daring in each "session," beginning to mutually explore their bodies, running their hands under their shirts, feeling their skin hot and smooth. The first time Eddie tweaked one of Philip's nipples, Philip thought he would die from the sensation that rocketed through him.

"A few weeks later, we actually did ask a couple of girls out on dates—since that seemed to be the thing to do. We took the streetcar into the city, went to a movie, then went out for burgers afterwards at the Dixie Diner."

"What movie did you see?"

"The Wizard of Oz, of course. What movie was everybody seeing in 1939?" He chuckled at the memory.

He took another sip of wine and ate a few more bites of his lunch, remembering the evening. "We took the girls home. They lived about a block apart so I walked my date to her house while Eddie went in the other direction."

"And...?" Phyllis smiled over her wineglass.

"And...I gave her a good night kiss, because that seemed to be what she wanted."

On the porch, under the light, Delores threw her arms around Philip's neck. "I had such a good time to-night...thank you for asking me out."

Philip looked at her face, upturned and expectant. He leaned in and gave her a quick peck on the cheek and waited for the feeling. Nothing. No racing heart, no beginning of an erection. Good Lord, what's wrong with me? he thought. And then he knew. He knew. None of it had been practice.

"Good night, Delores. I had a nice time too." He could sense she was not happy about the kiss—she wanted the real thing. Philip stepped back, widening the space between them. Delores frowned.

"Will I see you again?"

"I'm not sure. I'll call you."

He hurried off the porch and found Eddie waiting for him on the corner. "C'mon," he said, his voice almost a growl, and pulled Eddie by the hand through the shadowy streets. "Let's go back to my house," he said. "You want to spend the night?"

"Sure."

They tiptoed into the darkened house. It was almost mid-night. Philip's parents always went to bed early, even on the weekend. Philip dragged Eddie up the stairs to his room, pushing the door shut and turning the latch on the lock, something he had never done before. "Unbutton your pants," he ordered, his voice a whisper, and Eddie mutely complied, pushing them down off his hips.

Philip gasped at the sight of Eddie's penis, springing forth from the confines of his underpants. "Oh my God, I want it," he said, falling on his knees in front of his friend, kissing the tip and pushing the foreskin back with his tongue, tentatively holding it in his mouth.

"Yes," said Eddie hoarsely, and Philip's kisses turned into licks and licks turned into sucks and then he realized

that they both had reached the point of no return.

"I gather it wasn't a success," said Phyllis, intruding on Philip's thoughts.

"Huh?" answered Philip, feeling stupid. Maybe it was the wine. The second bottle might have been a mistake.

"The good night kiss…"

"Oh, yes." Philip gathered his thoughts. "All that practice and I…flopped." He laughed to himself. "I guess the good thing was that Eddie and I did figure out how we felt about each other and ended the charade with the girls."

The waiter appeared again, motioning towards their plates and they nodded they were done.

"Dessert, Philip?" asked Phyllis.

"I've always wanted to try chocolate mousse in France." He turned to the waiter. "Do you have any of that?"

"Bien sûr, Monsieur. Our *mousse au chocolat* is excellent. Would you like it *avec les framboises?*"

Philip looked at him, wondering why he didn't speak in just English or just French. He found his "franglais" confusing.

"Raspberries," whispered Phyllis. "*Framboise* is the word for raspberry."

Philip nodded his thanks. "Yes, please. I'd like a chocolate mousse with raspberries. And a cup of coffee, black."

"Bien sûr, Monsieur. Madame?"

"I'll have a *crème brulée,* please. And coffee, like the gentleman. Bring a small pot."

"Oui, Madame."

They sipped at the last of their wine, Philip remembering Eddie, realizing again he was just miles from his final resting place, probably only miles from the place where he had been killed. Forty years, and he was finally here.

"You said George knew…" Phyllis's voice came to him, as if traveling over a long distance. "Did he just guess?"

"Oh no." Philip laughed. "He caught us in bed together!" Now he knew he had had too much to drink. Laughing over the most embarrassing moment of his life? He had never been able to remember this incident without cringing in shame but now he wanted to blurt it out as if it were a stand-up comedy routine.

"Oh!" said Phyllis.

"You need to understand the situation. I was an only child so it was natural that Eddie tended to come to my house—lots of room and, like I said, the model trains. But I stayed at the Fiske's, too, plenty of times."

The waiter appeared with their coffee and Philip took a big gulp. He definitely needed to clear his head.

"Eddie shared a room with his brother John. George had his own room. But up in the attic, they had what they called 'the sleepover room.' If John had a friend over for the night, Eddie got kicked up to the attic. If *Eddie* had a friend over, it was supposed to work the same way—he got to sleep in the room and John would go up to the attic—but that never happened. John was sort of an operator like that." He laughed at the memory. "Eddie and I actually came to prefer the attic. It was quiet and private and no one bothered us up there."

Philip saw the waiter advancing towards them with their desserts, so he waited until they were served before continuing the story. He took a bite of the mousse, smiled at Phyllis and spoke again.

"One weekend that fall, after…well, after we started 'doing it,' my parents had to go out of town. Why?" He screwed up his face, trying to recall the reason. "Maybe my uncle was sick. Or my aunt was having a baby." He shrugged. "Who knows? Whatever, my parents wanted me to stay at the Fiske's, not be alone in our house.

"Eddie and I *promised* each other we'd behave. We knew what we could get away with at my house, but at the Fiske's it was a different story."

"I can tell where this is going," said Phyllis.

"I'm sure you can," said Philip, chuckling. "Two horny teenagers, fueled by testosterone? Our *promise* lasted all of five minutes." He took another bite of his mousse. "This is really good, by the way. How's yours?"

"Excellent," answered Phyllis, taking a bite of her dessert.

"We stayed up most of the night, fooling around and finally fell asleep, exhausted. The next morning, George came up to get us for breakfast and there we were—naked as the day we were born, twisted in each other's arms, sleeping the sleep of angels."

"Or devils..." said Phyllis, with a smile. "What happened then?"

"Nothing, immediately. But...that was the year that Eddie's father had died. George was taking his role as surrogate father very seriously. When he got Eddie alone, he gave him the sinner lecture, tried to do the same with me a few days later. But it was too late. That horse was long out of the barn...no closing the door for us."

"And George didn't belabor the point? Didn't bring it up again?"

"No." He scraped the last of the mousse out of the dish, licking his spoon. "I think," he said contemplatively, "that Mr. Fiske's death changed a lot of things."

"How so?"

"Well..." he paused. "Mr. Fiske was a very good man, don't get me wrong. But he was very strict, a real disciplinarian. And he was..." Philip searched for the right word. "Old-fashioned? Conservative?"

"Probably typical for a man of that era."

"Yes, he was. And...I have no doubt that he would not have tolerated having a son who was queer...er, I mean, homosexual."

"Gay," said Phyllis softly.

Philip shrugged. "I come from the old school. I think of myself as queer, always have. Eddie used the word too."

"What would Mr. Fiske have done, had he known?"

"That's a good question. Kicked Eddie out? Disowned

him? Probably...Eddie would never have acted on his impulses. He would have denied what he was feeling."

Phyllis nodded.

"That's what I mean when I say his death changed things. Now Audrey—Mrs. Fiske—she was different. Eddie was her darling boy and he could do no wrong in her eyes. He got away with things that George and John could only *dream* of doing."

"Such as?"

"He'd take the car and we'd go driving. Park way out by Loch Raven Dam and make out for hours."

"That doesn't seem so terrible..."

"He didn't have a license, Phyllis."

"Oh, well that changes things!"

Philip nodded. "Yup. Another time, we drank beer in his room. I know his mother found the bottles, but she never said a word."

"Somehow, that doesn't surprise me," said Phyllis, with a smile.

"Anyway, when Mr. Fiske died, Audrey was just numb. I think she was in a fog for about two years, oblivious to what was going on around her. She certainly never expected to become a widow at the age of 42. And—she loved her husband, even if he was a stern taskmaster. Her grief was obvious. The boys, too. Like I said, Mr. Fiske wasn't a bad guy, just strict."

Phyllis nodded, silently encouraging him to continue.

"I think...," said Philip, again drawing out the words slowly, "Eddie turned to me, at that time—well, one, because he loved me but also because of the loss of his father. There was a void there, a hole he was trying to fill. Does that make sense?"

"Yes, absolutely."

Philip nodded. "And the other piece is...well, Eddie knew he was queer. Or at least he was figuring it out, even if he didn't know it before. With his father out of the picture and his mother in la-la land, he probably felt it was safe to give in to what he was feeling. Safer than it would have been when his father was alive, that is."

Phyllis nodded again, then looked up at the waiter who had again reappeared at their table. He gathered up the dessert dishes. "May I bring you anything else, Madame, Monsieur?" he asked. "More *café*?" They shook their heads no and he nodded, leaving the check on the table.

Philip picked it up. "I assume I can charge it to my room?" Phyllis nodded and Philip carefully signed the bottom of the slip and turned it over, tucking it under the edge of his wine glass.

Philip pushed his chair back but Phyllis made a motion, stopping him. "One last question? Before we leave?"

"Sure. I feel like my life is an open book right now. What do you want to know?"

"Did his mother ever know? That he was gay, that is?"

"I don't think so, at least not that I'm aware of. I almost outed myself to her once, but ended up not saying anything. I wasn't sure how she'd react and... " He paused, running his finger along the edge of the table, "I didn't want to destroy her memory of her son. If she really hated queers, no sense in having her find out after he was gone."

"What do you think would have happened, if Eddie hadn't been killed?"

"We planned to live together. I had already rented an apartment. In that case, Audrey would have known. Eddie would have told her, if she didn't figure it out on her own. He couldn't keep secrets and he couldn't lie—and he certainly couldn't live a lie in front of his mother."

"No, he couldn't," agreed Phyllis. "That's how I found out."

"Found out what?" asked Philip.

"About you," she answered simply.

"Oh...I never knew."

"I didn't think you did."

"So...tell me," said Philip. "I think it is your turn for a confession or two."

Phyllis smiled. "Yes, well, when Eddie first sensed that I was falling for him, he told me he already had someone—a girl back home. I think he wanted to discourage me."

Philip chuckled. "A girl, huh?"

"Yes, her name was Philippa."

At that, Philip laughed out loud. "Philippa! Sounds like something from a romance novel."

"I know. Anyway, a few weeks before they went to the sausages..."

"Sausages?" Philip asked, interrupting.

"Sorry. That's what the soldiers called the containment area where they went before they were deployed to France. They would be in a type of isolation for about two weeks. The first D-Day soldiers were there for a month. Eddie left for the sausages at the beginning of July."

"Ah, I never knew the details. He couldn't write me about this stuff."

"Yes. Anyway, when the first D-Day reports started coming back, with the horrific number of casualties, the whole battle became very real. It wasn't about training and running around on the beaches of Slapton anymore. Everyone knew they might not live to see Christmas."

She paused and Philip could see tears welling in her eyes. "Like you said, Eddie couldn't lie. He invited me to Mass one morning and afterwards, he made a confession to the priest. Then he came and sat next to me in the pew and said, 'I have a confession for you, too.' And he told me that his 'girl' back home was really a boy and that he was hopelessly, desperately in love with a man named Philip."

Philip blushed at the mention of his name. "Were you shocked?"

Phyllis paused. "Not really shocked. More like dumbfounded. I was pretty naïve—remember, at that point, I hadn't even been kissed. The thought of my good friend

Eddie being in love with a man—and the implications of that—well, I really just didn't understand it at all."

"So, what did you say?"

"Nothing at first. I was silent and Eddie seemed to take that as condemnation. He said that if I didn't want to be friends with him anymore—because this revelation was too disgusting or something—he'd understand. But I just looked at him and said, 'You're the same person you were five minutes ago. I've known for months you're in love with someone else. Just because that person is a man, why should that change anything?'"

Philip smiled. "You really are a wonderful person, you know."

Phyllis shook her head. "No, I'm not. I'm just an ordinary person trying to make her way in the world and trying to be a good friend to the people she cares for."

Philip smiled again. "Go on. I'm interrupting you."

"Yes, well…after he told me, it was like the floodgates opened. We spent three hours sitting in that church and he told me all about you."

"*All* about me?" asked Philip.

"Well, he didn't mention the kissing practice," she said with a smile, "but he did share quite a few details—in a circumspect way, that is. He showed me the crucifix you gave him."

"Oh my God, my crucifix!" said Philip.

She nodded. "He even kissed it before he tucked it back in his shirt."

Philip pulled out a handkerchief and wiped his eyes, then blew his nose loudly.

"I'm sorry. Now I've made you cry."

"It's okay. I have a feeling the next few days are going to be pretty emotional. Might as well get started on it now."

"Anyway, it was at the end of that conversation that Eddie made me promise that if something happened to him, I would write you. He was afraid that you'd never get any sort of personal communication about his death."

"But how would you find out?"

"They posted names at the Council Office in town. So many of the villagers knew so many of the soldiers that it was done as a kindness to notify us. My mother, too, might have been able to find out something. She was pretty high up in the chain of volunteers. Besides, she was having an affair with one of the senior officers. She had ways to get information."

"Your mother?" said Philip, sounding truly shocked.

"Scandalous, isn't it?" Phyllis gave him a small smile. "Why do you think she was so protective of me?" She laughed softly, then paused. "Come to think of it, maybe she guessed about Eddie, and that's why she was so agreeable to our friendship. She knew that he...what's the expression? Batted for the other team?"

Philip laughed. "Something like that."

"And she knew he wasn't going to damage my virtue." She paused, refolding her napkin for the third time. "Anyway, in the end, it was Eddie who told me himself. He had a pre-written letter that they found on his body. They mailed it to me and his commanding General added a personal letter, explaining the circumstances of his death."

"General Baade," said Philip.

"Yes," said Phyllis, surprised. "How do you know?"

"He wrote me, too. Similar situation, I think. Eddie had a half-finished letter for me. The General included a handwritten note with it."

"So, I never really needed to write you."

"True, but if you hadn't we would never have met."

Phyllis nodded. "Yes. And that would have been the biggest loss of all."

They sat for a moment, in quiet contemplation of all that had passed between them. Then Philip pushed back his sleeve and looked at his watch. "It's two-thirty. Do you think we still have time to go to the cemetery today?"

"I believe so. It's open until five." She paused. "Unless you want to wait until the morning?"

"No, let's go now. It's the reason I'm here, after all."

Phyllis smiled. "Yes, of course. Give me a few minutes to freshen up, and then we can get a cab." She stood up, smoothing her skirt. "I'll meet you in the lobby."

~~~

The taxi pulled up in front of the Visitor's Center at the Lorraine American Cemetery. Philip noticed the stars and stripes flying overhead. "Welcome to the US," he said. He helped Phyllis out of the cab. "Or at least a little bit of America in France."

Philip looked at the Visitor's Center, flat and modular, with angled metal corners and plate glass windows. He held the door for Phyllis and followed her in, taking in the faux-leather couches and framed picture of Ronald Reagan hanging on the wall.

"May I help you?" came a voice from an office in the corner. A large heavy-set man emerged through the doorway.

"Yes, we're here to visit the grave of a loved one," answered Philip and the man nodded approvingly. Something about his manner irked Philip and he immediately felt on the defensive.

"Ah, of course." The man extended his hand. "I'm Glenn Tetford. I'll be happy to escort you."

Philip shook his hand, offering his name and introducing Phyllis. "We're here to see the grave of Eddie Fiske—PFC Edward G. Fiske," he added quickly, correcting himself.

Tetford pulled out an index card from his pocket. "Fiske, you said. With an E?" Philip nodded mechanically. "Are you a relative?" Tetford asked, his pen poised over the card.

"Close family friend."

Phyllis chimed in, "I knew him when he was stationed in England.

"Yes," said Tetford, making notes on the card. "Please

make yourselves comfortable. Sign the visitor's register. I'll only be a moment." He disappeared into the office.

Philip looked at the large leather bound book, sitting open on a table. He picked up the pen, glancing at the signatures. "We're the only visitors today," he said, as he signed his name. "In fact, we're the only visitors for three days."

"Well, it is an odd time of year. Not quite spring yet. Maybe it is busier in the summer."

"Or maybe everyone is forgetting." Philip had a trace of bitterness in his voice.

Tetford re-emerged from the office, carrying a bucket and two flags—one French, one American. A Polaroid camera hung around his neck and he wore a padded jacket, making him look even stouter and more rotund. "Shall we go?" He pointed towards the door.

They walked down a path and then turned left onto another path, a large memorial of some sort on their right. They continued then turned left again, his time stopping on the crest of the hill. The cemetery lay before them, more than ten thousand graves in a natural amphitheater, a sea of white crosses flowing down the gentle slope.

"Oh my," said Phyllis, her hand going to her mouth.

"Impressive, isn't it?" said their guide.

"Impressive isn't necessarily the word I would use," said Philip.

"Oh?" said Tetford. "How would you describe it?"

"Sad. Tragic." Philip pointed towards the scene in front of them. "Remember that under everyone of those gravestones is a young man who gave his life before he'd barely had a chance to live his life."

"Gave his life protecting *our* freedoms and democracy," retorted Tetford, an edge in his voice.

"I'm not arguing that. Just going on record that this is a visual reminder of the senselessness of war."

Tetford looked as if he was going to say something but didn't, compressing his lips in a straight line. He consulted a paper in his hand. "PFC Fiske is in Section C, over here to the right. Follow me."

He set off at a brisk pace, wending his way through the maze of paths and gravestones. Philip glanced at them as they walked by: California, New York, Maine, Tennessee. A few had Stars of David; most were white crosses. He noticed they didn't contain birth dates, only the date the soldier was killed.

After a few minutes they stepped off the path and turned into a row, treading lightly on the grass. Philip could hear Tetford counting under his breath. He stopped abruptly. "Here." He waved his arm with a flourish, as if he was announcing the opening act at the circus. Philip felt the bile rise in his throat.

They looked at the grave, seeing the neatly etched letters against the white marble. EDWARD G. FISKE. PFC 134 INF 35 DIV.

"Oh my God!" Phyllis clutched at her throat and immediately burst into tears.

"It's okay, Phyl." Philip put his arm around her shoulder and pulled her close.

Glenn Tetford was all brisk efficiency, bending down in front of the gravestone. Philip noticed that the bucket he had been carrying was one-third filled with sand. Tetford took a handful and wiped it across the marble stone, filling in the letters.

"Why are you doing that?" Philip asked.

"It makes the name show up better in a photograph," answered Tetford, pointing to the camera hanging from his neck.

"Oh," said Philip softly. "Who knew?"

When Tetford finished with the sand, he took the two flags and stuck them in the ground, one on each side of the base. He wiggled them a bit, making sure they caught the breeze correctly and that they were evenly positioned. Philip watched him, thinking that he was acting like a persnickety old queen.

"There," Tetford rose from his knees and wiped his hands on a towel in his bucket. "All set."

"All set?" asked Philip.

Tetford held up his camera. "I can take some pictures. If you want to be in them, that's fine."

Phyllis pulled a small camera out of her purse. "I can take pictures too."

"I'm glad one of us was thinking," Philip tightened his grip around her shoulders.

Tetford took one picture of the grave and as the picture ejected from the camera, he gave it to Philip to hold. "I can take one with the lady, one with you, and one both together."

"Is there a ration on Polaroid film?" Philip muttered under his breath and Phyllis covered his hand with hers.

"Philip, please..." she said softly and Philip nodded. *No point in making a scene.*

They finished with the pictures and Tetford moved to the grave, beginning to pull the flags out of the earth. "You can keep these...as a remembrance."

"Is there a fire somewhere?" Philip had a hard edge in his voice. "Can we have a few minutes?"

"Oh," said Tetford, blinking. "Our usual routine on the tour is to visit the grave, then I'll show you the memorial." He pointed to the large marble building that overlooked the cemetery.

"We're not here on a tour." Philip realized he was struggling to control his temper. "We're here for a remembrance. Go back to your office. We'll find our way out."

"I'll meet you at the Memorial," said Tetford, chastened. "Remember you are welcome to the flags." He gathered up his bucket and strode off, not looking back at the couple standing in front of the white cross.

"Asshole," said Philip, *sotto voce.*

"Philip, please! Not in front of Eddie!"

Philip smiled at her. "Eddie was in the Army. I'm sure he learned worse words."

They spent a few minutes in front of the grave, Phyllis taking pictures and Philip just standing and staring. "All these years..." he murmured, "I'm finally here."

Phyllis put her camera back in her purse and pulled her collar up around her chin. "I'm getting chilled," she said. "Are you ready to leave?"

Philip looked at her. "I need a few minutes alone. How about if you go up to the Visitor's Center and I'll meet you there?"

"Actually, I'd like to see the Memorial and Mr. Tetford said that's where he was going. I'll meet you there instead?"

Philip nodded. "Sure. I won't be long."

"Take all the time you need," she said, and kissed Philip lightly on the cheek before she left.

Philip looked at the grave again, watching the two flags fluttering gently in the chilly breeze. He sighed. "Why did you leave me?" he asked softly. "Why did you go and get yourself killed?" Another deep breath. His throat felt tight. "You could've let that officer get shot instead, you know. Why did you have to be a hero? I never wanted a hero. I just wanted my lover at my side."

He squatted down in front of the cross, putting himself at eye level with the gravestone. "Maybe I should have never promised to love you forever, Eddie. Why did you make me promise that, anyway? By loving you forever, I've never been able to love anyone else." He felt a rush of hot anger in his chest and his hand tightened into a fist, as if to hit some invisible opponent. He was surprised at his reaction. *Why am I angry with Eddie? He was the one who got killed after all.*

And then, the tears came. He let out a deep, gut wrenching sob and forty years of buried emotion burst forth. Philip felt the tears running down his cheek and dripping off his chin and didn't try to stop them, didn't wipe them away with his handkerchief, just let them flow. "I'm so sorry, Eddie," he said, "I shouldn't be mad at you. All I ever wanted was to be with you. Why did God take you away from me? Why didn't he take me too so we could be together?" He reached towards the marble gravestone but didn't touch it, just letting his finger waver in front of the engraved letters.

After awhile, Philip realized he was squatting in an awkward position when he started to feel his legs go numb and he stood up, wobbling a little. He pulled out his handkerchief and wiped his eyes, thinking he must look a mess, knowing that his face always got splotchy and red when he cried.

He made his way slowly up the hill towards the Memorial and when he got there, he slipped in quietly and stood in the back. Tetford was standing in front of a map, pointing to it and talking to Phyllis. Philip couldn't make out the words but he imagined that Tetford was describing the battle. He didn't make a move to listen. Knowing that Eddie had been killed was enough information for him.

When they finished, Phyllis and Tetford came over to where Philip was standing. "Are you alright, Philip?" Phyllis asked and reached out to touch his sleeve.

"Yes," he said, his voice shaky. "I just had…a moment." Phyllis nodded in silent understanding.

Glenn Tetford cleared his throat, offering Philip a blue folder. "This has information about the cemetery. You might want to show it to PFC Fiske's family."

Philip nodded. "He has a brother who lives in California, but I rarely see him. He probably doesn't care. But his nieces and nephews might be interested."

Phyllis extended her hand. "Thank you, Mr. Tetford," she said. "You've been very gracious."

Tetford beamed at this. "Thank you!"

"Can you call us a cab?" she asked, and Tetford nodded.

"Can we come back tomorrow?" asked Philip. "Visit again?"

"Of course, sir," said Tetford, suddenly deferential.

"We're open from nine to five."

"I might do that," he said. He cupped his hand around Phyllis's elbow. "Let's go, my dear. I'm ready for a rest."

~~~

Back at the hotel, Philip let out a big sigh, glancing at the restaurant. "I'm not sure I can put up with that obsequious waiter again," he said, "not after dealing with that officious prick at the cemetery. I suppose we'll have to go into the city to find a restaurant for dinner."

"Well, we could order room service," answered Phyllis.

"Oh, they have room service here? That's not just an American thing?"

Phyllis smiled. "I think the French invented it."

"Eating in would be nice. I'm sick and tired of being on my good behavior."

"Ah," answered Phyllis. "I understand. I'll just say good night, then, and plan on meeting you at breakfast?"

"Oh no, that's not what I meant," Philip replied quickly. "We can have dinner together. Nice and quiet in the room, just the two of us. I like that idea."

She smiled. "I like it too."

They walked down the hall to Philip's room and he inserted the key into the door, ushering her in. "Maybe there's a room service menu in the desk?"

Phyllis nodded and opened the drawer, pulling out a large laminated card. "There certainly is." She glanced at the menu, then looked at Philip. "Any idea what you are in the mood for?"

"You choose. Anything will be fine. Order some wine, too."

She nodded again, then picked up the phone, speaking quickly in French, hanging up when she finished. "Twenty to thirty minutes," she said. "While we are waiting, I'm going to go change into something more comfortable."

When she returned to the room, dinner had been served and Philip was pouring a glass of wine. "I noticed you ordered omelets." He handed Phyllis the glass.

She smiled. "Yes...French comfort food. You seem stressed."

"French comfort food?"

Phyllis laughed. "Well, that's what I call it. Watch any French movie—when the going gets tough, someone always goes into the kitchen and cooks an omelet."

"I've never noticed that," said Philip, chuckling. "But then again, I haven't watched too many French movies."

"After this trip, maybe you'll be more interested in all things *Francophone*."

Philip shook his head. "I don't think so. I'm enjoying traveling, but I am not sure I ever want to come back to France. It just seems too emotional to me."

"Maybe it's just this part of France. You might enjoy seeing the Dordogne, or Nice..."

Philip shrugged. "Maybe...but right now, I don't think so."

They sat down at the table, raising their wine glasses in a toast, and unfolding the heavy cotton napkins. Philip picked up his fork and took a bite of his omelet and realized that Phyllis was right. It was comfort food and it suited his mood perfectly. "Thank you for ordering this," he said softly.

They ate in companionable silence for a few minutes, Philip mulling over the events of the day, watching Phyllis, thinking about the revelations she had made about Eddie. He realized that there were very few people left in the world who actually *knew* Eddie when he was alive. It saddened him that the memory of Eddie Fiske was growing dimmer with each passing day.

He looked at Phyllis. She had changed into a lavender cashmere sweater which he realized set off her complexion and brought out the blue in her eyes. "You're a very pretty woman," he said, and Phyllis blushed.

"Why thank you."

"Phyllis..." He paused, taking another sip of his wine.

"Would you marry me?"

Her head snapped up in surprise. "Marry you? Is that a question or a proposal?"

Philip looked confused. "I guess when I asked it, I thought it was a question. But maybe it is a proposal."

Phyllis paused. "I'm not sure I'm such good marriage material," she said softly. "I've already gone through two husbands."

"Maybe the third time is the charm..."

"Maybe..." She hesitated again, carefully choosing her words. "Philip, I think you might be caught up in the emotion of the moment. I can't believe you love me and want to marry me—after all, we only met yesterday."

"We've been corresponding for forty years. I feel like I know you better than anyone else in the world. We only met *in person* yesterday but our friendship goes back decades."

"Well, true. And we would have met years ago if you didn't have that unfortunate—what was it? A family emergency?"

Philip groaned. "Oh God. I was afraid you'd bring that up."

Phyllis looked embarrassed. "Oh, I'm sorry," she said quickly. "If it is a bad memory..."

"It is only a bad memory because I was a stupid, drunken fool and that was one of the biggest fuck-ups," he put his hand to his mouth, quickly correcting himself, "oh, sorry, screw ups—of my life."

"We don't have to talk about it."

"Actually, I do want to talk about it—if only to give you a long overdue apology. I should never have stood you up and when I did, I should have told you the truth. Please forgive me."

"Of course I'll forgive you, if there is really anything to forgive. It's been twenty years, after all. No big deal, anymore. What happened, anyway?"

"I was there at the hotel...it was Friday night. I went

down to the bar to have a drink, got picked up by a hustler—went back to the room, got plastered, and he stole my wallet and camera. And my watch! A stupid, cheap Timex. I couldn't believe it."

"Oh, Philip, how awful. But he didn't hurt you in anyway, did he? Hit you?"

Philip shook his head. "No, nothing like that. The only thing wounded was my pride. Saturday morning, when I woke up, I was so hung over I could barely move. I couldn't imagine going to the World's Fair. So, I cancelled. Then I had to call George to wire me some money. I didn't have my train ticket or credit cards…nothing. I felt like an ass."

"But nothing like that has ever happened again, has it?"

"Oh no. I learned my lesson."

"And what lesson is that?" said Phyllis with a smile.

"Not to get picked up by good looking men in hotel bars, no matter how sweet and sincere they seem—and no matter how good the sex is, either." His hand flew to his mouth. "Good Lord, Phyllis—sorry about that. I don't know what it is with you. You have me saying things I've never said to anyone in my life."

"I told you, I'm happy to be your confidante." She paused. "But…since you bring it up, the sex part is another reason why it doesn't make sense for us to get married."

Philip waved his hand. "Sex isn't such a big deal for me anymore. I'm getting too old."

"Well," said Phyllis, "it is important to me…and, if I were to get into another relationship, I'd certainly want it to be one with an intimate dimension to it."

Philip flushed. "Well, yes…of course. Maybe I spoke too soon."

Phyllis peered at him. "You've never really been with anyone else? No other lovers?"

"Oh, I've been with people," Philip replied. "Off and on. There was a period when I was going to the beach in New York and that was pretty nice, actually. Relaxed, casual, friendly folks. But as far as having a relationship that included love, Eddie has been the only one."

Phyllis patted his hand. "You're really not that old and you are quite attractive," she said. "I'm going to respectfully decline your proposal because when you do meet the right person, I want you to be available for him. In the meantime, however...I am happy to be your friend."

"Thank you Phyllis." Philip's voice was soft. "Maybe a friend is what I need."

He stood up, gathering up the dishes from their meal and stacked them on the tray, then put it outside in the door in the hall. He poured the last of the wine into their glasses.

"I suppose it is time to say good night," said Phyllis, starting to stand.

"Actually, before you go, can you do something with me?"

"Do something?" Phyllis looked puzzled.

Philip went to his suitcase and pulled out a bulky manila envelope. "I have a bunch of letters and stuff from Eddie that George gave me a few months before he died. I've tried to look at them and I can't...maybe if you look at them with me?"

"Of course." Phyllis sat back down in her chair.

Philip sat down and put the envelope on the table between them. He opened it, pulling out a folder and two blue leather boxes. "Those must be his medals," he said, pushing them aside. He opened the folder which held a stack of thin envelopes, the paper aged and yellowed, the ink fading. "Mrs. Harold Fiske," he read aloud. "Eddie's letters to his mom."

Phyllis nodded, pushing through the pile. "There are a few addressed to George, too. Do you have any letters?"

"Oh yes. I saved them all. They're at home in Baltimore."

Phyllis nodded, choosing one letter at random from the pile. She pulled out the paper and unfolded it carefully, then started reading. She looked up at Philip, a funny smile on her face. "What a coincidence! Of all the letters I could have selected…I picked the one where he wrote about meeting me."

"Really?" said Philip, with a chuckle. "What does he say?"

She looked at the letter, reading carefully: *In other news here at the base, I met this really swell girl. Her name is Phyllis and she volunteers here, with her mother. We went to the dance at the Canteen last night. She's just as pretty as a picture and a great gal to talk to. She's making me feel less homesick and a little less worried about what's coming up in the next few months.*

She looked up at Philip and he could see her eyes were bright with tears. He touched her hand. "I'm sorry. Maybe this wasn't such a good idea."

"No, no…It's fine. It's just making me realize how young we all were. He was just a boy, really…writing to his mother about being homesick."

Philip nodded. "I know." He pushed through the pile of envelopes and picked out one with a typewritten address; the return address said "Department of the Army." He pulled the letter out and read it quickly. "Ah," he said softly.

"What?"

He passed the letter over to Phyllis. "Audrey mentioned this to me once. They gave her the option to have Eddie's body sent home—but she decided not to. I wonder if she ever regretted that?" he mused, partly to himself. "She never did get to see his grave."

"I think it's better that he's here…in the place where he died."

"I agree and obviously, that's what Audrey thought, too. But I know she was always sad that she never got here for a visit." He picked up one of the leather boxes. "Shall we look at his medals?" he said, pushing the latch and opening the cover.

The first one was his Purple Heart, the medal resting

against the blue velvet of the case, the top lined with white satin. "I know it's an honor," said Philip softly, "but it always seemed a bit of an insult to reward a man for getting killed."

Phyllis nodded, handing him the other box. "What's this one?"

"His Bronze Star. For bravery. He saved another man's life when he was shot."

"Really?" said Phyllis. "I never knew that."

Philip nodded. "An officer." He touched the metal of the medal and ran his fingers over the striped ribbon. "Audrey and I met him. He thanked her. Said Eddie changed his life."

He picked up a small tissue wrapped bundle that was tucked into the corner of the box. "What's that?" asked Phyllis.

"I don't know." Philip unwrapped the paper and spread it on the table. "His dogtags." He fingered the battered metal tags, then continued unfolding the paper. "Oh my God—I didn't expect this! My crucifix!"

Phyllis reached out and touched it, running her hands over the metal. "Yes, that's it. It's been so long since I've seen it."

"I can't believe it's been hidden away all these years." He held it up. "Of course, Audrey had no way of knowing that it was mine." He looked at it again and noticed a gold ring threaded on the chain. "What's this?"

"That's your ring," Phyllis answered.

"Mine?" Philip asked. "How do you know?"

"I was with Eddie when he bought it." She took the crucifix from Philip and unhooked the clasp, sliding the ring off the chain. "After our morning in the church, he told me he wanted to buy you a ring—that he had promised you one."

"Yes, he did," said Philip, nodding.

"He asked me to go with him to the jeweler, so when he had an afternoon leave, we set out for town." She handed Philip the ring and he turned it over in his hand.

"It looks like a wedding ring."

"It is. Eddie didn't really want a wedding ring...I think he had a signet ring in mind and wanted it engraved with your initials." She sighed. "But this was the fifth year of the war and everything was in short supply, including jewelry. The jeweler said he could order something from London, but Eddie was afraid he didn't have enough time for that. So he bought a traditional wedding ring, because that was all he had in stock."

Philip pushed it onto his finger. The ring slipped over his knuckle, settling on his finger in a natural fit. "He knew my size." He held up his hand, looking at the ring with a practiced eye. "I'm not sure I can wear it, though," He slipped it off. "I think I'll just wear it on the chain, like Eddie did." He put the ring back on the chain, then slipped the crucifix over his head, kissing it before he tucked it into his shirt. "I never thought I'd see this again. But Eddie promised me he'd bring it back to me. I guess he did."

Phyllis nodded. She started to gather up the letters, putting them back in their respective envelopes. "So, tomorrow? Another visit to the cemetery?"

Philip paused, fingering the crucifix through his shirt. "Yes...well...would it be all right with you if I went alone?"

"Of course! This is your pilgrimage. You need to do it in the way that feels right to you."

"I got a little emotional at the grave after you left and said some things. I feel like I need to go back and set it right...I didn't say the right kind of goodbye, if that makes sense."

"Philip, you don't need to explain to me," Phyllis answered. "You do whatever you need to do. You don't need me to approve."

Philip smiled. "Thank you. Maybe we could meet somewhere afterwards? For lunch?"

Phyllis nodded. "That would be nice."

"Where could we meet?" he asked. "I don't know my way around."

"Neither do I," said Phyllis, with a smile. "But I did notice that there is a clock tower right in the center of town. We could rendezvous there. I'm sure there is a restaurant within walking distance."

Philip nodded. "Sounds like a plan."

She rose, smoothing her skirt. "Good night, Philip...see you tomorrow."

Philip leaned over and kissed her lightly on the cheek. "Thank you for being a friend, when I needed a friend."

Phyllis gasped a little. "What did you say?"

"Thank you for being a friend..."

"...when I needed a friend," she said. "Eddie wrote that...in his last letter to me."

"Really?" Philip raised his eyebrows. "How odd that I should say that."

"Obviously he is talking to us tonight. Now I know why I selected the letter I did to read."

Philip shook his head. "I'm not sure..." he said, his voice trailing off, "I'm not sure I believe in that sort of stuff."

Phyllis leaned in and gave Philip a kiss on the cheek. "It's not a question of believing, it's a question of paying attention. Pay attention at the cemetery," she said softly, her lips close to his ear. "He may have another message for you." And with that, she exited the room, and headed down the hall.

~~~

Philip slept like a log, a deep, dreamless sleep that allowed him to wake early the next morning, full of energy and purpose. He ate a quick breakfast of croissant and coffee from the buffet in the restaurant, then headed out to the cemetery. He had noticed the day before that it was a short drive—probably less than a mile—and he opted to walk, glad for the chance to get some exercise. It wasn't a particularly scenic route, walking along the motorway, but it was early enough that traffic was light. To his surprise, there was a woman along the side of the road selling flowers from the trunk of her car. He bought a dozen yellow tulips. "Fresh from Holland," she said, and he smiled and thanked her.

The gate to the cemetery was closed but unlocked; Philip pushed it open and entered, then closed it carefully behind him. He headed off to the right, towards the memorial, avoiding the Visitor's Center completely. He didn't want Tetford to see or intercept him, although Philip realized he might not even be at work yet since it was just after eight-thirty.

He hurried down the path, finding his way quickly to Eddie's grave. He stopped and looked at it, then knelt down, the early morning dew quickly soaking the knees of his pants. He realized, too late, that he probably should have brought a towel. "Good morning, my love." He reached out and this time, he touched the smooth stone.

The sand from the day before was still caked in the letters. Philip tried to clean it out with a finger, thinking how messy it looked. *It might be good for photographs, but not every day.*

He studied the grave for a minute, then had an idea. He pulled his penknife from his pocket and wrapped the blade in his handkerchief, then carefully began to scrape the sand from the engravings. He worked slowly and methodically, brushing the sand from the marble with his handkerchief as he finished each letter. Eventually, it was clean, the stone returned back to its pristine white state. He wiped his hands then picked up the tulips, arranging them in a neat little bundle at the base of the grave.

He sat back on his haunches and stared at the marble stone. "Tell me what to do, Eddie," he said softly. "I've loved you all these years...I kept my promise. Please let me be free."

The silence in the cemetery was absolute. Philip realized there weren't any birds singing and the gardeners who had been mowing the lawn the day before hadn't yet come to work. The only sound was a sighing breeze in the trees. Long minutes ticked by as he stared at the marker, burning the name and date into his mind—not that he needed reminding, but something about finally seeing it in person...

Philip touched the stone again and thought of Phyllis's words from the evening before. He didn't know what he was expecting. Eddie's voice to come to him from beyond the grave? The sky to open up with a sign from heaven? But nothing happened. He wiped off his penknife and put it in his pocket along with his handkerchief, then started to rise. "I guess this is goodbye," his voice just a whisper. "I probably won't be coming back. It took me forty years to get here this time."

He bent over and arranged the tulips once more, then on impulse, leaned over and kissed the gravestone, the marble smooth and cold under his lips. As he did so, he started, and suddenly, everything was clear. He paused, then kissed the stone again.

"Thank you, my love." He smiled. "Message received and understood."

And without a backward glance, he headed up the hill and hurried out of the cemetery.

Florence, Italy, March 1985

Philip and Phyllis strode around the Piazza del Duomo, Philip hurrying and Phyllis struggling to keep up with him. "Don't you want to look at the cathedral?" She pointed to the magnificent building in the center of the square.

"We'll visit it on our way back. We'll take all the time you want—then. Come on!" He tugged at Phyllis's elbow.

"I don't understand the big rush! The Academy has been there for hundreds of years. It won't disappear in the next thirty minutes." But she was smiling as she said this and Philip knew her pique was just an act.

"I want to get there when it opens. The guidebook says it gets crowded..." He paused and looked at the map in his hand, then glanced at the streets. "There," he said, pointing. "Via Ricasoli. That's where we go."

They turned right onto the narrow street and quickly covered the three blocks to the *Galleria dell'Accademia*. The guard was just unlocking the door and there was already a cluster of people waiting to get in. "See, I told you! I'm glad we got here early."

The line moved quickly and within minutes they had paid their entrance fee. "The *Sala del Colosso* is to the right," said the docent, handing them the museum guide. "And the *Galleria dei Prigioni* starts here." She pointed to the hall in front of them. The *Tribuna del David* is at the end of the *Galleria.*"

"That's what I want to see." Philip took the brochure and

handed a second one to Phyllis. "Thank you. *Grazie.*"

The docent smiled. "Enjoy your visit."

Phyllis was trying to fish her reading glasses out of her purse as Philip was tugging on her arm again. "I want to read about the prisoners," she said, looking at the brochure. "There are four of them, I believe."

"We can look at them on the way out," said Philip. "Come on, we've come all this way, let's get right to the main attraction."

Phyllis laughed. "All right, all right! No arguing with an impatient man, I guess!"

They breezed down the corridor, past the knots of people admiring the unfinished prisoner sculptures, St. Matthew, and the *Pietà*. Philip barely gave them a backward glance. Then, as he passed through the doorway into the *Tribuna,* he stopped short, momentarily transfixed. "Oh my God," he said, looking at the statue in front of him. "It's more than I expected!"

Michelangelo's David rose in front of them, seventeen feet of splendid Carrara marble, the statue radiating and filling the space with its magnificent beauty. Philip stared at the lines of his nude body, the veins prominent in his long arms, his fingers curled around a rock, the muscles tense in his legs, his abdomen rippling with strength, his open eyes staring, preparing for battle, with only a ghost of a smile around his lips.

Phyllis reached for his hand, giving it a squeeze. "It's superb. More than I expected, too. Thanks for hurrying…"

They stood, staring at the statue, Philip lost in his thoughts but not thinking at all. He felt a powerful emotion that he didn't expect and couldn't name, but knew it had something to do with his heart, which was hammering in his chest.

His reverie was broken by a voice, speaking to his right. "He's a pretty fine specimen, isn't he?"

Philip started and turned to look at the speaker. Something about the choice of words triggered a long distant memory. "Fine specimen?" He felt disoriented.

"David...A fine looking man..."

"Yes, he is." Philip nodded. "More than I expected."

"I like watching the reaction of men when they see David for the first time. Am I correct in assuming that this is your first visit?"

"Yes, it is," said Philip, thinking about what the stranger had said. *The reaction of men?* "And you?"

"I am losing track but I think this must be visit number eight or nine. I try to get to Florence every two or three years—it rejuvenates my soul."

Philip managed to tear his eyes away from the statue and more fully look at the man who was speaking to him. He was surprised at how handsome he was. Six feet, Philip guessed, with a full head of dark hair, just the barest touch of silver at his temples. Clear blue eyes, smooth skin, freshly shaved, a whiff of cologne—something subtle. Philip noticed a pulse at the base of his throat and a tuft of dark hair just barely showing at the open 'V' of his oxford cloth shirt. He felt a flush rising in his cheeks. He forced his attention back to the statue.

"I had a friend once who said I reminded him of David," he said, trying to get his mind off the pulse in the man's throat, his own heart thundering in his ears. "We had planned to visit for a side-by-side comparison."

"Ah, and is your friend with you today? The woman I saw you with?"

Philip noticed that Phyllis had wandered off, studying the statue from a different angle. He was surprised that that man hadn't picked up on the 'him' in his sentence. Or perhaps that was intentional? "No, but she knew *him* too." He added some emphasis, trying to communicate: *I enjoy looking at men—statues and otherwise.*

"Maybe we need to do that comparison." The man pointed. "Go stand next to the big guy. Let me see."

"No." Philip felt embarrassed. "It's foolish."

"Nothing foolish in fulfilling a long held promise. Go on." He touched Philip lightly on the arm. Philip almost jumped. He swore he felt a jolt of electricity from the contact.

"Well, okay then," said Philip, willing himself to be calm, walking a few steps away and turning to face the stranger.

"Give me a rakish pose. Put your hand on your hip." Philip was once again struck by the choice of words. The thundering in his ears turned to a buzzing in his head. He worried he might faint and hoped to God he wouldn't.

"I was much younger then and when...the comparison was made, I was standing by a window, moonlight shining on me." He paused. "It probably heightened the effect—that I looked like marble, I mean. Not that I looked like him." He nodded towards the statue. *Christ, now I'm babbling!*

"Sounds romantic," The stranger gave Philip an appraising look.

Philip felt as if the man could see through his clothes and was studying his body, comparing him to David. *At least I never got fat,* he mused, thinking of all the other sixty-something men he knew. He stood there, not sure what to do, and finally nodded. "It was," he said softly, not sure if the other man heard him or not. "Romantic, that is."

He stood for a minute more, turning his head and looking up at the statue, admiring it anew. Then he crossed back to the man. "If I am going to be sharing such intimate secrets, perhaps we should introduce ourselves. I'm Philip Cormier." He stuck out his hand.

The man took his hand in a strong grip, shaking it firmly. "Pleased to meet you. David Gardiner."

"David? So does that explain your attraction to the statue?"

"I like to think so." David smiled at him.

"Were you named after him?"

"Well, depends on who you ask," he answered. "My father would tell you I was named after my grandfather. My mother would tell you I was named after St. David, since I was born on his feast day. But me..." he smiled again. "I like to think that I am the namesake of this magnificent creature."

"You could do worse!" Philip laughed. "All three options sound like distinguished forebears."

"Yes, they are."

They stood in silence for a minute, Philip trying to regain control of his heart and breathing. He was afraid if he lifted his hands, David would see them shaking. He jammed them in his pockets and began humming a noiseless tune under his breath. He was a jumble of nerves and couldn't believe how suddenly he was overcome by his emotions. He hadn't felt like this in years—in fact, he wasn't sure if he'd *ever* felt like this.

David looked at him. "So, you were saying, this is your first trip to Florence..."

"First trip to Europe, actually." Philip tried to breathe slowly, as he answered.

"Ah...and the purpose of your trip? Sightseeing? Business?"

"It started off as a remembrance but now we are sightseeing," said Philip. "This part of the trip is a little bit spontaneous—I hadn't originally planned on visiting Italy. Last week I was in France, visiting the Lorraine American Cemetery. I was there to see the grave of the friend I was talking about. He was killed in 1944 and is buried there."

"Oh, I'm very sorry to hear that," David replied. "My condolences."

"Thanks, but it's been good for me. The trip is helping me say goodbye, something I've needed to do for a long time." *Please understand, Eddie*, he thought, sending up a silent prayer. *I still love you.* He touched his crucifix through his shirt.

"And what inspired the side trip to Florence?"

"My friend," Philip answered. "Our conversation about David—the statue—was one of the last times we were together. I hadn't thought about it for years, then remembered when I saw his grave..." He paused, his voice drifting off.

"So this is very meaningful for you."

Philip nodded. "Yes, it is...and...," he paused, then, "meeting you seems to be special, too." He flushed again. *He must think I'm a fool.*

But if he did, he didn't show it, smiling at Philip and nodding understandingly. Philip felt his heart lurch in his chest at the look of sweet affection David gave him. *What is wrong with me? I think I'm going off the deep end...*

"I'm happy to meet you too," David was saying, as Philip tried to bring himself back to earth. "Now, since we're rapidly becoming the very best of friends, may I ask what city do you call home?"

"Baltimore. Born and raised. I've lived there all my life."

"Ah, Baltimore, home of the Orioles, steamed crabs, and National Boh."

Baseball, crabs, beer. Eddie's favorites. "Are you from Baltimore, too?" asked Philip, surprised.

David shook his head. "No, I lived in Chicago for many years, relocated to Tucson a few years ago. But I travel a good deal for my work and have several clients in Baltimore. I have spent quite a bit of time in your city. Lovely art museum."

"The Walters? Yes, I've been a member there for years. What do you do?"

"I'm a fraud accountant," he said. "A detective for white collar crime, uncovering nefarious deeds in the books of corporations..."

Philip laughed. "You make it sound like a mystery!"

David smiled back at him. "Well, I have to do something to make it sound interesting." He paused. "Seriously, I enjoy the work. It's varied and challenging—at least to me. Some people don't like numbers."

Philip gave him a smile. "I was in the insurance business my entire career. I can appreciate accounting."

David laughed. "Kindred souls, I guess. You said 'was'?"

"I retired two years ago. The business was being sold and it seemed like a good time to get out. You?"

"Not yet. I worked for Arthur Anderson for ages, then struck out on my own a few years ago. That's when I moved to Tucson. Needed a fresh break and some better weather. Now I have a small roster of clients which pays the bills and gives me the flexibility to do what I like…like this," he said, pointing to the statue.

"Meaning travel?" asked Philip.

David nodded. "Travel, look at art, eat wonderful food…my favorite things in life. Speaking of, would you like to go get an espresso and a pastry? There's a lovely bakery right close by which still seems to be undiscovered by tourists. They have wonderful *cornetti*."

Philip blinked. "Yes," he said. "I'd like that. Thank you." He looked around. "I need to find my friend Phyllis…" He spied her, standing and looking over the shoulder of a young man drawing in a sketch book.

"She's welcome to join us."

Philip nodded and went over to Phyllis's side, speaking softly to her, then guiding her back to his new friend. "Phyllis, let me introduce you to David Gardiner. David, this is my friend, Phyllis Lord Devine."

"My pleasure." David extended his hand and Phyllis shook it. Philip wondered if she felt the same shock of electricity that he did.

Phyllis smiled, returning the greeting. "Pleased to meet you."

"David has invited me—I mean us—out for coffee. Would you like to do that, Phyl?"

She waved a hand. "No, I'm still full from breakfast. You go ahead. I'd like to spend some time in the *Sala del Colosso*."

"You're sure? I don't want to abandon you."

"I'm a big girl, Philip," said Phyllis with mock severity. "You two go on, have fun, get acquainted. I'll catch up with you later."

"Well, all right." Philip felt a bit reluctant but then David touched his elbow and he felt that charge again and in that moment he knew that all he wanted was to have coffee with this man, and maybe even lunch, spending time with him and getting to know him better. It all seemed *so right.*

"How about if we plan to meet at the *pensione* at the end of the day," Phyllis said, interrupting his thoughts. "I'll find a special restaurant for dinner. David, you're welcome to join us, if you don't have other plans."

"Thank you," said David, gracious and open. "Maybe I will. Philip?" he said, gesturing towards the entrance of the building.

They strode down the corridor together, Philip once again not noticing any of the statues that lined the hall. He realized he only had eyes for David and he felt ridiculous, like a star struck teenager. But then David smiled at him, an extraordinary smile that lit up his face and Philip had the barest glimmer of hope that maybe David was experiencing some of the same wild emotions that he was.

At the door, David pushed it open, ushering Philip out with a motion of his arm. "After you, sir," he said, with a smile.

"Such a gentleman!" said Philip with a wink and the two of them grinned at each other, and exited the building into the brilliant sunshine of a beautiful Florentine morning.

The End

About the authors

Alex Beecroft was born in Northern Ireland during the Troubles and grew up in the wild countryside of the Peak District. Alex studied English and Philosophy before accepting employment with the Crown Court where she worked for a number of years. Now a stay-at-home mum and full time author, Alex lives with her husband and two daughters in a little village near Cambridge and tries to avoid being mistaken for a tourist. Alex is only intermittently present in the real world. She has lead a Saxon shield wall into battle, toiled as a Georgian kitchen maid, and recently taken up an 800 year old form of English folk dance, but she still hasn't learned to operate a mobile phone.

Mark R. Probst lives in Washington State, works in the computer industry, and writes in his spare time. He is an avid movie buff, and has a special admiration for the western films of the classic era. He's had a life-long interest in writing but didn't become published until 2007.

His favorite novels are The Lord of the Rings Trilogy, Maurice, and Gone with the Wind

Jordan Taylor lives in the Pacific Northwest with several pets; dividing time between training dogs, collecting canine movie memorabilia, reading classic and modern literature and writing.

E. N. Holland spent thirty-five years learning the craft of writing as a scientific and technical writer and editor, before finally deciding to pursue a lifelong dream to write fiction. She serialized two novel-length fanfiction stories online; positive feedback from readers gave her the confidence to tackle stories with original characters and settings. *Our One and Only* is her first published novella. It was inspired by visits to World War I and World War II cemeteries in Belgium and France in 2007. Ms. Holland has two other novels underway and dozens of ideas lined up in her brain. She lives in an antique cape (built in 1803) in southern Maine with her husband, two children, dog, and cat.

Lightning Source UK Ltd.
Milton Keynes UK
01 December 2009

146960UK00001B/239/P